Child of June

Child *of* June

Quillen deBruney

First edition

Library of Congress Control Number: 2023923556

ISBN: 979-8-9895564-0-3 (Paperback)
ISBN: 979-8-9895564-3-4 (Paperback)
ISBN: 979-8-9895564-1-0 (EPUB)
ISBN: 979-8-9895564-2-7 (Hardback)

For Kaitlyn, Emma, Aubrey, and Beatrice,
the next generation, and for all the ones
who came before them.

Woman is a riddle past all solving.
Within her soul, unknown to her, there sleep
A thousand possibilities . . . And she is soft as wax.
She bends to every hand,
And is Fate's plaything . . .

ॐBeatrice Dovsky,
Mona Lisa

PROLOGUE

Even now, a lifetime later, if I close my eyes for long enough, I can see it. The world we've lost.

Years pass, decades pass, and still, it lives on. In my mind's eye, it's as clear as an autumn night, fresh as spring rain. Like I was there only yesterday. Like nothing at all has changed. It's so close, I almost think I could touch it; all I need to do is reach out my hand.

I close my eyes, and there I am in the golden city, a step behind my sister. We run through the gardens, our laughter floating above the flowers. Mother looks on, smiles, turns her face to the sun.

I close my eyes, and there I am, tucked away in a cozy corner. I watch the light of genius ignite Father's eye. A spark, a flame, a wildfire. He gets lost in the force of his ideas; he sweeps me right along with him.

And there . . . There he is. That crooked grin. Those eyes that see through me, strip me down, right to my core. We rest side by side in a cradle of wildflowers. I speak soft words to my love, and he sings them back. His voice is a mountain breeze weaving the honeyed scent of edelweiss through my hair.

Was any of it real? Maybe I remember things as they never were. Perhaps I saw life through eyes too young to understand that happiness is a mirage. You touch it, and it dissolves, slips like sand through your fingers.

Some days I find comfort in that—in the idea that it was all an illusion. A trick of the mind. It lessens the enormity of the loss.

But some days, I convince myself that life really was that lovely. Once. Memories provide refuge when the days become too much. Beauty is possible, I remind myself. Great truths are possible. Love is possible.

But they are gone all too soon . . .

1914

HOLDING HER BREATH AND HER TONGUE

Before the bombs fell, there stood at the northern edge of the Rossau, in a quiet block of Stroheckgasse, a house with a copper door.

No one knew whose idea it had been to fit a copper door in the front of what was in every other way an unassuming structure. There were no gargoyles to keep the door company. No stonework, no columns, no turrets or cupolas. Nothing at all to make the door seem more at home in its surroundings. The house was, quite simply, a house, like countless others. And yet, someone had seen fit to lend it this one distinction. The logic of their choice had, of course, been lost to history. The improvement had been made generations before, far enough back that the once lustrous metal had long since crusted over with the patina of time, and the place had been known for many years simply as "the house with the green door."

Despite its somewhat peculiar entrance, it was a respectable enough house on a respectable enough street, filled with respectable—if slightly eccentric—people. It was home to Dr. Ansel Eder, esteemed chair of the Department of Political Philosophy at the University of Vienna.

A Sunday evening in early May found Dr. Eder surrounded by disciples. He sat, as he always did, in an overstuffed wingback chair next to the parlor fire. The very picture of a king holding court.

The night was warm, and though Dr. Eder had insisted on a fire to help light the room, its heat was a nuisance. He had already discarded his sack coat and rolled up his shirtsleeves, and still a bead of sweat crept down his forehead while he spoke, gradually picking up speed until its progress was interrupted by a wiry eyebrow that begged a comb and a trim. Perhaps it would have been more dignified of Dr. Eder to move to a cooler spot near one of the open windows—any among his guests would have been more than happy to give up their chair to him. But in typical fashion, the sovereign refused to cede his throne.

It was a familiar scene, this academic hotchpotch. The always affable Dr. Oppenheim with his balding head, a pair of wire-rimmed glasses lending a grandfatherly twinkle to his eye; Professor Leitner, the quiet prodigy, a pointed beard marking his intellectual prowess; Professor Neumann, his bushy mane scattered this way and that, his fervor so great that even his hair could not be contained; along with a smattering of less devoted followers who drifted in and out of Dr. Eder's orbit. For years, these men had huddled each week at the house with the green door to debate the finer points of political theory and philosophy. No appointment was needed where tradition reigned.

Just as familiar as the gathering itself was the specter lurking in the shadows cast by the firelight. This fair-haired phantom was Ilse Eder, Dr. Eder's youngest daughter, whose blue-green eyes echoed the verdigris of the door to her home. Over the years, Ilse had perfected the art of sitting in the corner of this room. With a book in her hands or a bit of neglected embroidery on her lap, she would blend in with the walls, assisted by the clouds of cigar smoke and an acute awareness of her own insignificance. She made not a sound, but her brow forever furrowed in interest and concentration. Undetected—or unremarked, at least, for even the intellectuals who flocked to the house with the green door could not help noticing a pretty young woman in their midst—Ilse silently captured the ideas that skittered about like birdshot, carefully stowing each one. The lofty ideals espoused were nourishment. Even the gentlemen's most fiery rhetoric, usually saved for night's end after the brandy had flowed for hours, never failed to give her something savory to chew on.

Ilse relished her glimpses into this world, which she knew would never truly admit her as one of its own. The weekly gatherings had been a constant in her young life. No matter what happened, she could walk into the parlor, breathe the smell of tobacco that clung to the upholstery, and feel comforted. Some things could be counted on. Some things would always be just as they had always been.

Lately, though, something *had* changed.

Lately, come Sunday evening, Ilse had been finding herself mildly queasy.

For weeks, she insisted it was merely indigestion. She told herself her tolerance for certain foods must be changing as she grew up. Surely, it was no more than that.

She chewed peppermint leaves, licorice roots; they did nothing to settle her. Ginger and chamomile proved equally fruitless. Confronted with such evidence, Ilse could persist in her delusions for only so long. Eventually, she had to admit it was not food that sat so uneasily in her stomach.

It was something closer to dread.

***

Two months earlier, Ilse had been sitting alone at her breakfast. She was always alone, it seemed. Generally, she had grown accustomed to isolation's persistent nibbling and nagging, but it ground its teeth into her bones at mealtimes. Precious hours that had once been filled with laughter and cheerful conversation. Therese's teasing, their mother's gentle chiding. Like sugar in a rotten tooth, the memories were painful in their sweetness.

How different the house had been before. How deafening the present silence.

In the months since Therese had left them, Ilse had learned how to hold loneliness at arm's length, never far away but not close enough to smother her. The trick was to keep her mind occupied. A volume of history at lunch. A novel at dinner on the nights Father stayed late at his office. At breakfast, it was a stained and crumpled copy of the preceding day's news, faithfully deposited on the Eder's doorstep each night after closing by Herr Hamerling, the owner of a nearby coffeehouse and one of Dr. Eder's many devotees.

It was just two weeks into March, and winter still held Vienna firmly in its grasp. The day was gray, and a squall of sleet was blowing through the city. Ilse could hear the sharp *flick-flick-flick* of ice pellets against the front door. Reflexively, she drew her shawl more tightly around her shoulders as she ate.

Dr. Eder had left for campus in the predawn darkness, and Ilse had spread the snow-dampened paper carefully across the table in front of her. She tore off bits of *semmel* with ink-stained fingers, slathering them with butter before popping them into her mouth. She paid little attention to the food. Her eyes were too busy devouring the day's main story: with the stroke of a pen, Count Stürgkh had dissolved the *Reichsrat*.[1]

Ilse read the story with interest, even indignation. But there was little risk her umbrage would turn into outrage. She was young and impulsive, easily provoked into excitement or passion, but seldom was she led into anger. Ilse sizzled; she did not boil.

As she read, she maintained a cautious disinterest. She

assured herself that everything would be fine. Indeed, it took little convincing.

The Eders lived close enough to the heart of Vienna to walk from their doorstep to the parliament without ever feeling winded. Yet the intrigues enacted behind that building's walls had always seemed distant affairs to Ilse. After all, the count and his contemporaries in the upper house were as far beyond her reach as she was beneath their notice. Archdukes, archbishops, peers of the highest nobility. She knew them only from the few political cartoons that evaded the *konfisziert* stamp.[2] To her, they were little more than flatfooted caricatures, laughable extremes. One moment they were despots; the next, they were hopeless bumblers. And as for the lower house . . . well, everyone knew they had been in disarray for years. Hundreds of men splintered into dozens of uncooperative factions with contrary aims. Even where their interests did align, they always found some detail to bicker over. More spectacle than statecraft.

They all could hem and haw or huff and puff, but it was the emperor, and only the emperor, who mattered in the end. He was all that ever mattered. If the emperor declared a man guilty of a crime, the man was guilty. If he wished to deny a manufacturing license, the machines sat idle. If he decreed that all grocers should wear red caps, red caps sprouted in markets from Galicia to Tyrol.

Ilse saw little reason to think the present slide away from suffrage would change much of anything in the long run. The government had fits and starts; this was nothing new. The sprawling labyrinth of imperial bureaucracy was at once heavy-handed and inept. Despite this latest setback, Ilse was sure they would muddle along. Muddling was their way. It had always *been* their way.

No one got much from the system, of course. But then, no one expected much either. That was the beauty of it. Rather liberating, really. Without the burden of fretting about politics, they could all attend to finer things. Like music and literature. The essence of beauty. Unlocking the human mind with all its powers and secrets. And these, after all, were matters worth pursuing.

Even for her father and his colleagues, men who made the study of politics the work of their lives, politics was rarely more than a mental exercise. A quest to discover truth, to discover good. They debated metaphysics and epistemology. They devised doctrines on the correct organization of human governance. But did any of them have even the slightest expectation their recipes might be tried? Of course not. Not in the realm of the Habsburgs. The academics and intellectuals could spend hours in smoke-filled coffeehouses arguing about the meaning of justice. The following day, they would open their curtains and look out at a system that defied every conception of the word, yet they would never raise an arm in protest. Not even Professor Neumann.

There was nothing contrary about this. It was simply rational. Reasonable. Why waste energy fighting for ideals you know to be out of reach? Apathy was a learned behavior and a hereditary trait. It had been internalized through years bearing witness, passed down from one generation to the next in a city where fine brocade papered over moldering walls.

Even at seventeen, the height of youthful romanticism, Ilse found little incentive to shake off her indifference. Its comforts were just so tempting. It whispered to her in her father's voice, *"Do not trouble yourself, child. There's nothing you can do, so there's nothing you should do. Best to simply leave things be."*

As Ilse sat reading her paper and chewing her roll, she began to second-guess her reaction. She wondered whether her father and his friends would be as unbothered by the day's news. After considering it for a moment, she felt certain they would. It was the only logical response. Confident in her decision to suspend herself in aloofness, she even dared to spread a thick layer of jam on her bread. Her hands were steady. No dollops of fruit would find their way down the front of her blouse.

Ilse assumed the future would mirror the past. She was not the first to make this mistake; she would not be the last.

It quickly became apparent that, on this occasion, Dr. Eder and his colleagues had reached a very different conclusion than Ilse had expected. In the weeks that followed, she watched, amazed, as the men transformed before her eyes. What was once a fussy knot of middle-aged scholars became something akin to a frenzied congregation of evangelists. With each point and counterpoint, their sermons foretold impending doom.

To his credit, the always-sensible Leitner had tried to model restraint. During their first gathering after Count Stürgkh let fall his heavy hand, Ilse watched Professor Leitner closely from her corner of the parlor. He took slow puffs from his cigar, closing his eyes, holding the warm smoke before releasing careful rings, then watching as the circles spread and diffused. A meditation to subdue any quake in his voice, any tremor that might betray him.

"The empire has had brushes with instability before," he reasoned from behind his smoke screen. "Even you, Neumann, cannot deny that."

"This is true," Oppenheim had replied, his eyebrows reaching up to grasp at this sliver of hope. "After all, no country or kingdom can boast our record of installing and removing heads of government. What is it, six times in the last decade alone?"

"Seven by my count."

"Precisely! The government does few things well, but instability . . . that is surely what it does best!"

A young associate who had joined the men for the first time that evening chuckled nervously. His eyes darted about, scanning the faces of the older men, reading them for cues.

"But it is not just the instability!" Professor Neumann cried out, practically leaping from his chair.

"Calm yourself, Neumann," Leitner urged.

But Neumann would not be calm. He ran his fingers back through his hair and pulled his hands away. His hair stood out from his scalp as if his body coursed with electricity. His patience was spent. He would not be pacified; he would not be talked out of his ire. He knew better.

"Something feels different this time; something *is* different. Can't any of you see it? This time, it's not that the body is replacing its head. This time, the head has forsaken the body!"

Neumann panted. The nervous young man froze. Everyone else in the room turned their eyes to Dr. Eder, who stared into his empty glass, searching for answers in the last traces of his drink like a seer reading tea.

"Neumann is right, Jozef," he had conceded at last, setting his glass on the side table and sitting back in his chair. He sighed, ran the pads of his middle fingers across his eyebrows. "Emperor or no emperor, without a legislature—even a feckless one—the government is a house of cards. A house of cards can't secure an empire as nationalists of every stripe fight to rend it apart. A house of cards will topple with the slightest jostling."

He was not Neumann; Dr. Eder did not rely on shouts or wild gesticulation to carry his point. He spoke softly, calmly, barely above a whisper. But no one missed how he dug his fingernails into the arms of his chair. The move might have been lost on a less observant crowd, but Dr. Eder's daughter and colleagues knew him too well. They all saw it for what it was.

The tension in his fingers screamed like a siren.

From that night forward, any pretense at debate had been set aside. In its place, the men had chosen instead to wallow in prophecy. Professor Neumann, eyes as wild as his hair, was unleashed. He raved about the coming authoritarian onslaught while the rest sat worriedly turning glasses of port and plum brandy in their hands and feeling their own importance—they, the elite few who could see the future so clearly.

Through it all, the ever-present specter sat in her corner, holding her breath along with her tongue.

***

After weeks spent twisting his hands behind the closed door of his study, Dr. Eder had settled his mind on just one thing: Vienna was no place for Ilse. Summer promised to raise both temperatures and tempers. It was better that his Ilse, so bright-eyed and impressionable, eager to try the world's waters, be kept far from those aching to write history across the streets of the capital. Therese, his eldest, had been established at her father-in-law's estate outside Linz for nearly a year. By now, the professor reasoned, Therese must be seen there as family. It only followed that, as Therese's sister, Ilse must be family as well. And so, as much as it pained him to part with his youngest child, he had made his decision. Ilse would go to Linz, to the Kassners, for the summer.

His edict had fallen with the force of a guillotine.

It was not that Ilse had no desire to see her sister. She loved Therese dearly, and she would have been thrilled under any other circumstance at the prospect of a visit. But this was not just a visit. Ilse was not being offered a holiday, not dashing off to go frolic in the mountains. She was being *handled.* Disposed of. To be so unceremoniously sentenced to a summer of seclusion felt like punishment for a crime she had not committed.

The fact that she was being sent away for *this* of all summers compounded the insult. Her father could read a calendar as well as she. He, too, had watched its agonizing trudge through the long winter months, approaching her June birthday at a crawl. He could not have forgotten his promise to finally introduce her into society once she turned eighteen. Indeed, he had often teased her about it. "Come this time next year, I suppose I shall have to wait on myself," he would remark as she poured him his nightcap and cut his cigar. "You'll be far too busy flitting about town to tend to a stuffy old man."

Her father had not forgotten. Moreover, Dr. Eder knew how much Ilse longed to be out. He had taught her the value of serious pursuits and enriched her mind with an unconventional education, but he was not blind. He could see that, despite his best efforts, Ilse's desires were not so different from those of any girl her age. Though she dedicated her afternoon hours to the study of Plato and Kant, Machiavelli and Rousseau, Dr. Eder had frequently observed the faraway look that would settle over her eyes each time she turned a page, as though her mind, for just that moment, had floated off to some sparkling scene.

Dr. Eder could not blame her, of course. Few raised within sight of Vienna's glitter could resist its seductive pull, and his Ilse certainly had not been born with a constitution that could withstand such temptations. Perhaps if she had been made of stiffer stuff, Ilse would not cherish visions of herself waltzing beneath the chandeliers of Kursalon. Maybe then she might dismiss as frivolous the idea of attending sunset concerts in Stadtpark, of strolling along the Prater, dazzling the young men not just with her looks but with her lively mind, as Therese had done before her.

No, Dr. Eder did not blame Ilse. But neither would he encourage her. And he certainly would not indulge her *now*. There was too much at stake.

For her part, Ilse knew deep down it was childish to cling to fancies as the city's bedrock eroded beneath her feet. She scolded herself each time she caught her focus drifting, reminding herself of the gravity of the situation. But logic could not dislodge her daydreams. Before long, her mind would run off again, and she would be twirling under a starlit sky, the sounds of an orchestra dancing around her.

In truth, it was not simply the dresses and music and plays that kept Ilse dreaming. She longed for *society* in the most basic sense. She longed for company. She had completed her formal schooling two years before and, since then, had continued her education privately under her father's tutelage. Since Therese's marriage and subsequent departure from Vienna, Ilse had scarcely left the house. She had spent the better part of a year alone, quietly resenting the constraints the world insisted on placing on young women.

Having no proper chaperone of her own, Ilse knew that even after she'd been introduced into society, her engagements would be more limited than those of other girls in her circle. Beyond his close cadre of colleagues, her father rarely went out in company, and though Frau Neumann had graciously offered to take her about town, Ilse knew that lady's primary focus must be on her own daughter, Lily, who had just recently come out as well. Being so dependent on the charity of their neighbors was bad enough. Yet, so long as she was *in* Vienna, Ilse could at least hope to have some broadening of her daily interactions. But now, it seemed, she would be denied even those pleasures charity might offer. Her father and fate demanded that she spend the summer on a quiet estate on the outskirts of Linz, tiptoeing her way through each day as an uninvited guest among her sister's chosen family.

Plainly put, it was unacceptable. Ilse refused to be cast off without a fight. She had pled her case repeatedly in the weeks since Dr. Eder had made his decision known, and she would make one final plea tonight, even as her trunks sat packed in her room.

***

The gentlemen, savoring their shared misery, were loath to

separate at a polite hour. The clock in the foyer was chiming eleven as the last of Dr. Eder's colleagues finally trickled out. He breathed a heavy sigh as he locked the door behind them.

Ilse had waited impatiently for the house to clear, listening to the gentlemen's ranting, feeling the now familiar grit of unease forming on her teeth. She knew it was late; she knew her father was exhausted. But what choice did she have? This was her last chance, her last night at home. She was determined to set her qualms aside and have her say, regardless of the late hour.

When the professor turned with a yawn and a stretch to drag his body upstairs to bed, he found his daughter blocking the path.

"Father, might I speak with you before you retire for the night?" Ilse asked, striving to inject into her voice the right balance of sweetness and maturity.

Dr. Eder was not fooled. "You may speak to me about any subject. Except, of course, the one you wish to discuss," he said. "I have said everything I wish to on that head."

"And how do you know what I want to discuss?" Ilse kept her voice even. Innocent, harmless. She would not let her father provoke an outburst. She would maintain a calm demeanor. She would show him how mature and womanly she had become.

"Because you are my daughter. You can bat your eyes and try to sound angelic, but I know you too well to be taken in. You have had my answer, and my answer is final."

"But how can it be final when I have more to say in my defense?"

"It's final because nothing you say will change my decision."

"But Fa—"

"My mind is made up. Now, it's late. I'm tired. I bid you goodnight, child."

"But can't you see, I'm *not* a child anymore!" Ilse insisted. Her father's mulishness rubbed away her air of calm. The tinny edge of adolescence found its way back into her voice.

"Oh really?" Dr. Eder replied, maintaining his composure in sharp contrast to his daughter. "You certainly have a charming way of showing it. Only a child would be so ignorant of the dangers at her very doorstep."

The barb landed with its intended effect.

"How can you think me ignorant to the dangers?" Ilse cried, incredulous. "Have I not sat in that room every night these past two months? Have I not listened to the debates, the conjectures, the predictions? I am fully aware of the climate and what it portends, and I am perfectly capable of navigating it. Have you so little faith in me, in my judgment, that you see no choice but to pack me up and ship me off to Linz?"

Dr. Eder knew that Ilse had every right to bristle at his words. It was unjust of him to suggest she was some silly girl who knew nothing about the world. He knew how she prided herself on her learning. He, too, took pride in Ilse's achievements. When properly corralled, her mind was, indeed, rather remarkable. But he meant to disarm her. She needed to understand the one thing that until now she had refused to accept: Knowledge and experience are two very different things. Without experience, too much knowledge breeds dangerous overconfidence, an assumption that one knows exactly how the world works. Without experience, the world is a precarious place.

He watched as Ilse cemented her lower lip, refusing to let it quiver, bracing it against her tongue to hold it steady. A portrait of willfulness. This daughter of his was so like her mother when she decided to dig in her heels. The memory hit him with force and freshness, draining his resolve.

"Dearest," he sighed. Gripping the banister for support, he lowered himself down, sitting on the third step. He took a handkerchief from his pocket and began to dab away the sweat that lingered on his brow. "It's not that I lack faith in you," he explained. "You are and have always been my brilliant girl. I'm sure you grasp the situation better than most grown men walking the streets. But these things, they're *merciless*. Chaos has a way of overwhelming even the strongest tower. And after losing your mother . . . I simply cannot bear the thought of losing you, too. I could not endure it. I won't allow you simply to be swept away."

Ilse looked down at her father, at his eyes that begged her understanding. He appeared to her suddenly diminished, extinguished, the smoldering remains of a once blistering fire. She loved him too well to continue her resistance in the face of such a pitiable sight.

And so, she relented. Without the advantage of the final word, Ilse let the subject drop. Swallowing defeat, she kissed her father on the top of his head and went upstairs to pass a sleepless night. With the first light of morning, she forced herself from her bed to prepare for her journey.

Later that day, the housemaid would cloak the furniture of Ilse's room in dustcovers that would not be removed for eight years.

AN UNSEASONED TRAVELER

Swept away. Her father had used those exact words. *Swept away.* They clung like spider webs, invisible yet impossible to brush off.

It was not only his words but his manner that troubled Ilse. Her father was a lion, always strong, forever infallible in her eyes. She had never seen him looking so thoroughly overcome as he had appeared when she'd bidden him pleasant dreams the night before. Not even in her mother's final days. It had not been Ilse's own words that had worked the change in him, of that she was sure. No, it was the unbearable weight of a future he could see coming but was powerless to stop.

As the train clattered through the countryside, Ilse relived their conversation in her mind. With each *chug-clank* of the railcar, Dr. Eder's words echoed off the distant mountains. *Swept away, swept away, swept away.* The train carried her farther and farther from danger; still, the words resounded. Reverberating like an alarm. A warning bell.

By the time the train eased to a halt at platform four of Linz *Hauptbahnhof,*[3] Ilse had worked herself into a spate of nervous jitters. After double- and triple-checking the car to ensure she had left nothing behind, she emerged from the train, lowering herself gingerly onto the platform. The moment her boot touched the pavement, steam from the engine hissed as though expressing its disapproval at her presence. Ilse, startled by the sudden burst, jumped and stumbled into a man who was trying to hurry around her. She stammered an apology, but he was already gone. He had no time for the fumblings of an unseasoned traveler.

A swarm of passengers and well-wishers soon buzzed all around. Ilse scoured the crowd for any sign of a familiar face, clenching the worn leather handle of her carpet bag so tightly that her knuckles whitened and her fingernails left little red crescents in the heels of her palms.

The clouds hung low, and the air was thick with drizzle that grabbed hold of soot from each puff of the trains rumbling in and out of the station. Ilse's lungs burned with each breath as she paced the platform. Her eyes reddened and teared as she squinted through the haze. She blinked to clear them.

Where on earth is Therese? The face of the station clock, glowing in the dim light of the murky afternoon, read ten minutes past three o'clock. Ilse drew her mother's silver watch from her coat pocket, confirmed the time, squeezed it to draw courage. *The train wasn't early,* she mused. *Therese should be here by now. If not her, then Friedrich, Amalia, a servant,* someone.

But to Ilse's mortification, she could find no sign of any of them.

The crowd on the platform began to disburse, and the conductor called straggling passengers aboard. Ilse wandered inside the station building. Finding an empty bench, she sat, striking as dignified a pose as she could muster while her mind spun out a thousand possibilities of what could have detained her usually exacting sister.

For all her father's fears about her spending the summer in Vienna, at least Ilse *knew* Vienna. Yes, there were rallies in the streets. Yes, the more radical young men could be a bother as they stirred up the crowds from atop their soapboxes. But she knew to avoid an overcrowded square. She could recognize the echoes of a forcefully shouted assent. The streets were her old friends. They would always offer her safe passage.

But here? Here, she was at a loss. Surrounded by strangers in a strange city.

Insufferable minutes ticked by, and Ilse's posture crept toward a slump. Frustrated and helpless, her thoughts again drifted back to the night before and every other night when she had pleaded with her father not to send her away. Vienna was no place for her, he had insisted, and yet here she sat, abandoned in a filthy train station, at the mercy of any passing criminal who might rob her . . . or worse.

Despite her best attempts to evict it, a sullen adolescent still found refuge within Ilse. It surfaced from time to time, stomping its foot when stress or strain forced down her guard. The longer she sat alone on the bench, the more her mind gave way to peevishness, her sober reflections from the train all but forgotten.

If I were to be taken at knifepoint, dragged into a dark corner by an escaped convict—some fiend who would slit my throat and rifle through the unmentionables in my traveling bag—that would be a sweet irony.

Adolescent Ilse relished the idea of meeting such a shocking end. Adolescent Ilse smirked as she pictured the police nabbing her killer right as he presented her lacy drawers to his lady love. But Ilse the Rational Young Woman quickly reasserted herself.

Then again, if that were to happen, I would be dead. And if I were dead, I wouldn't have the satisfaction of seeing the look on Father's face when he realized just how wrong he has been. So perhaps another form of vindication might be altogether preferable . . .

"Ilse!"

A familiar voice trilled above the din, disrupting Ilse's rumination. She looked up to see her sister crossing the lobby, the hint of a skip animating her quick steps.

Therese was impeccably dressed but ever-so-slightly flushed. Even in the muted light of the station, the pink of her cheeks drew out the red undertones in her neatly arranged auburn hair.

"I am so sorry we are late," Therese apologized as she rushed up. She pulled Ilse to her feet and straightened and smoothed her sister's traveling coat before brushing a kiss on her cheek. "Friedrich had business in town this morning," Therese explained, "and I told him very distinctly that he absolutely *must* return with the car by *two thirty sharp* so that I could come to retrieve you. An instruction that naturally he chose to ignore."

"Now, is that fair, my love?" said a dashing gentleman as he sauntered up to the pair. "Hello, Ilse." His smile was wide and genuine. He wrapped Ilse in an embrace, arching his back to lift her a few inches before depositing her, laughing, back on the floor. He grabbed her bag from the bench and steered the small party toward the exit. "You have no idea how happy I was to learn you were to join us for the summer. So delighted, in fact, that I urged your sister to come *with* me into town this morning, for I knew I would never be able to conclude my business in time to both fetch her from Bergesschatten *and* be here to greet you when your train arrived."

"And what, pray, would you have had me do by myself in town for all the morning and afternoon in this dreadful weather?" Therese and her husband continued to joust in this playful manner while they walked out of the station and toward the gleaming black Benz that awaited them. Ilse couldn't decide whether she should be amused at their easy rapport and spirited attempts to cast aspersions on each other or annoyed that they clearly had no need for her to participate in their dialogue, not even to return their greetings. She opted for the former.

Outside the station, Friedrich instructed the chauffeur to retrieve Fraulein Eder's trunks and head for home. The three of them then settled into the back of the car, where Friedrich finally made room in the conversation for Ilse.

"So, my dear sister, tell us about your travels. Did you have a pleasant journey?"

"Very pleasant, indeed," Ilse replied. "And the hours passed more quickly than I could have imagined. I shared a car with a nice couple who had been traveling all the way from Constantinople, where they had just spent their honeymoon. There was also an older gentleman, but he spent the entire trip napping with his fedora pulled down over his eyes. Had it not been for the occasional snore, we might have been tempted to check him for a pulse."

Ilse saw no need to mention that she had scarcely spoken to her car mates during the journey. Therese need not be burdened with the darker thoughts that had consumed her for most of the afternoon.

"Perhaps he wasn't napping," Friedrich suggested. "Perhaps he was just pretending to sleep and hoping you would step outside so he could observe the newlyweds in their natural habitat."

"Friedrich, you're terrible," scolded Therese with a roll of her eye and a gentle elbow to his ribs. "Really, though, I am relieved to hear you were in decent company. When I learned Father was planning to send you alone, without any sort of chaperone, I could scarcely keep my temper in check."

"*Pah!*" her husband guffawed with a whoop. "If you call the tirade you let fly after reading his letter *keeping your temper in check*, I should hate to see you when you lose it!"

"Really, Therese, you shouldn't have worried," Ilse assured her. "As you can see, I've made it to you in one piece. You forget that I, too, have grown a year older in the year since you left home. I am practically an old lady now. I can manage myself for a few hours on a train."

"Of course you can." Therese gave her sister's arm a patronizing little pat that said she didn't quite believe her. "But that's beside the point. It's not proper for you to be traveling on your own. It's very nearly indecent. You cannot go to the shops alone. What on earth possessed Father to think it appropriate for you to travel unaccompanied?"

Ilse made no reply but thought to herself, *Father has far more to worry about these days than society's ridiculous insistence that unmarried women are fragile flowers who must be shielded against the wind.*

"In any event," Therese went on, "I *am* glad you're here and that I get you for the whole of the summer. Having someone on my side for a change will be such a tremendous relief."

"Oh, come now, my love, I'm always on your side!" Friedrich exclaimed in his own defense.

"Yes, but you *have to* be. We have a binding contract, blessed by God, Father Theodor, and my father's attorney, which says you must always agree with me," she chided. "Ilse will be on my side because she *actually* agrees with me and takes pity."

There was something in her sister's voice and manner of speaking that Ilse did not quite recognize. Something unnatural. An affectedness. Ilse chased away the thought almost as soon as she'd had it. It was probably just the novelty of the situation. Welcoming a visitor to her new home for the first time, Therese must simply be on edge.

The train station being on the city's south side, and the Kassner family estate being on the northern and opposite bank of the Danube River, the drive home took them through the heart of Linz. As they made slow progress up the Landstrasse, Friedrich pointed through the jumble of carts and pedestrians to various sites of interest. The Carmelite convent with its modest façade. Just up the street, the magnificent Ursuline Church with its buttery-smooth stucco, impressive baroque columns, and twin bell towers, each topped with an onion-shaped copper cupola that glowed bright turquoise against the gray sky.

Without warning, the narrow avenue burst into a broad and

bustling market square. A marble pillar rose at the plaza's center, its carved surface twisting twenty meters to the sky. Perched at its zenith, the figures of Father, Son, and Holy Ghost, unironically gilded in gold, kept watch over their flock below. "The Trinity Column," Friedrich explained. "A grateful city's expression of thanks to God for sending them success and prosperity."

"Also known as *good chance*," Therese translated. Friedrich feigned offense, and Ilse laughed, glad despite everything to be in their company again after so many months apart.

The car passed out of the square and, within seconds, was crossing over the river, leaving the busy commercial center behind them.

Thrust again before Ilse's view were the craggy forests of the Alpine foothills, which she had admired for much of her journey. Amid the crowded streets of Linz, she could have almost pretended that she had strayed into an unfamiliar section of Vienna, but as they made their way west along the Danube, she felt for the first time that she was away from home. As much as she wanted to marinate in disappointment at having been exiled, an irrepressible sense of adventure began to stir. Brooding was, in general, against her character, and as she stared up at the rocky prominences and thickly forested hills, she found it impossible to sustain a sour mood.

After about a quarter of an hour, the road pulled back from the river, and shortly after that, they turned and drove through a pair of ornate iron gates onto the lane that led to Haus Bergesschatten, home of the Kassner family. As the house came into view, Ilse instantly saw that what she had always suspected was undeniably true: her sister had married into a world of wealth beyond anything Ilse had ever seen up close.

No wonder Therese was at a loss for what to do with a few free hours in town this morning, Ilse thought as she stared ahead in awe. *Where can Therese possibly fit in this world?*

QUITE AN ALTERED CREATURE

Friedrich Kassner was the eldest son of Andras Kassner, the latest in a line of staunch capitalists. With the savvy to match even the most grizzled old courtiers and industriousness to rival their American brethren, generations of Kassners had clawed their way out of obscurity. As the Habsburg Empire expanded, the Kassner family's business empire grew into new markets, and by the turn of the century, they had amassed a considerable fortune. Though the family continued to reside in their ancestral estate—a "modest" twenty-eight-room retreat on the Danube River built by Andras's grandfather—it was general knowledge that their affluence now bordered on the obscene. This, along with a stubbornly unblemished reputation, assured the Kassners freedom to move among the finest of Linz society, even absent the dignity of a noble rank.

You would never know any of this on meeting Friedrich. With an easy manner and a playful charm, Friedrich Kassner moved freely in *any* society. Intelligent and quick-witted, with an imposing physique, dark hair, and a face that was far from off-putting, the first-born child of Andras Kassner and his wife, Helene, strolled through life paying little mind to the expectations heaped on his shoulders.

With so much working in his favor, the Kassners had had every reason to hope their son would make an advantageous marriage. Friedrich's presentation, then, of Therese Eder as his chosen bride had evoked considerable consternation. Lovely and lively she might be, but Therese was still the daughter of, in Helene's words, an "eccentric educator" and, therefore, unworthy of joining their ranks. Friedrich's younger brother Kurt, then just seventeen, launched no such attacks. He demanded only that the lady not be opposed to frequent games of Consequences and Fictionary.

Andras, Helene, and their daughter, Amalia, barely one year Friedrich's junior, had tried for weeks to convince him of his folly, but Friedrich held firm. Loving their son too much to risk an estrangement, the Kassners eventually surrendered, albeit begrudgingly. They conceded that the distasteful name of Therese Kassner would sour their tongues and burn their ears until that blessed day when death might part the upstart from their golden child.

Acquiescence was not acceptance, though.

"Apparently, Mrs. Eder died quite young," Amalia had consoled her mother as they examined floral arrangements for the engagement party. "Perhaps it will turn out to be a hereditary trait."

"That we could be so lucky!"

Only the stoutest of affections could have sustained Friedrich through such intrafamilial gamesmanship. And, indeed, his engagement to Therese was not the product of some fleeting infatuation. It was the culmination of a love affair years in the making.

Five years earlier, on arriving in Vienna to begin his studies at the university, Friedrich's quick and enquiring mind had caught the notice of the slightly bumbling but unquestionably brilliant Dr. Ansel Eder. Despite differences in age, demeanor, style, and perspective, this unlikely pair established an affinity. Dr. Eder delighted in the young man's spirit, and Friedrich felt something bordering on reverence for his professor's intellect and experience.

It was only a matter of time before Dr. Eder invited his acolyte to join him for a family dinner at the house with the green door. After that, it was only a matter of time before the young man became a fixture at Dr. Eder's salons. And after that, it was only a matter of time before Friedrich fell madly in love with Dr. Eder's eldest daughter.

This series of events, inevitable though it may seem, was not a foregone conclusion. Far from it.

When he first embarked on his weekly visits to the Eder home, lovemaking was the farthest thing from Friedrich's mind—if lovemaking can ever be said to be far from the mind of any young man of nineteen. Friedrich's joking manner belied the mind of a determined scholar. Early on, he courted the professor's company solely in the hopes that a bit of the old man's genius might rub off. He had attended Dr. Eder's salons for months, listening to the men and their quibbling. The professor and his colleagues even began to consider Friedrich as something of a mascot, like a well-mannered dog who performed tricks on command but otherwise sat quietly beside his master no matter how rowdy the party became.

Friedrich's defenses eventually wore away, however. In Therese Eder, he had found more than a pleasing face with a pair of hazel eyes that lit the room whenever he spoke. Therese had a mind ready to challenge his. She could sit listening for hours and then suddenly say six words that made each man present question his every assumption. She constantly surprised him. The love of a woman like Therese Eder was no trifle and not something to be casually cast aside.

And so, after three years of courtship, on a glorious day in May, Dr. Ansel Eder walked his eldest daughter down the aisle of Votivkirche, surrounded by cold gothic arches and even colder glares from a handful of Kassners.

Any triumph Therese might have felt in securing a husband

like Friedrich quickly dissipated. The reality of her new situation set in before the end of her first week at Bergesschatten. While not ostensibly cruel, Helene and Amalia thought little of the newest member of their family. They offered compliments through gritted teeth, critique with the faintest glimmer of glee.

Friedrich saw none of this. Though brilliant in his own right, he was still a man, after all, and largely oblivious to social nuance.

But each and every pinprick was felt keenly by Therese.

Therese Eder had come of age in a world where she was the equal—and frequently the superior—of every other girl in her company. Nature had blessed her with beauty and intelligence. To this, her father had added a careful education, and her mother had refined her manners to pragmatic politeness. Being looked down upon was a new and entirely unwelcome sensation, a pill that stuck in her throat. Beyond merely surviving, it became her life's mission to gain the approval of her mother- and sister-in-law.

Therese's desperation to please was not lost on these two fine ladies. Unfortunately, instead of having the intended effect, her efforts made her the subject of many a private joke and much outright derision behind closed doors.

After a year in such an inhospitable climate, Therese had become quite an altered creature. Without her father's steady hand and counsel, she unconsciously resorted to mimicking Helene and Amalia's manners and conversation in her daily pains to impress. Though Friedrich still loved his wife, he often caught himself wondering what had happened to the sensible girl he had known in Vienna and if he would ever see that girl again.

***

The car rolled to a gentle stop in front of the house. A footman, bearing as stiff as his livery, stepped forward to open the door and hand the ladies out.

"Thank you, Franz," said Therese, taking the hand he offered. "My sister, Fraulein Eder," she noted briefly, motioning back to Ilse with a breezy gesture.

Ilse stepped down and felt the grit of finely crushed gravel beneath her boot.

"Fraulein." The footman acknowledged her with a click of the heel, a brisk nod. Without waiting for a reply, he pivoted and turned his attention to her trunks, working to untie them from the back of the car, muttering under his breath as he struggled to loosen the knots.

Ilse scarcely noticed the servant's lapse in decorum. She didn't see how, for just a fraction of a second, his eyes lingered over the scuffs on her boots, the cheap cloth of her skirt. Sizing her up. Deciding he would have few demands from this visitor.

While the footman was busy making these calculations, Ilse's gaze fixed on the face of Bergesschatten. It rose up before her, looking down its nose at them. Smooth yellow stucco, high windows, ornamental cornices, undulating columns. It was clear the architect had drawn inspiration from the Ursalines, clearer still that Friedrich's ancestor had commissioned this building to be grander than even the most impressive structure in Linz. The former Herr Kassner had not been building a house; he had been making a point.

"Come, Ilse," Therese beckoned as she followed her husband inside.

Ilse shook off her trance and scurried after Therese through a pair of elaborately carved double doors into the grand foyer. To Ilse's surprise, Friedrich had already disappeared into the depths of the house, leaving Therese to introduce her to a kind-looking housekeeper, Frau Brunner, and the butler, Herr Wimmer. Ilse couldn't help noticing the latter bore a striking resemblance to Schmusen, her neighbor's pug.

Introductions complete, Ilse started to remove her traveling coat to hand to the awaiting Frau Brunner, but Therese set her to rights.

"No, no, leave it on," she said authoritatively, waving the housekeeper away. She positioned herself in front of Ilse. "Now, let me inspect you."

Therese batted at the stubborn creases in the front of her sister's skirt and tugged at her coat, brushed dust off her shoulders. The effect was marginal, but the effort seemed to placate her. "Hat off," she instructed, and Ilse obeyed. She fussed at Ilse's hairpins, hoping to capture a few wisps that had pulled free. She moistened her fingers, ran them across the curls that had frizzled in the damp weather, sighed as the hairs seemed to stick out even more.

"Now, let me look at you," Therese said. She stepped back to survey her work while Ilse stood there, anxiously rolling up on the sides of her feet and back down again, an eyebrow cocked in impatience. Therese frowned at her sister's fidgeting but finally sighed and forced a smile. "Well, you're still a bit of a rumple, but I suppose it will have to do. We certainly won't manage any better today!" She tittered. Her laugh had a hollow, metallic quality that grated against Ilse's spine.

"All right, hat back on."

"What?" Ilse did not bother to suppress her confusion.

"You heard me. Hat back on."

Ilse obeyed, dumbfounded, and watched as her sister stepped over to a mirror near the door and began performing this same ritual on herself. Scrutinizing her reflection in the glass, Therese noticed a bemused Ilse standing a few feet behind her.

"Don't look at me like that," Therese chided as she pushed a strand of hair behind her ear and pinched color into her cheeks.

"Like what?"

"Like I'm trying to blow music from a banana."

"I wasn't—"

"I know how wild your hair can get, so that, of course, had to be fixed. But it would be positively insolent to present ourselves without traveling attire before Mother Kassner and Amalia. They must be assured that your very first business upon arriving was to pay your respects to them."

Ilse wondered at Therese's newfound superciliousness, but she accepted these rules of engagement without question.

Shaking any traces of anxiety out of her face, Therese threw her shoulders back and led the way toward the back of the house, where the entrance to a large drawing room was tucked beneath one side of the double staircase that wrapped the back half of the great hall.

The room they entered housed exquisite antiques, priceless vases, and two respectable ladies. Ilse immediately recognized the latter from the wedding as the arrogant Frau Helene Kassner and her equally-condescending daughter, Amalia. Neither lady stirred when Therese and Ilse arrived.

Frau Kassner sat perfectly erect on a divan near the fireplace, ankles crossed, mouth pinched, hands clenched in her lap. Her elbows jutted stiffly to her sides. She gave the impression of a housecat eyeing a butterfly—contained, not wanting to draw notice, yet ready to pounce without warning. Amalia lounged in a far less intentional pose on a settee by one of the large arched windows overlooking the river. Had Ilse never met this pair before, the tableau into which she had stumbled painted so accurate a portrait of their characters as to tell her everything she needed to know. Contempt was the motivating emotion of Frau Kassner's life; ennui, Amalia's.

"Here we are!" Therese chirped, removing her hat once again. Ilse, following her sister's cue, took off her own hat as well. "Good afternoon, Mother Kassner. Good afternoon, Amalia. Allow me to present my sister, Ilse."

"Yes, we know who this is," sighed Helene. Her expression

did not change, but her eyes managed to roll. "Good day, Fraulein Eder," the lady continued. She deployed a more formal address than Therese's introduction, a distinction Ilse did not fail to notice. "You are welcome at Bergesschatten."

"Thank you ever so much, Frau Kassner. It is such a pleasure to see you again, and you also, Fraulein Kassner." Ilse bobbed a demi-curtsy to them both.

Curiously, no one said a thing in reply. Feeling exposed in the charged silence, Ilse kept speaking.

"I really am delighted to find you both looking so well, and I want to extend my warmest gratitude to you both—and of course, to Herr Kassner—for welcoming me so graciously into your home. Although I suppose I will see Herr Kassner soon enough and can thank him for myself when I do." Ilse spoke rapidly, her eyes on Frau Kassner's knees, unable to meet her hostess's iron stare.

Therese stifled a groan. Her sister, she knew, tended to ramble when nervous. It usually was charming in a vaguely pitiful way, but the quirk was sadly inappropriate on the present occasion.

Frau Kassner roused herself to speak again, if only to silence her guest. "Please don't fawn so, my dear. It is beneath your dignity. I'm forever trying to correct the same bad habit in your sister."

Therese's heat rose at this unconcealed barb. She knew full well that where *she* was concerned, her mother-in-law could never be shown too much respect.

"Tell me, how was your journey?"

"Very pleasant," Ilse replied. She had taken her lesson. She kept her answer short.

"And you are to be with us for the whole summer?"

"I believe so, madam." A pause. "I do hope the length of my stay will not inconvenience you." Ilse's eyes jumped from Helene to Amalia, back again.

"Not at all, not at all. Your father was quite right to send you to your sister, things being what they are," Helene replied, showing much more grace than when Friedrich had first presented the idea of a houseguest to her. "As it is, we will not be at home for most of your time here. Amalia and I will travel to Pula with my husband early next month. Friedrich and Therese will remain here, of course. With you."

"I had thought you had no idea of heading south until July," inquired Therese, her statement taking the tone of a question. Her mother-in-law's pronouncement had taken her by surprise.

"Our plans changed," stated Frau Kassner flatly. "My husband finds he has business in Trieste that cannot wait. Amalia and I decided we had just as well travel to the coast with him and spend the extra month by the sea."

Very likely, thought Therese, suspecting this was merely a pretense. Her in-laws would avoid an unwanted guest as much as basic civility could excuse.

Ilse could feel the temperature of the room rising. "I have never seen the sea, but I've heard that Pula is beautiful," she offered. "I'm sure you won't regret extending your stay there."

"Well," interrupted Therese, eager to close this initial interview before her sister could start chattering again, "Ilse has had a long afternoon of travel and is, I'm sure, quite anxious to change out of her traveling clothes and freshen up. But, good creature that she is, she insisted on wasting not even one moment before coming to pay her respects to you. Dinner is at seven tonight, I presume?"

"Is dinner not at seven every night?" said Amalia, finally deciding she needed a place in the dialogue and spotting an opening to needle Therese.

"Yes, of course," Therese muttered. Her cheeks burned, but she wrenched her lips into a cloying smile. "We will see you this evening."

And with that, the only traces of the Eder sisters left in the room were the faint echoes of their footfalls as they hurried back across the foyer and up the stairs.

MORE THAN A PASSING IMPRESSION

Ilse Eder was a quick study. Before many days had passed, she learned that the dominant feature of life at Bergesschatten was a busy monotony.

Each morning, she awoke to the first burst of light as the sun surged over the mountains. She rose, she bathed, she made herself presentable with the unsolicited assistance of Therese's maid, Maria. She bore Maria's constant *tut-tutting* at the lack of finery hanging in Fraulein Eder's wardrobe. Where were the brocades? Where was the beadwork? And such a shocking lack of silk charmeuse! Ilse's attempts to explain that her father encouraged simple dress so her mind, not her person, might be the focus of the world's attention drew nothing but giggles and headshakes.

After Maria bestowed her needless assurance that Ilse would not shame herself, Ilse joined the family in the breakfast room. She ate her meal without speaking, without being called on to speak. She waited patiently as sections of the daily news made their way around the table, starting with the venerable Herr Kassner before circulating to Friedrich, then to his mother, followed by Therese, and then Ilse herself. (Amalia saw no need to trouble herself with the drudgery of world events.) Frequently, by the time Ilse had read a word, Herr Kassner had retired to his study to squint over figures and reports, and Friedrich was placing a peck on his wife's forehead and departing to oversee the activities of their offices in town.

After breakfast, the ladies departed for their own corners of the house to spend the daylight hours carefully avoiding each other's company without ever giving the appearance of doing so. It was a dance they had perfected, and Haus Bergesschatten was an able dancing partner. Given the size of the house and the expanse of the grounds, were it not for bells calling them to luncheon at midday and to coffee when Friedrich returned from the city, the paths of the Kassner and Eder contingents on most days would not have crossed.

After coffee came an hour for dressing, an hour for cocktails, dinner, cigars for the gentlemen, music and reading for the ladies, and a glass of wine. Then the family made their way to bed to restore themselves for the next identical day.

Indeed, the only variation to their daily equation was the number of ladies and gentlemen present, as neighbors, acquaintances, and business associates came and went, seeking to curry favor with this influential family.

Stifled by the tedium of such routines, Ilse sought refuge outdoors. Far beyond the walls of the pristine and prickly mansion, she found solace exploring the woods lining the Danube and the surrounding foothills. Therese permitted this freedom so long as Ilse stayed within easy sight of the house.

Ilse obeyed her sister's dictate on the first afternoon.

She tried her best to obey it on her second afternoon.

By the third day, she ignored it entirely.

On this third afternoon after her arrival, a bout of ennui began to well up within Ilse. She refused to succumb to it, felt compelled to chase it away. After first glancing around to be sure no one was in sight, she raised her skirts, just enough to free her gangly legs, and then burst into a full sprint, running as fast and as far as she could until, at last, she collapsed into a heap of breathless laughter.

Anyone chancing upon Ilse in this private moment would have found her wholly enchanting or completely mad. In truth, Ilse was not mad. After three days of constrained conversation, she was homesick. Desperately so. It was not so much the sights and sounds of Vienna that she missed; she longed for the unreserved confidant she had once known in Therese.

Try though she might, Ilse could not find the sister she had known in the fussy and fashionable woman who haunted the halls of Bergesschatten. This new Therese moved like a ghost across the spotless floors, the fine carpets. There but not there. Screaming to be noticed while using as little air as possible. This new Therese was artificial and detached. Shallow, somehow. A shell of the vibrant young woman she once was. Endlessly absorbed in her own concerns, this Therese scored every move Ilse made, every word Ilse spoke against some unknown system based on how they might reflect back on herself.

Lying in the untamed grasses, Ilse stretched her arms above her head, soaking in the sunshine, and tucked her hands behind her neck. With the clouds racing east across the blue expanse above, she allowed her thoughts to drift away on the breeze. She followed them to the distant streets of Vienna. As she took in the crisp mountain air, instead of smelling alpine honeysuckle and early purple orchid, she could smell the roses of Volksgarten, just starting to bloom. Instead of hearing the rock wrens flitting across the sky, she imagined she heard the squeaking of cartwheels as she and Therese, arm in arm, darted across the busy boulevards on their way to Naschmarkt, gasping, laughing as they narrowly avoided collision after collision. She could practically taste the pretzels, dripping with butter, served in thin paper bags at their favorite market stall, its boisterous proprietor offering a wink and a pert word to each smiling face he served.

It had been a brief but wondrous window—after they'd boxed up their mourning clothes following their mother's death but before Therese became engaged to Friedrich. For one year, Ilse had been free to roam the city with no other chaperone than her sister. Had their mother been alive, she would never have allowed it, but Dr. Eder couldn't be bothered to enforce the constraints society placed on otherwise capable young women. With his encouragement, or at least his blind eye, Therese and Ilse had spent hours beneath their parasols, strolling through parks, arms amicably linked, watching street performers and sharing every thought that passed through their heads. Aside from Friedrich, there was no one in the world in whose company Therese had delighted so much as in Ilse's, and Ilse looked on her sister as an extension of herself. A wiser, more experienced version who would always be an advocate and advisor and would steer her away from serious missteps.

But that was before. Before Therese met Friedrich's family, before coming home from her first dinner at their townhouse in Vienna and declaring she would no longer go out without Friedrich or Father or one of her friend's mothers to accompany her. Back when Therese had lived to push boundaries. Before she started keeping her eyes on the ground, watching where she placed each step, fretting that her foot might land on the wrong side of the line.

Lost in memory, Ilse at first did not hear the sound of a lone guitar echoing through the hills. Not until the music rose in a crescendo did she stir from her reverie. She sat up, startled, looking about, searching for the source of the melody. The musician was concealed from her view. Disconcerted by the presence of an unseen stranger, Ilse stood and brushed herself off. With eyes scanning the horizon, she hurried through the fields and returned to the house, pulling bits of grass and stem from her hair as she fled.

***

Friedrich arrived home the next day to find his wife alone

on the terrace, reading in the shade of the newly leafed oaks. He stood there for a moment, leaning against the frame of the broad French doors, taking in the sight of her. The way she tensed her shoulders, sucked at the corner of her lower lip, completely lost in her reading. The way little triangles of sunlight filtered through the leaves, falling like lace across her forehead, glinting off her auburn hair. In these moments, when she thought no one was watching, Friedrich could still catch glimpses of the girl who had captured his heart. Unpolished, raw, beautiful. He wanted to freeze time, to live in this moment. With his Therese, as she ever was, here in this place that he loved, framed by the trees and the mountains beyond.

Too soon, Therese sensed her husband's presence. She looked up at him and smiled. Setting her book aside, she rose to greet him as quickly as her narrow skirt would allow.

Friedrich could not help laughing at his wife's struggle with mobility. "Ten years ago," he teased as he took her in his arms, "my mother wore bustles so broad she couldn't fit in a streetcar. And here you are today, on the verge of toppling because my sister has convinced you to wrap yourself in a skirt so slim you can scarcely move your legs."

"Do you not like it, my dear?"

"I think you are a vision. I simply worry you are a vision I will have to scoop up off the paving stones."

And, indeed, she *was* a vision, in her dusty-rose hobble skirt[4] and flowing ivory tunic, a delicately painted silk scarf dancing behind her on a gust of wind. She was life breathed into a fashion plate.

Therese gave her husband a playful punch to his gut. "Well, at least today, unlike ten years ago, your mother is at liberty to climb in and out of a streetcar without taking out four rows of children with her bustle." She wandered back to the table with her husband's arm draped around her shoulder, adding, "Not that your mother would ever stoop to riding in a streetcar."

"Oh no, heaven forbid."

They exchanged the usual assurances that each had passed a pleasant day, and then Friedrich asked after Ilse, how she was adjusting to country life.

"Oh, you know how it is," Therese replied, giving a dismissive shrug. "It has certainly been a shock to her system. She's used to being able to step outside her door at any hour of the day and, within a moment, be surrounded by people. Living with all this open space can be very confining, you know, to one unaccustomed to solitude. But I think she is enjoying the change of scenery; she spends hours each day walking about the estate. And I'm not surprised. It's so beautiful here." She inhaled deeply and let her gaze wander toward the river. "I can't imagine anyone not being captivated."

"I do hope she won't be lonely, spending so much time on her own," Friedrich said.

"She may be. But I must say, I think it will be good for her."

"How so?"

"I'd be lying," Therese confessed, "if I said I haven't been worried about Ilse coming out with only my father to guide her. Being here, she will at least be able to observe Amalia and me in company for a time before being sent back to fend for herself again. I'm sure she will benefit from it."

"But your father is a sensible man. You can't be worried he would allow Ilse to get herself into a scrape."

"My dear, you confuse brilliance with sense," she replied with a pitying smile. "Father is exceedingly learned; I would never dispute that. But, you know, even for a genius such as him, there are limits to a man's expertise. His understanding may be unmatched when it comes to statecraft, but when it comes to the finer points of etiquette and social conduct . . . well, let's just say he feels the real estate in his mind is too valuable to waste space on subjects he finds unworthy of his time and attention."

Therese paused for her husband to reply, but Friedrich was unwilling to approach anything bordering on a slight against his mentor. He found something interesting to examine in the cuticle of his thumb and avoided his wife's eye. Sensing she would get nothing resembling an opinion from her husband, Therese continued.

"After my mother died, knowing I would soon be coming away, I tried to convince Father to take on a governess for Ilse. He wouldn't hear of it, of course. He insisted there could be no one better suited to superintend Ilse's education than himself."

"Surely, you could not have questioned him on that point."

"Oh, certainly not. No, it wasn't Ilse's education that concerned me. It was her lack of *guardianship*. You have no idea how important it is for a young woman at Ilse's time of life to have someone she can consult and confide in, someone who has marched across the battlefield and come out the other side reasonably unscathed.

"When I first knew you, I can't tell you how many nights I would sit in my bedroom, with Mother behind me, brushing out my hair and talking. Just talking. Of my hopes, my fears, and yes, even of you. After she died, I still had all those memories of her, so even though she was no longer there, I could still have those conversations. I could still hear her whispering to me, advising me when to be cautious, when it was safe to take chances. Let me tell you, if not for that voice in my head, there were nights I might have given in and allowed you to compromise me." Therese smiled archly at her husband.

"And I assure you, I would not have minded that in the least," Friedrich teased, reaching under the table and giving his wife's thigh a squeeze.

"Friedrich Kassner, you'll bring scandal on my name yet!"

"Well, if I do, it will be a scandal on *both* our names now," he replied impishly.

"But you know very well the point I'm getting at," Therese continued, forcing a serious tone again. "Ilse, she's not practical like I am. Don't get me wrong, she's no carouser, not by any means. But she can be hard to contain. She's a dreamer. Her mind likes to wander away with her. And there's a very fine line between getting lost in the political debates among the old men at Father's salons and losing oneself in the words of an ardent young man. And with no one there to guide her . . ." Therese's voice trailed off. She hesitated even to finish the sentence out loud. "Her heart is simply too open for her own good, whether she knows it yet or not. I know it's not quite the thing for ladies in your circle, but a part of me hopes she will marry young, simply so I know she is out of danger."

***

On the far edge of the Kassner property, Ilse was enjoying the day, unaware that her future was the subject of her sister and brother-in-law's conversation. Blessedly ignorant, she scampered across moss-covered rocks, carefully traversing a frothy brook that trickled toward the Danube, carrying crystal clear waters from the melting mountain snows.

She had just paused to watch a cuckoo surreptitiously slipping its egg into another bird's nest when, suddenly, it came to her again. Music. From nowhere, just as it had the day before. A lilting melody played by skilled hands. It floated along the river like a breeze off the distant hills.

Ilse followed the sound and soon found the musician. A young man, not much older than herself, sat on a dried-out log that had washed up on the riverbank. He seemed oblivious to everything around him. His world consisted of the log upon which he sat, the guitar in his hands, and the vibrations it emitted. He was dressed only in trousers and shirtsleeves; his waistcoat and sack coat had been strewn across the log. A sweep of dark hair fell across his forehead as he played, shielding his face from Ilse's view.

Leaning against a tree just out of the musician's sight, Ilse let the melancholy music wash over her, fill her up, possess her. She knew it was improper, watching this stranger in such a private moment. She blushed to think what Therese would say if someone were to catch her in so unguarded a pose. But Ilse could muster neither the courage to reveal herself nor the will to tear herself away. *Just a moment more*, she told herself. *One more moment, and I will go. I will go.*

But then the young man began to sing, and her feet refused to move. Her breath caught in her chest at the sound of his voice. It was at once weak and haunting, singing to her a song she had not heard since childhood.

> *The world is wholly still,*
> *Within the night's sweet shell.*
> *So intimate, so pure.*
> *Here in this peaceful place,*
> *Far from the pains of day,*
> *In dreaming you are lured.*
>
> *You, in the pride of youth,*
> *Who cannot see the truth.*
> *You hopelessly vain child.*
> *We spin our webs of air,*
> *And flee what good is there*
> *As we hone our many guiles.*

At the end of the verse, the young man stopped. He stared at the river, motionless, seemingly lost in thought.

The sudden silence left Ilse exposed. She was painfully aware of every movement of her body. The tight rise and fall of her chest, each blink of her eyes, the sinking of her teeth into her lower lip, every twitch of every muscle. Self-consciousness took a physical form. It ran a finger up her spine, hollowed out her bones. She shouldn't be there; she knew she should not. She thought she might be able to slip away undetected, but the moment she turned to go, the young man spoke.

"It's not polite to spy, you know." He did not turn to face her. His eyes remained affixed to a spot on the water in front of him.

"I wasn't spying!" Ilse exclaimed. Her tone surprised even her in its defensiveness, mortified as she was at having been discovered. "I was merely walking along the river when I came across you, sitting here in what I must say is a rather shocking state of undress. If one of us is impolite, it's quite clearly— But wait," she stopped herself. "How did you even know I was here?"

"Your reflection," he said matter-of-factly, motioning toward the water. He turned toward Ilse at last. "I could see you up there the whole time." He tried to maintain a stern expression, but one corner of his mouth pulled up, and his eyes shimmered with a merriment that betrayed him.

Ilse felt heat creeping up her neck; her cheeks fired. She wanted to offer a brilliant retort to regain her footing after having been so thoroughly found out, but she struggled to come up with an appropriately biting remark. Luckily, the young man spared her the inconvenience of responding.

"A bit dangerous, isn't it?" he said, resting his guitar against the log and rising to don his discarded articles of clothing.

"Isn't *what* a bit dangerous?" Ilse asked, taking full advantage of the change of topic to recover her composure.

"You. Here. Just walking through the woods. *Alone.* Aren't you afraid of the roving bands of rogues one hears tell of?"

"What *roving bands of rogues*?" she asked incredulously. "The only person I've seen in these woods this entire week is you."

"Ah, yes, but that is where you seem to have erred. How do you know that *I* am not a rogue? I could be their leader. Perhaps they are just beyond that knoll, waiting for me to lull you with my song, ready to strike the second I give the signal."

"Ah, yes, but that is where *you* seem to have erred, sir," she said, mimicking his theatrical tone. "You see, I assumed from the first that you are the most roguish of rogues. *You* mistakenly assume that I cannot handle one." Ilse declared this last with an obstinate look. Her expression dared him to contradict her.

The young man stared at her intently for a moment, his blue-gray eyes stripping away layers, trying to decide if she was serious or in jest. At last, he broke into a laugh.

"Touché," he said, tipping an imaginary hat toward his new acquaintance. "One point for the spy."

His laugh set Ilse at ease. She allowed her shoulders to drop and took a few steps forward. A pair of swans glided past on the river. Ilse kept her eyes trained on them as the young man climbed up the embankment to where she stood.

"I haven't seen you here before. I would remember having encountered such a self-sufficient young lady as yourself. Are you visiting our fair countryside?" he inquired formally.

"Yes," she said, turning to face him. She sensed he was mocking her and hesitated, not wanting to share too much. "I arrived this week to stay with my sister and her husband."

"Ah, you *are* Fraulein Ilse Eder, then. I thought you might be."

Ilse flinched at this unexpected recognition. The young man saw her start and sensed her apprehensiveness. He laughed at the alarm he had caused but quickly explained. "Don't worry, don't worry. Friedrich told me you would be coming. The Kassners are practically family to me. I grew up with Friedrich's younger brother, Kurt. Even spent a year living at

Bergesschatten when my parents were abroad. Junius von Hess, at your service." He offered with his introduction a bow so ludicrously exaggerated that Ilse smiled in spite of herself.

"Funny, Friedrich never mentioned having a rogue in the family," she quipped.

"Well," Junius said, "Friedrich is rather a rogue himself, don't you think? So, I'm quite sure he's never noticed."

"And that's one point for you, sir," she remarked with a wry smile.

"I suppose we are even now?"

"Yes, I suppose we are."

Silence settled over them, and they turned their attention back to the river. "Well," Junius said after a moment, retrieving his guitar and straightening his jacket, "I sense you are a young lady who appreciates being on an equal footing with others. So, seeing as we are now even, I should bid you good day." He gave a slight bow and turned to go.

"Oh, please don't," Ilse said. She placed a hand on his shoulder to detain him but instantly recollected herself, snapping back her hand as though regret had burned her fingers. "I'm the one who interrupted you, after all. And when you were playing so beautifully. Really, I should be the one to go. Please, stay and keep playing."

"Did you really like it?" he asked. He stared into Ilse's face, his eyes earnest, inviting.

"Very much," she replied, blushing, looking down. "I've never heard anyone play 'Evening Song'[5] like that. I hardly know how to describe it. It was like . . . listening to rain falling on the water."

Junius flushed at the sincerity of her praise, embarrassed for her as much as for himself. The brash and teasing young man was suddenly shy, flustered. "Thank you," he said. "I've always thought the best songs are the old ones that can be made new again. Where you can evoke something completely unexpected while at the same time helping people remember little pieces of themselves they thought they'd lost long ago."

As he went on, speaking of his music, his embarrassment was replaced by passion, a fire that radiated behind his icy-blue eyes. Ilse began to feel that she was not, in fact, on an equal footing with this boy. Not at all. She was a silly nymph romping through the woods who had wandered into the presence of Orpheus.[6]

"*Ilse!*" The thought had only started to germinate in the back of her mind when it was yanked out at the roots by her sister's voice. "*Illllse!*"

"That will be Therese," Ilse said, her voice colored with flecks of exasperation. A moment later, her sister emerged from behind the very knoll that was meant to be hiding Junius's band of misfits.

"Oh, there you are," called Therese. Waving an arm, she rushed over to Ilse and Junius, who each felt like they had been caught in a lovers' tryst. "And I see you've met our Junius. Good afternoon, Herr von Hess," Therese said genially, lifting a gloved hand to him.

"Good afternoon to you, Frau Kassner," Junius replied cordially, taking her hand and politely lowering his lips to it.

Ilse felt a stirring in her stomach at the sight of Junius offering this gesture to her sister. Jealousy? Her face grew warm as she recognized the emotion. It couldn't be. Why should she be jealous?

"Yes," Junius continued, "Fraulein Eder and I crossed paths entirely by chance. Seeing your family resemblance and feeling certain this must be Friedrich's sister-in-law, I had the audacity to introduce myself. I hope you will pardon my having taken the liberty."

"Of course, of course," said Therese, her smile warm,

dismissing any trace of offense. "You're practically family. It's only natural you should want to become acquainted with my little sister. Really, I will more readily excuse your taking from me the honor of the introduction than I will the affront of hearing her called *Fraulein Eder*. I may have been a Frau Kassner for the past year, but it is still jarring to hear anyone besides myself being called Fraulein Eder! She will always be Fraulein Ilse in my book." Therese beamed at the blushing girl who stood beside her.

"Come now, is that fair?" Junius replied. "You made such good use of the name Fraulein Eder. The best use of it, in fact—you traded it in for an even better one. Let the poor girl have it, now you've so smartly cast it aside."

Ilse kept her head down during this exchange of neighborly small talk. Therese and Junius spoke of her as if she weren't there, and that suited her rather nicely for the moment. She didn't know what to make of Junius concealing the true nature of their meeting, and in her confusion she could feel rosy splotches creeping up her neck. As long as Therese and Junius remained focused on each other, there was some hope that Ilse's fluster might pass unnoticed.

As far as her sister was concerned, Ilse had little cause to worry. Therese was still intent on impressing upon the neighborhood the legitimacy of her claims to the status that came with the Kassner name; she was far too focused on perfecting her own manner to give a moment's thought to the nuances of her sister's behavior.

But Junius stole frequent glances at Therese's pretty sister. He parted from the ladies a few minutes later, feeling unusually confident that he had made more than just a passing impression.

***

"So, what did you make of our Junius?" asked Therese—a bit archly, Ilse thought—as the two sisters strolled back toward the terraces leading up to Bergesschatten.

"Herr von Hess?" Ilse examined her sister's expression, searching for the safest response. "I make very little of him. I had only just come across him when you found us. Really, I didn't have much opportunity to form an impression."

A benign answer. Not an outright lie, but nothing too candid either. Still, the deception sat on Ilse's tongue for long moments after she had spoken it, bitter as soap. She could wash her mouth clean and tell the whole truth, but her instincts were screaming warnings. How many times in the last few days had she dissembled in front of Therese, *her* Therese, the one person in whom she had always placed her every trust? But then, this wasn't *her* Therese. Not anymore. That much was becoming more evident with each day that passed. The woman who lived here among the Kassners was so different from the one who had left Vienna a year before. Therese Eder had been a warm and caring protector; Therese Kassner seemed entirely focused on self-preservation. Somehow, Ilse could not stomach the idea of *this* Therese having anything to hold over her.

"So many of the daughters of the neighborhood are quite mad about him. I suppose it's the eyes. Or maybe that devilish smile of his," Therese mused. Prodding, pulling at threads, trying to coax Ilse into revealing more than she wished to at present.

"Or perhaps the music?" Ilse suggested. The words were out before she could stop them.

"The music?" Therese raised an eyebrow and looked at her sister. "What do you know of his music?"

"Oh, you know," Ilse retreated. "The guitar he was carrying . . . I can only *assume* it was his and that he plays it. I'm sure plenty of girls would be taken with that sort of thing."

"Hmm . . ." Therese examined Ilse, looking for even the slightest trace of evasion. Not finding any, she went on. "Perhaps. Though that doesn't seem terribly likely."

"Of course *you* would say that," Ilse teased. "Miss Practical. You who's never had a romantic bone in your body."

"That's *Mrs.* Practical now," Therese corrected, smiling. "Go on and scold me, but I never have seen the point in falling for an artistic temperament. All that gets you is a reem of sonnets interspersed with mood swings. I always advise falling for a pair of fine eyes if you can possibly manage it. Even better if they come with a fine estate." Her grin was sardonic as she made an ostentatious gesture at the beauty surrounding them.

"Well," Ilse laughed, "it's lucky for Herr von Hess that he seems to join all three."

"Two of the three, perhaps," Therese said. "Poor dear is only a second son. His brother is to inherit the house, their father's title, and most of the estate. Junius will get only the satisfaction of making his own way in the world."

"Well, at any rate," said Ilse, hoping to close a subject that seemed fraught with traps, "he seemed good-natured enough for a neighbor."

Therese glided past Ilse's cue to move on. "Oh yes, I suppose he is good-natured enough. He's certainly good for a lark when it suits him to be. But he does have a tendency toward melancholy that tries my patience. Still," she sighed affectedly, displaying how much she was put upon, "Friedrich and Kurt adore him, and he would do anything for them in his turn, and so I try to take his moods in stride. And even I must admit that it's been a blessing having Junius here these last few months. Especially now that Kurt will be staying away for the summer. Friedrich does so relish being the older brother, and Amalia certainly does not allow him an outlet for his brotherly exertions."

"Just these last few months? Is Linz not Herr von Hess's home?"

"He certainly grew up here. But no, generally, he is away. Since he is not to inherit, his father, Baron von Hess, insists

Junius have a career. The baron had always intended that Junius should become an officer in the Imperial Navy like he had been himself. But he indulged his son's rebellion ever so slightly on that point. Instead of attending the Maritime Academy, Junius is at the Theresianum."

"At Wiener Neustadt?"

"Yes, that's the one."

"So, he will be an officer on land instead of by sea."

"Precisely."

"Quite the rebellion!" Ilse tried to imagine the young man she had just met standing at attention, marching in column, running drills with a weapon in hand. The discordance bordered on the comedic.

"Sadly," Therese went on, savoring the opportunity to speak with authority to a captive audience, "he was pulled away from the academy this past winter. Baron von Hess and his eldest son were attending to some interests abroad when the baroness fell gravely ill. We were really quite worried they would lose her. Junius was released from his studies to come and attend to his mother. She is much recovered now, of course, and the baron has returned to take her to the sea to restore her strength further. I suppose they are simply awaiting the start of a new term, and Junius will return to school in the autumn. It will be a sad loss for Friedrich when he goes."

Sensing her sister's eagerness to play the expert, Ilse decided it was safe to indulge her own curiosity. "And what do you know of the Hess family?"

"The Hesses? Well, they are well respected enough, I suppose. Though the family certainly is not what it once was. Not so very long ago, they held everything you can see here. But the current baron's grandfather took on a lot of debt and was forced to sell off a large swath of the estate to Friedrich's great-grandfather—that's how the Kassners came to settle here, you know.

Then the baron's father was forced to sell land on the opposite side of the estate to pay a rather sizeable tax bill when *his* father died. I am not much acquainted with the man, as he has been away for most of my time here, but as I understand it, Baron von Hess is terribly proud. He's determined that his family's position should degrade no further on his watch. His greatest ambition is to pass on what remains of the estate intact and to secure it in such a way that it is in no danger in the future. It's an ambition, I fear, that Junius has shown little interest in thus far."

"If that's the case, it's probably a good thing his brother will inherit." Ilse spoke these words lightly, not betraying the anxiety tightening her throat. She couldn't be sure, but she thought she sensed a warning in Therese's words. Though of what Therese might be warning, Ilse hadn't the slightest idea.

They were approaching the main terrace where the Kassners had gathered for afternoon coffee, so any further pursuit of the subject would have to wait. Therese reluctantly put aside her interesting history in favor of less sensitive topics. From the banter passing between them as they joined the party, the family had little reason to believe the Eder sisters had discussed any subjects more serious than the security of their hat pins.

THOSE WHO PROMISE ONLY BEAUTY

"Well, of all the . . ."

Ilse's attention at breakfast the following day was drawn from her buttered toast to an exasperated Helene Kassner. Herr Wimmer had just brought in a message for her, which she now unceremoniously tossed across the table.

"What is it, my dear?" enquired her husband, his tone curious but cautious. He had lived enough years with his wife to know that even minor inconveniences could rile her.

"Oh, it's Cardinal Baumgartner," she said with a sigh. "He's been called away to his sister and won't be able to join us for dinner this evening."

"The countess? Is the poor dear ill?" asked Therese.

"Dying."

Watching this little melodrama unfold, Ilse couldn't help noticing that her hostess's voice was tinged with more annoyance than sympathy.

"What, again?" asked Amalia. She did not mask the rolling of her eyes. "Heavens, isn't this the third time in a year?"

"Fourth," sighed her mother. "And have you noticed how she always seems to be dying at the worst possible moments? You remember in January, she had everyone in such a fret at the Hoffstein's Fasching[8] ball? People were quite ill, and it had little to do with the *gluhwein.*"

"The old bird is unforgivably rude," Friedrich declared

sarcastically. "She times her brushes with death most inconveniently. You must tell her as much when she's next at tea."

"Don't you think I won't! I know it sounds rather heartless, but mark my word, that woman has one, *maybe* two visits to her deathbed left before the entire world writes her off as an utter nuisance."

"Well, I suppose there's nothing to be done about it now," Herr Kassner said, patting his wife's hand.

"No, there's nothing to be done now." She took a careful sip from her coffee. "Without the cardinal, we are an odd number for dinner, which will completely ruin the aesthetic Frau Brunner has planned for the table."

"If a warm body is all you require, why not send for Junius?" Friedrich offered. "He has few aspirations at present higher than preserving Frau Brunner's table aesthetic."

Ilse's stomach fluttered at the mention of this name, so full of intrigue. She reached for her coffee, burning her tongue wretchedly in an ill-fated attempt to conceal her interest.

"Of course!" Therese exclaimed. "What a charming idea, my love! The Hesses are away, and I can't imagine Junius will have any prior engagements. I'm sure he would be more than happy to stand in."

"Junius von Hess sitting across from the mother of Freiherr von Auersperg? You must be out of your senses! I don't care if he is the son of a baron," Helene scoffed.

"If Kurt were here, he would be at our table, would he not?" her husband intervened. After more than twenty-five years of marriage, his patience with his wife's crises was quickly exhausted. "I dare say, one nineteen-year-old man is much the same as any other. If you are so worried about impressing the old lady, then by all means, have Brunner change the arrangement. But I see no reason why we cannot have Junius solve our problem and be done with it."

And so he did, and so they were.

***

The day passed in a blur of jumbled thoughts and confused spirits. Ilse's nerves bounced about with the boundless energy of a herd of kid goats, bleating for attention, kicking up dust, vaulting around the room. She dropped her book on the stairs. She spilled a cup of tea. She paced restlessly from the music room to the drawing room and back again, driving her sister to distraction. More than once, Therese asked if she was well and suggested she lie down.

Ilse reproached herself for not having better mastery over her emotions. She knew the cause of her agitation, yet it seemed utterly ridiculous that the prospect of spending an evening in the same room with Junius von Hess could work her into such a lather. Who was Junius von Hess to her, after all? No one. A complete stranger, a passing acquaintance. Certainly not worth going to pieces over, she reasoned with herself.

Still, she knew that even the most rational among us are never truly masters of ourselves. We are all human, mere animals, really. Animals with brains manipulated by a million years of evolution and instinct, which we will never fully understand. Viewed from a certain angle, irrational behavior is the very *essence* of being human, isn't it? Or, at least, this is what Ilse told herself as she scampered down the stairs to join the family before dinner, the swift *click-click* of her shoes echoing off the marble.

"You're late," was the curt greeting offered by her hostess as Ilse entered the drawing room and situated herself on a small sofa next to her sister.

"My apologies, Frau Kassner," Ilse said, lowering her head. She channeled her unease into smoothing the silvery-blue satin of the sheath she had borrowed from Therese.

"Ilse was taking extra care in dressing this evening, Mother Kassner. She knows how important your guests are to you and wants to represent the family well," Therese interceded.

"Hmm," Helene replied flatly.

"It matters not," Herr Kassner assured his wife. "Our guests are late as well."

"I suppose. But next time, I hope, Fraulein Eder, you'll avoid taking such a risk and appear early."

"Of course, Frau Kassner," Ilse nodded.

"Good evening, all," Amalia greeted them, wafting into the room in a burst of burgundy silk organza, gold lamé, and fringe.

"Good evening, my dear," Frau Kassner replied, accepting her daughter's quick kiss on the cheek. She said nothing, Ilse noted, about the tardiness of Amalia's entrance.

"You look lovely tonight, Amalia dear," Therese said, convincingly feigning genuine affection. "And what a striking frock. Is that one of Monsieur Poiret's[9] creations?"

"Yes," Amalia said. "It has just arrived from Paris. How good you are to notice." She gave a little twirl, modeling the sheer, shimmering dress. Its knee-length skirt was suspended by a hoop over a set of flowing chiffon harem pants. Ilse thought Amalia looked rather like a lampshade but said nothing. Smiling, she tried to give the impression that she was admiring the effect.

"You're coming along quite nicely, Therese," Amalia said as she first considered and then determined the best way to approach a seat without crumpling her new couture. "When you came to us last year, you were quite hopeless. I swear, you didn't know a Poiret from a *poisson*.[10]" She laughed at her own cleverness. "But look at you now! Friedrich dear, I think, with a bit more work, we might make something of this wife of yours yet."

Friedrich smiled proudly at his sister's words, in which he heard only a compliment; Therese smiled insincerely at what she knew had been no compliment at all.

***

For the next hour, guests entered and were greeted,

cocktails were poured, and polite topics of conversation were thoroughly canvassed. A high-profile business associate of Herr Kassner's was the first to arrive, a portly little man with thinning hair, ostentatious ruby cufflinks, and an attractive young wife on his arm. Passing through Linz on his way from Budapest to Munich, this distinguished visitor received a considerate welcome from all the family. He and his wife were the sole focus of their attention until the arrival of the Freiherr and Baroness von Auersperg, along with the former's aging mother. This most elegant and revered trio immediately commanded the full notice of the ladies of the Kassner family, none of whom seemed to appreciate that their standing in the world depended much more on pleasing their first guests than on impressing a family of titled but declining aristocrats.

Throughout, Ilse did her best to do what was expected of her under the roof of Bergesschatten: to be introduced, to smile prettily, and to draw as little attention to herself as possible. She managed to play her part admirably until, shortly after his arrival, Junius von Hess sidled over and asked her for an actual opinion.

"Pardon my rudeness, Fraulein Eder," he said thoughtfully, "but I find I cannot endure another moment without seeking the answer to a question that has burned in my mind since I arrived this evening."

Astonished at his forwardness, Ilse leaned in slightly. She cautiously bade him, "Go on?"

"Do you find my attire tonight more appropriate than yesterday?"

A burst of unchecked laughter escaped Ilse, surprising them both and loud enough to elicit a momentary pause in the conversations throughout the room. She was sure her lapse in decorum would cause Therese a pang, but there was no helping that now. All she could do was recover and reply with as much solemnity as she could muster. "Indeed, sir. You are attired most appropriately on this occasion."

"I'm glad to hear it." He smirked, obviously proud of the reaction he'd provoked.

"Well, now," said Friedrich, joining them, "you two seem to be old friends already."

"We *are* old friends," replied Junius. "Already we have known each other at least seven-and-twenty hours."

"I can think of no older or dearer friends in the room," agreed Ilse, leaning into the jibe.

"I am glad to hear it," Friedrich laughed, clapping Junius on the back. "Therese mentioned you had met. I must admit, I have been hoping you would get on well. I've been wild to get Therese out on the river all spring. I can't row the boat alone, and Therese refuses to go out with just Junius and me. And heaven *forbid* Amalia risk getting murky river water on any of her frocks. But now, we will have a perfect foursome all summer."

"I would have no objection. So long as Therese does not," Ilse stipulated.

"You just leave your sister to me," Friedrich advised. "Now that we have that settled, Mother is giving me her best evil eye. I'd better get back to our guests, lest we invite her wrath." He winked and was gone.

"What, and we don't count as guests?" Junius called after him.

"Of course not, my boy." Friedrich turned and grinned. "You're both family."

***

Five days at Bergesschatten might have been sufficient to remove any surprise Ilse might otherwise have felt on discovering the dinner menu, but they were not enough to remove the novelty of the experience. Her hostess insisted on making the family's habits distinctive. While the rest of the country dined heavily at midday, guests at Bergesschatten always knew to expect a lavish spread when spending an evening with the Kassners. Accustomed as she was to simple dinners of cold meats, sausage salad, cheeses, and bread, Ilse could not but appreciate the culinary delights that paraded before her: rich liver dumpling soup; white asparagus, blanched to perfection and drizzled with a lemony hollandaise; exquisitely boiled veal *tafelspitz*,[11] served with the creamiest horseradish sauce she had ever tasted. Throughout the meal, her focus remained almost exclusively on her plate until a particular conversation between Frau Kassner and Baroness von Auersperg drew her attention.

"I cannot tell you," the baroness said, "how disappointed my Gertrude was to learn that the youngest Herr Kassner would not be returning from Vienna this summer."

"I confess, I was dreadfully disappointed myself when we learned he would not be coming home," Helene replied, sighing her maternal longing. "I had hoped he would come to us for a few months. But, alas, it was not to be. He is summering in Paris, though it is beyond me why anyone would choose to suffer the heat of summer in that filthy city."

"Come now, Mother," Friedrich said. "Surely, you can see there is value to be had in Kurt broadening his perspectives. He can only benefit from it. Indeed, it's the infusion of perspectives that has made Vienna the envy of the world! Why, you can sit down to read a newspaper at Café Central, and before you know it, you are picking apart Freud's theories of psychoanalysis with a group of total strangers, among them a Bohemian physician, a Hungarian poet, and a Carinthian railman. After a summer shadowing Dr. Bergson, Kurt will be infinitely better prepared to hold his own in the coffeehouse."

In her surprise, Ilse nearly choked on her veal. "*Henri* Bergson?" she exclaimed from the other end of the table, unable to contain her amazement.

"Yes, yes, I believe that is the gentleman's name,"

responded Frau Kassner, trying her best to disguise her annoyance with Ilse's outburst.

"Are you acquainted with the gentleman's work, Fraulein Eder?" inquired Herr Kassner. His words, as always, were at once dignified and entirely uninterested.

"Oh, yes!" Ilse gushed. After nearly a week of inane small talk, her academic fervor shoved aside any attempts she might otherwise have made at silencing herself. "I mean . . . no . . . I suppose I'm not so well acquainted with his work. But I do admire what I know of it. Kurt must be a very deserving scholar to be so distinguished!"

"Thank you, my dear. I'm sure Kurt would—"

Frau Kassner's attempt to curtail her young guest was lost on Ilse. Enlivened by the unexpected turn the conversation had taken, Ilse rolled right through this hint that she hold her tongue. "Father's associate, Professor Kleinmann, attended Dr. Bergson's address at the Congress in Bologna a few years ago, and he returned full of the man's ideas. That at the core of every philosophical system is a single, simple truth about the world that the philosopher strives his entire life to articulate. And at the core of this truth is the philosopher's own intuition, the driving force of which is not observation but *negation*. How does it go . . . ? *Faced with accepted ideas that had passed as scientific, intuition whispers one word in the philosopher's ear: Impossible!*[12]"

This unexpected surge, not only of zeal but of understanding, coming from one so young and insignificant, was met with decidedly mixed reviews. The family von Auersperg appeared dumbstruck, unsure what to make of this strange creature who, until now, they had scarcely bothered to notice. The baroness and freiherr sat frozen, with forks half raised, mouths agape, staring at Ilse as though there was an oversized cockatoo perched on her head. Frau Kassner and Amalia said not a word, but their nostrils flared their irritation at this second breach of decorum from Ilse that night. Therese clenched her jaw, bulged her eyes, and jutted forward her chin in a subtle warning; her husband, on the other hand, leaned in, suddenly transported back to his university days and the evenings spent philosophizing in Dr. Eder's parlor. Herr Kassner merely looked bored.

Reading the faces around the table, Ilse was astute enough to take her cue from the Kassner women. "The beef is positively delicious, Frau Kassner," she offered, hoping to turn attention away from herself.

"Thank you, Fraulein Eder. Our cook, Frau Bauer, grows the herbs in our gardens."

"And quite successfully, it would seem," offered the baroness. "The meal is a triumph. Herr Wimmer, please give my compliments to Frau Bauer. We will have to have her share some of her knowledge of herbs with our Frau Steiner."

And with that, the conversation propelled forward, and Ilse found she could breathe again. Her comfort was short-lived, however. She soon realized two eyes still watched her with interest: those of Junius von Hess.

***

After dinner, the gentlemen and ladies divided. The former remained seated around the table to enjoy their brandy and smoky cigars while the latter filtered into the music room. Knowing that Ilse had still to redeem herself in the eyes of the Kassner women following her two lapses earlier in the evening, and also knowing how charming her sister could be when seated behind a piano—mainly because while playing, there was little risk of her *speaking*—Therese immediately suggested that Ilse take up a post at the instrument in the corner. As no other lady wished to exhibit her skills, Ilse obliged.

In truth, she was not a strong performer. Ilse had a zest for melody but insisted that music was made for joy, not toil. She played; she did not practice. She flitted from song to song as the muse moved her, rarely exerting herself. Therese often scolded her, insisting that if Ilse only labored more, her playing might not sound so *laborious*. Indeed, there was a clumsiness in her strokes. She cheated her way through difficult bars, hid behind the *sostenuto*. These tendencies were particularly acute when Ilse played before company. What she lacked in discipline, she made up for in self-awareness. She was so well acquainted with her deficiencies that her hands shook whenever she was called upon to perform.

But there was a purity in her singing. Not unlike the rasp that had made Junius's song so entrancing to Ilse herself the day before, something in Ilse's technically weak soprano conveyed unalloyed emotion. Her voice reached inside her listeners, breathing life into the gray and lifeless corners of their souls and rendering all but the severest critics deaf to the flaws in her execution.

She had just moved on from Mozart to Shubert's "Erlkö-nig"[13] when the gentlemen joined the gentler half of the party. Junius barely made it past the threshold before he was transfixed. He moved slowly, not taking his eyes from Ilse's face, feeling his way through the room and settling into a spot in the opposite corner where he could hang on every word she sang.

> *Who rides there so late through the night dark and drear?*
> *The father it is, with his infant so dear;*
> *He holdeth the boy tightly clasp'd in his arm,*
> *He holdeth him safely, he keepeth him warm.*
>
> *"My son, wherefore seek'st thou thy face thus to hide?"*
> *"Look, father, the Elf King is close by our side!*
> *Dost see not the Elf King, with crown and with train?"*
> *"My son, 'tis the mist rising over the plain."*

"Oh, come, thou dear infant! Oh, come thou with me!
Full many a game I will play there with thee;
On my strand, lovely flowers their blossoms unfold,
My mother shall grace thee with garments of gold."

"My father, my father, and dost thou not hear
The words that the Elf King now breathes in mine ear?"
"Be calm, dearest child, 'tis thy fancy deceives;
'Tis the sad wind that sighs through the withering leaves."

"Wilt go, then, dear infant, wilt go with me there?
My daughters shall tend thee with sisterly care
My daughters by night their glad festival keep,
They'll dance thee, and rock thee, and sing thee to sleep."

"My father, my father, and dost thou not see,
How the Elf King his daughters has brought here for me?"
"My darling, my darling, I see it aright,
'Tis the aged grey willows deceiving thy sight."

"I love thee, I'm charm'd by thy beauty, dear boy!
And if thou'rt unwilling, then force I'll employ."
"My father, my father, he seizes me fast,
Full sorely the Elf King has hurt me at last."

The father now gallops, with terror half wild,
He grasps in his arms the poor shuddering child;
He reaches his courtyard with toil and with dread—
The child in his arms finds he motionless, dead.

Ilse finished her song, and Junius watched as she raised her
hands from the keys, as the rawness of feeling lifted, and she
slowly came back into herself. He was convinced. Perhaps she

lacked skill; she would never master the great works of Rachmaninoff or Liszt. But Ilse Eder was a young woman of taste and discernment whose love of music rivaled even his own.

The company applauded politely. Noticing that the gentlemen had entered, Ilse rose from the piano and, walking with her head down, made her way to a seat next to Therese.

"What a dreadfully morbid song that was, Fraulein Eder!" complained Frau Kassner. "I'm sure you could find something cheerier to play for us."

"But it is Goethe, Frau Kassner!" cried Junius. "Surely, we should do all we can to keep Goethe alive and well, shouldn't we? Or would you prefer she play us a rag?"

"Certainly not," interposed Amalia. "But even you, Herr von Hess, must admit that the lyrics are rather dreary for a dinner party."

"I admit no such thing!" he replied defiantly. "Would you have me pondering Goethe while at home by myself, sitting in a dark, musty library? How dismal that would be! No, I make it a point only to think on such bleak tales when among close friends or particularly good company. That way, I know someone will be around to help me shake off the gloom they are bound to produce."

"But invisible elves killing children? It's positively ghastly!" Amalia declared.

"You must interpret beyond the words, Amalia love," Frau Kassner nudged. "It is about the danger of those who would promise only beauty. One can never make such assurances, so anyone who does must be unworthy of our trust."

"No, no, Mother," Friedrich chimed in, grinning his mischievous grin. "It is about one essential and universal rule."

"And what might that be?"

"That parents should always listen to their sons."

Even Frau Kassner could not help laughing at that. She

gazed adoringly at her firstborn for a moment before turning to her guests. "And what say you, Herr Baron?"

"Me? Oh, I prefer Haydn."

A CREDIT TO THE NAME

The next morning's sunrise inexplicably revealed more blue skies. No one cared to ask where the May rains were hiding, least of all Ilse. Any excuse to escape outdoors was to be embraced, not questioned.

The air in the house was brittle as sugar glass; Ilse worried she might break it simply by drawing breath. Therese had taken it into her head to punish Friedrich for some perceived slight. What his offense had been and whether it was the product of Friedrich's thoughtlessness, Therese's imagination, or simply a miscommunication was a mystery. Whenever he inquired, Therese maintained she shouldn't have to tell him; Friedrich should *know* what he had done, and if he couldn't figure it out, he did not deserve her forgiveness. She was determined to sustain an icy cordiality for no less than two days. That, at the very least, was due punishment for Friedrich's crimes.

Justly delivered or not, Therese's pains to educate her husband made them awkward company, and Ilse selected the earliest pardonable moment to extricate herself.

She set a westward course, away from the river, toward the mountains. Before long, a now-familiar sound began to swell. As she pressed farther into the foothills, the song grew louder, and she was not surprised when Junius's form came into view. He sat on a blanket in a shallow glen, legs crossed, guitar balanced across his lap, head bowed in reverence.

Ilse decided it would be best not to risk being thought a serial skulker. She approached with long strides, swinging her arms in exaggerated arcs, announcing loudly, with a word on each step for emphasis, "I . . . am . . . not . . . spying!"

Junius stopped playing and broke into a hearty laugh at the sight of her.

"Not in the least," he conceded, chuckling and rising to greet his new acquaintance. "I wouldn't dare accuse you of spying today, Fraulein Eder."

"Good."

"Although," he added, a twinkle of mischief lighting his eye, "an accusation of stalking might still be in order. How is it you always seem to find yourself in the exact location I have chosen?"

"Could I not ask you the same question?" She raised a brow and tried to appear dubious but could not keep a smirk from curling her lips. "I suppose I'll just have to credit our faultless judgment; we each have an equal knack for searching out the most perfect spot in the countryside on any given day.

"Will you join me?" Junius offered, motioning to the blanket.

Ilse looked around nervously. Her brain furiously worked the equation of propriety. Junius was of noble birth. A lesser noble, perhaps, but noble, nonetheless. She should consider his invitation a distinction, an honor. Would it be an insult to refuse? The last thing she wanted was to offend him. And yet, wouldn't it be improper to lounge in a secluded field with a young man she scarcely knew? Any young man, for that matter. In Vienna, it was rare for a respectable unmarried woman even to be allowed out of the house without a chaperone. The wealthier families would hire French or English matrons for the sole purpose of escorting their grown daughters about town. Of course, things may have been different here in the countryside.

Here there was no one around to judge her. But did their isolation render the breach lesser or worse? Her books and studying had left her completely unprepared to answer these questions. She wanted to run, to find Therese, ask what she should do. But she did not want to seem foolish. She was not a child. She should know the proper course.

"Well, perhaps just for a moment . . ." Her voice trailed off, draped in wariness. She slowly lowered herself onto the very edge of the blanket, her posture alert, her feet tucked tightly beneath her. Junius sensed her unease and placed himself in the grass several feet away.

They were not alone, though. Embarrassment was a presence—invisible, yes, but physical, tangible, impossible to ignore. Both could feel it, the awkwardness of the situation. They had committed to this intimate scene, but neither quite knew how to engage the other. And so, neither said a word for a time. Ilse leaned back on her hands and turned her face to catch the sunshine, trying to appear perfectly at ease, hoping Junius could not see how her body trembled as she drew in the clean air. Junius distractedly plucked a long blade of grass and pulled it back and forth through his fingers, refusing to raise his eyes to her.

"I do hope," he finally ventured, "you did not find the dinner conversation too staid last night, Fraulein Eder. I'm sure you must be used to much livelier discussions in Vienna." He smiled impishly, peering at her from the corner of his eye.

"You must be referring to my little outburst during the main course," she said with a self-deprecating snort, a slight blush.

"A girl with a habit of running about the country unattended is the last person one might expect to speak on French philosophers with such authority."

"Is it so surprising that an independent spirit should be united with an independent mind?"

"I suppose not," he replied, "though I maintain my surprise.

It's been my experience that few young ladies can speak so eloquently on philosophy."

"Few young ladies could be raised by my father and avoid it. Really, coming up under his roof, it would be more surprising if I could *not* quote you Bergson."

Junius looked at her with interest, his expression nudging her forward.

"For as long as I can remember," she continued, "our house has served as a private coffeehouse of sorts. My father seems to attract the more raucous members of Vienna's intellectual set— men who feel stifled holding conversations and debates anywhere so public as an actual coffeehouse. At least once a week, they gather around our fire. Always on Sundays, sometimes spilling over into Monday, Tuesday, Wednesday . . . When I was little, I remember crawling out of bed when I was meant to be sleeping, creeping down the stairs. The pocket doors that open to the parlor have always refused to seal all the way shut, and I would sit there for hours, peeking in through the gap, hanging on every word spoken on the other side of the door. I'm sure I didn't understand above half of what they said, but their passion still mesmerized me. Whether the subject was politics or science or literature, you could feel the weight of every word. The air was so thick with conviction, you could practically scoop it up with your bare hands. I would stay put, listening, until I couldn't keep my eyes open any longer. Eventually Mother would find me there, curled up on the floor like a cat, fast asleep."

"It must have been difficult, always being outside the door."

"To be honest, in those early years, I was in such awe of them all that if Father ever had thrown open the door, I'm sure I would have been petrified. But," she went on, "time passed, and I grew older, as we all must, and eventually, I was allowed to enter, to sit in the corner of the room. Much to my mother's chagrin, of course. While she was alive, she tried her best to make my father see that it was not proper for a young woman to sit up at all hours in a room of strange men. But my father always insisted it was crucial for the *cultivation of my mind*, as he called it. And being the intractable man that he is, he always won out. Not that Mother didn't have a stubborn streak as well—she absolutely did—but Father has a high tolerance for discord. When he thought he was right, he was always willing to disturb the balance of the house for longer than my mother was. She cared more about peace than being right, so she tended to give in."

Ilse paused and smiled to herself in fond remembrance, recalling how her mother would set her face in determination but gradually let it soften into a smile, an exhale of breath, a roll of the eye, a laugh, an indulgence.

"So," Ilse continued, recollecting herself, "I listened, and I learned, and each morning at breakfast, Father would quiz me and challenge me on my opinions until I could withstand just about anyone's interrogations."

"I don't know if I should be impressed or terrified," joked Junius.

"Both, preferably," Ilse rejoined with a wry smile.

"Have it your way. I am impressed *and* terrified. And," he ventured, "quite delighted to see that what they say is not true." Ilse raised her eyebrows in silent inquiry. "I had always heard that such rational exertion would make a girl lose her figure, cause her hair to fall out, or some other such nonsense. And here you are, having suffered no apparent ill effects."

Ilse could only blush, embarrassed at such forced gallantry. She was beginning to regret having been so open. When she said nothing in reply, Junius changed course, adopting a more sincere tone. "And did your sister undergo this same education? Knowing her for these last six months, I'm having difficulty imagining it."

"Yes, I suppose you would. Believe it or not, Therese is more than capable of challenging you on the theories of Dr. Freud, Aquinas, or Kant."

Junius's face showed his amazement.

"I confess," Ilse sighed, "I barely recognize Therese here. She's changed. She seems so determined to mimic Frau Kassner's every move and manner. Doesn't she realize Friedrich loves her *because* she is nothing like his mother, not despite it?"

"Perhaps it's simply that she knows she has secured Friedrich's affection, but she's still trying to earn it from the rest of the family. After all, her happiness here depends quite as much on them as on her husband."

"Perhaps." Ilse turned her gaze to the sky, thinking about what Junius had said, while Junius admired his view of her, the breeze sweeping a tendril of fair hair loose from her braid, blowing it across her forehead. After a moment, Ilse called his attention upward.

"I always wonder," she said, motioning to a pair of birds with her chin. "I never can tell if what I'm watching is a battle or some sort of romantic entanglement."

Junius looked up. High above them, two jackdaws danced a violent *pas de deux* across a cerulean stage, swooping towards each other, jousting and parting, only for one to dive back for another tussle.

"I imagine it's a bit of both," he mused. "Every great love has an element of war about it. Hate without love, love without hate . . . one without the other is mere apathy. Don't you think?"

"I see I am not the only philosopher present," she noted.

"A philosopher, I certainly am not," he replied modestly. "But I have always imagined that love, if it is to call itself *great*, must be layered, multifaceted. Pure and positive feelings alone are not food enough to sustain it."

"How do you mean?"

"No two minds are so alike that they never differ in their opinions. And if two people *are* so very similar, the pair cannot be balanced. Either they will both be obstinate and end up arguing about the most trivial things, or both be gregarious, constantly vying for attention. Whether similar or dissimilar in perspectives and personalities, there are bound to be quarrels between any two people."

"True."

"It's in having and moving past those quarrels, in the humility of forgiveness. That's where love—real love—is nurtured and strengthened."

"You seem to have thought on this subject a great deal," Ilse observed.

"Not so very great, but I do enjoy studying the people around me. I have so few other sources of amusement!"

Ilse considered his words a moment before saying, "It could be as you say, I suppose. I'm sure my father loved my mother, but they were different in so many ways they could not help clashing. But they always forgave. What they had together was worth a little wounded pride. And one of them, at least, was always willing to suffer the wounds."

"And Friedrich and your sister?"

"A love story, I'm certain."

"But not always peaceful."

"It pains me to say it, but I think not. I love my brother-in-law, but seeing him here, I admit he does baffle me. I question his goodness no more than his love for Therese. I have the utmost faith in each. But I don't know how he can tolerate the way she is treated every day by his own mother and sister." Ilse sighed and shook her head to chase away the unwelcome thought. "Forgive me. I mean no disrespect to the Kassners. They have been gracious hosts, and I owe them much. I'll simply say I can make no sense of it all."

"Would you like to know what I think?" Junius asked.

"Very much. You've seen them all together much more often than I have."

"I think it is precisely *because* he loves your sister so much that he says nothing. He is not blind to her pain, but he is blind to the injuries. When Friedrich looks at your sister, he sees only perfection. Quick as he is, he still cannot imagine anyone looking at his wife and seeing otherwise. So, for every backhanded compliment his family volleys in Therese's general direction, he hears only well-deserved praise."

Ilse contemplated this theory and decided to accept it. She was not entirely convinced, but Junius's explanation offered one compelling benefit: it comforted her. Though she was still worried about her sister, Junius's theory eased her mind by restoring Friedrich more solidly to her good opinion.

"And what of your family?" she asked.

"My family?"

"Yes, your family. You didn't think I'd let you prod and probe into all my family's concerns without ever turning the spyglass back on you, did you?"

"Fair enough. My family is, shall we say, old-fashioned," Junius said, plucking a small weed and tossing it forcefully into the field in front of him. "They are much more concerned with waging *actual* battles than battles of the heart. With them, everything is position and power, respectability and family duty. My poor pawn of a brother must cover the first two. His mission in life is to marry the right girl from the right family with the right name and *especially* the right fortune, whereas I, lucky fellow that I am, need only trouble myself with respectability."

Just that quickly, Junius's tone had turned from thoughtful to bitter, and his focus shifted from his companion to the blades of grass he was uprooting from the soil.

"Being a credit to the Hess name," he went on. "And, surely, the only way to be a credit to the Hess name is by following the same path my father followed. Or something close enough to it, at least. So come autumn, regardless of what I might choose, I'll be on a train back to Wiener Neustadt."

"Well then," Ilse interjected, her tone upbeat, hoping to interrupt his increasingly sullen train of thought, "it is lucky I am here. I will have to make sure you make the most of the time between now and then. I will make that *my* mission in life. At least for the next few months."

Junius looked over at her, forced a half-smile, but said no more as he slipped into a bout of brooding.

"If you don't mind my asking," Ilse continued tentatively, "if it *was* in your power to choose for yourself, what would you choose?" Her instincts warned that she was pressing further into dangerous territory, but she was not ready to abandon the subject.

"What would *I* choose?"

"Yes, you. What would you choose for yourself?"

"Truth be told, I would stay here."

Ilse blinked in surprise. It was a wholly unexpected response.

"I can see I shock you with my boldness," he said, some of his former liveliness returning to his voice. "Of course, I don't mean *here* in this field or even here on this estate. But here in Linz. There is a music institute in town. If I had any say in the matter, I would live a life filled with music—performing, composing, teaching. But the son of his greatness, Baron Otto von Hess, a meager music master? Unthinkable!"

He delivered this last sentence with spirit and animation, but Ilse sensed the sarcasm masked a more profound sadness. Sure enough, Junius became pensive again, slipping back into silence. Early as it was in their acquaintance, Ilse was unsure how to navigate this mood that had taken hold of him. She dared not pursue the topic further but worried any attempt to change the subject might seem unfeeling or insensitive. Lacking a better alternative, she opted for retreat.

"Well," she said amiably, "I should be getting back. Thank you for inviting me to rest with you for a moment."

"Oh, please don't run off," Junius replied, clearing out the fog that had settled over him. "I apologize. Really, I do. Stay, and I promise to be better company. I will speak only of pleasant things. We can talk about this fine spring weather. Or about that clever lampshade Amalia was wearing last night."

Ilse scolded Junius for his wicked remark but couldn't help laughing; Amalia's dress, fashionable though it must have been, *had* been quite ridiculous. But she could not be persuaded to stay. "I really *should* be going. But," she offered as she rose to her feet, "you may accompany me if you'd like. I'm sure Friedrich would appreciate a caller. Anything to break up the silence in the house today."

"An offer no man could refuse." He sprang to his feet with the energy of youth and sloppily folded his blanket. With guitar in hand and the blanket slung across his arm, he motioned for Ilse to lead the way back to the house.

***

Monday arrived, as it is wont to do, marking the end of Ilse's first week in the mountains. The week had left her with much to think about during her afternoon ramble.

Seven days had not been sufficient to remove Ilse's unease regarding her sister. Therese had always been persnickety. She fussed and fretted and wanted everything to be just so. She set high standards, and she would never settle for less from herself than she knew she was able to achieve. In another person, this tendency might have been insufferable. But Therese had always managed to pair her perfectionism with an infectious warmth that reduced it to an eccentricity. A foible. A quirk. Something to be smiled at, something those who loved her best could laugh fondly about in her absence.

Here at Bergesschatten, though, that warmth was all but gone, lost beneath an excess of deference. Desperation, almost. For praise, for acceptance, for simple acknowledgment. It was impossible to tell.

Not that Ilse could blame her. The steady flow of jabs and jilts that flowed Therese's way from Frau Kassner and her daughter was enough to make even gentle Ilse seethe. Every hour in their presence was a test and a trial, every day a battle to maintain her composure and confer upon her hosts the respect she owed them as an unsolicited guest.

Still, empathy had its bounds. Ilse's heart could ache for Therese. It could boil and pull and shred into a thousand pieces, but it could not ignore the wall of reserve that had built up between them. There were still moments when something in their surroundings would trigger a wave of nostalgia. Like a pebble dropped in a pristine pool, it would ripple through Therese's polished façade. In such moments, shared memories were still enough to foster tenderness. But the wall was still there, and Ilse did not know how to bring it down.

Rather than try, she simply vowed she would not add to her sister's distress. She would try not to, at least. What more could she do?

And then there was Junius.

Ilse had never thought of herself as a flirt. She was not coy; she did not tease. She was not the type of girl to dreamily pluck petals from a flower or to spend nights tossing on the edge of sleep, unable to chase a particular face from her mind. And yet there was something about Junius von Hess that interested her more than she could explain. He could be puckish. He could be bitterly moody, as she had so recently seen him. But rather than repelling her, these moments drew her in. When he spoke, she clung to every word. If he moved, her disobedient eyes followed him. Even when he was nowhere near, all she had to do was think his name, and she would find herself smoothing stray hairs behind her ears, biting color into her lips.

Lost in the labyrinth of her own thoughts as she strolled along the river, Ilse failed to notice that storm clouds, absent for so many days, were gathering to the west. She did not see their change from white to gray to inky green. The first raindrops had hit her cheeks before she even realized the blue had been crowded out of the sky. She paused a moment, considering whether she thought it would amount to anything, but before she could resolve on returning to the house, the skies opened. A torrent poured down over her.

Ilse shrieked at the shock of the cold, driving rain and looked frantically about for refuge. Seeing that she was near a small boathouse at the edge of the estate, she made that her target and scurried toward it as quickly as the slippery grass would allow. Alas, her scamper was in vain; Ilse reached the boathouse only to find it locked. She could do nothing but huddle under its narrow overhang, shivering and miserable, as thunder echoed off the mountains and a fierce wind whipped the hem of her skirt.

Within a few minutes, the rain let up enough that she could again see her surroundings. As she stood there, bouncing to keep warm, her eye wandered up the riverbank, running over the dock, the rowboats, the trees, and coming to land on a gazebo in the distance. Therese had pointed it out to her a few days before; she knew it was part of the Hess property. Ilse watched as thin waterfalls poured off its roof, allowed them to lull her into a daydream, hypnotize her into believing she was sipping a cup of tea before a crackling fire . . .

Suddenly her eyes landed on a figure in the gazebo, and her breath caught. There, lounging on a bench with a book, was Junius.

It was bad enough to be soaking wet, hair dripping, hat askew, dress clinging to her skin. But to be in such a state within easy sight of a person so interesting, who by all accounts was comfortably warm and dry, aroused in Ilse a vanity she had not known she possessed. Flushing at the thought of Junius seeing her in her current bedraggled state, she desperately searched for an escape. But there would be no running away, not without throwing herself on the mercy of the storm.

Her one consolation was that he had not yet seen her. His eyes were safely buried in his book; he paid no mind to the tempest on her side of the glass. With any luck, the rain would abate quickly, and she could slip off unnoticed. Ilse allowed herself to be reassured by this prospect. She even convinced herself it was the most likely outcome. Breathing came easier; her pulse slowed.

But then, as if on cue, Junius looked up, saw her, and laughed. He stood and waved. Ilse gave a quick wave in return before crossing her arms again over her chest and throwing a wretched glance up at the sky.

Junius watched her for a minute, contemplating her situation. A moment of decision—born of chivalry, kindness, perhaps even folly—found him whipping off his jacket and rolling it into a ball. Cramming it under his arm, he left the safety of his shelter and sprinted across the lawn.

And then he was at her side.

She laughed. "What on earth are you doing?"

"Well, you looked like you might be a tad chilly over here," he said, wiping his brow and shaking out his jacket from its tightly wound bundle. "And who am I to deny a damsel in distress?"

"You're insane!" She laughed again as he wrapped the coat around her shoulders. "Completely mad."

Junius did not deny the allegation, merely gave a complacent shrug, followed by a crooked half-smile that melted Ilse's knees. He did not immediately draw back as she pulled the jacket tight around her. He held his hands on her upper arms, ran them up and down to warm her. Quickly at first, firmly, but then more slowly, gently, his hands barely grazing the fabric, the fabric barely touching her rain-dampened skin.

Ilse was shivering, but she no longer felt cold. She had never been held by a man, never stood this close. So close she could hear his breathing. So close she could feel the heat rising off his body, infusing her with warmth. The world blurred. Ilse began to feel lightheaded. Her heart raced. Her legs felt weak. Numb. Like they might fall out from under her, like she might crash right into his arms. She lowered her eyes, shy, confused, scared someone might see them and get the wrong impression. And yet she could not pull herself away, was unwilling to remove his hands from her.

In a moment of boldness, she met his gaze. Behind her eyes, a flame burned. Innocence on fire. Her expression was an invitation, one Junius readily accepted. He leaned toward her, slowly, and she toward him. She closed her eyes, felt his thumb gently raising her chin, his breath on her lips . . .

Suddenly, a clap of thunder rang out—vibrating and deafening and close. They jumped apart, startled, shaking with desire and anxious laughter. As the shock wore off and their laughter subsided, Junius resigned himself to accepting this hint. God had urged caution, and Junius would heed the advice. Leaning against the wall, he took in Ilse from a safer distance.

It was Ilse, in all her youth and inexperience, who refused to let the moment pass. Maybe it was a hunger for human connection, so long unfulfilled. Maybe it was the electricity that still charged the air. Whatever its source, Ilse found herself empowered, fueled from within by sudden, unaccountable daring. She stepped toward Junius, reached out, and pulled him back to her. Their lips met in a soft, slow kiss while the rain washed the world clean around them.

AWAY FROM PRYING EYES

June arrived, and the Kassners departed. A hazy Tuesday, its sunlight filtering through a scrim of pollen and morning mist, saw the elder Herr and Frau Kassner safely deposited at the train station. With Amalia in tow, scowling and complaining of crowds but immaculate as ever in her traveling suit, they climbed aboard a southbound train.

With their departure, a cloud lifted from Bergesschatten.

The rain of arrows that had assaulted Therese for the better part of a year suddenly stopped. In its absence, Therese let down her guard. She slowly began to lower her shield, to remove her armor, piece by steely piece.

She could by no means be called *easy* during this time. The house still had servants, after all. The servants still had eyes that could see. They still had ears to hear and mouths watering for every salacious morsel. Any breach of decorum risked becoming the subject of maids' gossip and eventually reaching her mother-in-law and Amalia. Of that, Therese had no doubt.

Still, without the constant cracking of eggshells under her feet, whispers of the old Therese began to sound, albeit faintly.

For Ilse, the weeks that followed were some of the happiest in her young life. She was relieved to see traces of her sister returning. But more than just this, there was Junius. To her evenings was added the thrill of private smiles, knowing glances, feet stretching out to graze each other beneath the table, unexpected flushes that had to be laughed away during dinner. *So funny how the heat of the day can creep up on you at the strangest times!*

Afternoons were for clandestine meetings, trysts that proved surprisingly easy to arrange. From her first day in the country, Ilse had established a habit of taking solitary strolls whenever the weather permitted. So each day, assuming the sun and its sentries kept the rains at bay, Ilse could simply sneak away for an hour or two to spend precious moments alone with Junius. In doing so, she aroused no suspicion, caused no curious eyebrows to lift. She was simply doing what she had always done.

As their attachment grew, so did Ilse's desire to keep the affair secret. She may have felt it her right to give her heart where she chose, but she was not so naïve as to think this was the prevailing opinion. The Kassners would disapprove. There was no question about that. They would see in her another Therese, another interloper set on conning her way into their world. They would see a guest under their roof bringing scandal to sully their name and mar their precious reputations. They would feel the ire of the baron, their noble neighbor. And they would blame Therese, making her even more miserable than she already was. Therese would, surely, anticipate all this and more. She would force Ilse to give Junius up.

It was a risk Ilse refused to take. Therese mustn't know. And as long as they were discrete, Therese *needn't* know.

And so, Junius and Ilse fed their passion in secret, away from prying eyes, fueled by the rush of deception, each meeting a relief and a release. They lived for the stolen hours, moments that melted away as fingers intertwined, as hands brushed against cheeks. Concealed beneath the cover of the woods or tucked away on the far side of a hill, they would sing to Junius's guitar or lay side by side on a carpet of wildflowers, swaddled in the scent of edelweiss.

During these escapes, Ilse learned to avoid any allusion to

the future. The mere mention of it sent Junius spiraling into an abyss, summoning in him the melancholy Therese had once described. The future was not Ilse's ally. And so, she and Junius spent their days blessedly tethered to the present, living in a fantasy of their own creation. Reserve, ceremony, propriety, caution—all were banished to the thoughts of another day. They basked in idle banter, sweet nothings. They canvassed the usual subjects important to young love: music, art, and books; the most minute details of their short personal histories; the idiosyncrasies of their shared acquaintances and far-off friends.

Where their opinions aligned, their conversations were animated. Junius's voice resonated with the fervency of one who feels every emotion keenly. Ilse sparkled with the joy she derived from bringing Junius to life.

Where their opinions diverged, there could be no ill will, only spirited debate. Lighthearted jabs ending in pokes and tussles and rolling in the field, sending up clouds of dust and dandelion seeds.

Ilse knew it was wrong, of course. Both the affair itself and the dishonesty. It disturbed her how easily it all came. How quickly she silenced that voice in her head urging restraint. How effortlessly she evaded detection, omitted truths. In private reflections, she wondered whether she was walking down a path from which she could not easily return. But then the afternoon would come, and she would be racing away from reality again, her hesitations smothered by the insatiable sway of infatuation.

First love strikes fast; its victims fall hard. Rare is the mind that can resist the chemical pull of pleasures so foreign, sensations so new. Who pauses to think? Who lays a foundation? Such hastily built affections are bound to waver. Whether it is the lovers themselves who grow distant as they grow older or the fickle world that rips them apart, even the most brilliantly burning flames eventually flicker and fade.

A SHIFT IN THE BALANCE

The telegram came on a Sunday.

It had been an entirely unremarkable day, notable only in its commonness. That such an unexceptional day was destined to be etched in the memory of generations seemed incredible.

And yet it was, indeed, etched on their memories.

Unyieldingly so.

It was late June, the evening of Derby Day. Parties and balls, concerts and carnivals marked the end of the social season in far-off Vienna, but those gathered beneath the roof of Bergess-chatten were engaged in much more domestic diversions. They were passing a quiet evening in the drawing room at the end of the first truly hot day of the summer. The windows had been thrown open, and a gentle breeze swept in and out of the room, lifting the dusty rose chiffon of Ilse's sleeves each time it passed, tossing them this way and that before letting them float back down to caress her shoulders.

Therese was seated at the piano, dressed in puce satin covered in exquisite ivory lace. The day's heat had drained her, and she played languidly, no song in particular, simply stringing together notes and chords within her chosen key. Still, the music was not altogether unpleasant, even to Junius's discerning ear. While Therese played, Friedrich slouched in a chair in the corner, his feet stretched out before him, shamelessly reading a red leather-bound copy of *Venus in Furs*,[14] something he never would have dared were his mother in residence. Meanwhile, Junius and Ilse were locked in a fierce battle at the chessboard.

Years later, Ilse would recall every detail of the scene. She could reconstruct it all with perfect clarity. The exact shade of her dress. How glorious the chill night air had felt against her skin. The sharp arc of Junius's brow, the wrenching of his lips each time she declared "check." The flecks of gray and blue in his eyes. The way he locked them on her face after each move, trying to break her concentration, trying to force a stumble. The muffled rumble of the motorbike coming up the driveway. How she had given it no thought. None whatsoever.

Ilse was about to slide her bishop across the board and declare checkmate when the young footman Franz burst into the room.

"Pardon the intrusion, Herr Kassner, sir. An urgent telegram from Vienna." Franz had a strange look in his eyes. Was it embarrassment or anxiety of another sort?

Friedrich waved the boy over to him and accepted the message. After thanking and dismissing Franz, he wasted no time tearing open the envelope.

Three sets of eyes attached to Friedrich. Something was amiss; that much was immediately clear. The color drained from his face as he leaned forward, resting his elbows on his knees. For a moment, he did nothing, simply stared at the telegram hanging limply from his hand, like he didn't know what to do with it, as if trying to convince himself the page wasn't even there.

"What is it, my love?" Therese asked. She rose from the piano and approached him tentatively, like she was coming up on a wounded deer, not wanting to frighten it.

Friedrich, still speechless, waved the letter in his wife's direction, inviting her to read for herself. As soon as she had taken it, he dropped his head into his hands and pressed his fingers back through his carefully slicked hair. He closed his eyes, threw back his head, exhaled loudly. Like the simple act of pulling air in and out of his lungs was exhausting.

Therese read the message and gasped. She read it again, sputtered, "Good god." She read it again and again, each time thinking she must be missing something, that there must be some mistake. She was not even conscious that her free hand had found its way to her chest, that her fingernails were digging holes in the delicate lace of her dress. "This can't be true." She turned wide eyes to her husband. "Tell me it isn't true."

Friedrich looked up at her. His only response was a shake of his head before he rose to pace the room.

"What's wrong, Therese? What's happened?" Ilse asked.

Thinking it must be a family matter, Junius shrank back, not wanting to draw unnecessary attention to himself. All he could do was watch the scene unfold.

When Therese didn't respond, Ilse pressed her. "Please, Therese, you have to tell me. Has something happened to Father?"

"No, no, it is nothing like that."

"What, then?"

Therese looked at her sister. Even now, when her expression was contorted by worry, Ilse's face was still so young, so innocent. Luminous in the lantern light, like an angel sent to walk among mortals. Therese could not bring herself to say the words. She could not be the one to shatter that innocence.

"Therese. Please." Ilse entreated her sister with a command that declared her capable, young though she was, of coping with whatever news the message contained.

After collecting her thoughts for another moment, Therese forced herself to share the truth. There was no point in hiding it, after all. Ilse would learn everything once the papers began spreading the news. "It is a message from Father," she said.

"The heir has been shot. He is dead."

"The archduke? Killed?" Ilse looked from her sister to Friedrich and back again. Therese nodded, fighting to maintain her composure. "But what does this mean?"

"Father says nothing more. 'ARCHDUKE SHOT DEAD IN SARAJEVO[15] WILL WRITE MORE WHEN KNOWN.' That is all it says."

"Good god." The dam that had kept Junius silent finally broke. He exhaled the words in an overflow of disbelief, much as Therese had done moments before. "And he says nothing about who has done it or why? Do they know?"

Therese shook her head, blew out air, and blinked back tears. "There is nothing but what I have told you. Leave it to Father to feel he had to go to the expense of delivering such news in a telegram and then worry about his word count! It would have been kinder to leave us in ignorance until we had the full account in the papers!" Therese lowered herself onto a sofa and sat in silence, stunned. She was joined by her husband, who clasped her hands between his.

Never until that moment, as she sat watching Therese and Friedrich, had Ilse noticed the difference in their sizes. Therese looked small and fragile; Friedrich's massive form loomed over her, a mighty protector, shielding her, soaking up all her hurts. In their company, Ilse felt utterly alone. Junius was so near, and yet he could not comfort her. She longed to reach out to him but knew she didn't dare. She couldn't even look at him without giving herself away. The only thing she could hold on to was the bishop, still clenched in her hand. She rolled it back and forth between her fingers, focusing on the smooth ivory, its ridges and curves. Trying to transfer her fears into the cold hard bone.

For a time, no one said another word. Yet, though no one said it, each was thinking the same thing.

The balance of the world had shifted.

And nothing they nor anyone else could do would put it back.

***

Dr. Eder's promised letter was several days in coming. Friedrich, Therese, and Ilse, so accustomed to relying on his wisdom and guidance, became increasingly frustrated with each day that passed. Was he waiting to know *everything* before writing? Close as he sat to the pulsating heart of Vienna, by now, he must have known *something* more.

A lack of answers didn't keep people from talking, though. Each day's newspaper was filled with conjecture and speculation. The killer was a madman, working alone. No, he was not alone, but part of a network of more than twenty radicals, rogue actors all! No, no, there were not twenty, but six, and they weren't rogues but covert operatives sent by Serbia. No, no, no, it was surely some domestic agitator. The Archduke had been so reviled, after all, that the Derby Day orchestras in the Prater didn't even stop playing after news of his murder broke in Vienna; clearly, the act required no foreign influence.

The family put little stock in any of these early accounts. They waited to hear the real story from Dr. Eder.

During these first tense days, Ilse and Junius continued their rendezvous. Yet, even between them, something had changed. Neither would own it, of course. But they couldn't deny what they lived and felt every day. Lost was the easy rapport, the flirtatious jostling and laughter. In their place were hours of quiet contemplation. Lying together in silence, watching the passing clouds, trying and failing to read the future in them. Instinct told them they were on the precipice of something, but that something remained just beyond their sights.

***

One night, about three weeks after news of the assassination had first arrived, Therese made an unexpected announcement at dinner.

"Ilse, dear, what would you say about our taking a little trip?" Her tone dripped with cheerfulness, at odds with the more subdued moods that had characterized their gatherings of late.

Junius, who had been among them most evenings while the senior Kassners were away, stopped chewing mid-bite. He fixed his gaze on Ilse's face.

"A trip?" Ilse, too, was caught off guard.

"Yes, a trip," Therese replied, glancing quickly at Friedrich, who smiled and squeezed her hand. "We have all been so morose around here lately. And Friedrich's aunt, Selde, has been quite wild for me to pay her a long visit in Boston so she can get to know me. Really, for the last six months, her letters have practically begged for it. So, I thought, what better way to cheer us up than by taking a little trip?"

"Boston? In America? I would hardly call that a *little* trip, Therese. I can't suppose Father would consent to my going so far."

"Oh, but that is the brilliant thing! Father has already consented!" Therese proclaimed. "I didn't want to get your hopes up only to have them disappointed, so I wrote to him last week. He most heartily agreed it is a wonderful scheme. You know he has always wished for us to have an opportunity to travel. He even provided names of connections at Harvard University. He is sure they would be only too glad to host us for dinner if we should tire of Aunt Selde's company. Though I hardly think that is possible. Aunt Selde is such a fascinating woman. And, you know, you would not need to be gone from Vienna for longer than Father should desire. So, all things considered, he thinks we had just as well go."

This little speech of Therese's was not entirely disingenuous. Indeed, she *had* suggested this journey to her father, and he *had* readily embraced the idea of their going to Aunt Selde. But Therese failed to mention Friedrich's receipt of an earlier letter from her father. Of *that* correspondence, Ilse was kept entirely ignorant, and in the confusion of the moment, Ilse did not think to inquire about it.

"But I was to be back in Vienna by the end of September. To pay a visit of any length to make such a journey worthwhile, we would need to leave almost this very instant, wouldn't we?" inquired Ilse with some concern.

"This very instant? You silly thing! Certainly, we do not leave this very instant." Therese laughed and turned her attention to cutting her meat. "No, no," she said into her plate, "we do not leave until Tuesday."

"Tuesday! But that is the day after tomorrow!" Ilse protested, her concern edging toward panic.

"Yes, the day after tomorrow."

"But—"

"There is nothing special we will need to prepare for the journey. It is not like we are going on some great expedition. It is Boston in summer, after all, not the Baltic in winter. You came to us with everything you could possibly need. We will have all day tomorrow to pack, more than enough time, especially with Maria to help you. And Friedrich has already arranged for our travel. We are to take the train to Paris on Tuesday afternoon, where Kurt will meet us and take us on to Le Havre. From there, we will board our ship and set sail on Wednesday evening."

The day after tomorrow. Ilse's head was spinning. It hardly seemed real. To be uprooted so soon, yanked away from Junius with so little warning. To lose for the next two months the joy of his company, the thrill of his gaze, the warming reassurance of his arms around her. How could she bear it? And yet, how could she even attempt to counter this plan? She could claim a fear of homesickness, but was she not already away from home? She could fabricate a dread of the ocean crossing, but had she not always expressed a fond desire to travel abroad? What argument could she possibly make that would not arouse Therese's suspicions?

"It sounds like you have everything settled," Ilse said, her voice weak, defeated. She dared not look her sister in the eye. She stared instead at the candle on the table between them, at the flame that danced with the breeze from the open windows, until black-orange spots blotted her vision.

"Yes, quite," Therese replied, confident this plan would satisfy her and her father's wishes while giving her sister nothing but pleasure. "We shall be such a gay trio for the rest of the summer—three fabulous European ladies taking an American city by storm! I believe Friedrich is quite jealous of us."

"I am indeed," replied Friedrich. He smiled at his wife, but Ilse thought she saw a flash of something like sadness behind his eyes. "You will be gallivanting around Boston while I am left here to toil away at the office. Really, I will have to give Aunt Selde a firm talking to when next she is here. I had not enjoyed married life for six months before she began lobbying to whisk my wife away from me!"

Friedrich and Therese continued to chat in this way, but Ilse struggled to focus on their words, to hear them over the thudding of her own pulse in her ears. Everything they said was a distant echo, as if she were listening to them from beneath a deep pool of water. She tried her best to maintain a neutral expression, though she felt like she was drowning, about to be swallowed by her misery.

Junius had said nothing through all of this. He now scooped up several peas but could not bring himself to take another bite. He held his fork in front of him, watching it tremble in his hand, blinking as the peas rolled off, one by one, and bounced across his plate. Seeing this and fearing his reaction would draw Therese's notice, Ilse gave him a soft kick under the table. He looked over at her, his eyes pleading.

All she could offer him was a grief-stricken smile.

Ilse prayed that her look, brief though it had been, had said everything to Junius that she could not put into words. That the idea of leaving him pained her more than anything. That she would come back to him as quickly as she could. That in resigning herself to this separation, she was not giving him up. But also that they were not at liberty to make their cares known.

Ilse and Junius did their best to don dispassionate masks for the rest of the evening. Under the ever-present eye of Therese and Friedrich, one of whom was always in the room with them, there was no opportunity for private conversation. Hours passed, and they did what both knew they must. They maintained their carefully manicured appearance. They were disinterested acquaintances, nothing more.

But in their hearts, they were anything but indifferent. Ilse longed to throw her arms around Junius, cover his face with kisses and assure him that if she had any choice, she would not leave him for anything in the world. For his part, Junius fought the urge to throw himself at her feet and beg her to drop their ruse, to tell her sister the truth, to plead their case that Ilse be allowed to stay. But he would not breach Ilse's trust. He would not breathe a word of his feelings to Therese. He cared for Ilse too much.

And so, the evening was simply allowed to pass. When the clock on the mantle chimed nine o'clock, Therese proposed that she and Ilse retire to get an early start on their preparations the next day, and Ilse acquiesced. She bade the gentlemen goodnight and followed her sister out, slowly shutting the door behind them, keeping her eyes on Junius's face until the very last.

The click of the latch was like cannon fire, sending out shrapnel that ripped into Junius's gut. He closed his eyes tight as his anguish manifested in physical pain. His suffering was not lost on Friedrich, who asked his young friend if he was all right.

Junius waved away Friedrich's concern, blaming the onset of a sudden headache.

"Too much time in the sun today," he lied. "Nothing more. I'm sure I'll be fine come morning. If you don't mind, though, I think I might take myself home rather earlier than usual tonight."

"Of course," Friedrich replied, patting Junius on the shoulder as he rose to refill his drink. "No need to sit around here in pain on my account. Only, if you think you can bear it, might I keep you here just a few more minutes?"

As sympathetic as he was to Junius's headache, Friedrich, too, had troubles weighing on his mind. He, too, was desperate for relief.

***

The next day, Ilse's last at Bergesschatten, was gray, both in weather and mood. She longed to run out and find Junius, but a steady rain drenched the countryside all afternoon, leaving her with no pretense for venturing out of the house. She made slow progress folding her garments and filling her trunks, only half listening as Maria prattled on. She paused frequently to look out the rain-streaked window, scanning the sky for a break in the clouds, only to be disappointed.

By the time she joined Therese and Friedrich in the drawing room before dinner, her preparations were all but complete. Though the dark skies had fed her melancholy all day, she performed admirably before her sister and brother-in-law. To them, she appeared almost excited about the coming adventure. The worst Therese could say was that her sister seemed a bit distracted. But that was no surprise; agitation was always the mistress of expectation.

Shortly before dinner was announced, Junius joined them. He greeted Friedrich and Therese cordially as he entered the room but locked eyes with Ilse as he seated himself in a chair across from her, his look piercing in its urgency. She received his message as clearly as if he had shouted it: he needed to speak with her alone. When Herr Wimmer called the party to the dining room a few minutes later, Ilse rose as slowly as she could. Inventing a problem with the strap of her shoe, she bade her sister and Friedrich not to wait for her; she would follow in a matter of seconds. Junius politely offered to remain with her, watching Friedrich lead Therese out the door by the small of her back. As soon as they were gone, he rushed over to Ilse, pulling her into a tight embrace but releasing her again instantly, always careful to avoid discovery.

"We only have a moment." Ilse's voice was low, almost a whisper. Her gaze darted between Junius and the door.

"I need to speak to you alone, but there isn't time to explain everything now," Junius said breathlessly. His eyes were frantic. "Can you meet me tonight?"

"Meet you? But how? Where?"

"Slip away. It doesn't matter when—whenever you think you can without being seen. I'll wait all night if I must. I'll be at the place we met, the downed tree by the river. Can you find your way in the dark?"

"I can find it. But Junius, please, you're frightening me. What's this all about?" Ilse searched every corner of his face for an explanation, from the wildfire in his eyes to the clenched jaw to the vein in his forehead that twitched rapidly, betraying his racing heart.

"There's no time; I can't tell you now. Will you come?"

She knew it was wrong, shockingly improper, to meet with a man alone, under cover of night. Therese would be furious. Even her father, who typically cared little about etiquette and propriety, would turn his head in shame. Yet, Ilse could not refuse. She owed it to Junius to relieve him of whatever had thrown him into such a frenzy. But it was not only a sense of obligation. She *wanted* to see him alone again; there was no use denying that. She needed to part from him in a way that exulted everything they had come to mean to each other. The thought of leaving with no more than a cordial pressing of the hand in the Kassners' drawing room was an affront.

"I will come," she said, then rushed out of the room.

***

The clock had long since struck midnight, the candles long since extinguished when Ilse creaked open the door of her bedroom. She crept down the hall, past the room where Friedrich and Therese were drinking in each remaining moment of each other's company. Knowing it could be their last night together for much longer than the six weeks they had acknowledged to Ilse, they had no attention to spare for anyone outside themselves. They did not hear the soft padding of Ilse's feet as she tiptoed down the hall, shoes in hand, a towel under her arm.

Ilse slinked out the back of the house, closed the doors behind her without a sound, slipped on her shoes, and tucked the towel behind a planter on the terrace. The rain had stopped shortly after dinner, but Ilse knew the mud would be unforgiving and had the foresight to bring the towel, worried even her bare feet might leave tracks that would reveal her indiscretion.

She hurried across the terrace and down the slope of the lawn toward the river. After every few steps, she paused, glanced back, reassured herself no one was watching.

Mud sucked at her shoes, slowing her progress, but before long, she could see Junius sitting on the embankment. She slowed at the sight of him. In the moonlight, his white shirt-sleeves and pale complexion glowed, and Ilse had to fight off the feeling that he was already a ghost to her, already a distant memory.

As she approached, a twig snapped beneath Ilse's foot, and Junius started, his head whipping toward her. He rose to his feet but did not run to her. He had spread out a tarp and several blankets so he would have somewhere dry to sit in the hours he might have been waiting for her, and he had removed his shoes to avoid muddying the blankets. Ilse removed her shoes as well before joining him with a tender embrace.

"You're here," he sighed, pressing his cheek to hers. Ilse felt his breath against her ear, whispering through her hair. He took her face in his hands, kissed her gently, then rested his forehead against hers. "I was so scared you would change your mind . . . that you would leave, and I would—"

Ilse placed a finger over his lips. "I'm here," she said, closing her eyes, covering his hands with hers, pulling them down, letting him feel her heart, the rise and fall of her chest, their rapid breaths slowing, synchronizing as they melted together.

"Did anyone see you?" he asked, pushing back a strand of hair that had fallen across her face. She pressed her cheek into his hand.

"I don't think so," she replied, looking back toward the house. "Have you waited long?"

"I hardly know. But I would have waited forever."

The July night was heavy after the day's rain, and Ilse could feel tiny beads of perspiration beginning to moisten her forehead as they sat on the blankets facing each other, Junius sitting cross-legged like a child; Ilse tucking her legs demurely beneath her.

Ilse wore only a pale-blue dressing gown over her white night shift. Other than her traveling clothes for the next day, they were the only things that hadn't already been packed. Her fair hair fell in loose waves over her shoulders. Staring at her in the silvery light, Junius found himself warding off unwelcome thoughts. That Ilse was not here with him at all. That she was already lost to him. That it was only her memory sitting so close, a vision shimmering in the moonglow.

"I'm sorry to have asked you to come out like this," he finally said, hardly able to meet her eye. "I know what a risk you took in doing so, and I love you all the more for it."

"You know I could never refuse you anything."

"I know you wouldn't," he said, "which makes the liberty I've taken all the worse."

Ilse reached over and took his hand, absolving him of all guilt, forgiving his sins, past, present, and future.

"I just couldn't let the last time I saw you be under your sister's eye and under Friedrich's roof," Junius went on. "This secret we've kept, it's been a betrayal to them both. But saying goodbye to you, perhaps a final goodbye, in the manner of a common friend . . . that's an injustice I could not have lived with."

"For the last time? A final goodbye? You're talking like we're never going to see each other again. Surely, we can survive being apart for six weeks. I'll be back before you return to school. And even then, you will not be far from Vienna. We will see each other. I know we will." Even as Ilse tried to lighten the mood with assurances, her voice began to tremble. "This is not the end," she said, hoping to convince herself as much as him. But there was something in the look on his face. The fear in his eyes unmoored her. Unbidden, connections were crystalizing in her mind. Like the final pieces of a puzzle snapping into place in rapid succession, it began to dawn on her that there might be something more to her and Therese's journey than had been openly acknowledged. "Right? Therese and I . . . we will return by September?"

Junius inhaled deeply. He grasped her hands more tightly—to calm her, to ground himself—and pressed ahead with what he had come to do. "There is something you should know." And then he revealed everything that had tormented him since their parting the night before.

After the sisters had retired, Friedrich had shown him a letter he had received from Dr. Eder just a week after the archduke's assassination. Friedrich and Therese had intentionally concealed it from Ilse. While he could not recall all the details, Junius remembered enough to say one thing with certainty: Dr. Eder was convinced that war was imminent, and now Friedrich and Therese shared that conviction. Ilse's father had pleaded with Friedrich to shield his daughters from the truth for as long as possible, but he had begged Friedrich to do everything he could to keep them safe. Friedrich had ultimately determined he had no choice but to share the letter with his wife. It was the only way to convince her of the need for her and Ilse to leave the country. Together, he and Therese had contrived the idea of her and Ilse's visit to Aunt Selde, a plan Dr. Eder acceded to readily and gratefully. Friedrich had carried this knowledge for two weeks, but the strain of pretending to be happy about Therese's leaving finally had proved too much. Emotionally exhausted, he had unburdened himself and told Junius everything.

Ilse listened quietly to Junius's story, suspended in denial. When she spoke, her voice was detached, as though she were simply musing aloud, not talking to the man just inches away from her. "How can this be? You must have misunderstood. I can't believe Therese would have hidden this from me."

"You have often said you feel estranged from your sister."

"Yes, but how could she not trust me to handle something like this?"

"Can you really be surprised that she would keep something like this from you when you have not even trusted her enough to tell her about us?"

"That's not fair, Junius."

"Perhaps not, but it's also true. And so is what I'm telling you now."

Ilse thought for a moment, trying to make sense of it all.

"But I just can't understand how my father could have reached such a conclusion. Unrest after what has happened is to be expected. But all-out war? It just makes no sense, Junius! The latest reports are that the assassins weren't even connected to the Serbian government."

"Given everything else at stake, the opportunity to make an example of Serbia is simply too tempting. If the emperor's response is weak, what is to stop further secessionist agitation from the Serbs in Bosnia or any of a dozen other nations across the empire? But if he is strong, he doesn't only quiet the Serbs; he can quell the ambitions of others as well. Or that is the thinking, at least."

"But even if the emperor is set on taking Serbia as you say, there can be no threat to us. Father can't believe little Serbia could push back to such a degree that we would not be safe here in Linz."

"Think about it. If you work through it, I'm sure you can see what your father sees."

Ilse did think about it, and with assistance from Junius, she reached her destination.

"What happens if we declare war on Serbia?" he nudged her. "Who is allied with Serbia?"

"If the emperor declares war on Serbia . . ." At last, the answer came to her. "Russia!" she gasped. "Russia is allied with Serbia. If we declare war on Serbia, Russia will almost certainly strike back at us."

"And if Russia declares war on us?"

"Germany!" It was getting easier now, the answers coming more quickly. "Germany is sworn to come to our aid in any incursion from Russia. If we declare war on Serbia, Russia declares war on us, and Germany declares war on Russia."

"And if Germany declares war on Russia?"

Her mind raced through the pages of the histories she had

read, both ancient and modern. Terror crept across her face as the full implications of the tangled web began to emerge. "France. God help us. France is allied with Russia. If Germany declares war on Russia, France will declare war on Germany. And if France declares war on Germany, we will not just be at war with Serbia, we will simultaneously be at war with Serbia, Russia, and France!"

Junius could only nod, his pride in his young love's genius checked by the horrifying implications of what she had worked out. It was the same thing her father had foretold in his letter.

"But I still can't understand," Ilse said, mind still working, resisting. "It makes no sense. If an eighteen-year-old girl can see this after two minutes' consideration, how is it that those around the emperor have not foreseen the futility of such an endeavor? Surely, his counselors would have told him all this."

"It's not that they don't see it," Junius replied defeatedly. "According to your father, the German chancellor thinks he has a plan to counteract these forces and is goading the emperor along. I cannot recall all the specifics of his rationale, but your father is convinced they all have miscalculated. *Seriously* miscalculated. They depend on weakness where instead they should see strength, wavering where instead they should sense resolve. Your father has concluded the emperor is choosing to trust those who see the world as it suits him, not the world as it is."

Ilse was astounded. This was beyond anything she could have imagined. It was not just that Vienna was unsafe. It was not that Linz was unsafe. Her father was convinced that all of Europe was unsafe. Tears began to well in her eyes as the enormity of it crested over her like a wave in a violent storm. "But what about you? What of Friedrich and my father?"

"Your father, I cannot say. But from what I've heard, I am sure he's shrewd enough to navigate whatever is to come. Friedrich may be able to avoid conscription. Herr Kassner has influence; he has contracts with the government and, if it comes to it, will likely argue that Friedrich's presence is essential if they are to ramp up production and supply the war effort."

"And you?"

Junius didn't have to say a word. The look he gave her said everything she needed to know. He had long ago started his military training. He was committed to returning to the Theresianum in the fall. There was nothing he could do. When war came, he would be there to greet it.

"And so, this . . . tonight . . ."

"Yes." He gulped, forcing back tears of his own. "This could be the last time we see each other."

Ilse could no longer hold back the torrent churning inside her. Fear, loss, longing, hopelessness all poured forth, and she threw herself into Junius's arms. It was an unsteady pose, with Junius still sitting cross-legged on the blanket, but he would not disrespect her grief by toppling to the ground. With all his strength, he managed to keep them upright, to hold her tight as she wept on his shoulder.

They stayed that way for some time, Ilse's head buried in Junius's chest until her sobs subsided into slow, deep breaths. Only then did Junius gently pull her up, just far enough so he could look into her tear-streaked face. Her eyes were red and puffy, her mussed hair plastered to her forehead. It was a sight both pathetic and crushing. Seeing her suffer was worse than any injury to himself. Junius could not live with her pain. He needed to take it away somehow. He needed to lead them back to the fantasy they had so recently known. To the place where no one could touch them, where nothing could come between them. Where the world was only the two of them, and the only things he knew were her smile, her lips, her hands, the beating of his own heart. A rush of ardor swept over him, powerful and impossible to deny. He desperately kissed her forehead, her wet cheeks, every inch of her face until, at last, he found soft lips.

Ilse returned his kiss, gently at first, then with depth and urgency. Overwhelmed by the weight of the moment, something inside her released. Her fears about the war, her pains to hide her feelings for Junius from her sister, the opinions of the Kassners or her father or anyone else—it all fell away. None of it mattered anymore. The only thing that mattered was Junius.

She held him close, running her hands through his hair, across the sinews of his back, breathing in the scent of him.

But it wasn't enough.

She felt heat rise from his body, his mouth on her neck, the scrape of stubble across her skin, hands finding places that had never been explored. She trembled. Her heart sent blood coursing through her veins. Sensation fled her fingers, her hands, her arms. They were no longer under her control; they took on life of their own, separate and apart from her. The only thing she could feel was an aching, like nothing she had ever known. It swelled within her, low and deep.

She held to him even more tightly, pulled him over her, felt the weight of him, the growing tension, the surge and surrender.

It still was not enough.

No matter how she tried, she could not hold him closely enough. She was overcome by an urge, primal and all-consuming, to join with him, be one with him, merge body and soul. She needed him in a way she had never needed anything.

If she couldn't be with Junius, she would be with no one.

She was his.

Only his.

Forever.

And just like that, in a pool of moonlight on the banks of the swollen Danube, as her father had feared but in a way he never imagined, Ilse got swept away.

THE STAIN OF BETRAYAL

Within night's sweet shell, the world lay wholly still. All was silent, save the rushing of the river, the crickets droning their lullaby, so intimate, so pure.

Junius's arm was draped around her, her body enveloped in his. She could feel his chest pressed against her back, his steady inhale and exhale telling her he slept. As gently as she could, she lifted his arm, freezing for a moment as he let out a low sigh, almost a purr, then eased herself out from under it. Slowly, soundlessly, she rose to her feet, slipped on her shoes, and stole away into the darkness.

When she had put a safe distance between Junius and herself, Ilse paused and looked back at his sleeping form. Only then did she whisper a tearful, "I love you," so the wind might carry her words to his ears, so he might hear them in his dreams.

She knew it was wrong, slinking off without a word. But what about anything she had done that night had been right? Had it been right to sneak out of her sister's house, risking Therese's reputation as well as her own? And what she and Junius had done, had that been right? Naïve as she was, she knew the answers to those questions.

Ever since she had laid eyes on Junius, she had tossed aside her moral compass and allowed herself to be guided by instinct alone. She had abandoned any modicum of restraint, willingly plunging into a hole. For she *had* thrown herself in, she knew well that she had. She was no hapless victim; she had not been led. No, she had relished every second. And the fact that it had come so easily, with hardly a second thought, appalled her. On some level, she had always imagined she was somehow different, better, beyond reproach—that in some intangible way, her superior education set her on a pedestal above every other girl. Were she not so sickened, she might have laughed, thinking how flawed those presumptions had been.

At last, her eyes were open. She did not recognize herself, yet felt she could see herself clearly for the first time. She was no pillar of fortitude. She was ordinary and weak, just like everyone else. And she loathed herself for it.

She imagined Junius waking up alone, finding her gone. Would he think her heartless? Would he assume her indifferent? Either possibility made her ill. But the alternative—to look into those eyes she loved and perhaps see that they now despised her as much as she hated herself—was unthinkable.

And so, she ran. Ran from him. Ran up the muddy slope. Ran across the cold, hard tiles of the terrace. And after slipping off her shoes and stepping into the house, she ran as quietly as she could up the pristine marble staircase, down the hallway lined with fine Turkish carpets. She did not stop running until she had safely closed herself behind the door of her own room.

But she could not run from what she had done. She could only pray it would never be known to anyone beyond Junius and herself.

Alone in the darkness, she washed herself, scrubbed until her skin was red and raw, desperate to remove the stain of her sin, the stench of her betrayal. She brushed her long hair over and over, scraping the bristles against her scalp, stripping away any leaf, any stray blade of grass, any speck of dirt that could reveal her transgression.

Fighting against a tangle, Ilse was slammed with a sudden,

horrific thought. *Dear God, what would Therese say if she knew?* Worse, what would her sister *think* without bringing herself to say? What sentiments would fester just beneath the surface? Disappointment, disgust, shame? A chasm of dread opened as she thought of sinking so low in Therese's opinion, and Ilse choked back both alarm and bile.

Painful as these reflections were, the torment was a blessing. As long as Ilse focused on her own failings, her own weakness, she could avoid the other knowledge that every moment seeped into the corners of her consciousness. The information Junius had shared with her awakened Ilse to dangers she had never imagined. Her father's certainty was now her own: their homeland was on the brink of war. Everything she knew and all those she held dear faced untold peril.

And with this certainty came the possibility that she had just seen Junius for the last time.

Junius. Her Junius. Simply thinking his name, picturing his face, stirred in Ilse such a storm of emotions she strained to draw breath. Fear, sorrow, shame, desire . . . each fought for supremacy in every second she allowed her thoughts to linger. This storm still raged within her when she finally laid herself on the clean, white bed. And as the first bursts of morning light found their way through the window, the manic onslaught continued to electrify her brain unabated, ensuring Ilse's wearied mind would receive no repose.

***

Ilse entered the breakfast room late. Her eyes were red and puffy, and her skin sagged with a sickly pallor. Fortunately, her sister and brother-in-law were too preoccupied to notice.

Had Therese bothered to look at her sister, *really* look, she might have seen a young woman who carried a heavy secret and an intense longing for one from whom she would soon be parted. She might have seen a woman stalked by fear of all the terrible possibilities that lay ahead.

Had Ilse, in her turn, bothered to look at *her* sister, she might have seen much the same thing.

Their last meal at Bergesschatten was devoid of conversation. Friedrich pushed food around his plate and stole frequent glimpses of his wife, trying to memorize her face. Each curve, each crease, every streak of green and amber in her eyes. Ilse, likewise, had appetite for neither food nor conversation. She sat holding her coffee. Raising the cup to her lips, blowing on it, watching the ripple of the dark liquid, lowering it again without taking a sip. She did not set it back on the table; she kept it in her hands, let its heat singe the tips of her fingers, clasping it for as long as she could bear. The pain was a deserved yet insufficient punishment.

The only banter was an occasional remark from Therese. About how she wondered what kind of breakfast Aunt Selde served and if her jams could possibly match the standard set by Frau Bauer. About how thrilling it was to imagine that in less than two weeks they would be tracing the steps of the American rebels through the streets of Boston. Therese did not direct these comments to anyone in particular. No one was listening to her anyway, and she decided that was for the best. If she was going to keep up her charade, she could meet neither Friedrich's nor Ilse's eye. She was too close to breaking, close enough that one straight and solid look would reveal to Ilse the crack opening in her veneer. Ilse would see it, and she would prod it and work it until it split Therese in two. And yet Therese couldn't stand the silence. The void threatened to swallow her up. She sank her teeth into a strawberry and gazed out the window. "Would you look at that sky! The day promises to be perfectly exquisite for traveling!"

After breakfast, the trunks were carried out to the car, and the sisters took their leave of Frau Brunner and Herr Wimmer.

They made their way toward the city in silence. Even Therese had given up pretending everything was normal. Simply holding herself together took all the energy she had to spare.

Ilse stared out the car window, watching as they passed hills and woods that had been witness to such perfect felicity for so many weeks. She longed to turn back the clock. Just two days—that was all she needed. It had been that short a time ago. When she was innocent. When she was happy.

She wondered what Junius was doing at that moment, where he was, what he was thinking. Did he ache for her the way she ached for him?

Did he understand why she had done what she had done?

Did he still love her?

Did he loathe her?

They arrived at the train station and made their way across the platform, three stoic and silent figures. Onlookers saw not refugees, but prisoners walking to the gallows.

Angry as Ilse was with Therese and Friedrich for colluding to remove her under false pretenses, she pitied her sister. There was no helping it. She knew all too well what Therese, who must have seen and understood the implications of their father's letter, was feeling. After quickly embracing her brother-in-law and thanking him for his hospitality, Ilse boarded the train ahead of her sister, leaving Therese to bid her husband an unreserved farewell.

From the train car, Ilse could observe their parting: Therese, inconsolable, head down, unable to look Friedrich in the eye; Friedrich, sturdy and supportive, lifting her chin with one hand and wiping away a tear with the other, speaking words of comfort, pulling her into his embrace. Always soothing, always so strong. Only when the whistle sounded did Therese tear herself from his arms and rush onto the train.

Friedrich remained where he stood, alone on the platform,

as the train lurched forward. Ilse continued to watch him from the window. She wondered when they might meet again. *Whether* they would meet again. As the train began its crawl forward, she craned her neck to look back, watching until his figure receded from the corner of her vision. Just before he slipped from view, Ilse saw him drop onto his haunches, defeated, cradling his head in his hands.

***

Agitated and exhausted, Ilse departed on the longest journey of her life. She scarcely knew where she was and noticed little of the sights rushing past. Salzburg, Munich, Stuttgart, Strasbourg . . . They all came and went in a blur of blue mountain, green grass, yellow field, gray walls. Across from her, Therese was lost in thought, hypnotized by the rhythmic *click-clank, click-clank, click-clank* of the train's wheels across the rail ties. She did not speak; she did not look at her sister. Saying goodbye to Friedrich had taken too much. She had nothing left.

The hour was late when the train screeched its way to a halt at *Gare du Nord* in Paris. They emerged into the steamy summer night to find Kurt Kassner brimming with the exuberance and gallantry of a nineteen-year-old entrusted with his first assignment of consequence. Oblivious to their sorrows, Kurt greeted them with unrestrained smiles, delighted to welcome his sister-in-law and the lovely Fraulein Eder to Paris. Despite his satisfaction in seeing them, he was ignorant neither to the lateness of the hour, the strain of their journey, nor his obligations as host; he escorted them directly to the lodgings he'd arranged near the station, a courtesy for which both sisters expressed their gratitude.

The drive was short, clattering over cobblestoned streets into the village of Montmartre, situated just north of the station. The guesthouse where they were to spend the night was near the newly erected Sacre Coeur Basilica. When Ilse stepped out of their taxicab, she could see its majestic dome glowing in the moonlight, keeping watch over the sleeping city. She had but a moment to consider this holy sentinel. No sooner had her feet hit the paving stones than Kurt was ushering them inside. He stayed just long enough to see that they were safely settled. Assured of this, he gave a salute and a *"Bonne soir, mes dames"* and promised to return by noon to dine before escorting them to Le Havre, where they would board the boat that would carry them across the sea.

The room was comfortable—small but sufficient for a single night's residence—yet both sisters passed another sleepless night. Not that either would admit this to the other. They lay in their shared bed, back to back and silent, pretending to submit to the rest that evaded them. With the first hazy light of dawn, they rose, weary, to face another day in the world as strangers.

At breakfast, their hostess remarked on how pale they each looked. Therese thanked *madame* and assured her nothing was amiss. The fatigue from the previous day's journey, nothing more. To Ilse's relief, Therese indicated a desire to relax in the small courtyard garden until Kurt joined them. Ilse suggested a walk through the village streets promised to be of far greater benefit to her. At first, Therese resisted this plan. The city's streets were such a maze, and Ilse, either from fatigue or simply being unfamiliar with their twists and turns, might get hopelessly lost in them. In this, their proprietress turned out to be a welcome ally for Ilse. She was more than happy to draw out a map of the immediate area on a scrap of paper for Mademoiselle Eder, as well as their address in Rue de Steinkerque, should she happen to need assistance. Therese, too exhausted to put up a fight, was quickly overcome by Ilse's insistence and their hostess's reassurances.

Immediately after breakfast, Ilse emerged onto the narrow streets. Able to think of no better salve for the agitation that continued to rattle her mind, she turned her steps toward the basilica.

The Eders had never been a particularly devout family, but at this moment, Ilse's soul craved absolution. She longed to unburden herself, be forgiven for what she had done, be freed from the grim knowledge she was not even supposed to have. There was no hope for the latter, but for the former . . .

With slow but determined steps, she made her way up the hill to Sacre Coeur. On and on she went. Up, always up, as though ascending to the clouds themselves. On tired legs, she finally reached the crowded plaza in front of the basilica, filled with men and women strolling arm in arm, grimy children hocking trinkets no one wanted to buy. Ilse neither saw nor heard them. Her eyes were fixed on the doors of the great church. She traversed the plaza and climbed the last of the steps.

Her ascent complete, Ilse stood before three intricately carved doors, panting, breathless after her long climb. She approached the doors and grasped one of the iron handles. It would not budge. She heaved with all her strength but to no avail. She tried the second door and then the third. None would admit her.

What could this mean? Was she unworthy of confession? Was even God denying her reprieve? Like a sullen child, Ilse marched back down the steps, put out and perturbed, pausing only once to take a last exasperated glance at the doors that had refused her.

Back in the plaza, she called the attention of a man passing through and asked in heavily accented French why the church doors were barred. He laughed, tickled by the ignorance of a silly foreigner. "Does Mademoiselle not know that construction has just been completed? The church has not yet been consecrated. Not until October!"

His amusement stung more than it should have. Ilse's mind

was in no state to brush off an affront. After brusquely thanking him for the information, she found her way to the low balustrade lining the plaza's perimeter. She lingered there for some time, leaning against the barrier, absorbing the coolness of the travertine, looking down the hill at the expanse of land that sloped steeply away from her.

From this vantage at the apex of the martyr's mountain,[16] Ilse felt sure that, if not for the smog, she would have a view of all Paris. She imagined what she might see if only rain would come and wash the smoke from the air. Below her, people were going about their lives. Men were rushing off to their places of work; children screamed and laughed as they raced through the streets to school; women haggled in markets, tended their homes, made house calls. Babes were coming into the world, and the elderly and infirm were leaving it. Life, in short, went on. Stubbornly. Heedless of Ilse's misery. Each of the million souls below carried secrets and cares of their own. But how many of them saw what was coming? How many of them read the morning paper and recognized in its headlines the inevitable march of events that would drag their sons and brothers, fathers and husbands and lovers to war?

Ilse remained at this overlook until the heat of the approaching midday and her own sense of the time urged her back to the guesthouse. Her sister was waiting. *Therese.* Ilse wanted to run to her and pour forth everything that weighed so heavily on her heart. She longed for Therese to confide everything Ilse knew she must be feeling, that through their troubles, they might stitch together some semblance of the bond they once shared.

But this was not to be. Ilse's own feelings—of fear, of pride, of regret—absolutely forbade it.

Where could she turn? Her sister was near yet wholly estranged. Even God and the balm of confession remained just out of reach. Ilse felt entirely alone. And yet, as she made her way down from the mount, she resolved to embrace the solitude. She was young; she had made mistakes. But she was also strong. Flowing in her veins were her father's wisdom and her mother's grace. Surely, when things seemed most bleak, she could look within herself and find consolation there.

She could shoulder her burdens on her own. She knew she could. She could because she *must*.

A WOMAN WHO MADE AN IMPRESSION

Long and stormy was the week at sea. The skies may have been clear, the ocean blessedly calm, but the waters to be navigated with Therese were rockier. Considerably so.

From the moment Kurt left Therese and Ilse at Le Havre, Therese came undone. Within the ship's claustrophobic quarters, a dark mood took hold. She dressed, made herself ready, but spent the better part of each day in bed, staring at the cabin walls, rejecting sunlight, refusing air. As a matter of duty, she accompanied Ilse to meals, but she took no food and scarcely attended the conversation. She had simply collapsed in on herself. Like a flower in frost.

When anyone inquired, Therese offered up excuses of seasickness. There might have been some truth in that, but Ilse suspected her sister's condition had more to do with the state of her mind than the state of her stomach.

Ilse watched Therese's decline with growing concern but felt helpless to lift her back up. How could she hope to comfort Therese without first countering her claims of illness? And yet, she could not dispute Therese's claims without revealing that she knew what was really ailing her. But even to hint at this awareness could raise unwelcome questions about how Ilse came to learn the true nature of their journey. She could invent a story, say it had been Friedrich who had told her. But if Therese were to question Friedrich . . . No. It was impossible.

Any time she started to broach the subject, her voice choked off, an invisible force robbing her of air and crushing her will to speak.

And so, Ilse left her sister to her own defenses, to recover in her own time, without consolation or support. It was selfishness, abandoning Therese—a selfishness born of fear. Ilse felt that keenly. Once again, she saw her capacity for cowardice and self-interest. It shamed her. Worse was the discovery that simply recognizing her deficiencies did not enable her to correct them. No amount of self-reproachment would fix her. *Wanting* to be good and *being* good may have been similar hues, but they were dramatically different shades.

As the week wore on, Ilse spent much of her time alone. Walking the deck alone. Reposing on a deck chair alone. A solitary figure, leaning against the guardrail, contemplating the vast emptiness of the ocean.

Her own mind, for the most part, settled after the first few days. Aided by youthful resilience and the cradlelike rocking of the ship, the early frenzy subsided.

Still, there were moments when Ilse was visited, unbidden. Ghosts crept in, found openings, worming into crevices and invading the vacant corners of her consciousness. She tried to force herself to think of other things, but her thoughts always returned to Junius. His smile, his laugh, his moods and her ability to pull him out of them . . .

Such harmless daydreams inevitably yielded to less delicate ones. Of hands on thighs and steam and sweat and Junius's body pressing into her own. Illicitly acquired memories brought waves of desire so intense that Ilse, face flushed, skin ablaze, would have to expel Junius from her mind the only way she knew how. She would curse herself and quell her arousal by envisioning the impending war.

So often did Ilse's reflections follow this path—from

innocence and love to sex and betrayal, to war and death and waste—that her tormented psyche became a hopeless jumble of cause and effect. An open heart led to sin, sin to suffering and sorrow. In her confusion, she could almost have been convinced that the coming war hearkened the arrival of the apocalypse, brought on by her own trespasses.

In this uneasy way, the Eder sisters made their slow way across the Atlantic. But by the time the ship trudged into the port of Boston, each had moved past the initial stings of grief. They were ready to find comfort. Or, at the very least, distraction.

Luckily, few ladies were better equipped to meet both needs than Aunt Selde.

***

If anyone could be said to personify mirth, it was Selde Knight, née Kassner.

A stout widow in her early forties, Selde had lived with one aim since the day she disposed of her mourning clothes eight years earlier: to delight in life. Selde delighted in art and theater; she delighted in good company; she delighted in fine wine and good food, as evinced by her ample bosom, belly, and arms. But far from detracting from the loveliness of her youth, these habits had added to it. Though firmly in middle age, her skin, smooth as marzipan, radiated affability, and her dark, sparkling eyes still could command the attention of even the vainest audience.

In short, Selde Knight was a woman who made an impression, and that impression was always exceedingly pleasant.

When Therese and Ilse tramped down the gangway, their feet filled with lead, their legs unaccustomed to firm ground, Aunt Selde was waiting on the dock, ready to bathe them in her overflow of goodwill.

It was a delicate business, this little welcome reception. Not only did Selde have the pleasure of receiving her nephew's bride, but she was also the bearer of dreadful news: their country was at war. The emperor's declaration against Serbia had come over the wires that morning, and the news had been splashed across the front page of the evening papers mere hours before. Selde was still struggling to adjust to it herself. There were so many unknowns, so many open questions. A banner headline had been crammed in at the last minute, but they had little so far by way of concrete information. A minimalist story tacked in alongside the murder trials and stock reports. What had it told them? Not much. There would be more to come soon enough. She knew how the American press worked. Constantly balancing the desire to break a story against the desire to keep the people buying papers. Buying, buying, always buying. The coming days would be like a leaking faucet, a slow *drip-drip* of details. A parched public would hand over their pennies morning, noon, and night, desperate to quench their thirst.

Selde was determined not to pass on her anxieties to her young charges. She would not create a panic. Not until more was known, not until there was reason for it. After greeting Therese and Ilse with warm smiles, she broke the news, right there on the dock, and executed her duty so gently that anyone watching would have thought she was consoling her own daughters rather than two young ladies she had never met. For their part, Therese and Ilse received her intelligence with such sobriety and good sense that Selde was proud to claim the Eder sisters as her nieces.

As much as Aunt Selde had hoped they would spend their time together in the pursuit of merriment, even she saw the need to retrench as each day's reports from Europe brought some fresh outrage. Within the first week came word that Germany was at war with Russia, Belgium, and Britain. Austria-Hungary herself was likewise at war with Russia, Montenegro, Britain, and France. Each morning's headlines shocked and dismayed Selde.

Yet, the sisters bore it all with the same equanimity they had previously demonstrated. It was a remarkable thing. Watching them, Selde wondered whether they were hard-hearted or simply too young to grasp the implications of the news. She refused to believe it was the former. *No,* she thought, *they are sweet girls. It must be the latter. Just because Dr. Eder is supposed to be some sort of genius, and just because the girls speak intelligently, does not mean they inherited their father's understanding.*

To Therese, though, Ilse's reaction, or lack thereof, could not be explained away so easily. How was it that Ilse did not seem surprised by anything that was happening? Therese asked her sister about it one afternoon as they were strolling across Boston Common, a green expanse of fields and parkland not far from Selde's Beacon Hill townhouse.

"Why am I not surprised?" Feeling a bit ambushed, Ilse repeated her sister's question to carve out a moment to gather her thoughts.

"It's just curious, that's all," Therese said. "You don't seem the least surprised by anything that is happening. I want to know how that is possible."

Ilse looked away, pretending to watch a young boy on the other side of the field trying to launch a kite. The blue box trailed behind him, lifeless, refusing to catch the wind. Ilse shrugged. "It wasn't hard to see coming. It's no secret the emperor has wanted to annex Serbia for some time. His nephew's death gave him an excuse to act. Everything that followed was obvious. Not inevitable, but not surprising."

Therese observed her sister, trying to perceive some sign of dissembling—a darting eye, a fidgeting hand—but could discern none.

"I might ask you the same question." Ilse turned, locked eyes with Therese, testing how far she could wade in these waters. "Why don't *you* seem surprised?"

"Me?" Therese stumbled. She hadn't considered that Ilse might fling the question back in her face. And was that a note of impertinence in Ilse's voice? That wasn't like her. Stubbornness, yes, but never impertinence, never disrespect. Therese was thrown.

"Yes, you. Why don't you seem surprised?"

"Well," Therese stammered, "as you said, it was all fairly obvious—certainly not inevitable, but hardly unexpected. I, too, had worked it out before." Her voice quaked.

Faint though the tremor had been, Ilse knew she had gained the upper hand. "So that's why we're here?"

"What?"

"You heard me." Ilse looked her sister square in the eye. *Try it,* the look said. *Just try to evade me.* "I asked if that is why we really came here. No, I guess I'm not asking; I'm certain that's why we came. But I want you to confirm it."

Therese paused, tried to look away, but folded under the weight of Ilse's stare. She sighed. "Yes. That's why we came."

"And how long are we to stay?" Ilse could have answered the question herself. But she felt she was standing level with Therese, perhaps for the first time. The surge of power was intoxicating. She wanted to force the confession. Simply because she could.

Therese said nothing, merely looked at her sister. Her eyes begged Ilse not to make her say the words out loud; she could not bear it. Ilse relented and nodded her understanding. She took a deep breath, blew it out in a chuff, and walked resolutely on.

The two continued in silence for some minutes before Therese ventured, "Are you angry with me?" Her voice was meek, like a child caught in a lie.

"Am I angry?"

"For bringing you here. Under false pretenses, I mean."

Ilse thought about it for a moment. She fixed her eyes again on the boy, the kite, which at last had seen fit to take flight. The sky behind it was clear but dingy, shrouded by the soot of a thousand stoves, a million hearths. The blue paper of the kite popped in contrast. Ilse wondered if the skies in Vienna had been like that. Polluted. Dirty. Impure. They must have been. She had never noticed it. But then, until she left home in May, she had never known a sky could look any other way. She had not yet seen the skies in the mountains, where an unspoiled heaven spread above you like a field of hyacinth. How experience colored her view of the world.

"No, Therese," she said at last, "I'm not angry with you. A bit sad, perhaps. That you didn't trust me. That you thought you had to hide it. But I'm not angry you brought us here. Not anymore. With the world falling apart, how can I be angry with you for wanting us to be safe?"

And that was the truth. Therese's lack of faith still stung, but Ilse could not begrudge her the result.

Therese took her sister's hand and gave it a light squeeze. With tears moistening the corners of her eyes, she tucked Ilse's arm under her own, and the Eder sisters walked together, arm in arm, for the first time since they were girls on the streets of Vienna.

***

With one barrier removed, Therese was freed. She could share her anxieties, every doubt and worry that nipped at the back of her mind. They poured out of her over the next few weeks as she awaited each new letter from Friedrich. And though Ilse continued to conceal the depth of her concerns for Junius, she was glad she could finally be an outlet for Therese. That was something, at least.

As for Aunt Selde, she was simply relieved to see a normal emotional response from one of her guests. Female hysteria she had seen before. She knew what to do with it. She knew when to tut and coo her sympathies, when to encourage exertion, and when to simply shut her mouth.

But the hard shell that seemed to have formed around Ilse was a mystery to Selde. She had never seen anything like it. Perhaps in a weathered old crone, but certainly not in anyone so young and vibrant as Miss Ilse. It was like the girl had stepped off the boat and decided then and there that she would feel nothing—that if she could feel nothing, she might, in turn, have nothing to fear. So odd. Very nearly off-putting.

Ultimately, she decided the same medicine would cure both sisters' ills. Selde Knight was not a woman who walked on egg-shells. She did not coddle them. Helplessness and mourning must have their moment; Selde did not deny that. But she also saw value in application. She insisted on getting the sisters out and introducing them into Boston society generally and, more particularly, into the small Austro-Hungarian community of which she, after nearly two decades in the city, was the undisputed center of gravity.

Ilse marveled at the ease with which Selde moved through the world. There was no embarrassment, no sign of nerves, no fawning, no excess of formality. Selde floated in and out of drawing rooms and parlors on a breeze. And though she was far from being the wealthiest or most fashionable lady around town, the residents of these rooms always seemed glad to welcome her into their intimate circles, grateful for any moment she could lend to their company. Thanks to this lady's patronage, it was not long before Therese and Ilse began hearing, "*Mrs. Kassner, Miss Eder, how lovely to see you!*" any time they left the house.

By the end of their first month in Boston, it was clear the conflicts in Europe would have no quick or easy resolution. Therese began to hint that she and Ilse should start searching for rooms to rent. She had no intention of imposing on Selde's kindness and had planned all along to set up house for Ilse and herself by summer's end. Their hostess, however, would not hear of it. Selde's sense of family duty would never permit her to turn her nephew's wife out on the street.

It was not merely duty, though. Selde genuinely enjoyed having Therese and Ilse under her protection. As much as she found ways to fill her time, she was nevertheless a wealthy single woman of a certain age, childless and alone in a big house. In her rare sour moods, Selde worried her life had become rather shallow. A bit silly. Having Therese and Ilse to watch over gave her the sense of purpose she had been sorely lacking for many years.

And so, it was settled. The refugees were to consider Selde's home as their own until Europe was again blessed with peace, however long that might be.

***

Around this time, Friedrich's letters to Therese started to contain more than the usual professions of love and hopes for their imminent reunion. Friedrich became a wartime correspondent. Intermingled with tenderer sentiments were updates that, though perhaps not worthy of gracing the pages of the daily papers, were of much more interest to his readers.

One morning in late September, the post arrived as the ladies ate their meal in the cozy breakfast parlor. Therese abandoned her toast and jam and watched as Selde inspected one letter, then another, until she finally waved in Therese's direction an envelope made out in Friedrich's hand. Therese snatched it up and hurried out of the room without a word, bumping the table and leaving the china and cutlery rattling in her wake.

"Don't you worry, my dear," Selde called after her with a chuckle, "I take no offense at playing second fiddle to a piece of parchment!" To Ilse, she whispered more sympathetically, "We must allow for such lapses. After all, the poor woman has practically worried herself into a fit these past weeks. And it's no wonder, devoted as she is to my nephew. It can't be easy, being away from him for so long. And so early in their marriage, too! When I pestered him into sending her to me, I assure you, I had no intention of stealing her from him for an age! And with everything else going on besides . . ." Selde's voice trailed off. Her look grew distant as she sank her teeth into a thick slice of sweetbread with a sigh.

What heartaches were memorialized in that sigh, Ilse could only imagine. Selde said no more.

Therese returned a few minutes later, eyes glistening but tolerably composed. She seated herself and took a sip of coffee.

"Well, let us have it, my dear. What news from Linz?" Selde inquired.

"Nothing to celebrate, to be sure," Therese said resignedly, "but nor was there anything we haven't been expecting. Kurt's letters of conscription arrived last week. He reports for training on the first of next month. Mother and Father Kassner—your brother and sister-in-law—remain in Pula for now. He is monitoring the expansion of the shipyard, and his wife and Amalia continue there with him. Naturally, they refuse to upset their lives a moment sooner than necessary. Friedrich is working day and night, overseeing the shifting of production in the factories in and around Linz. At least for now, it seems that will be the extent of his service to the realm, thank God. Oh, and Junius von Hess is back at Wiener Neustadt and has received his orders. He'll be moving to the eastern front in a matter of days. Possibly he is there already. Herr von Hess—or I suppose I should call him Fähnrich[17] von Hess now—is the youngest son of the neighboring estate," Therese explained for Selde. "He's quite close to Friedrich and Kurt and spent a good deal of time with us lately before Ilse and I came to you."

"Ah yes, the Hess family. I knew his father well. Vile man. My own father tried to promote a match between us when I was a girl. But I wasn't nearly high-born enough for his grandness, the future baron. The daughter of an industrialist? Heaven forbid!" Selde recollected with a derisive snort.

Therese couldn't help smiling, amused at the idea that the sister of the great Andras Kassner had ever been thought too low for anyone.

"Just as well," Selde went on. "If I had married into that family, I would have had all that pressure to be forever popping out heirs for them. Ha! I see from your faces that I've shocked you. Miss Ilse, you are positively peaky! But I assure you, children didn't interest me in the least. Don't misunderstand me; there's nothing *wrong* with motherhood . . . assuming it's what you want out of life. But I just never could bring myself around to the idea. All I saw was pain and mess and loss of self. It simply wasn't for me, was all. Not that I ever could have said that out loud to anyone, mind you. No, no, our situation back then was far too precarious. You see, we were in the club but only just barely. One wrong move, and out they would have tossed us all.

"It was a big part of what drew me to my Hugh, actually." Selde had skewered a bit of fried hominy and gestured with her fork to emphasize points in her story. "He was older than me, *much* older, and everyone thought I married him only for the money. Don't get me wrong; money was part of the equation. Don't you ever believe a woman who marries a rich man and claims his money has nothing to do with it. It *sweetened the pot*, as they say around here. But it was more than that. None of the other ladies seemed to see the appeal of a husband who, in addition to being delightful company, had no desire for sons to succeed him. My Hugh may have immigrated from Ireland, but he was so exceedingly *American*. He built his own fortune with little more than his two hands and the brain between his ears.

He worked and worked until, eventually, he got tired. Then when he was tired, he sold his business, and that was that. By the time he met me, he simply wanted to enjoy what was left of his life. I could help him do that, and in exchange, I could gain an independence without regularly paying the marriage debt. To me, that sounded like an absolute dream!

"Oh, but I've lost the thread again, haven't I? What were we talking about? Oh, yes, now I remember. Young Hess is shipping out, you say?"

"Yes," Therese replied, smirking. Selde's stories always seemed to ease her mind. They did not remove her burdens, but they made them lighter, easier to carry. "He's to have charge of a cavalry unit. Bohemian volunteers, apparently."

"Bohemian volunteers? Well, that certainly doesn't promise well, does it? I suppose they won't have more than a hundred words in common. How dreadful!"

Wrapped up in the contents of the letter and Selde's stories, Therese and Selde failed to notice the color draining from Ilse's cheeks, the sheen of sweat wetting her forehead. Friedrich's letter had brought the first news of Junius since their arrival in Boston, and it confirmed Ilse's worst fears.

Junius was engaged in the war effort.

He would soon be on the front lines.

Perhaps he was there already.

Perhaps he was already dead.

Ilse tried to swallow this news, brush it off and carry on as if nothing had happened. After all, she had known it was just a matter of time. Still, it was real now. It was really happening. And there was nothing she could do about it.

Selde and Therese continued to chat, but their voices grew distant, echoing inside Ilse's head. She willed herself to be still as the walls around her swirled, undulated, rose and fell, crested and collapsed. Like waves. Like the ocean that stood between her and Junius. Ilse blinked hard, stared at Therese's lips, tried to focus on the words coming from them. But it was too late. A hot churn was frothing within her, about to boil over.

She had just enough time to mutter, "Please excuse me," and run for the toilet before her stomach relieved itself of her breakfast.

***

Half an hour later, on legs that strained to carry her weight, Ilse joined the others in the salon. Therese and Aunt Selde watched with concern as she eased herself into a chair near the window to drink in the fresh air. Their gentle, fussing voices washed over Ilse as they expressed their hopes that she was not coming down with an illness.

"I'm sure it's only the accumulation of these past two months," Ilse assured them. "Being uprooted, adjusting to new surroundings, meeting so many new people, worrying for Father and Friedrich and all our friends. It all just caught up with me, that's all. I'll be fine now."

But Ilse wasn't fine. The morning saw her twice more running out of the salon.

When Ilse had no appetite at lunch, Aunt Selde ignored her protests and ordered her to bed for the rest of the afternoon. Selde spent the rest of the day admonishing herself for having ever imagined Ilse unfeeling. There was no longer a doubt in Selde's mind: Ilse had felt each blow as it had come. She had simply been absorbing them all, hoping not to trouble anyone with her worries, displaying a level of self-control that was foreign even to Selde. But Ilse's struggle had been unsustainable. Selde now saw the toll it had taken.

Evening fell, and Ilse remained languid and weak, with sharp pains stabbing and twisting in her belly. She insisted there was no need for a doctor but did not resist Therese's order that she go to bed early and get a good night's sleep.

THE SLIGHTEST CREAK OF A BOARD

Fog hung in the air, thick and disorienting, obscuring Ilse's vision, playing games with her mind. She stood on the boathouse dock, looking across the water, searching, squinting to see through the curtain of gray.

Gradually, the fog lifted, revealing not the gently flowing river but wide, open prairie. Waves of tall grass rolled in the wind. As Ilse watched, the scene transformed. It was no longer a rich, verdant plain but a grassless field, stretching out bleakly before her. Bare land scarred with craters. A desolate place. A land of decay. Where things go to die.

Ilse jumped down from the dock and landed hard, catching herself. Shards of rock bit into her palms. She didn't feel the scraping sting, didn't brush off her hands. She stood and walked, plunging into the void, propelled by an unseen force. The ground was wet, the mud thick, sinking and shifting beneath her feet. Her progress was labored, but she kept moving, willing herself on as the mire dragged her down. Her feet grew heavy; her steps became slower and slower until, at last, she could not move. She was help-lessly cemented in place.

That was when she saw it. In the distance. A lone horse. She could not see the rider's face, yet instinctively she knew.

It was Junius.

She called to him, but no sound escaped her. Again and again, she silently cried out. Panic welled. And then, cutting through the quiet, she heard it. The sharp metallic hiss.

An explosion lit the horizon.

A voiceless Ilse fell to her knees.

"*No!*" Ilse, awakened by her own scream, shot up in bed, shaking, still caught in the nightmare.

"Hush now." Therese was at her side, taking Ilse's frightened face in her hands. "It's me. It's only me. You were dreaming. You're here. You're safe." She pushed back sweat-soaked hair and brushed a thumb across a damp cheek.

"Therese?" Ilse panted. Her feral eyes stopped darting around the room and found her sister, focused on the familiar face, the brow knitted with concern. Gradually, she became oriented, recognizing the bureau, the bed, the overstuffed armchair in the corner where Therese had insisted on sleeping, all of it lit by a sliver of light seeping between the panels of the thick curtains.

"I'm sorry," Ilse said, catching her breath. "I'm fine. I'm fine now. It was just a bad dream." As soon as she uttered these words, reassuring herself as well as Therese, an intense pain wrenched her belly. Ilse let forth a low, guttural moan. Between her legs, she felt wetness, warmth.

"Ilse, are you okay?" Therese laid a hand across Ilse's forehead, checking for fever.

"Yes, I'm fine," Ilse groaned, waving her sister away. "I think my courses have finally started, that's all. That must be what had me feeling so ill yesterday."

She had bled a bit, hardly more than a spotting, shortly after they arrived in Boston, but nothing since. Ilse had thought little of it; it was not unusual for her to miss months. Stress and anxiety always left her susceptible to disruptions. After her mother died, when Therese moved out, even when she first traveled to Linz. She had never had such a long gap before, but the last two months had been unlike any she had ever lived through.

Ilse dragged herself from the bed, modestly pulling down her nightgown, which she had tugged up past her waist in the distress of dreaming. She pushed back the curtains to better light her way to the small chest, where her menstrual rags were discretely tucked away. The dim glow of early morning filled the room.

Therese also began to rouse herself, opting to start her day rather than try to wrestle from the dawn another hour's sleep. She moved to throw back the blankets to air out the bed, but something in the space her sister had vacated caught her eye. She gasped, recoiled.

A moment was all it took for Therese to pass from horror to recognition to outrage. "Ilse, what have you done?" she asked breathlessly. "*What have you done!*"

"Calm yourself, Therese," Ilse replied groggily as she rummaged through the drawer, searching for her rags. "It's not as if I am the first girl to have bloodied her bedclothes."

But Therese would not be calm; she was throwing herself across the room. She whipped Ilse around and grabbed her by the shoulders, shaking her, shrieking. "*Whose is it? Whose is it?*"

Stunned and confused, Ilse searched her sister's face, looking for some clue, a hint as to what had triggered the eruption, the violence of the onslaught. "Therese, are you out of your senses?" she cried, prying herself from Therese's grip. "What on earth is the matter? What have I done?"

Therese shoved Ilse toward the bed and pointed at the blood-soaked sheet. "Look. *Just look!*"

Ilse, still dazed, obliged. She saw what had sparked her sister's hysteria. Not just blood. Amid the stain, dark red clots. And a mass, no larger than a bean. Grayish-pink and sickly. Her inexperienced eyes struggled to process what they saw. She stood transfixed, unable to move, unable to speak, yet unable to look away.

Therese positioned herself across the bed, putting intentional distance between them as she fought to regain self-control. "Who was it?" she said slowly, her voice quaking and low, practically whispered. Muted fury.

Ilse, still speechless, looked over at her sister, begging for an explanation that Therese was too enraged to offer.

"I said, who was it?" Therese hissed again.

Ilse looked frantically from the bed to her sister and back again, trying but failing to understand. Excruciating seconds ticked away as she groped in the darkness. Her mind raced to connect what lay between them on the sheets to Therese's ire and questions. *What have I done . . . ? Whose is it . . . ? Who was it . . . ?*

And finally, it all made sense.

The night with Junius.

The missed courses.

Her recent illness.

Ilse stared at the strange sight on the bed and began to comprehend. Signs of life. Or, more aptly, signs of death. Signs that life had, for the briefest of moments, rooted itself within her but now was no more.

Ilse looked to Therese with imploring eyes. Her voice failed her. She could squeak out just one word, barely audible. "Junius."

Therese stared at her sister—her beautiful, spirited, innocent little sister—for a moment but could stand Ilse's presence no longer. Disgust was too thick. It choked her. She could not breathe. Without another word, Therese left Ilse to clean up the mess she had made. She walked back to her own room, slowly, cautiously, as though the slightest creak of a board might obliterate her entire world.

***

The door was closed between them.

Ilse stood with her feet planted, nailed to the floorboards. She stared at the tiny lump on the bed, horror mixing with awe. Part of her was drawn, wanted to reach out, touch it, felt there must be some sort of power to be drawn from it, this strange and mystical thing. Part of her wanted to hide, wanted never to have seen it, felt it somehow knew her, knew each secret desire, every shameful act she'd ever committed or imagined.

Blood trickled down her thigh. She wiped her leg with the rag she still held in her shaking hand. Then she threw the rag over the mucus-covered mass and scooped it from the bed. Mindlessly, she dropped the evidence of her disgrace into the embers of the fire Aunt Selde had insisted on lighting the night before. As the bundle began to smolder, the smell of burning tissue made Ilse's stomach lurch. She opened the window and gulped down fresh air until the feeling passed.

Numbed, she sat on the edge of the bed. Mind devoid of thought, soul delivered of emotion. How long did she sit there? She couldn't say. Seconds, minutes, hours melded into each other, a homogeneous hum of time.

Eventually, Selde's maid, Ginny, appeared with a dish of oatmeal and a cup of ginger tea, along with her mistress's inquiries about Miss Eder's health. Ilse thanked Ginny for bringing her breakfast and asked her to convey to her mistress that Miss Eder was improved but still much fatigued and wished to remain in bed for the morning.

"'Course, Miss." Ginny bobbed a curtsy and made her exit.

After staring at the food for several minutes, Ilse attempted a bite. She held it in her mouth, working up the will to chew, to swallow, and finally managed to force it down. It took all her remaining energy to keep the food from rising back up. Pushing the tray away, she sank back into the pillows and fell into the deep sleep of one fleeing the world.

***

Around midday, Ilse awoke, huddled to one side of the bed. For a moment, she thought it had all been some horrible dream, another nightmare. But then she saw the angry stain in the middle of the bed and knew she had not imagined it.

She got up, splashed water on her still-pale face, changed her clothes, ran a brush through her hair, tied it back with a powder-blue ribbon. Catching a glimpse of herself in the mirror, she yanked the ribbon out, letting it drop to the floor. She could no longer stomach it, that ribbon. It felt dishonest—the girlish innocence it suggested. It made her feel like a fraud.

Perhaps she *was* a fraud. But she didn't have to perpetuate the lie, not anymore. The world could see her for what she was.

She cracked the door open, listening. Hearing nothing, she assumed Selde and Therese had gone out and ventured to remove herself to the salon so that Ginny might have a chance to set the room to rights.

The assumption proved wrong, however. Half wrong, at least. On entering the salon, Ilse found Therese sitting near the window, looking out at the slow fall of autumn leaves. A book lay open across her lap, a sure sign to anyone who knew her well that Therese's thoughts were as tangled as her sister's. Ilse edged backward, hoping she might retreat unnoticed, but was betrayed by a loose floorboard. Its deep groan startled Therese out of her stupor.

"Ilse," Therese said.

"Therese. I thought you had gone out."

"No." She closed her book with a sigh. "I told Aunt Selde that I preferred to stay in today. In case you got worse." Her voice had an acidity, a bite. It brought to Ilse's mind images of a dog with raised hackles.

Ilse crossed the room, eyes lowered, and sat in the chair farthest from her sister. "Did you tell her what happened?" she asked, holding her breath. A knot of fear inched up her throat.

"Of course not. What kind of simpleton do you take me for?"

"Thank you." Ilse's fear receded.

"Don't think for a moment that my silence is for you alone. Yes, you are my sister, and no, I don't want your future ruined by this. But never forget that everything you do affects me. Every blemish on your reputation blackens mine."

Ilse could say nothing in response. She knew Therese had every right to be incensed. Ilse could not justify herself. She simply sat in her chair, staring at her hands as they twisted the fabric of her skirt, like a little girl being scolded for muddying the carpets.

Therese rose and walked to the open window. For a moment, she remained silent, closing her eyes and breathing in the late-September air, letting the breeze stroke her cheek. Outside, people were passing on the sidewalk: a hunched old man, tottering by, leaning on his cane; a mother pushing a pram, bending as she walked to coo at her child; two rowdy boys kicking a tin can; a well-dressed man weaving his way around the others. Therese waited for them all to pass. No one, not even a stranger, could hear what she was about to say. When the street was clear, she turned back to Ilse.

"I just need to know one thing. Did he force himself on you?"

Ilse stared at Therese. For half a second, she was affronted by the question. But then she recollected the circumstance and lowered her eyes again. "No," she said softly. "I was not forced to do anything."

Therese sucked in a breath, held the air in her lungs. She closed her eyes and bit down on her lip as if absorbing the jolt of a slap. Ilse's words both relieved and substantiated her fears. She would never have to sit across the table from Junius von Hess and see in him a villain who had raped her sister without being at liberty to have him removed from the house. For this, Therese was thankful. But the price of this blessing was great. It meant her sister was not the victim she had both feared and hoped her to be. It meant Ilse had been reckless enough to put a moment's passion above the future happiness of those who loved her. It meant Therese would never again look in Ilse's face and see that sweet, innocent child over whom she had doted since the day she was born. That girl was gone; the one who sat before her was a stranger.

"When?" Therese asked.

"What?"

"I asked when it happened."

"The night before we left. I went to meet him. After everyone had gone to bed."

And then, like a flood, powerful and unstoppable, it all came out. Everything Ilse had concealed from her sister for so long. How she and Junius had met for weeks. How they had hidden their relationship from everyone, fearing the truth might make Therese's life at Bergesschatten even more miserable than it already seemed. How Junius had begged her to end the charade, and she had refused. How he had asked her to meet him one last time and shared with her the contents of Dr. Eder's letter. How, at that moment, she had been blinded, acting without thought, fueled by raw emotion.

"I know it was wrong, Therese. I know how much I am to blame, and I regret that more than you could ever imagine. But nothing you can say will make me regret loving him."

Therese had managed to hold her tongue while Ilse narrated her story, but this was too much. "Love?" she spat. "You know nothing of love. You barely know him! You run around for a few weeks, romping in meadows and hiding in the woods, and you call that love? That's a fantasy. That's what little girls imagine love to be. Love is no fantasy, Ilse. It's gritty, and it's trying. It's working together to build something stable and solid, something worth fighting for."

"You're wrong," Ilse cried. "I do love Junius, and he loves

me with all his heart! I know he does! And what we have *is* worth fighting for!"

"Maybe you're right," Therese replied with a cold frankness to counter Ilse's fervor. "Maybe what you *had* was worth fighting for. But I guarantee you, it's not a fight you would have won. You should consider yourself damn lucky you won't be saddled with Junius von Hess's bastard for the rest of your life."

"How dare—"

"Because it's the truth!" Therese shouted Ilse down, invalidating her indignation. "Are you such a fool that you can't see that? That child would have been the end of you!"

"You're wrong," Ilse replied with the surety, not of pride, but of one who has no doubt in the truth of their own words. "Junius loves me. He never would have let me suffer. He would have married me."

"You really are a fool, aren't you?" Therese said in exasperation. She sat, leaning forward, forearms on her thighs, hands clasped in her lap, as if in prayer. She took a deep breath, preparing to shatter her sister's delusions. When she spoke, her words were more considered than before, her tone kinder. "Did Junius ever say anything to make you think he had any thoughts of marrying you?"

"He told me he loved me. Every day he told me, both through his actions and in words," Ilse replied defiantly, her lower lip trembling.

"But did he ever talk of marriage? Did he ever talk of a future with you?"

Defenses still raised, Ilse began to reply in the affirmative but stopped herself. Every conversation she and Junius had ever shared flashed before her. Her breath left her. The future was the one topic she had learned to avoid; it was the one thing Junius could never bear to discuss. "No," she admitted. "He did not."

"Because Junius knows his future is not his own. He knows his course has been charted for him. His father would never allow him to bind himself to someone of so little significance."

"But Friedrich's family objected to his marrying you, and you were able to overcome it."

"Because the Kassners have half the pride and twice the love for their son as have the Hesses. You heard what Selde's said yesterday about the baron. A *Kassner* was not good enough for him; do you really think an *Eder* would be good enough for his son? Baron von Hess would never give his blessing to your marriage."

"But, surely, if I was carrying his grandchild, the baron would have too much a sense of duty—too much pride—to deny us."

"Perhaps. But it will be months, maybe years before you see Junius again. And that's assuming he . . ." Therese stopped herself. Angry as she was, saying the words aloud seemed too cruel.

". . . survives the war." Ilse finished the sentence. It came easily to her. It was a thought she'd had all too often.

"The point is," Therese continued, shaking away the morbid notion, "by the time you see Junius again, who knows how much time likely will have passed. The baron would have every reason to deny your claims. You gave yourself to Junius after barely more than a month's acquaintance. What's to say you wouldn't do so again? How could they trust your word when you said the child belonged to Junius? It would have been the easiest thing in the world for the Hesses to keep you from him. And Junius is a sensitive soul; it would not be hard for them to convince him you had broken faith."

Ilse opened her mouth to refute these points, but even in her current state, she was far too intelligent a creature not to feel the truth in her sister's words. She knew Junius would never go against his family. Worse, after the way she had left him, she knew he would spend the months and years they were apart questioning the strength of both her feelings for him and her character. If he still cared for her at all.

"I'm sorry I have to say these things," Therese went on, seeing that she had finally gotten through to Ilse. "To cause you pain brings me no joy. But you must see the risk you have taken, the danger you've put yourself in."

Ilse nodded. It was all she could do; words failed her. Silent tears rolled down her cheeks. She did not bother to wipe them away. She let them fall, watching as they landed on her skirt, dotting the fabric with dark circles.

"Well," said Therese with a sigh, "we should put this subject away. Aunt Selde will be home soon. I'll leave so you can collect yourself before she arrives."

Therese began to walk out, but Ilse stopped her. "Therese, wait."

"Yes?"

"It's just . . . I just wanted to say . . . I want you to know . . . that I am . . . . sorry."

"I hope that's true. And now, I am going to leave this room, and we will never speak of this again."

END VOLUME I

1922

We make one choice, and then another, and then another. Pretty soon, we pick up speed, go flying down a path we aren't sure we've chosen.

That's how it was for me, at least. I made choices, choices I'm not sure I even chose. Not really. Sometimes I think they were thrust upon me, that my fate was ordained from the start, that the options were just for appearances.

Still, I kept on choosing. I was glad to do so. I chose, and I did what I thought was best. Always what was best.

It's funny, when you stop to think about it, how convinced we are that the best thing is to deprive ourselves of everything that makes life worth living. We think it makes us wise. We believe the sacrifice somehow makes us holy, as if joy itself is a sin. So unyielding is our belief that the road to paradise must be littered with suffering that we never stop to question it. We simply choose the responsible thing. The safe thing. The thing that is best.

Even if, on some level, we know it will never make us happy.

Sounds rather trite, doesn't it? Happiness. Really, I ask you, who gets to be happy? Happiness is for children, we say. Happiness is for bedtime stories, to get restless little ones to close their eyes. "And they lived happily ever after. The end." So tidy. So simple. So simplistic.

I had happily ever after once. The trick is to stop the story at just the right moment. My story ended on a spring day, standing by a river in the rain.

And we lived happily ever after.

The trouble lies in the ever after, of course. It suggests nothing else happens. It requires time to stop in that one perfect moment.

But time does not stop. Time keeps moving.

And we keep choosing . . .

For the old, a year passes in an instant. The withered old man looks about and asks how it can be November when just yesterday it was June. But for the young, a day can feel like a week, a week like a month, a month like a year. Time stretches out. A boy in a schoolroom swears the hands on the clock are ticking backward.

With the bloom of youth still clinging to her, Ilse Eder can be excused, then, for any impatience she felt as she sat aboard a train chugging into Vienna. It had been eight years—a youthful eternity—since she had watched her beloved city shrinking into the distance. Nearly a third of her life had been lived on foreign shores. A third of the steps she had taken. A third of the lunches she had eaten and teas she had sipped. A third of her sunrises and sunsets.

This, in short, was a homecoming long awaited.

Of course, she showed neither anxiety nor excitement. Chaos pressed against her ribs and hammered the walls of her chest in a syncopated rhythm. She felt like a balloon growing larger and larger, stretching thinner and thinner. But she would not burst. Whatever she felt, she kept tidily contained.

Ilse liked to think of emotion as a large sheet of that colorful gift-wrapping paper that had recently become so popular in America. Garish but malleable. She could take the tawdry display, and she could fold it up. Fold it once; it got smaller by half.

Fold it again; it was smaller still. She could fold it over and over until it shrank down to practically nothing. A pill she could swallow without water.

It was a trick she had learned years ago from Selde. *"Imagine your feelings as a tangible thing,"* Selde had advised. *"Anything tangible can be tamed."* For Selde, it was light. She pictured her emotions as a diffusion of light, spread all through her body. As she breathed in, she imagined the light pulling together, condensing—in from her fingers and toes, up her arms and legs, and down from her head into her core, all the way to her lungs, where it became a tiny, glowing orb. A pellet so small she could expel it in a single breath.

There was a certain beauty in Selde's metaphor, an elegance. But Ilse preferred her paper. Paper had weight; it had heft. She could not only see it but feel it, hear it, smell it. It was a real, physical thing she could double over. Or, in her worst moments, she could crush it, crumple it up with imagined violence and hurl it far away from her.

Of all the skills she had acquired—her knowledge of politics, her finely honed social savvy, her mastery of languages, both spoken and unspoken—this was the one of which she was most proud. Her heart may have been racing, her mind in bedlam, but any onlooker would see only a lovely woman with a distant expression, an undefined spark lighting her blue-green eyes.

Ilse inhaled slow, deliberate breaths. *Breathe in, fold the paper; breathe out, press the crease.*

Across from her, her two traveling companions slept soundly: her father, legs outstretched, arms crossed over his chest, fedora pulled over his eyes; Aunt Selde, slumped against his shoulder, mouth wide, emitting a low snore. A trickle of drool moistened both her cheek and the tweed of Dr. Eder's jacket.

Ilse smiled.

She couldn't blame them. The rough waters had afforded

little rest during their crossing, and her ever-frugal guardians had insisted on traveling through to Vienna without stopping in Le Havre or Paris to recover. Ilse hadn't protested. God knew she held no nostalgia for either of those cities. Still, hale as she was, even Ilse was looking forward to a long night's sleep in a stationary bed.

Not that sleep would come easily. She was home. A different home, she knew, than the one she had left. Years of war and rebuilding would have changed many things. Not to mention the dissolution of the Austro-Hungarian Empire and the birth of the Austrian Republic. Strange, when she stopped to think about it, that she had spent the last three years of her life promoting the interests of a country she had not yet set foot in.

Soon, though, she told herself. *So very soon.*

Boarding the train in Vienna eight years before, Ilse never could have imagined how long her absence would prove or what the coming years would bring. How naïve she had been; it almost made her laugh to recall it. Those brief months she spent outside Linz before leaving for Boston had seemed such a monumental epoch. In retrospect, it was scarcely a blink of an eye. And yet, so much of her life since then had been shaped by what had happened there.

As she sat watching the warehouses and factories on the city's outskirts sweep past her window, the events of Ilse's life lined up before her like a daisy chain. Each distinct, all connected. Pull out one link, and the whole thing fell to the ground. There was nothing rare in this, of course. The same could be said for any person, any life. And yet, in all its commonness, the fact was no less remarkable. Had her father never brought Friedrich home to dinner, Therese never would have known him, never married him. Therese never would have moved to Linz. Ilse herself never would have been sent there. She never would have met Junius, never betrayed Therese, never made so many terrible mistakes . . .

As it often did, her mind wandered to that awful day early in the war. The day when so many truths had come out. Therese had sworn she would never again speak of what had transpired at Bergesschatten, and she had been true to her word. They never did speak of it. No passing allusions, no underhanded digs to score points in a quarrel. Still, the battle had left them each scarred in different ways. Disfigured. Practically unrecognizable.

***

After their confrontation, Ilse had been a clumsy fusion of insight and upheaval. Therese's harsh words about Junius and his prospects, and what they meant for Ilse's own hopes, had spawned an eddy, frothing with indignation and relief, acuity and loss.

At last, Ilse saw how close to the brink she had walked. Perilously close. Right up to the cliff where, by some grace of God, she had been yanked back before plunging over. The extent of her lawlessness and its consequences were thrust before her. She saw them with razor-sharp clarity.

She had allowed herself to be ruled by her basest appetites, purchasing a moment's release at an exorbitant price. She was diminished in the eyes of a sister who, for all her faults, had taken Ilse in, kept her safe, and shown her only kindness. Worse, Ilse was tarnished, perhaps forever, in Junius's opinion. Would she ever know what he thought of her now? And then, knowing that for more than two months she had carried a part of him inside her. A little piece of them both, united in the form of another life. A life that had been blotted out, that in the rawness of shock Ilse had tossed in with the cinders of her bedroom fire to burn away until it was nothing but dust. Ashes that Ginny swept up to be scattered in the gutter, to float away with the rainwater and the waste.

Against all reason, Ilse mourned the loss of something she

had never even known she possessed. It was a strange kind of mourning. Not an ache exactly, not even a longing. Just an emptiness. A dull but endless dread. A feeling that something was amiss. Like she had left home without a key or had forgotten to snuff a candle somewhere in the house.

Logically, she knew Therese was right. She was lucky to have escaped with so little damage. Blessedly lucky. But relief left an aftertaste. She swilled it in her mouth, tried to accustom herself to the bitterness. The flavor never improved.

Injustice would always taste foul.

That was what it was, after all. An injustice. She could think of no other word for it. Had she borne Junius's child, her life never would have been the same. She would have been destroyed, forever tainted in the eyes of the world. But what of Junius? Was he not equally to blame for what they had done? What sentence would he have faced? None. That was the truth of it. He could simply have denied her claims and walked away. Ilse felt the disparity keenly. She carried with her a simmering resentment, not just toward the world, but toward Junius. Surely, he had known the danger was hers and hers alone to bear. If he loved her, could he have been so careless with her future? If he really loved her, shouldn't he have put an end to it—kissed her on the head and sent her off to bed like the silly child she was?

Well, Ilse decided, never again. Never would she allow herself to approach such a cliff.

Therese, in her own way, was shaken as well. In truth, she was infuriated. To learn that Ilse had deceived her, not just once, but day in, day out, and for weeks! Running about, carrying on an affair with Junius under her very nose, betraying her confidence with every move! That Ilse could have taken such liberties with both of their reputations, even after witnessing the ordeal that was Therese's life at Bergesschatten . . . it was unconscionable!

How could she ever trust her sister again?

Therese ruminated for weeks, and her awareness of her own role in the affair only heightened her indignation. Whether she would admit it or not, deep down, Therese knew she, too, had done wrong. She had been a feckless guardian to Ilse. Therese knew, or should have known, that a young woman coming into independence needed more guidance, not less. But she had been so consumed by her own world, her own troubles, that she had allowed Ilse to run wild from the very day she had arrived in Linz. Therese knew this, and she resented Ilse all the more for making her regret her own actions.

Well, Therese decided, never again. She would not make that same mistake twice. She would keep up appearances before Selde and treat Ilse with whatever love and kindness she owed her as a sister. But trust was impossible, freedom out of the question. She could not risk a repeat of what had happened at Bergesschatten. As long as Ilse remained under her care, Therese vowed not to let Ilse out of her sight.

And so, while all of Europe warred, the Eder sisters settled into an uneasy détente, quietly nursing invisible wounds. Weeks passed, then months. Gradually, it became easier to be in each other's company. They found their way to enjoying moments together, laughing over some story of Selde's or sharing a sidelong glance, a suppressed smile over a quirk of one of their new acquaintances. But the bond of confidence that once existed between them—the bond that for months had been fraying—was severed beyond repair.

To the outside world, they were inseparable. Ilse never appeared in any shop, parlor, or dance hall without Therese's wing wrapped protectively around her shoulders. And yet, in their divided hearts, each stood alone.

Therese survived the war years buttressed by a faith that kind and loving words from Friedrich were always on their way.

Her faith never proved unjustified. Friedrich's habits were as regular as his wife's confidence was unflinching. Even during the worst of it, his letters somehow arrived each week, providing all the updates he could scribble onto their pages.

If any of these letters contained news of Junius, Therese did not share it, and Ilse dared not ask. Though she never stopped wondering where he was and praying for his safe delivery, Ilse eventually stopped hoping to hear of him. Instead, she devoted her life to study: to perfecting her English, which improved by the day; to devouring every book about history and art and science she could get her hands on; and most especially, to making a study of Aunt Selde.

In Selde Knight, the Austrian widow of an immigrant entrepreneur, Ilse found an unexpected mentor and muse, and Ilse was as devoted an apprentice as any master could desire. For nearly five years, she watched and internalized the way Selde tiptoed along the bounds of impropriety without ever crossing the line; how she bore her own scars with dignity and grace; how she made everyone around her feel loved and important and yet never allowed her own heart to be touched.

Ilse and Therese remained with Selde for the duration of the war. Life became an exercise in endurance, marking time until the present became the past, never knowing if they should wish to hurry the future. The days were a uniform blur of house calls with Selde and strolls in the park. They held their breaths and crossed themselves each time they passed a newsboy on the street, as if doing so might alter reports already written about events that had already happened.

At social gatherings, Selde steered conversations away from politics. Though confident America was too much a melting pot to ever take the side of one party over another in Europe's war, privately, they all carried a sliver of fear that one day America, too, would be drawn in.

Fear proved more prescient than logic. Foolishness can spread like a contagion, rendering neutrality unsustainable. In April 1917, a pacifist president stood before his Congress, entreating them to bless a war.[18]

Though only Germany was named in the initial declaration, the three imperial ladies knew it was only a matter of time. They lived on a knife's edge, smiling dead smiles all the way to December, when their host country finally declared war against their homeland.

Though they had been in Boston for over three years by that time, the sisters' accents clearly marked them as foreigners. Anyone with an attuned ear could hear the inflection of the enemy in their words. Therese and Ilse spoke as little as possible to shop clerks, constantly fearing their voices would leave them vulnerable. They cloaked themselves in anonymity. They kept their heads down. Their circle contracted to the few Austrians among their acquaintance.

Even Aunt Selde, beloved as she was in Boston society, largely isolated from company. She could not know where she would be welcome and where she would not, and Selde refused ever to suffer the indignity of being turned away at a door or ejected from a drawing room. It seemed altogether preferable simply to stay home.

During this time, when the ladies had only each other, something resembling a more genuine friendship regained a footing between Therese and Ilse. Certainly, they could never return to what they had been. They were no longer carefree girls tripping through the streets of Vienna. But as women who had each known sorrows, they could at least begin to draw strength from each other's company and their shared memories of home.

Armistice came in 1918, just in time for the Thanksgiving holiday. Though it meant the defeat of Austria-Hungary, peace was celebrated in the townhouse in Beacon Hill. Aunt Selde dug the last bottle of champagne out of the cellar. She invited Ginny, the cook, and the laundry maid to join them in the sitting room for the evening, where they all raised a glass to mark the close of an era where foolhardy men risked gambits with bets staked on other people's lives.

As soon as she could safely do so, Therese returned to Austria to help her family rebuild. The loss of Kurt at Caporetto was not the only casualty suffered by the Kassners. The indomitable Herr Kassner had taken on substantial debt to supply the war effort, fully expecting his largess would be rewarded after all was said and done. But a failed state does not make good on its obligations. When the dust settled, Austria-Hungary was not the only empire to fall; the Kassner business empire was left in tatters. Bit by bit, the factories were sold off or repossessed; Bergesschatten was auctioned to an Italian speculator with grand plans of converting it into a health resort. Swallowing their pride, the Kassners took the remains of their once-great fortune and relocated to their one remaining asset, a townhouse in Vienna, determined to start anew. They were not alone in their suffering; others had lost so much more and been left with so much less. If anyone in the family appreciated their relative prosperity, none dared to voice such traitorous sentiments.

Ilse did not return to Vienna with Therese in the spring of 1919. Instead, at her father's request, she traveled south to Washington, the American capital, arriving just in time to see the forsythia blazing in golden flames and the cherry trees dusting the sidewalks with a snowfall of soft, pink petals.

Despite his keen understanding of statecraft, Dr. Eder had never been a particularly political being himself. He was happy to comment on the events of the day and did so frequently, even during the war years when honest discourse was largely relegated to whispers and dark corners. But never in his wildest imaginings had he envisioned or desired that he might become one of the figures on the chessboard.

And yet, in unprecedented times, fate takes extraordinary turns.

Throughout the war, the professor's writings came to the attention of several men who would eventually be influential in forming the new republic. Recognizing the sharply strategic turn of Dr. Eder's mind, these gentlemen often sought his counsel in the months after the ceasefire. They showed particular interest in the question of the Americans. How might they best engage the ascendant power across the sea? In advising these men to seek someone from outside the political establishment—someone less likely to be accused of sympathizing with the Habsburgs—it never occurred to Dr. Eder that he was writing his own letter of recommendation.

When it was first suggested that he, Dr. Ansel Eder, move to Washington and begin rebuilding diplomatic ties, the professor demurred. "He was no emissary," he insisted. "He was just a silly old man with a pen." His modesty started to wane when pressed on a second and third occasion. Upon receiving a visit from Herr Renner[19] himself, the professor began packing his trunks.

Dr. Eder was confident in his ability to manage the official aspects of the job. Yet, he had a firm enough grasp of how the world worked to realize the *informal* elements of the position—what happened beyond the stuffy offices and marble columns—would be just as important to his success. It was this that worried him; in these situations, he feared he would be found wanting.

Social intelligence had never been Dr. Eder's strong suit. He had never been adept at reading a room, even in familiar Vienna. If he was to navigate foreign shores, he required a guide, an interpreter of sorts. Someone who might smooth his rough edges. He needed one of his daughters by his side.

For Therese to be parted from her husband for longer than

she had already been, that was out of the question. He could not even bring himself to ask it. No, it must be Ilse. But at twenty-two, and having never been properly brought out, was Ilse ready to take on such a challenge? Dr. Eder had observed with satisfaction through her letters that her mind had continued to expand and refine during their separation. But was she a social creature or an academic like himself? Were her manners awkward like his own or womanly and endearing like her mother's had been? Was she discrete and self-contained? In short, was she prepared for what would be asked of her?

Before even broaching the subject with his youngest daughter, Dr. Eder did his homework and wrote to consult his eldest.

Ilse has quite grown up in our time here, Therese confirmed in her response. *She is much more reserved than she once was and represents herself well. No longer is she prone to those little outbursts that used to leave me so often shaking my head. She has mastered emotions of every sort and will, I believe, be a credit to you. But, if you will permit me to presume so far, I will give you a word of caution. You must take care, Father. Matured though Ilse is, I worry she may be inclined toward romantic fantasies, being run away with by infatuations. I know this has never been something you've much concerned yourself with, but in a position such as yours is to be, affronted egos and wounded feelings could risk the failure of the entire mission. You must leave Ilse in no doubt that if she is to join you, personal relationships of a romantic nature will be entirely out of the question.*

To her credit, Therese never gave her father a hint as to the history underlying her assessment; she was a model of sisterly discretion. But Dr. Eder trusted his eldest daughter enough to accept her advice without question. His letter to Ilse proposing that she extend her stay in America presented the task as one of perpetual distance, always putting their country's needs above her own.

"*I know, my dear,*" he wrote, "*that you are now of an age where you must be thinking to your future—marriage, a family of your own. To ask you to put aside such dreams for several years more is asking much. I would not do so if I was not certain that you and I can achieve great things for the Republic. We can help carve out a place in this new world for our Austria. We can help rebuild our people from the heaps of rubble left behind by the Habsburgs. But doing so will require much. You will have to give an appearance of openness while always remaining closed, to acquaint yourself with many strangers but only from a safe distance. I am afraid it will feel, at times, a very inauthentic existence. I am sure there will come a day when you will be forced to deny your heart. If it were only for me, I could not ask this of you. But I do not ask for myself alone. I ask for Austria."*

Awaiting Ilse's reply, Dr. Eder tormented himself. What kind of father asks such a sacrifice from his child? He had no way of knowing that his call to duty had filled Ilse, for the first time in a very long time, with something akin to satisfaction, something like pride. Dr. Eder's words had given purpose to patterns she had already begun to establish.

Though much time had passed, no one had supplanted Junius in Ilse's affections. No one had even come close. Therese had made sure of that. Ilse knew she and Junius would never be reunited. Even if their paths should happen to cross, it had been too long; too many things had happened. Yet, she could not bear to give her heart to another. It was not a sense of loyalty that held her back but an aversion, one she could never quite define.

Love came in many forms. That much Ilse knew. She had seen it with her own eyes. Sometimes love was nourishment, like soup, warming you from the inside, filling you up. But sometimes love was a drug, an addiction. Its victims clung to it not because it made them happy but because they had no choice, because they feared they would die without it. Looking back, Ilse didn't know what her love for Junius had once been, but she knew what it had become and what it would be every day for the rest of her life. For her, love was poison. She had survived the toxin once, but it had marred her. She still saw traces—the scars and pocks—every time she looked in the mirror. She would not expose herself to it again. The risk was too great.

And so, slowly, brick by sharp-edged brick, Ilse had built a wall around her heart. It was not a conscious decision, more like a reflex. The more she polished her surface into a shining artificial perfection, the higher and more impenetrable the wall became. It was only behind this wall that the real Ilse lived, where the real Ilse's thoughts were housed, safely hidden away from anyone who dared get too close. If no one knew the real her, no one could love the real her, and since she could never love someone who did not love her in return, she was safe.

In forging these convictions, in practicing such detachment, Ilse had molded herself into exactly the woman her father would one day call on her to be.

In the end, Dr. Eder's instincts proved astute. Though much admired in his own little corner of the world, the professor was an acquired taste. He did not excel at ingratiating himself among those who did not share his brand of erudite eccentricity. That he made a success of his new position was thanks in large part to the efforts of his daughter.

Within no time, Ilse established herself as a fixture of Washington society, an ornament sought to decorate every dining table and salon. Scarcely a week went by during their first year that did not hear some Mrs. Mitchell or Mrs. Baker saying to her husband, "I met the most fascinating woman today; we simply *must* include Miss Ilse Eder on the list for our next dinner." And as a young lady must have a chaperone, where Ilse was invited, her father must and could follow.

Dr. Eder no longer objected to any finery in Ilse's dress or the pains she took in her appearance. Quite the opposite. If Dr. Eder was anything, he was a pragmatist. He was not blind to reality. He knew that first impressions are almost always visual, and opportunities to make a second impression often depend on the first. Vanity in the name of strategy was a worthy pursuit.

And so, Ilse transformed herself.

She became the personification of past imperial grace, the taste of royalty the steadfastly democratic Americans secretly craved.

She was regal glamor with republican ideals on her lips.

She was a tool with which Dr. Eder fashioned his own fortunes.

Ilse swam through the sea of arrogance and self-aggrandizement with the easy strokes of an Olympian. With the ladies, she was open and engaging, happy to express views that would intrigue without shocking, and these women delighted in the novelty of a woman who matched their husbands in both education and strength of opinion. Rarely did their husbands notice that, with them, Ilse's strong views were seldom shared. Ilse could discern exactly what these men needed to hear—which, more often than not, was the echo of their own voices. She knew how to sparkle while letting them shine, sparring but never offering a perspective of her own, teasing without ever challenging their inflated valuations of themselves. If asked for Miss Eder's thoughts on the prospects of this new treaty or that trade proposal, she would laugh, touch a wrist, and say, "Now, Senator, why would an important man like you care to hear my opinion? Honestly, I wouldn't venture even to form one. You might take it as representing the views of all my people, and, really, I've been living in America for so long that would do neither of us justice. No, no, I'm much more interested in hearing *your* thoughts on the subject."

By offering a rapt audience as they espoused their own views, Ilse became enchanting in the eyes of even the most cynical politicians. How, then, could they resist when she later would suggest, "My father would find you positively fascinating—you absolutely *must* meet him"? Through Ilse's maneuvering, Dr. Eder had only to suffer through an uncomfortable dinner or an awkward cocktail party to secure a formal meeting where he could impress in his own right.

Admired though she'd been in these circles, Ilse was never at risk of an attachment that might introduce complications into her father's work. Her flirtations were as harmless as they were overt, always delivered with a studied and ironic air. Even among the gentlemen with whom she was most closely acquainted, she was a "chap," a "fellow." As much as they enjoyed her company, none considered her a romantic prospect. Her practiced warmth left them cold. She was too ordered, too perfect. There was a hardness there. They would never live up to her standards. Miss Eder could not possibly understand their defects because she had none; she could never relate to their anxieties because she felt none.

No, this was not the partner to lend comfort in their darkest hours.

This force of a woman was no safe harbor for their hearts.

***

The train began to slow, and Ilse laid her memories aside, bundled them up and tucked them away in the corners of her mind until the next time she wished to peruse them.

Memories had the lure of familiarity but held no promise for the future. Their realm was the past; for now, she must leave them there. It was time to start the next phase in her life.

What that phase might consist of, Ilse could not yet say. For the first time in many years, she was arriving in a city that promised permanency. This was no summer trip to Linz, no escape to Boston, no detour to Washington. The idea of firmly affixing herself to a world again offered refreshing prospects. And terrifying possibilities.

The train lurched into the station, and Dr. Eder and Aunt Selde were jostled awake. They stretched and rubbed their eyes.

Selde noticed the spot of drool on Dr. Eder's shoulder, blushed and fussed, dabbed at the tweed with her handkerchief.

Dr. Eder smiled at his daughter. "Well, my dear," he said through a yawn, "are you ready to go home?"

Yes, she was ready.

A MILLION TINY REVULSIONS

"Ilse! At last!"

The moment Ilse entered the parlor of the Kassners' townhouse in Landstrasse, Therese was struggling to her feet. She waddled forward as quickly as her swollen body would allow and embraced Ilse tightly, blinking back joyful tears before they could smudge the line around her eyes or leave tracks in her face powder.

"My dear sister, just look at you!" Ilse stepped back to survey Therese, breaking her normally steely composure. Without a second thought, she laid a hand on either side of Therese's rounded belly.

Therese didn't mind. Maternal pride was all-consuming, leaving no room for quibbles about personal space. "Are you surprised?" she asked, beaming.

"I could not be more so! But you sly thing, you didn't say a word about it, not in any of your letters! You must be six months along by now!"

"Seven, actually. I would have said something, but I knew you would be coming home before it was time, and I just couldn't resist the opportunity to stun the famously unflappable Ilse Eder." Therese's face lit with mischief. "And I see I have succeeded."

"Indeed, you have. I admit I am astounded. Does Father know?" Ilse couldn't stop staring at the curve of her sister's stomach.

"Oh yes, he's known for months. But I made him promise to let me share the news with you in person."

"Some things never change, I see," Ilse chided, though without any trace of malice or bad humor. "So good to see the two of you still enjoy conspiring against me after all these years."

"You may be a formidable figure these days, but you will always be my baby sister," was Therese's reply as she eased herself back onto the small divan where she'd been sitting and patted the space next to her.

"I'm not sure I would call myself formidable," Ilse replied, answering Therese's summons and joining her on the sofa.

"Don't think you can fool me with false modesty. Your reputation precedes you. Father has told me how invaluable you were to him in Washington. And I've heard glowing reports from others as well."

"Well, if you consider it invaluable to be universally inoffensive and unfailingly pleasant to look at, then I suppose—"

"As a matter of fact, I do." Therese wagged a finger to silence her sister's protest. "Men may not take seriously a young woman who is nice in her appearance, but they won't even take the measure of a woman who is not."

"And what of the woman who they *actually* take seriously?"

"I shall tell you once I've met her."

Ilse laughed in commiseration, taking Therese's hand and squeezing it. Both knew well the frustrations of being an educated, capable woman in a world that preferred its women to be neither.

Putting on a mulish expression that silenced further debate, Therese continued. "Besides, you and I both know that diplomacy is achieved as much at the supper table as at the conference table. Your *inoffensiveness*, as you call it, got Father to that supper table. Perhaps if you had been at St. Germain, one of our people could have wriggled their way into the negotiating room![20] I'm very proud of my baby sister."

Ilse was touched. How could she not be moved by such compliments? And from Therese, of all people. For so long, her sister had looked at her and seen only flaws and missteps. To now receive such praise instead was truly gratifying.

"And I am so very happy for you," Ilse replied, glancing again at Therese's belly. It was now Ilse's turn to blink back tears.

In truth, she was not only thrilled to learn of Therese's pregnancy, Ilse was relieved. She knew Therese had miscarried at least twice since returning to Vienna—a predisposition that had afflicted their mother and very likely herself also—and she knew of the emotional toll it had taken. While their shared history made it impossible that Therese would confide in Ilse on such matters, Ilse had maintained a frank and open correspondence with Friedrich, who a year earlier had written to her seeking advice on how to remove the cloud of a particularly stubborn dark mood that had settled over his wife following her most recent miscarriage. But sitting with her sister now, Ilse was pleased to find her completely at ease. The cloud was gone. Therese's long-troubled mind was finally at peace.

"Where are Father and Aunt Selde?" Therese asked, suddenly remembering she was expecting more visitors beyond her sister.

"Father sends his apologies; he had to report to the office this morning. But he promises to stop in before dinner. And Aunt Selde says to tell you she is still recovering but will be here to see everyone . . . well, I'm not quite sure when. But I'm sure it will be before long."

"I suppose I'm not surprised," Therese sighed. "Whenever I've asked about her promised visit over the last few years, she's put it off. She always said she loathed the idea of an ocean crossing without good company, but I suspect it is more than that. She has been avoiding seeing what has become of the family. It must be very hard on her, knowing her childhood home is gone and her brother is so reduced when she herself is still so comfortable in Boston."

"And how *is* the family?"

"Muddling through as best we can," Therese replied. "No one pretends to be happy about our current circumstances, but I do think everyone is starting to adjust. And our prospects have brightened a bit lately. Friedrich and his father secured some investors for their new venture. They were great once; I'm sure they can be so again, eventually. Until then, we get by. Amalia even asked me last week to recommend a *modiste* to help her alter her old dresses into more modern silhouettes! Can you imagine!" Therese laughed. To Ilse's surprise, there was more love than derision behind Therese's words. "I must confess," she continued with her voice lowered conspiratorially, giving a quick glance toward the door to ensure neither Amalia nor her mother would walk in while she was expressing forbidden sentiments, "our way of living now really does suit me better than our life at Linz ever did. It's more familiar. Here I feel like I can hold my ground, stand on something of an equal footing with the rest of the family. I can be of some use."

Ilse smiled fondly at her sister. It occurred to her that it might not have been the anticipation of her first child alone that had brought forth the change in Therese's demeanor. Perhaps it had as much to do with the Kassners; perhaps through their trials, they had finally come to accept Therese as a member of the family, fully and truly. As much as Ilse still held on to former prejudices against Amalia and Frau Kassner, if this was the case, for her sister's sake, she was glad of it.

"Well," said Therese, "should we walk out?"

"Are you able?" Ilse asked warily.

"Of course! For now, at least. And the day is fine. Soon it will be too hot for *anyone* to be walking about. Heavens, I abhor to think I will be nine months pregnant in the heat of July! So, while the weather is still lovely, I get out whenever I can."

"Well then, by all means, lead the way."

***

The morning was cool but pleasant, with brilliant sunshine and a clear sky interrupted only by sporadic wisps of white cloud. As the Ringstrasse, with all its impressive and familiar sights, was but a short distance from the Kassners' home, Therese steered them in that direction.

They spoke little. Therese was acquainted with her sister's habits and knew Ilse would be taking in every detail, every change that the passing of eight years had rendered on the face of the city. She could have commented on the modern fashions, the unchallenged supremacy of cars in the streets, the reduced need to mind one's step in the wake of the horses. But she trusted Ilse was observant enough to perceive the transformation without commentary.

Though not blind to such changes, Ilse was grateful to find that, at least where the fundamentals of the scenery were concerned, Vienna had changed little. Franz Joseph[21] may have been dead and buried, his kingdom crushed and splintered, but his vision for Vienna lived on unblemished, grand as ever in the regal boulevard. Its eclectic buildings still mingled like ladies at a winter ball: the classical parliament whispering to the gothic Rathaus;[22] the opera and the Imperial Hotel, dressed in Italian neo-renaissance, gossiping behind the back of the Hofburg,[23] passé in her multiplicity of melded styles.

A thousand memories rushed at Ilse as they approached each familiar edifice. Her feet remembered these sidewalks. The exact drop of each curb, the clap of her heel against the hard gray slabs. It was as if she had never gone away. Like she had walked this path every day for the last eight years. Her Vienna was still here, steadfast, unchanged.

But then there were the people, their faces . . .

Gone was the glow of a golden age in a golden city. Tales of struggle were written deep in the lines of each creased brow. The eyes looking out from beneath them told of weariness, defeat, resignation. Years of war and deprivation, the shame of international scolding, famine, disease, unemployment, poverty. Misery kept finding ways to reinvent itself, and the men and women of Vienna wore injury as a badge of honor when no other honor was offered.

But perhaps, Ilse consoled herself, *it is not that the people of Vienna have changed so very much. Perhaps it is me. Maybe I have come home older, wizened. The love of beauty, the devotion to ideas, perhaps they were never more than a veneer, through which I now can easily see. Perhaps . . .*

Their progress along the avenue was slow, accommodating both Therese's size and Ilse's wandering eyes and thoughts, but soon they had walked as far out as Therese dared and returned to the vicinity of the Kassners' home.

Given how close they lived to Stadtpark, though, Therese felt it safe to propose a slight detour so Ilse could see the new monument to Johann Strauss, which had just been unveiled the year before. Ilse had no objection to this plan, so the sisters strolled into the park.

The monument had been erected in the gardens that spread before the lofty Kursalon, that lavish concert hall. As they approached the gardens, they came upon a large group of schoolgirls, chattering and laughing, ignoring the pleas of their escort—a stout and sour-faced nun—that they conduct themselves as proper young ladies. Pushing through the throng, Ilse held her breath, a habit she'd developed back when influenza ran rampant in Boston and still found herself unconsciously practicing. Only this held breath kept Ilse from gasping as she emerged on the other side of the crowd. Instead, she expelled the air forcefully, as though she'd been punched in the gut.

Not far from where they walked rose the bronze likeness of Strauss, gleaming in the morning sun. But it was not the monument that took Ilse's breath away. There, in the shadow of the composer, stood a gentleman with strong shoulders, an even stronger jaw, and piercing gray-blue eyes. In his arms was a child, not yet two years old, with devilishly curly hair. The girl squealed as the man tossed her in the air and danced the moment he set her on the ground next to a delicately beautiful blonde dressed in white linen and lace. The woman gazed adoringly up at the man, who was obviously her husband, and then opened her arms for the child to come toddling into. The girl fell into her mother's embrace, and the two of them tumbled back into the grass, not caring about the dirt.

The gentleman's figure was more filled out than Ilse remembered, more of a man than a boy. His hair was cut shorter and greased back. Yet Ilse knew him within an instant and without a doubt.

The man standing before them was Junius von Hess.

Ilse stopped, placed a hand on her sister's arm to halt her progress. Therese, seeing what Ilse had seen, gasped and looked to Ilse in alarm. Ilse showed no visible sign of emotion, merely steered them toward a different path where they might retreat unnoticed.

The two walked in silence for a few agonizing minutes. Ilse's mind filled with colored papers; she furiously folded them, one after the other. Therese searched for words that might skirt catastrophe. "I didn't know if I should say anything," Therese said meekly, "if I should tell you he was in town."

"He lives in Vienna now?" Ilse asked.

"No, no . . . He is only here for the week, on some business or other. They dined with us the evening before last. He and

Friedrich remain quite close, so we see him whenever he is in town. Which isn't often," Therese assured her sister.

"And the woman is . . ."

"His wife. Arabella. And the child, their first. Juna. Bella is expecting their second. If it's a boy, they plan to name him Kurt, after our dear boy." Mourning was still fresh in Therese's voice, though more than four years had passed since they'd received the news of Kurt's passing. She watched Ilse closely as they walked, but Ilse kept her gaze on the path ahead, refusing to let it wander.

Ilse was quiet for a time, and Therese gave her space to process the news. When she finally spoke, she asked the one question Therese dreaded answering.

"Is he happy?"

"Yes," Therese admitted, truthfully though reluctantly. "Yes, I do believe he is happy. He and Bella married shortly after the war, and his father died not long after that. And with his brother having been lost at Kraśnik, Junius inherited his father's estate about two years ago."

Therese's revelation sent Ilse's mind hurtling down the road of regret. Baron von Hess had died. Had Junius not been forced into a loveless marriage, he would have been free to choose his own path in life. She could have returned to him. They could have been together.

Though Ilse revealed nothing, Therese could guess where her sister's thoughts were straying, and so she offered more intimate details than she might have otherwise thought tactful. "Though she was his father's chosen match, I have no doubt Junius loves her very much. You would see why if you knew her. She's smart and sweet and very kind. She reminds me of you when you were younger. Before . . . well, before everything."

"Well, consistency is certainly an admirable quality in a man, I suppose." Ilse twisted her lips into a wry smile to mask her misery. After another uncomfortable pause, she continued her line of questioning. "I need you to tell me just one thing more, and then we can have done with it." Her sister looked at her expectantly. "Has he ever asked about me?"

Therese hesitated. "Yes, he has," she answered. "He has asked where you are, if you are well, that sort of thing. The way one might inquire about a common acquaintance." She immediately regretted her phrasing. "Oh, Ilse, I'm so sorry. I didn't mean to suggest that—"

"Think nothing of it." Ilse waved her off, forcing indifference. "He must ask *something*; it would be rude if he did not. And I'm not surprised he's never brought himself to ask more. I'm not proud, you know, of how I left things with him. Our parting hurt him. I'm sure it did. No, that's not quite right; I'm sure *I* hurt him. It was not our parting; I can't pretend it was some passive event over which I had no culpability. It was me that hurt him. My choices, my actions. I would not expect him to harbor any particular interest where I'm concerned."

They walked on in silence, Therese watching with alarm every breath her sister took, every subtle, involuntary twitch of Ilse's mouth. While Ilse maintained a placid expression, Therese looked like a stray kitten, eyes wide and troubled. Ilse could bear just about anything, but she could not stand the excess of Therese's concern, the lack of faith it represented. "Oh, for heaven's sake, Therese," she blurted in exasperation. And then more calmly, "I assure you, I am fine. I have withstood much more significant blows than this."

They were by now far enough away from the Hesses for safety, so Therese requested they take a short rest on a bench. She was, after all, carrying twenty pounds more weight in her front than usual. As they sat observing the passersby, Therese turned to Ilse and said in a burst of wonder and relief, "I must say, I'm amazed by how well you handled that. I have often thought about what would happen if the two of you crossed paths again. In my head, it was quite the pitiful scene!"

Ilse took her sister's hand and gave it a patronizing pat. She considered Therese's comment, then asked, "Have you ever seen a cicada?"

"A cicada? Of course. Nasty little beasties!" replied Therese with a grimace and a shudder. "But what have cicadas to do with anything?"

"Father's and my first year in Washington was a summer of cicadas. Did I ever tell you about it? They are around every year, of course. But now and then, I suppose every fifteen years or so, they emerge there by the millions, crawling out of the soil and up into the trees for a few weeks to mate before dying or burrowing back under the ground. We had only been there for a month or so when they emerged that summer, and I had managed to secure an invitation to this very elite garden party. There I was, Miss Never-a-Hair-Amiss, charming senators and cabinet secretaries, completely unflinching as these revolting creatures crawled up my shins and snagged at my stockings, feeling the rush of their wings as they flew about beneath my skirt, their spiky little legs pricking at my thighs. All the while wanting to howl in disgust but never allowing myself to lose control.

"But that's what it's all about, isn't it?" She looked at Therese, who was narrowing her eyes, trying to discern Ilse's meaning. "Being a woman, I mean. It's about keeping up appearances. The constant battle to choke off the screams of a million tiny revulsions."

Therese clasped Ilse's hand and held it to her heart. Estranged for so many years, the Eder sisters finally understood each other again.

***

Ilse refused to let Junius enter her head as she escorted Therese home, as she deposited her sister safely back onto the little sofa in the parlor, kissed her cheeks, and passed along her regrets that she had missed seeing the rest of the family.

She kept him from creeping in as she hired a cab to take her back to Stroheckgasse, stopping along the way to call on her old friend, Lily Neumann, who was no longer the gawky girl Ilse remembered, but a married woman with a crop of little ones running about her knees.

At home, she managed to remain tolerably focused while giving instructions to the new housemaid on the arrangement of her books and while nodding along to the details of Dr. Eder's first day at his new office. Her mind absorbed the names and titles of individuals who would expand their social circle as if it had nothing else to occupy it.

Not until much later, after Ilse had bid her father goodnight and closed the door to her room, did she allow her thoughts to wander back to the garden.

There, in the room of her discarded youth, Junius flooded Ilse's senses. Memories of the boy she had known—the smell of his hair, laced with strains of cedar and rosemary and wet grass; the salty-sour taste of his kiss; the way his voice took on that nervous tinge whenever he edged toward sullenness—competed with flashes of the man she had seen that day. His easy cheer, the smile that reached from the curve of his lips up to the crinkle of his eyes. Those eyes that could still undo her, that exuded so much love. There was a lightness about Junius now, a joy. Never, not even in their sweetest moments, had she seen him like that. The intensity, the weight that had always pressed in on him from every direction, was gone. Somehow it had lifted away. The same years that had left her jaded and worn down seemed to have had the opposite effect on Junius. His clock ran in reverse. Within the body of a man, the spirit of youth had reasserted itself.

But more even than the ghost of Junius von Hess, the vision that tormented Ilse as she slipped into bed was that of Arabella, the new Baroness von Hess. Every time she closed her eyes, Ilse saw her. Her warmth, her vibrancy that, by some force of God, seemed to have survived the war untouched. The woman practically effervesced. Ilse couldn't help suspecting that the change in Junius was due to Arabella.

No, she did not suspect; she knew.

Ilse, too, had been luminous once. It was so long ago she struggled now to remember what it felt like to be that weightless, that free, but she was sure it had been so. She, too, had once radiated life. Junius had loved her *because* of her brightness; it had balanced his dark.

But life had stolen Ilse's flame. Stolen it from her and given it to Junius. In its place now was nothing but stone. Her false warmth left a hint of a chill; her practiced softness lent no comfort.

She knew this.

Junius's life had not paused when she left him; Ilse knew this, too. She had always known it. The rational side of her brain shouted at her to forget what she had seen that day; it was no more than she had expected, after all. Of course he had looked to the future after the war. Of course he had married.

But the audacity of his happiness, the fact that Arabella didn't just balance his darkness but had pulled him out of it entirely . . . that was what was so hard to swallow.

The more Ilse tried to be reasonable, the more she found her common sense competing with a far shriller voice. This second voice cherished being the victim, wrapped itself in the sting, reveled in it. She could feel its sensuous breath on her ear, its forked tongue tickling the back of her mind, sparking thoughts she longed not to have. *You were betrayed*, the voice whispered. *Junius betrayed you. Therese suffocated you. Even your father . . . he, too, was more than happy to exploit you. It's their fault you're cold, their fault you're so hard and distant. They made you what you are.*

But you don't need them. You're better alone. You're stronger alone.

These words would be her tonic, and the day's wounds would heal over, leaving new scars, pink and raw, that she would bury alongside the rest. Ilse allowed herself one night of tortured thoughts, one morning of puffy eyes and aching head.

She hid herself away for one day.

Then she left Junius von Hess to the dust of memory.

BRIEF BUT INFECTIOUS

Houses, too, have memories. History nestles into soot stains above the fireplace, burrows into the threads of the curtains on the backs of dust mites. But decay is a cunning foe; it lives in plain view but is spotted only by comparison, when fresh hues are discovered to have survived in the hidden spaces, unwashed by the sun, safe from the accumulation of grime.

Moving about her childhood home, Ilse marveled that everything was exactly as she had left it. But then she would go to replace a painting, and there it was: the passage of time, written in the paint on the wall. Lifting frames, Ilse would see it. *Oh, yes,* she would say to herself, *there you are. Life has marked this place.*

No one told Dr. Eder's former colleagues how his walls had faded or how the cigar smoke had turned stale beneath the dust covers. Three years was nothing to them. Far from having moved on, these gentlemen seemed to have been waiting in the wings. They flooded back into the house with the green door before their old friend had even unpacked his trunks. Arriving home from dinner with the Kassners just three days after she and her father had returned to Vienna, Ilse was welcomed by booming tones of debate echoing out from the parlor. She latched the front door and rested against it, closing her eyes, smiling, soaking in the familiar sounds. Now she was truly home.

The time abroad had wrought little change in Dr. Eder. He still relished the company of his old friends and encouraged them to join him whenever they could. What *had* changed, though, was his place in the world. With his new position as a confidential advisor to the foreign minister, Dr. Eder was now a man of influence. Soon, a very different set of men began flocking to the modest house on Stroheckgasse.

Dr. Eder's Sunday salons were no longer characterized by intellectual and moral homogeneity, where educated men of essentially the same worldview deliberated over the nuances of what was empirically correct or ethically sound. Now these voices competed with those espousing more vulgar notions: those who promoted the *advantageous*. Climbers crowded into the Copperdoor Club (as the Eder home came to be known) to sell both their causes and themselves. Not a month after the Eders' return, Professor Neumann—hair now salted with streaks of white but disobedient as ever—found himself sandwiched between a pair of pomaded men in dinner jackets and shined shoes, in a tug-of-war over the benefits and threats of labor unions.

The mild-mannered Dr. Eder did little to discourage these changes, and before long, he found his gatherings drifting into unfamiliar territory. Somehow or other, they had become fashionable.

***

One newcomer, in particular, was destined to become a frequent visitor at the Copperdoor Club. He came not to curry favor, not to cultivate contacts or pedal pet proposals. As a man of a certain standing who cared little for his position, he had just two aims: first, to honor his late father's memory by living up to, or at least close to, society's expectations; and second, to achieve the first while putting himself out as little as possible. Showing his face in any venue deemed "acceptable" by the upper crust was all he required, and he could do so with minimal effort in Dr. Eder's parlor. He first arrived on the Eders' doorstep in the company of an old school chum and, by the end of his first night, found that the lively conversation and fast-flowing brandy were rather to his liking.

His name was Heinrich Jörger. Heinrich, the Baron Jörger von Tollet, to be precise, although he felt legally obligated to wave away the honorific any time it was used. The nobility had officially been abolished in 1919, which suited the modest Heinrich just fine. He had no need for attention or grandeur. It was Viennese society that insisted on keeping the aristocratic titles alive. As terms of respect. As miniature rebellions against the changing times.

The baron was a stocky yet handsome man. Despite a nagging birth certificate that reminded him he was well past forty, he had managed to maintain a boyish charm. Exceedingly well-read but with a modish air, Heinrich Jörger mixed effortlessly with the varied sorts that Dr. Eder attracted. The baron joined with these qualities an easiness and wit that perhaps was surpassed only by Ilse herself, and from his very first visit, he established himself as a favorite jousting partner of the lady of the house.

On that muggy August evening, the topic heating up the conversation was a scandal that had rocked the legal world that week: the lady barrister. A woman had not only dared to study and seek a license to practice the law, she'd had the audacity to attempt to represent a client before the court. The lady's presence was too much to be born; the prosecutor had been forced to storm out of the courtroom without so much as acknowledging her. Was the prosecutor wrong for walking away, refusing to argue against a woman and, thereby, causing a delay in justice? Or was the woman in the wrong? Surely, she knew she would create a sensation, yet she had persisted in her course of action, regardless of the risk she posed to her client. This was the great debate of the day.

While the battle raged, Ilse found a quiet corner from which to watch and bite her tongue. It was like observing a spectacle of nature. She had read the works of the naturalists; she knew the many ways males fight for dominance. The displays of plumage, the howling, the boxing, the sparring. Listening to the bombast, she pictured a consortium of fiddler crabs waving their claws around, skittering about on spindly orange legs, their dance at once mesmerizing and comic. The only difference between such exhibits and the one playing out before her eyes was the target. Rather than trying to woo a mate, these men sought to impress her father.

Ilse was content in her corner. It was home. She had spent many nights here, had been formed many years ago in this very chair, watching some of these same men batter each other with their intellects. But in taking up her place again, she was not slipping back into adolescent habits. In her youth, she had done everything she could to disappear into the walls. Invisibility no longer interested her. Ilse was no longer a wraith; she was a full-bodied presence, and she made her presence known. But that did not mean she felt the need to throw herself into the center of the debate. Standing in the middle of the room, proclaiming her brilliance, insisting everyone listen to her every word—she left such peacocking to the men.

The men didn't know any better.

"There is no need to stamp your foot and demand attention," Selde had advised all those years ago. *"You do not dance about like a fool. Dancing is for circus bears and grinder monkeys. You are no bear. You are no monkey. You are a lady. It is in the way you hold yourself. It is an energy that burns from within. Let that energy speak for itself. They will come to you because they cannot help themselves. They will look to you because they cannot possibly look away."*

Perhaps even more than Selde herself, Ilse had come to embody that quiet energy. It was not Ilse's actions that commanded attention but her presence, her being. All she had to do was walk into a room. Or sit in a corner.

As she fanned herself in the stuffy parlor that night, listening to the men's shouting about a woman's proper place, the cries of *hear-hear* and *tosh,* Ilse knew she would not be alone for long. Someone always found his way to her side. Though, at least in this crowd, their interest was rarely in her conversation. She knew she was their ploy. If they failed to impress Dr. Eder on their own merits . . . well, why not try the daughter?

Had Ilse been less assured of her own worth, she might have resented these attempts to inveigle her. As it was, she found it mildly amusing. Where once her father had used her to gain access to the seats of power in Washington, now it was her father who had the influence, and these men used her to gain access to him. There was a certain deliciousness in the symmetry. The tables had turned, yet she was cemented in the same place. The axle around which the wheel spun. Always the means to some man's end.

On this night, however, she had caught the attention of the newcomer, Baron Jörger. He slid into a chair next to Ilse as his friend was detailing the scientifically proven biological limitations of females in stressful situations, points Neumann declared to be "scientifically proven bunkum."

"I don't believe we've been introduced," the newcomer said. "You are Fraulein Ilse Eder, I believe?"

"A remarkable guess from one to whom I've not yet been introduced," she replied.

"You will have to forgive my forwardness; I've heard much of you from Herr Wasegg . . . who does not seem to be carrying his point very well this evening, I'm afraid." He nodded toward his friend, who was now standing chastened, arms crossed, on the other side of the room.

"Indeed, he does not," Ilse agreed, suppressing the urge to

giggle. She permitted herself only a slight, bemused smirk. "If you've heard of me from Herr Wasegg, I wonder you bothered coming over at all, given all of my *scientifically proven* limitations."

"On the contrary, he's done nothing but sing your praises for two weeks together. If I were you, I would pay his words no heed, Fraulein Eder. I suspect he got caught up in the game just now, trying to score a rhetorical point, and doesn't even believe that drivel. Or he simply has failed to notice you're a female. Knowing Karl, either possibility is equally likely."

Ilse laughed. "Well, since you have learned my identity on such reliable authority, I will own that you are correct; I am Ilse Eder. And you are Heinrich Jörger, I believe?"

"A remarkable guess from one to whom I've not yet been introduced," he answered, mimicking her, simpering.

"You are not the only person here with sources, Herr Baron."

"Please, I beg you," he said with the obligatory shake of the head and wave of the hand, "I am merely Heinrich. To borrow a phrase from Count Sternberg, my family may have been enno-bled by Josef II in 1784, but I was respectfully *un*-nobled by Karl Renner in 1918."[24]

"Herr *Jörger*, then."

"An acceptable compromise. For now."

"And how do you find the conversation this evening, Herr Jörger? Is it everything Herr Wasegg promised you?"

"Hmm . . . How to answer . . . ? It is quite, shall we say, *in-teresting*. But it's missing one crucial element that would make it truly stimulating."

"And what might that be?"

"Why, a voice from the sex at the center of the controversy, of course."

A hoot of laughter escaped Ilse, brief but infectious. It was a reaction she had succeeded in suppressing for years; she was astonished her body could still produce such a sound. "Forgive me, sir. I don't mean to laugh at you. Your response simply took me by surprise."

"Surely, it can't be so very shocking for a man to be interested in a woman's opinion. I should think the need for it is rather obvious in this instance. I came over here with no other objective than to solicit yours."

"My opinion?" she deflected. "Since, as you say, Herr Wasegg has told you so much about me, you must know I am a woman of some education and experience who has seen a bit of the world. I'm sure you could guess my opinion on such a topic. I would much rather hear what *your* thoughts are. Your stance is rather more a mystery than my own."

"*My* thoughts? Nonsense! I can think of no world where the opinion of a lazy, privileged aristocrat should carry more weight than that of a woman of your accomplishment. Come now, let us have it."

She couldn't say what, but something in this man's manner rubbed away Ilse's usual defenses. There was nothing she had to gain from him, and she sensed, instinctively and against her better judgment, that he likewise sought nothing from her. For once, she felt no need for artifice. For just that moment, it seemed safe to let someone peek behind the velvet curtain.

"Well," Ilse leaned in, lowering her voice, "if you must know, I think it all perfectly absurd."

"Go on."

"To think this prosecutor would abandon his duties and flee the courtroom rather than argue against a woman! Did he imagine he was being gallant? Was he afraid he would dishonor himself by making her cry? Or is his ego simply too fragile to deal with the possibility that a woman just might best him? I suspect it was the latter. Rather than risk it, he fled the scene with his cowardly tail between his legs."

"Ah, there are all kinds of flights from responsibility. The most convenient, of course, being the flight into stupidity. For most of us, it is but a short journey." Heinrich's words were wistful, as though he were reciting a cherished childhood rhyme. He looked to Ilse with a sly twinkle. "That is not mine," he confessed. "It is something I heard Herr Schnitzler say once."[25]

"Schnitzler? Herr Arthur Schnitzler, the writer?"

"The very one. He was an old university fellow of my father's. Not often, but from time to time, he would join us for a dinner or on some other occasion. I always felt wiser afterward. Though, in all honesty, I'm sure I was no wiser. I simply walked away with another man's wise words to go around repeating."

"Let us test how much of his wisdom truly rubbed off, then. What do you, in your own words, have to say on the matter at hand?" Ilse probed, glancing back toward the melee.

"I say the prosecutor is a vile embarrassment to the court. His behavior is almost as unpardonable as this group of men, who love the sound of their own voices so much they would discuss a subject such as this for over an hour, and not one— until now of course—"

"Of course."

"—has thought to ask the thoughts of the only woman present."

"Wiser words have seldom been spoken. Now was that so hard?"

"No, I suppose it wasn't."

They both took deep, satisfied breaths and chuckled over their own audacity, looking rather proud of themselves. After a moment's consideration, Ilse turned to her new conspirator and said, "Could you do me a small favor?"

"Consider me your servant."

"Would you hold this for just a moment?" Ilse handed him the drink she'd been nursing. "I shall be back shortly; there's something I must see to."

"That is the very smallest of favors, and one I could not possibly refuse."

Though slightly confused as to why he was left holding her glass when there was a perfectly serviceable table between their chairs, the baron was more than happy to be of use to such a charming lady.

***

In the months that followed, Ilse's path often crossed with that of Baron Jörger. He became a frequent, if atypical, caller at the Eder's home in Rossau. Unlike other gentlemen to visit, he was more a spectator than a player. Far from striving to dominate the conversation, he appeared content to occupy the periphery, whispering in the corner and critiquing the others' performances with the daughter of the house.

Beyond the confines of Dr. Eder's parlor, either by chance or by design, Ilse seemed unable to move about the city without happening upon the baron. If she appeared at Kursalon, he was there; if she attended a private party, he was there. They joked that the alignment of their tastes and social circles destined them to grow weary of each other's company. Were they a less compatible duo, this might have been the case. As it was, intimacy blossomed.

Heinrich found diversion to fill many a dull hour simply in observing the way Ilse moved through the world. Only he saw the effort behind her effortless grace. How she stole peeks at her reflection—in mirrors, windows, spoons, champagne flutes—to ensure her finger curls hadn't rebelled. How her face retained its focus, but her right pinky finger twitched almost imperceptibly when she'd been caught talking for too long with some tedious braggart.

When Ilse had done her duty by everyone else in the room, she would take refuge in the quiet corners Heinrich preferred to inhabit, where they would indulge in the sanctuary of candid conversation. It was in these moments that Heinrich caught glimpses of the real, complete human being who lived beneath Ilse's polished surface. How very different *this* Ilse was from the false idol the rest of the world so worshiped! How much livelier; how much more interesting!

These routines were not lost on their shared acquaintance. Before long, Vienna whirred with the hum of speculation. The beguiling Ilse Eder had not only conquered cities on distant shores; it seemed Heinrich Jörger, that famously indomitable bachelor, had been conquered as well. He finally had found a lady he deemed worthy of wearing the empty title of Baroness Jörger von Tollet.

The subject came up before dinner at the Kassner home one evening in November as Ilse bounced her nephew, then four months old, on her knee.

"It is so very nice to see you without your shadow this evening, Ilse," Amalia teased as she carefully swirled a glass of wine. Having observed how quickly Ilse's standing in Vienna had eclipsed her own, Amalia had finally dispensed with the formality of calling her sister-in-law *fraulein*. Whenever they saw each other in company, Amalia now embraced Ilse with a showy "Ilse, dear!" claiming Ilse as an intimate and shoring up her own standing in the social order.

"I quite agree," Friedrich said with a smirk. "Wonderful that she is able to bestow her undivided attention on little Ansel for a change."

"I am *always* happy to give my undivided attention to my nephew. He is the best company of anyone I know. Yes, you are!" Ilse cooed, leaning in and planting kisses on the child's chubby cheeks, making him squeal and speckle her satin with a spray of spittle. "Although I'm not sure I follow your meaning, Amalia dear."

"Oh pish," Amalia chided. "Of course you do!"

Ilse maintained that she hadn't the slightest idea.

"Shall I illuminate her?" Therese asked, directing the question to her husband.

"Please do. We'll know whether we've scandalized her by how deeply she blushes."

"Oh, I don't depend on that at all," Therese replied. "My sister would never allow herself to do anything so undignified as blushing."

"Well, they will simply have to take my word as to whether or not they have shocked me, won't they?" Ilse said to the infant.

"We are speaking of the baron, of course."

"The baron?" Ilse's heart stopped. Inured as she had become to this title being bandied about in her presence of late, the word delivered from Therese's lips instantly brought forth images of Junius, the Baron von Hess.

Therese balked at her sister's blank expression. "*Heinrich Jörger*," she clarified in mock exasperation. "We might not get around quite as we used to, but it's not like we are entirely isolated. We know what people are saying."

"And pray, what are people saying?" Ilse asked insouciantly, her heart regaining its normal function.

"Come now, drop the charade," Amalia pressed her. "I refuse to believe you're oblivious to the gossip."

"If people *are* saying things, they would hardly say them in front of me, so I am quite at a loss."

"Ladies, I'm afraid you will find no sport here tonight. Your sister is determined not to give away a thing," Friedrich declared.

"Hmm. She might not give anything away, but I know my sister too well to think her in ignorance," Therese replied to her husband. To her sister, she said, "You must be aware of the expectations you've raised, Ilse. You seldom go anywhere that the baron is not."

Ilse shrugged noncommittally. "We have many of the same acquaintances."

"And rare is the evening when you are not seen engaged in some intensely private tête-à-tête," Friedrich inserted.

"We enjoy each other's conversation immensely."

"And whenever you are *not* talking to him, his eyes follow you around like a poor little lost puppy!" Amalia added gaily.

"Well," Ilse replied coolly, "I cannot answer for that, nor would I vouch for its veracity without first referring to Heinrich."

"Ooh, she calls him Heinrich!" Amalia squealed, giving a delighted little clap.

"*Heinrich*," Ilse continued, darting a warning glance at Amalia, who composed herself but could not keep a giddy grin from her lips, "is a dear friend. We enjoy each other's company and conversation, but that is all."

"Oh, fine," Therese relented. "For now, I will accept what you say. We will save our fun for your engagement announcement. Then we will all sip champagne while watching you eat your words."

ON SO PRECARIOUS A LIMB

Ilse and Heinrich were not ignorant of the rumors about them. But trying to slow gossip was like trying to bottle the wind—a futile struggle that left them with nothing to show for their efforts. So, rather than moderate their behavior, they leaned into it. People would talk about them regardless, so why not have a bit of fun at their friends' expense? The glasses raised in Heinrich's direction, the mirthful whispers and knowing smiles of ladies watching from across a room became sources of endless entertainment.

It was not until her conversation with the Kassners that Ilse began to worry their jests might also be raising expectations in Heinrich—expectations she could not rise to.

She was not in love with Heinrich Jörger. Loved him, yes. Dearly. Respected him. Valued him beyond measure. But was she *in* love with him? No, she was not.

What's more, her resolution not to marry had not changed. On principle, Ilse knew she could never marry a man, especially one she esteemed as highly as Heinrich, without being totally open with him. But she could only open herself to someone she loved and trusted completely. And she could only trust someone who knew her, knew every dark and damaged corner and loved her despite her deficiencies. Yet, she could never shine light in these dark corners without first being assured of unconditional love.

It was a disastrous circuitous logic that led nowhere. Only to solitude.

There was just one thing to be done. She must put Heinrich on his guard. Unpleasant though the conversation might be, she cared for him too much to risk toying with his affections. She resolved to waste no time; it would be done at the first opportunity.

***

Heinrich called on them a few nights later. Rather than excuse herself and retire upstairs at a reasonable hour, as was her habit, Ilse remained downstairs, counting the minutes as the bottles slowly drained and the parlor slowly emptied. One moment, she was wishing the other men away; the next moment, she found herself dreading their departures.

Heinrich seemed in no hurry for the evening to end. As the clock approached midnight, only he, Ilse, and a yawning Dr. Eder remained. Unable to outlast his final guest, Dr. Eder wished them both goodnight. He did not think twice about leaving his daughter unattended with a single man. After all, Ilse always took such pains to stay on the right side of propriety; he had long ago stopped worrying about either appearance or actuality. Kissing Ilse on the top of her head, he entrusted Baron Jörger's enjoyment to the lady of the house.

"I should turn you out this instant," Ilse teased after her father had disappeared up the stairs. "I'm sure it is most improper, the two of us sitting here alone like this. But I confess, I enjoy our conversations far too much to do any such thing."

"Selfish girl! Just think of the scandal that would attach to my name if someone was to see me slinking out of here in the middle of the night."

"And what of my name? Surely, I should be just as worried."

"Oh, hardly. Ilse Eder? Such an obscure name would sell few copies. But the Baron Jörger von Tollet embroiled in intrigue and disgrace? I can practically hear the papers flying off the stands."

"And then we cannot forget about those poor newsboys. What, with the rags being so violently snatched from their little hands and all, they will get such wretched paper cuts."

"*Tsk, tsk*, I had not even thought of them."

"Really, Heinrich darling, for your good and theirs, I should toss you to the curb."

They chuckled but then went silent. Each sat turning a glass slowly in their hands, watching the dwindling fire dance and pop, searching for meaning in the movement of the flames. Ilse knew the time had come. The glass in her hands was empty, but she raised it to her lips anyway, drank air, hoping some residue of courage might find its way into her veins.

"While I have you here," she began, "I feel I should thank you."

"Thank me? Whatever for?"

"You have been a good friend to me, a very good friend. Perhaps the best I have ever known. Which seems a strange thing to say after so short a time, but there it is. It has been a great relief having someone with whom I feel I can be myself. Or something resembling myself, at least."

"And can you not be yourself with others?"

"Oh, heavens, no," she laughed. "There are few things for which the world has less appetite than a woman who is authentically herself. All that time in Washington with my father, I hadn't a soul in whom I could confide."

"Such a pity to be so admired and yet reap so little reward!"

She waved the compliment away. "And just what makes you think I was admired there?"

He shrugged. "People talk."

"And you take them at their word?"

"Naturally. With such evidence before me, how could I

doubt them? You, my lady, could never be anything but perfectly enchanting," he said with overdone gallantry.

Again she laughed, swatting his arm and rolling her eyes. "Oh, I could. *Believe me.* That woman they all rave about is the result of extensive study."

"Well, you must have been an excellent student."

"I take no credit; I had the very best of tutors."

"Can you possibly mean your sister?" He had met Therese on several occasions. She was pleasant enough in her way, and he had nothing to say against the woman, but he couldn't imagine her being described as "the best of tutors."

"Hardly!" Ilse exclaimed. "Therese has many endearing qualities but being—what were your words?—'perfectly enchanting' certainly is not one of them. She craves approval far too much for her own good. No, I was referring to Frau Selde Knight, my brother-in-law's aunt. Did you ever happen to meet her while she was in town?"

He replied that he had not had that pleasure.

"Well, you certainly missed out," she continued. "For all the Kassners are today . . . well, I guess not *today* exactly, but . . . for all they were at the height of their influence before the war, when Selde was a girl, they were the dreaded *nouveau riche*. Back then, society treated the Kassners much like the Kassners treated my sister when she first joined their ranks. And I can assure you, that was not particularly well. It was Selde who opened the door for them all, who earned their acceptance. She has this ability to be exactly what anyone needs her to be at any given moment. I would almost swear she is an *alp*.[26] She knows how to ask questions without ever committing herself to answers, so she never offends anyone. And just when a conversation is about to lull, she has this knack for extracting herself from it, so no one ever wearies of her company. For years, I observed her and learned from her, tried hard to master every little trick."

"Ah, I see now what you've been about. Lucky for us, I was too clever for your games by half," Heinrich gloated.

"Oh, you think so, do you?"

"I absolutely think so. I remember the night we met perfectly. You were sitting right over there. I came to ask your opinion on some trifle or other, and you tried to turn my question back on me. But I was a step ahead. I forced it out of you!"

"And how do you know I didn't simply get a better read on you and change tactics?"

Heinrich studied her. The arched brow. The mischief in her eye. He thought about it, and then a wave of incredulity swept over his face. "Beautiful thou art, but dangerous too![27] You little minx!" he cried, slapping the arm of his chair. "I held your drink!"

Ilse nodded. "You held my drink." She couldn't help smirking.

"And why on earth did I hold your drink? I remember thinking it odd at the time, and yet I did it anyway."

"Of course you did it anyway. I had asked you to, hadn't I?"

"You had. And if you don't mind my now asking, why exactly did I sit there holding your drink like some sort of after-hours aide-de-camp?"

"Oh no, the magician never gives away all her tricks."

"Oh, come now, is that fair?" he protested. "I know now I was bested. At least give me the satisfaction of knowing for what insidious purpose I was duped."

"Oh, fine," Ilse said with a playfully exaggerated sigh. "If you really must know, that is another of Aunt Selde's devices. Whenever she meets someone she wants to warm to her quickly, she always asks them to do her a favor. It doesn't have to be a large favor. Any trivial thing will do."

"Well, now you've hooked me. Why a favor?"

"Because, Heinrich darling, we humans are nothing if not

self-interested creatures," she explained. "If you enlist some-one's help, even with something silly—something like, say, holding a drink—they become invested. They have exerted themselves on your behalf, so your interests become more aligned. They care more about you and your welfare because if something were to befall you . . . well then, their exertions would have been completely in vain."

He looked at her dubiously.

"I know it sounds like nonsense," she laughed, "but it works. We mortals were not designed with logic in mind, after all."

Heinrich leaned back in his chair in a posture of defeat, pouting. "Well, if nothing else, I suppose I ought to be flattered that you wanted me to warm to you. Though I must say, at the moment, I'm feeling rather chilly," he said with a shiver.

Ilse reached over and patted his arm, batting her eyes at him dotingly. In a moment, though, she recalled herself and became serious again. "Well, now you have me off on a tangent, which you are so very good at doing, but there really is something I need to discuss with you while we have this chance to speak privately."

Suddenly, as if taken by a fit, Heinrich blurted out, "Ilse, I *cannot* marry you!"

For a moment, she was too flabbergasted for words. But after the first shock of Heinrich's outburst wore off, all Ilse could do was laugh, and she did so heartily.

"The lady laughs at me. That's wonderful," he said, floating between injury, humiliation, and relief.

Ilse tried to reach over, to lay a hand on his arm, but she was still doubled over. "I'm sorry . . . I'm sorry . . . I'm not laughing at you," she said in gasps, forcing herself to regain her composure. "Really, I promise I am not laughing at you."

"All evidence to the contrary."

"It's just the absurdity of the situation. I couldn't help my-self! You see, I had stayed downstairs tonight intent on making clear that I cannot marry *you*." Her composure was again spent. She was lost to hilarity, but this time, she had company. Hein-rich, too, burst. The weight of worry having lifted off them, they laughed until they could not breathe, until the muscles in their stomachs ached.

"We are quite a pair, aren't we?" Heinrich said once their mirth had finally subsided into contented sighs. "Both so sure of our own irresistibility we feel the need to actively ward off suitors, even when those suitors want nothing to do with us."

"Quite a pair indeed," Ilse agreed. "How I agonized over it, too!"

"*You* agonized? Look at these circles under my eyes. I've been worrying myself sick! Oh, sure, it was all good fun at first. But the more winking congratulations on my future happiness came in, the more I began to fear you would be receiving the same and that some part of you might begin to take them seri-ously, and I might be breaking your heart!"

"What, break this heart? Impossible!"

"You may have fooled the rest of the world into thinking you indestructible, but I know better. Or I thought I did, at least."

Ilse responded with a shrug, a vague half-smile.

"In all seriousness, though," Heinrich continued, "I'm curi-ous. Why couldn't you marry me?"

"Ah, curiosity can be a dangerous thing, darling."

"And yet, I would still like to know."

"It's no great mystery. It is simply this: lovely as you are, I am not in love with you."

"Oh, is that all?"

"Is that not enough?"

"Not in my experience, no," he said, half joking, half in

earnest. "We get on extremely well. I'm rich. Handsome to boot. Mothers have been unsuccessfully forcing their daughters upon my notice for at least two decades. You could do a lot worse, you know."

"Now you are arguing against your purpose. If I didn't know better, I would think you are trying to convince me *to* marry you, not the opposite."

"Not at all. Simply trying to better understand the outlier that is Ilse Eder."

She sighed. Her expression grew distant. "It is a promise I made myself long ago. That I would never marry."

"Curiouser and curiouser," he said, crossing his feet, reclining into a relaxed pose as if settling in for a long story. "'The world is a prison, in which solitary confinement is preferable.'[28] Is that it?"

"I suppose you could say it's something like that," Ilse replied. She offered no further explanation and could not bring herself to meet his gaze. Even with Heinrich, there was a limit, and she had reached it.

For several minutes, they were silent, staring into the dwindling fire, the mood in the room more sober than before. Ilse stole glimpses at Heinrich, who was lost in thought, brow knitted, sucking on his lower lip, something Ilse had never seen him do. She longed to know what he was thinking but couldn't bring herself to ask.

When he did speak, he did not look at her. "Damn it to hell, Ilse! The thought of you being alone your entire life . . . I must tell you, it breaks my heart. It really does."

She was surprised by the strength of his words, the emotion behind them. It was not like him; he was always so even, so unbothered. It put her on the defensive. "You are alone. I don't see there's much difference."

"The difference is I am not unmarried by choice. I *cannot* be with the one I love."

"No," she confessed. "Nor I."

"That may be. But our situations are *not* the same." He took a breath, calmed himself. He then continued, slowly, each word chosen with the utmost care. "You see, you might hope to love again. Nothing is holding you back but your own heart, and your heart might one day change. I, on the other hand, know I will never be able to marry *any* person I love."

Heinrich lowered his chin and locked eyes with Ilse. He dared not say more. But he did not need words; his meaning was clear. That one look told Ilse everything he was too afraid to say out loud. She knew his truth now, knew it with absolute certainty.

She could have been shocked. That would have been the "proper" reaction. What Heinrich was alluding to was illegal; her religion taught that it was immoral. But her father had also taught her the limits of religion as a moral philosophy. Every religious text was, after all, written by a man. Even if they represented the word of God, they were still the word of God as translated by men, with all their biases, their all-too-human imperfections. She had never taken them at their literal word. They were a north star to be looked to for guidance in the dark, but they were not a map. They were a reference point; she consulted them alongside her own conscience.

In that moment, she turned to her conscience for counsel. In her heart, Ilse was not affronted by what Heinrich had shared. She found no sin in it. He was speaking of love. How could an expression of love be immoral? If God was infallible and he had made a man to love another man, how can that love be wrong? Is not declaring it so tantamount to questioning God's will, God's plan for us?

She looked at the man sitting beside her—this brilliant, besieged, lovely man. Ilse had never cherished her friend more than in that moment. Heinrich had found in her someone he could trust enough to keep safe the secret he hid from the world. He had placed his confidence in her, and in his faith, she had never felt more secure. Ilse wanted more than anything to wrap Heinrich, who had walked out onto so precarious a limb, in the same security she now felt, in the safety of mutual confession. And so, propelled by friendship and fidelity, for the first time, she told her story. The whole messy story. The short weeks with Junius and the night of their parting. The miscarriage. The rupture with Therese. The years of isolation. Everything.

The night ticked away, and the two friends continued to confide, each lessening their burdens by inviting someone else to help carry them. Through the confidences exchanged, they forged a bond as intimate as the ties linking any two lovers.

Hours later, the sun rose over Stroheckgasse, and Ilse and Heinrich embraced and parted. He strolled up the street in the soft morning light, wearied but weightless, pausing just once to glance back, to raise his hat to the woman watching him walk away.

Heinrich did not look back again. He felt unusually sure he had made the right decision. Even as the choice would have been unthinkable only a few hours earlier.

He had left Ilse in the completely opposite state from what either had intended when he had arrived the evening before at the house with the green door.

He was engaged.

EPHEMERAL AS A PUFF OF SMOKE

Myriad are the motivations for marriage. There are marriages of love, marriages for position, marriages for profit. Love fades, positions change, money runs dry. Who is to judge whether one incentive is superior to the others? Can anyone really know what best promotes the future happiness of those who would bind themselves to another person until death parts them?

In an ideal world, Ilse and Heinrich both would have found themselves united to their true love, and that love would have lasted a lifetime. But the world was far from ideal, and they both knew it. Each had felt the sting of injustice. Ilse knew how easily a woman could be labeled and brought down. Heinrich, too, knew the very real danger that came with certain labels. No matter how much each had become accustomed to the idea of remaining unmarried, on some level, each knew such a situation was unsustainable.

Ilse was a single woman in a world that reviled single women. Had the Eders been wealthy, she could have been a respectable spinster, escorted everywhere by a hired widow companion, devoting her life to charitable causes—a force for good in a heartless time. But they were not wealthy, far from it. As much as Dr. Eder's current position provided them with a comfortable living, and as much as her own experience in America offered her some freedom to move about unaccompanied without drawing whispers, the political world into which Dr.

Eder had entered was capricious. Ilse feared relying on it too much. And yet, their position was still too high for her to eschew the dictates of respectability. With Therese's coup of a marriage, Dr. Eder's high-ranking post, and Ilse's own burgeoning reputation, the Eders had managed to wedge themselves into that fickle world of the upper-middle class. Too affluent for Ilse to dirty her hands earning her own keep, but not so well off that her single status could be sustained. She was a songbird in a gilded cage. The only path for a woman in her position was marriage.

Heinrich's position was no less precarious, though for very different reasons. For years, he had been able to set himself up as a curiosity, the intriguingly unattachable bachelor. But that charade could be kept up for only so long. One misstep—that was all it would take. One slip, and the whole thing could come crashing down. First would come the laughter, the comments dropped in jest. Then would come the speculation. Then the smears. Then the law.

The solution had become obvious as these two kindred spirits shared their stories and secrets under cover of night. If they would eventually have to marry anyway, why not marry someone who understood and accepted them completely?

It was not merely a marriage of convenience that they plotted, but a partnership in the truest sense. They would not have children. That side of marriage was out of the question for Ilse as much as it was for Heinrich. In every other way, however, it would be a *union*. They would share their lives. They would stand by each other and against the world. They would help and support each other, no matter what the future might bring. And they would love each other. Not romantic love, of course, but still a love built to last. The love of friendship and family. The love that all too often was debased as being of secondary importance, but that Ilse was convinced was worth more than any other.

***

The next evening Ilse arrived at Heinrich's office by appointment. The two friends had agreed to dine together to discuss how best to announce their engagement to Dr. Eder and the wider world.

"Hello, Streusel!" Heinrich greeted her cheerfully as she entered the room.

"Streusel?" Ilse threw him a quizzical look.

He offered a shrug and a smile. "I just figure, if we're going to make a go of this and make it believable, we'll have to have pet names for each other. I thought I would give one a try."

"Try again," she laughed.

"If not Streusel, what do you like? *Zimtschnecke? Kugelhopf?* It must be something sweet if the world is to be convinced that I'm sweet on you."

"Well, if you insist, I guess I don't mind chocolates."

"Hmm . . . Coco?"

"Better, I suppose. *Marginally* better," Ilse replied. "So, if I'm to be sweet, then you must be savory. What shall I call you? Wiener Schnitzel? Sauerkraut?" Heinrich twisted his face in disapproval. "How about I simply call you *darling*, like I already do."

"If you—" Before completing his sentence, Heinrich sucked in his breath in a spasmodic gasp.

"Hiccups?" Ilse asked.

He groaned. "Yes. Infernal things have been plaguing me all day."

Ilse looked him in the eye and said firmly, "You are not a fish."

"And you are not a parakeet. What an odd thing to say!" he laughed.

"Just wait," was Ilse's only explanation.

Heinrich did wait, though he wasn't exactly sure what he was waiting for. After a moment, he tested two deep breaths and cleared his throat. His hiccups had vanished. "Remarkable!" he exclaimed. "How on earth did you do that?"

Ilse shrugged. "Another one of those tricks I picked up while living in Boston."

"In Boston, you say? Isn't Boston near Salem? Is witchcraft one of the arts you studied under your aunt's tutelage?"

"If that was a spell, it is news to me. But it certainly does work like magic, I've always found . . ." Her voice trailed off as her attention was drawn to an object on the conference table in front of them, a map of Vienna, dotted with red triangles and blue squares. She leaned in to examine it. "What's this?"

"It's this revolutionary new thing they're calling a map."

Ilse gave him a backhanded swat on his arm. "I had worked that much out for myself, thank you very much. But what are all these symbols?"

"Those would be my residential holdings. *Our* holdings now, I suppose. Or they soon will be, at least. Red are town-homes; blue are apartment blocks."

"But these are all in Leopoldstadt . . ."

"Yes," he replied tentatively, scrutinizing her face as she studied the map. "All of my family's business ventures passed down from my mother's side." He cleared his throat again. "Her family built up much of the area."

"Your mother was—"

"Jewish? Yes, she was."

"So that means you're Jewish?"

"Yes, I suppose . . . in a way. According to matrilineal descent and all. Is that a problem for you?"

"Not at all," Ilse replied honestly. "I'm only surprised you've never mentioned it before."

"I suppose that's because religion isn't central to my life. We never practiced my mother's faith. Never really practiced my father's either, for that matter.

"You see, at the time my parents wed, Vienna was not as accommodating of Jews as it is today. Oh, sure, they had been emancipated under the constitution of 1867, given the right to live and worship freely across the empire. But the old prejudices didn't simply disappear with that stroke of the pen. Had my father had a brother or a less rebellious temperament, I have no doubt his parents would have risked a rift and tried to block the marriage entirely. As it was, they only required that my mother not make a show of her faith and that any children would be brought up in my father's. Mother loved my father very much, and her parents, though not quite so enamored with my father as she was, very much loved the idea that their daughter might one day be introduced as *baroness*. And so, they accepted my grandfather's terms. By the time I came along, my parents had established very secular habits, and they raised me with very secular traditions. And in truth, that suits me just fine. Neither my mother's faith nor my father's will have me as I am, so I am content to live without either."

Ilse could not argue with his logic. Still, it pained her to think what his mother had been convinced to sacrifice. So many of Dr. Eder's colleagues had been Jewish that, though the Eders were themselves Catholic, Jewish families had comprised the greater part of Ilse's social circle while she was growing up. The Neumanns, the Leitners—their practices and traditions were almost as familiar to her as her own. There were aspects of the faith that she could never hope to fully appreciate. She could never grasp, for instance, the strength of their emotional connection to past generations, ancestors they had never even met. Yet she had the utmost respect for these differences, saw beauty in the distinctions. To think that the baroness might have been compelled to bury an integral part of her identity was heartbreaking. But maybe she had never been particularly religious to begin with. Ilse hoped that was the case.

"You are very quiet," Heinrich said.

Wrapped in her thoughts, Ilse realized she hadn't the slightest idea how long it had been since she had spoken. "I was simply thinking of your mother. I wish I'd had the opportunity to know her."

Heinrich smiled. A bit sadly, Ilse thought. "That's good," he said. "I was worried you were thinking of all the ways my background might throw up obstacles to our plan."

"Not at all, Heinrich darling," she said confidently. "Not with me, at least. And I can't imagine it would pose a problem for my father. You forget we are academics, first and foremost. We understand that, despite the passions religion always seems to rouse, all the Abrahamic faiths are at their cores the same. Simply different ways of describing the same god. You are an intelligent, good man who finds me endlessly fascinating. My father will be positively thrilled with you."

***

Ilse's assumptions about her father proved mostly correct.

When Heinrich approached him a few days later to solicit his daughter's hand, Dr. Eder assented without hesitation. He regarded the baron highly. Heinrich was no bumbling professor who would be incapable of holding his own at Ilse's side. Nor was he one of those preening sycophants, constantly seeking to impress and cultivate contacts. The baron was an educated, reasonable human being. Did he have a mildly aggravating tendency to hide behind the words of others a bit too often? Perhaps. But this was immaterial. Dr. Eder had no doubt Ilse had chosen well for herself.

Dr. Eder saw nothing in the differences in their family backgrounds to prevent the match. True, Heinrich was of noble birth, and Ilse was not. But it was 1922, not 1912. The aristocracy was on its way out, and Ilse was establishing herself as a force in Vienna quite as quickly as she had done in Washington.

And, happily for Ilse, Heinrich's parents had both been lost to the influenza a few years before. At the very least, she would not face the challenges at home that Therese had suffered early in her marriage.

There was just one point on which Dr. Eder privately urged caution. "The baron is a fine man," he advised, "but I just want to be sure you've thought carefully about linking your fate to his."

"What do you mean, Father?"

Dr. Eder tugged nervously at his eyebrow. "On the matter of Heinrich's heritage . . ."

Ilse could not believe what she was hearing. "Oh, Father, you cannot mean to say that you object on the grounds of his mother's—"

"No, no, no, do not misunderstand me. I have no concerns about Heinrich's faith. You know my feelings regarding matters of religion. I would never object on those grounds," he insisted. "But I am your father, and it is my duty to protect you. I would not have you blindly enter a life that could hold significantly more struggles than you bargained for. I simply want to be sure you are going into this with your eyes open."

He paused, arranged his thoughts carefully. He could not have her mistake his meaning. This was too important.

"You see, my dear," he explained, "you grew up in a blessed age. The Vienna you remember from your youth was a world of art and ideas. You knew a diverse and cohesive city where prejudice was overcome through a shared love of beauty. It was not always that way. That city you remember was an illusion, ephemeral as a puff of smoke. It was not beauty that held it all together but prosperity. The moment prosperity fades, everyone goes looking for someone to blame. And since no one can bear to shoulder the blame themselves, they lay it at the feet of whoever they can find who is least like them.

"The years you were away were not kind to this city, Ilse. You cannot imagine the suffering that has been endured, that people are *still* enduring. With suffering comes fear. And with fear, unimaginable demons can be released. We are trying to rebuild what's been lost, but if we should fail . . ."

His voice broke off, and his gaze grew distant and melancholy as he stared into the uncertain future, the future that would come for them whether they were prepared for it or not.

Ilse had seen that look in his eyes once before. It was the look she had seen the night before she left for Linz.

Kissing him on the cheek, she thanked her father for his concern and assured him she knew what she was about. She poured him a brandy, clipped and lit his cigar, as she had done so many times before. Then she left him to his thoughts and headed upstairs to ready herself for bed.

As she sat before the mirror applying cold cream, wiping away the day's makeup, carefully wrapping her hair in a silk scarf, Ilse may have felt certain she knew where her father's mind had drifted. She might even have believed herself the master of every perilous path his imagination had explored.

She was wrong.

Ilse was not yet able to swim to the depths her father had reached. For all she had lived through and all she had learned, Ilse had been spared so much. In many ways, she was still a child of June. A child of June can never imagine the chill of winter's storm.

THE FULFILLMENT OF EVERY EXPECTATION

On a gray afternoon in March, not one year since his return to Vienna, Dr. Ansel Eder stood next to his daughter in front of the Rathaus, the seat of city government.

Looking to his left, he thought he could see the spires of Votivkirche just a few blocks away, peaking over the skyline. Nearly a decade had passed since he had walked beneath those spires in his simple Sunday suit, steeling himself to give away his eldest to a cadre of finely attired Kassners.

A decade, and still, there was a rawness to the memory.

To watch a child wed is to fuse grief and joy. They mix an indelible ink, stamp the moment permanently on the heart. Today, another memory would be inked. With a tear in his eye, Dr. Eder offered his arm to his youngest daughter. Taking a deep breath, he led her through the Rathaus's lavishly secular halls.

On that chilly afternoon, Ilse Eder wed a famously uncatchable baron. They were joined not by a cardinal, not even by a priest, but by a bureaucrat in a flannel waistcoat.

The fact that Ilse and Heinrich were married in a civil ceremony and not in the church raised no hearsay as to the motives or reservations of either bride or groom. Most attributed the decision to Dr. Eder, saw it as a savvy political statement. Even in such turbulent times, the aging diplomat placed his full faith in the state.

Ilse and Heinrich knew how to skirt gossip of the dangerous sort and stoke it when it worked in their favor. They chose a date for their wedding that was far enough out to prevent ladies from speculating about the reason for so short an engagement, yet soon enough to prevent gentlemen from wondering why the baron would and how he possibly *could* wait so long to wed and bed a woman like Ilse Eder.

At the wedding banquet, as it had been throughout the preceding four months, Heinrich and Ilse's devotion to each other was on full display. No one doubted that the union was inspired by anything but the deepest of passions. No one suspected the kisses performed before company were the only ones exchanged. Who would question what their own eyes told them to be true? The marriage, after all, was the fulfillment of every expectation.

Pretense was nothing new for Ilse; it came quite naturally. She smiled adoringly at Heinrich as he bent to kiss her hand, as he expressed his thanks to all who had come to help them celebrate their happiness. She beamed as her father jested about how Heinrich had found his way to Ilse's side the moment he set eyes on her. She laughed along as Therese regaled the company with the story of the night when Ilse had so confidently assured the Kassners that she and Heinrich were "merely good friends who enjoyed only each other's *conversation.* Friends who not a week later realized they could not bear the thought of ever being apart!"

One guest did not laugh quite so convincingly. Martin Rezek, Heinrich's long-time friend and financial advisor, looked so grim throughout that several guests wondered how much the extravagant dinner could possibly be costing the baron.

***

Having obtained Ilse's commitment to the engagement, Heinrich had wasted no time introducing her and Martin. He secured an opportunity for them to meet within a matter of days. Though it was not openly acknowledged during that first meeting, which took place within full view of the other patrons of Restaurant St. Annahof, Ilse knew Herr Rezek was no mere business associate; much more than friendship existed between him and her intended.

As the weeks and months passed, Ilse chipped away at Martin's disapproval. She gave him space and time to get used to the arrangement. After all, he had not been consulted. Heinrich had thrust his plans on Martin without warning, certain the scheme was so obviously beneficial to them all that Martin would have no choice but to come around to the idea. Working slowly and deliberately, like a sculptor coaxing Venus out of marble, Ilse impressed upon Martin how much she respected what he and Heinrich had together, hoping to convince him that her and Heinrich's marriage would offer some degree of protection not just to the man he loved, but to himself as well.

***

Logic was central to the character of Martin Rezek. Even while nursing his wounds in those first days after Heinrich had told him of his plans, Martin had seen the logic in them—he didn't like it, but he *saw* it. In the months since then, he had even come to view Ilse as a friend and defender.

Still, to be standing in that room, watching the world rejoice in the union of this woman to his Heinrich, he felt deflated. Emptied. Like a hog bled before butchering.

It didn't matter how often Ilse reassured him that the arrangement would not fundamentally change what he had with Heinrich. That was the whole problem, wasn't it? Ilse or no Ilse, his relationship with Heinrich never would nor could change. State and society were both so eager to bless Heinrich's marriage to a woman who did not love him, yet no amount of love would ever sanction what he and Heinrich shared. No matter how he tried, Martin found it impossible to suppress his discontent.

The dinner had been cleared, the cake had been cut, and the guests were in high spirits, floating on champagne bubbles through the grand foyer and sitting rooms of Heinrich's opulent house, when Ilse came to Martin's side. She laid a hand on his arm. "Marty dear, you break my heart."

"Ah," he said with a rueful smile, "the unbreakable lady has a heart that can break?"

"Don't be unkind. You know I have, and to see you so downcast does indeed break it."

Martin said nothing. He glared down at the cube of ice melting in his glass and swirled it around in what remained of his scotch.

Ilse sighed and looked out at the room. The flower-filled vases, the dancing, the champagne flutes zipping about on carefully balanced trays. Everything spoke to revelry and enjoyment. She knew all of it must be a torment to Martin.

"I wish we lived in a different world, Marty," she said, keeping her expression placid to avoid attracting attention. "You know I do. For your sake, for Heinrich's . . . for my own, even. I wish we were free to live our lives as we would have them be. But we aren't. None of us draws our own hand. We all must play the cards that have been dealt us, and unfair as it is, some are dealt a worse hand than others. The best we can do is choose the least objectionable of the flawed choices that present themselves. I hope Heinrich has done that today. I hope one day you will agree that he has."

"I already do," Martin sighed. "That doesn't mean I have to be happy about it."

"I'm glad of it. Not that you are unhappy, of course. But that you have come to see the situation as Heinrich does."

Across the room, Ilse's new husband was waving for her to come over to the cluster of guests that had gathered around him.

She motioned that she would join them in a moment. Before leaving him, she turned to Martin. Her back was to the room so no one could see her face, her voice hushed so only he could hear it above the din of the crowd. She took his free hand in her own and gripped it tightly. "I know I have said this before, Martin, but today I am a bride, so I feel like repeating these words now will solidify them into a vow. I will always welcome you in our home. Perhaps there might come a time when you and Heinrich quarrel or drift apart, or perhaps you will always love each other as you do now. But I promise you this: no matter what happens, you will never be turned away from this house on my account. Never."

She pressed his hand, offered a bolstering smile, then turned and glided away, leaving Martin to think how life had misused him and to wonder whether Ilse meant what she had said . . . or if, even with him, she was only acting. Simply playing the part everyone needed her to play.

END VOLUME II

1934

It becomes a habit after a while. Performing. Playacting. The hair, the makeup, the dress, the glitter. All just part of the costume.

At first, the boundaries are clear. There is who you are, and there is who you have to be. The dividing line between the two is unmistakable. You can keep one foot in each stream and still stay tethered to something resembling reality.

But eventually, the line blurs; you start to lose yourself, lose your sense of where the character ends, where you begin.

Being yourself. What does that even mean? Who out there knows who they truly are, what they really want? If it were up to you and you alone, if it had only ever been up to you, perhaps then you might know.

But it's never just about us, is it? There's always someone else. Some expectation you must rise to, some standard you must meet, someone you can't bear to let down. So, we do what we are told. We put on a show and hope to God no one can tell the drama is a farce.

Ask ten people who I am, and you will get ten different answers. She is fascinating. She is charming. She is steadfast. She is impervious. I am to each who they need me to be.

Only I know who I really am.

I am a shapeshifter. I am a master of disguise.

I am a coward.

AND THEN THE LIGHTS WENT OUT

Vienna had always been a city of masks. In a manner of speaking. Dandies feigned flawless taste, suppressing more raucous interests that fell out of fashion long ago. Tormented geniuses haunted the avenues, nagged by self-doubt, constantly glancing over their shoulders, always watching for the one who might yank off their veil, expose the imposter lurking beneath. Pristinely pious ladies gasped for air. Sitting in the confessional cell, rosaries wrapping their wrists like manacles, they admitted their sins but never their desires.

And then there was the mask for which the Viennese were most famous. *Gemütlichkeit.* That distinctly Viennese art of pretense that made even the most irksome visitor feel their presence was the most pleasing in all the world.

During Fasching season, the masks took on an entirely different form: they manifested in the physical. For three months each winter, before spring blossomed into forty days of deprivation, the city's inhabitants relished delights that could only be tasted from behind a mask.

At the height of its decadence, Fasching Vienna abounded in balls—scores held in a single night, hundreds across the season. Behind the safety of their masks, the upper and lower nobles, middle class and bourgeois mixed without shock or scandal. Thousands of repressed young ladies savored freedoms denied during the rest of the year. Under cover of darkness, obscured by candlelight, they surrendered to a parade of nameless strangers, allowing themselves to be swept around the dance floor in a flurry of feathers and lace. And for the space of a waltz, any upstart could claim the hand of a future countess. By the light of day, they might never speak a word. But in the early hours of a Fasching morning, on the wings of a sweeping melody, he could hold her in his arms, breathless, basking in pleasures that would dissolve with the dawn.

Of course, by 1934, Fasching season was not what it once had been. Glimmers of glamour and glitz remained, but they were the privilege of the shrinking few. For the unfortunate masses to whom the march of history had been less obliging, the season's enjoyments were restricted to a baser kind.

And yet, the masks endured. An undying reminder of a golden time, drawing colorful contrast with the dinginess of daily life.

As the end of the season approached, Baroness Ilse Jörger, the mistress of masks, found herself in a disguise she had not yet worn. Sitting next to her husband in the office of Dr. Leschetizky, Vienna's preeminent diagnostician, she cloaked herself in a shroud of stalwart reassurance, concealing infinite dread. She prattled on as though they were sipping coffee in a sidewalk café, as though they weren't sitting in a drab room that reeked of disinfectant, waiting for the doctor to deliver his sentence.

It was a new experience, dissembling before her husband. For eleven years, Heinrich had been the one person with whom Ilse was perfectly at ease, perfectly herself. Today was different, though. She could not let him see what she was really feeling. He must not know of the anxiety that had gripped her for months, clutching her throat like invisible hands as she watched him growing thinner, paler, more drawn . . . .

No. She would not think of that. She would not give in to the fear, would not have him feeling he needed to console her.

Today was not about her. Today was about him. She must show him that she was fine.

She was fine because she knew *he* was fine.

Everything was fine.

Come what may, *they would be fine.*

Minutes ticked away, and Ilse talked. Talked about funds raised at the Metternich's weekend ball and all the wonderful charities waiting to put the money to good use. Talked about what she expected for the Mardi Gras carnival the next night.

If she kept talking, the doctor could not come in.

If she could keep talking, he could not take the light out of her world.

But he did come in. He entered the room, impeccable and stiff in his pressed white coat, test results tucked under his arm, glasses sliding down his nose. He shook their hands, exchanged pleasantries, pushed up his glasses with his middle finger. When he sat, the chair groaned under his weight. Disregarding the sound, he folded his hands atop his unornamented pine desk and did what he had to do.

He uttered the word Ilse had known was coming.

And then the lights went out.

***

Ilse did not hear Dr. Leschetizky apologizing for the power outage. She did not hear Heinrich's assurances that neither he nor his wife held the doctor responsible for the faulty electrical grid.

Ilse could only hear one word.

Cancer.

It thudded in her ears with each beat of her heart as the doctor and Heinrich spoke and as she and Heinrich later fumbled their way through the unlit halls and down the pitch-black stairs of the medical office.

As they sat in the car riding home through unregulated

streets, Ilse paid no mind to the blaring horns or the shouts of impatient drivers. Still she heard only Dr. Leschetizky's voice grinding through the vile word, over and over, like a pestle in a mortar.

Heinrich said little. A remark here and there to note that the electrical outage afflicting the doctor's office was also affecting this street and that.

When they arrived home, he instructed the housekeeper that he was not to be disturbed. He kissed his wife on her forehead and retreated into his study, locking the door behind him.

***

Hours later, Ilse sat alone in silence. Evening was setting in, and the maids were scurrying about lighting candles to ward off the encroaching darkness. Ilse ignored their efficient comings and goings. All her attention was on the abominable word that still was playing in her mind, like the drone of a tympani. Like a scratched record that refuses to advance. *Cancer. Cancer. Cancer.*

It wasn't unusual for Heinrich to sequester himself after receiving bad news. Ilse had seen it play out many times. The night the Palace of Justice burned. During the banking crisis of '32. He had lived alone for so long that he needed time to make space for her before Ilse could join him in his anger, worries, or sorrow. She didn't hold it against him; she always knew that if she just gave him his breathing room, eventually he would emerge, ready to enlist a partner for whatever trial he faced. And then, together, they would fight whatever monster waited at the gate.

And fight they had.

Indeed, sometimes it seemed the great achievement of their marriage had been their dogged determination simply to carry on.

With inflation running rampant and rents in Vienna frozen at pre-war levels, maintaining their building portfolio had become increasingly unviable. Yet they could not sell to tenants whose savings had dwindled to nothing, nor would any investor in his right mind buy a private building with rents that would never recover the cost of upkeep. A rational businessperson would have written them off and allowed the buildings to fall into disrepair. But Ilse and Heinrich both abhorred such miserly rationality. If they let their properties become unlivable, where were the residents to go? The only housing available seemed to be in the newly built government tenements, controlled by the patronage of the Social Democrats who ran Vienna. The solidly middle-class Jewish residents of Leopoldstadt would top no official priority list. If the Jörger's could not think of them, who would?

And besides, what need did they have for profits? Thanks to Martin's clever management, Heinrich's inheritance, safely stowed away in Swiss francs, was enough to support them through ten lifetimes. Along with their privilege, in such difficult times, did they not also have a responsibility to their tenants to carry on as before?

Martin, ever cautious, ever thinking toward Heinrich's bottom line, cringed at this silent charity but gritted through it. Profits from the non-residential portfolio—the canneries, the breweries, the mills—could subsidize Heinrich's residential benevolence and keep the company solvent.

"And don't forget," Ilse frequently reminded him, "paying more for something than it is worth is the hallmark of importance in society. If the *nouveau riche* can flaunt their consequence by overtipping, the former nobility can exhibit theirs through hopeless business endeavors. In a world of fading social distinctions, it will ensure Heinrich's relevance!"

But then came the Depression. Trade plummeted; factories shuttered. Across the country, nearly half of all industrial workers lost their employment. On every street, the hands of the hungry reached out for compassion. Wretched souls looked out from sunken eyes, desperate not just for food but for reasons to hope.

Ever diligent, Martin had implored Heinrich to face reality and cease production. The cost was too great; it could not be sustained. But Heinrich stood firm, and Ilse stood beside him. His bank accounts could starve, but his workers would not. The Jörger Corporation would not create more desperate men on the streets, not so long as he could still afford to employ them.

When Ilse later suggested they index their salaries to the price of bread, Heinrich had praised it as a splendid idea, and Martin had thrown up his hands and marched out. In eleven years, it was the only time Martin had stayed away for longer than a week.

Yet despite the endless battles, despite the turbulent times, this unlikely trio—Ilse, Heinrich, and Martin—had carved out something resembling a happy life. In the eyes of the world, Ilse and Heinrich were a couple to be reckoned with. Between his money and her charm, few matched their influence in Viennese society. Their guards never dropped. No one ever had cause to wonder if perhaps their relationship wasn't exactly as it seemed. No one saw that the marriage was unconsummated, that behind closed doors, Heinrich and Ilse shared the love not of husband and wife but of brother and sister.

The baron and baroness had rather eccentric financial priorities—this was no secret—so no one questioned that their financial advisor was such a fixture in their lives. Martin's comings and goings from the Jörger home at all hours of the day and night were as unexceptional as the arrival of the milkman or the post.

To Ilse's surprise, the darkness did not keep Martin away that night of the blackout. As she sat in the drawing room window looking out into the deepening twilight, she saw his silhouette hurry up the street and bound up the front steps before disappearing from her view. The bell rang, and a maid's quick steps clipped across the foyer to admit him, followed by a muffled rise and fall of voices and the sound of Martin's fading footfalls as he made his way to Heinrich's study at the back of the house.

Ilse closed her eyes and let her breath drain out in a slow, pinched stream. She tried not to imagine the conversation that was about to take place just a few meters away.

Despite all his single-minded efficiency when it came to business, Ilse liked Martin. His wit was sharp, as was his tongue. His tastes were discerning, and he saw little need to hide his disapproval when he felt it. There was an honesty in his callousness that she couldn't help respecting. And for all his egoism, all his snark, when Martin thought no one was looking, there were moments of humanity, rendered even more beautiful by their rarity. They softened him, made him almost endearing. Plus, she knew he loved Heinrich and was unfailingly loyal to him and, by extension, to herself.

It pained her to know that, at that very moment, her friend's heart must be breaking.

She and Martin had not yet spoken of Heinrich's health. The subject had sat between them like an unwanted guest for weeks, straining every conversation. Though neither would broach the subject, each knew what the other was thinking: they wondered who would be most afflicted when the end came. Most of the time, Ilse hoped she would be the one to feel that despair. She couldn't bear the thought of watching Martin suffer and being helpless to comfort him.

A few minutes later, Martin entered the room, looking wild and shaken. The candlelight cast shadows across his face, accentuating the rabidity of his expression. He was even more discomposed than Ilse had feared. She braced herself.

"He's told you, hasn't he," she said.

Martin blinked, stared at her, tried to make out her meaning. His eyes struggled to focus. He could manage to spit out only one word before motioning for her to follow him to the study.

"War."

FOLLY

It was the revolution that wasn't.

Four days. That was all it took to put down the workers' uprising. Still, those who had watched the country's politics unravel were surprised it had taken even that long. When would-be leaders focused more on rhetoric than execution, was it any surprise when the action itself was fumbled?

The thing had been a folly from the start. The blackout—the result of an electrical workers' strike—was to have triggered a general strike in protest of the national government, decrying its increasing repressiveness, its hostile labor policies, and the continued erosion of life in a state that most had come to view as hopelessly unviable. Yet, in their zeal to be heard, the union leaders had thrown the switch too soon. Far too soon. Without electricity, the printing presses ground to a halt; without the presses, pamphlets went unprinted; without the pamphlets, most of the would-be strikers remained in the dark, literally and figuratively.

But four days had been enough. The damage had been done.

Four days saw a government turn its arms on its own people.

Four days saw the blood of hundreds spilling in the streets.

Four days saw thousands imprisoned, thousands more cut from their all too rare sources of employment.

Four days left ample opportunity for devils to pose as saviors.

***

Ilse sat alone at the breakfast table, reading the morning paper by the light of the May sun beaming in through the window. She ate alone most mornings these days. Heinrich had been allowing his usually militant schedule to slip in recent weeks. *So much the better*, she thought, her mood soured by the content of her reading. *At least if I am alone, I don't have to moderate my disgust.* She shoved the newspaper away, lest it ruin her appetite. Its pages may have contained only half-truths—the press was so restricted in what they could publish—but half was more than enough to sour her stomach.

She should have been accustomed to revulsion by now. For years, as the country languished, parliament had ground itself into a stalemate. The ruling Christian Social Party and the opposition Social Democrats had such diametrically opposed visions for the country that fighting seemed like an achievement. Any actual achievement was regarded as a compromise, and everyone knew compromise was tantamount to capitulation. An exasperated Chancellor Dollfuss had taken to avoiding the people's representatives altogether. He ruled by emergency decree. By the time the ministers had lowered their sabers for long enough to be offended by his overreach, there was little to be done: Dollfuss had suspended parliament, and terrorist bombs had rocked the capital in retribution. In the name of stability, Dollfuss further tightened his grip. Any pretense of popular government, the long-held dream of democracy, had been swept from the table like so many trash-bound crumbs.

"Good morning, Coco." Heinrich's appearance put an end to Ilse's brooding. She did her best to don an unbothered expression as he planted a kiss on the top of her head.

"Good morning, darling!" she answered in singsong cheer.

"What is it this time?" After more than a decade, Heinrich knew her moods all too well. He quickly saw through her too-shining demeanor to the annoyance sputtering beneath.

"Oh, it's that preposterous man Bauer," she said offhandedly, rolling her eyes, trying to keep things light. "He talks and talks and seems to believe speech is action. Men lose their jobs, he talks; people starve, he talks. Even after everything that has happened, he still thinks the Socials will advance if only he can find a way to be *more* unyielding. Does he think it's 1905, that he can just bang on pots and pans[29] and expect the bureaucracy to hold everything together?" Of all the things Ilse loathed about the dominant factions, perhaps it was the ineptitude of their leaders that she despised the most.

"You really must stop reading that hogwash at breakfast," Heinrich said, motioning to the pile of papers on the table. "You know it does nothing but put you in a mood all day."

"What would you suggest? That I read it before bed and then spend the whole night stewing when I should be sleeping?"

"Of course not. I would have you do what I do: ignore it altogether. No good can come from knowing what's happening in the world these days."

"I'm sorry, but not everyone can go through life as unbothered as Master Biedermeier."[30]

"I don't see why not. It has served me rather well," Heinrich said. "Look at this head. I might be a dying old man, but there's not a gray hair on it! Besides, we are Austrians. Ambivalence toward politics is practically a birthright. It comes in right behind our impeccable taste in music and our boundless patience for regulatory muddle."

Ilse threw him a disapproving look as he filled a cup with coffee. "Well," she conceded, "ignorance seems to have done you some good today, at least. You look well rested; I'll admit that much."

"Yes, tolerably so," he replied. "Today will be a good day, I think."

In the months since Heinrich's diagnosis, they had taken to

dividing their life between good days and bad. On good days they could still maintain some semblance of normality. He could go to the office, take some meetings; in the evenings, they could entertain company, dine out, or simply enjoy time at home, just themselves and Martin. On bad days, his strength failed him, and he could do little beyond reading in his bed or going for short walks. Increasingly, the bad days were starting to outnumber the good. It was becoming harder and harder for Ilse to avoid thinking of a future without her beloved friend by her side.

"I am glad to hear it," Ilse said, looking at Heinrich tenderly. "And what would you like to do with your good day?"

"Well, I forgot to mention it last night, but I have invited a guest to dine with us this evening."

Ilse thought she heard a bit more caution than usual in his tone. "A guest? Who might that be?"

"It's a new acquaintance of mine. An old friend of Martin's, actually. They served together in the Great War. I had lunch with them yesterday."

"I'm sure any friend of Marty's will be a friend of mine." She smiled and took a careful sip from her cup.

"Well, you see, that's the thing," he continued, clearing his throat. "I believe you are already acquainted with the gentleman."

"Oh really, who is it?" Ilse inquired, trying to sound unbothered. She saw that he was avoiding her gaze, concentrating far too intently on the milk he was pouring into his coffee. His tentativeness unsettled her.

"He's visiting from Linz, or there about." Heinrich raised his coffee and blew on it to buy himself another second to work up to the revelation. "His name is Hess . . ."

Across from him, Ilse froze. The color drained from her face. She said nothing, just sat there in stunned silence, a teaspoon hanging from her fingers.

"Ilse . . ." Heinrich cautiously nudged, hoping to rouse her without unleashing the forces mobilizing within.

With effort, Ilse collected herself and said in the most detached tone she could muster, "Baron Junius von Hess?"

"Well, he styles himself Oberst[31] Junius Hess. But, yes, I believe they are one and the same," Heinrich replied, trying to match her nonchalance. If she was going to play cool with him, he would play it right back. "He seems to remember you from many years ago. Do you recall him?"

Ilse closed her eyes and took two slow breaths. Then, without another word, she lifted the napkin from her lap, folded it and gingerly placed it beside her plate, then stood and walked slowly out of the room, minding each step. As though she feared anything she touched might shatter. As though she herself might disintegrate at the slightest jostling.

Heinrich stayed where he was. He had never seen that reaction from his wife before and did not quite know what to make of it. Just as he was beginning to worry that he'd overplayed his hand, Ilse burst back into the room.

"How *dare* you!" she cried and then marched back out, an unspoken invitation for him to follow her.

"There it is," he sighed, wiping his mouth and unceremoniously dropping his napkin on the table. He could hear the angry slapping of Ilse's shoes against the marble floors of the foyer as she retreated to the drawing room, where she could better channel her fury into pacing. He followed her there.

As expected, he found her stalking back and forth like a caged jungle cat. "You invited Junius von Hess to dine in this house? Are you out of your mind? What were you thinking?"

"Fold the paper, Coco."

"Don't you tell me to *fold the paper*, you insensitive—" She bit off the end of her sentence. Even at the height of indignation, she could not disparage her husband. Clenching her jaw, she tried to speak more calmly. "Don't tell me to control myself, and don't stand there pretending you don't know my history with Junius. How could you do this? Do my feelings mean nothing to you?"

"Ilse, please," he implored. He had been prepared for this kind of reaction, but that didn't make it any more pleasant to endure. "If you will just sit down, I can explain."

Ilse's eyes shot arrows at her husband as he motioned to a chair. She flumped down and sat in a huff, arms crossed, refusing to look at him.

"Where do I start," he sighed, running a hand back through his hair and sinking into the chair across from her. He leaned forward, elbows digging into his knees, fingers knitted behind his neck. For several seconds, he stared at the floor between his feet, organizing his thoughts, until Ilse coughed to signal her impatience. With a deep breath, he began.

"A few nights ago, Martin came by while you were dining with the Kassners. He stayed only for a few minutes, as he was meeting up with an old friend to go to the theater. When I asked with whom he was going, he said it was a fellow by the name of Hess. I recognized the name, of course, and asked him if it was Junius, and Martin confirmed that it was. He was surprised I knew the name and asked if we were acquainted. I brushed it off, said Oberst Hess is a friend of your brother-in-law. At first, I didn't think much of it, merely wondered if there was a way I could request that he avoid mentioning their friendship to you without arousing his suspicions. But then Martin said something that piqued my interest. He said he wasn't much looking forward to the evening, that the oberst had been good company once but had grown insufferably dull since having had the misfortune to lose his wife."

Ilse started at this news. "Oberst Hess is a widower?" she asked, trying without much success to sound disinterested.

Heinrich nodded. He could see the change this knowledge had worked over Ilse. She was becoming more receptive to what he had to say. "About four years since. The Baroness von Hess died, it seems, shortly after giving birth to their youngest child.

"As Martin was getting up to leave, I mentioned that, if he could bear it, I should very much like to meet the oberst. There was nothing remarkable in this request; after all, I've heard Friedrich speak so highly of the man over the years. Why shouldn't I be interested in meeting such a valued family connection? Well, Martin could never refuse a dying man and certainly could never refuse *me*, so the introduction took place yesterday."

Heinrich paused his story, but Ilse said nothing. Her pulse thrummed in her ears. Heinrich's words seemed to echo and bounce around the room. It took effort to catch them, assemble them, make sense of them. But she was determined now to hear him out.

"Coco, you know I would never do anything to hurt you. You are as dear to me as anyone in the world. We have loved each other, you and I, in our own way. We have built a life, and it's been a good one. For me, it's been a happier life than I once thought possible. I've had your constant friendship and support, and I've been able to go on with Martin, the love of my life, by my side, freed of the constant worry about exposure. You have done that for us. I know you, too, have gained something in this bargain. Marrying me gave you greater freedom, security, all that. But still, I've had to watch all these years as you lived but half a life. You have sealed yourself off from the world, even more so than when I met you, and I have sat quietly by and let you do it. You think it makes you clever; you think it makes you stronger, somehow safer, living behind these walls of yours, closing your heart to love. But I know better. I know what it is to love and be loved every day. I want that for you.

"Yesterday was a good day," Heinrich continued, "and it

seems today will be too. But it's not lost on either of us that my bad days are starting to win out. I don't know how much longer I have left in this world. Maybe a month, maybe a year. I'm not afraid of dying. I've thought a great deal about it lately, and I think I look at death much as Bahr did: it will take nothing from me yet give me so much. It will be the great consummator. Anything I lack, it will bring to me.[32] And I lack so little, thanks to you. The only thing missing now is the solace of knowing that you, too, will feel as complete as I do when your days near their end."

Her husband might have been prepared to die, but Ilse was in no way prepared to lose him. Heinrich's words overwhelmed her, and she could no longer sit there looking at him. She crossed the room and stared out the window. Heinrich followed, placing himself behind her, laying reassuring hands on her shoulders.

"Our days together are growing fewer and fewer," he pressed on, "but now is not the time for you to mourn. Now is the time to prepare, to set the scene for your third act.

"The Oberst is a widower; he is unattached. But for how long can that last? With four children and interests that keep him frequently from home, I cannot imagine it will be much longer. Can't you see, Coco? This is your chance. I beg you, don't throw away this opportunity. Reintroduce yourself into his life. Let him see that, one day, in the not-too-distant future, the two of you might finally be together."

It was all too much. The thought of losing Heinrich. The shame of allowing a childish hope to enter her heart. The fear of that hope being stamped out as quickly as it had sparked. Silent tears ran down Ilse's face, but she would not let her husband see them. She stayed where she was, standing in the window with Heinrich safely behind her. "You presume too far," she said flatly. "Not only do you assume I still harbor some girlish infatuation for a man I have not spoken to in twenty years, but you also assume he would leap at the chance to be with me. But I assure you, you have miscalculated. He has not been pining for me. On the contrary, I'm quite sure the man despises me."

"He accepted my invitation, didn't he?"

"He was being polite, Heinrich. Junius von Hess could not care less whether I lived or died."

Heinrich sighed and began to leave the room, pausing when he reached the door to look back at his wife. She would not turn to him; she obstinately fixed her eyes on the window.

"We are living in mad times, Ilse. No one can say what the future will bring, but I don't want you to face it alone. Please, at least think on what I've said."

***

Think on it. How could she possibly think on it? Ilse's mind was a firestorm of leaves caught in an autumn gale, every color and texture swirling in frantic disarray.

She was angry. Not just mad, but physically, viscerally angry. She could feel the anger sinking in claws, twisting each muscle of her back. But she was also hurt that Heinrich could knowingly wound her, and the hurt ripped the air from her lungs. All while her teeth gritted with irritation at the way he'd presented it as some grand romantic gesture, depriving her of her right even to resent him for it.

Worst of all was the fact that she believed him. She believed he was only trying to further her happiness. His good intentions left her no recourse. She could only lick her wounds and let his parting words fester. *I don't want you to face it alone.* Like she was a child. As if she weren't strong enough to carry on without him.

But then, she understood what he meant. Of course she did. She knew as well as anyone what was happening in the world. Her imagination had spun forth cynical threads, weaving them into disturbing tapestries. None of the thousand scenarios she'd envisioned ended well. Some were downright terrifying. The future would be easier to face with a partner, someone to whisper comforting words and make her smile through the desperate days. Even she had to admit that.

But Junius? After all these years, could Junius be that person? It seemed impossible, and yet . . .

No. Ilse swatted away the possibility.

The fact that her heart stopped at the thought of seeing him again—even now, after twenty years, after she had seen and done so much—made her cheeks burn. She had spent two decades treating sentiment like a contagion to be eradicated, cleansed, or otherwise leached from her body. Yet, somehow, she had failed to inoculate herself against Junius von Hess. How could she still allow him to hold such sway over her?

It was unacceptable. She would not be infected by fancy. Junius von Hess would not come back into her life and unmoor her in a single sweep. She was better than that now. She must go about her day. As though nothing had happened.

Over the years, Ilse had gradually taken on a more prominent role in the running of Heinrich's company. Not only did the work interest her more than it did her husband, but he would also be the first to admit she was far better suited to it. Since the start of his sickness, she had taken over for him almost entirely.

Determined not to let her quarrel with Heinrich and the news he had delivered over breakfast derail her, Ilse left the house. But the churning in her mind left little room for rational thought. She went to an early lunch with the board of one of her favored charities. Which charity had it been? She could scarcely say, so little had she attended to the presentation. In the afternoon, as scheduled, she visited one of the canneries. She must have given some instruction or other to the floor manager, but sitting in the car being driven back into the city, she struggled to recall what instruction she might have left.

In the seat next to her, her secretary was shuffling papers and scribbling away to clean up and clarify his shorthand. Filip. Dear, dear Filip. So eager, always so assiduous. He would have taken down anything meaningful from her conversations. She sighed out the tension in her shoulders, reminding herself that she could review his notes tomorrow.

Even with Filip to cover for her distraction, Ilse decided it would be a mistake to risk any more damage that day. In her current state, she was useless, little more than a figurehead, a role she revolted against. It was better to return home early.

Blaming the onset of a headache, she asked Filip to clear her calendar for the rest of the afternoon. He told her not to worry about a thing, assured her everything would be done to her satisfaction. When they arrived at the office, Filip instructed the driver to continue to the Jörger residence and climbed out of the car. After wishing her a speedy recovery, he closed the door behind him as softly as possible.

As the car pulled back into traffic, Ilse raised her eyes, silently thanking God for having sent young Filip to her and inviting His punishment for her weakness.

Not that she needed to be punished further. Dinner that evening would be punishing enough.

NAVY WILL HIDE ANYTHING

On one side of the glass, the bright white of day was softening into the orange pink of sunset. On the other side of the glass, the bulbs surrounding Ilse's vanity hummed with electric life, filling the room with an ersatz glow.

Ilse had been sitting at her make-up table for nearly an hour, making needless adjustments and critiquing the reflection that stared back from the mirror.

She was still a beautiful woman; she did not doubt that. Her hair was still the color of spun honey, its wild locks tamed into obedient waves. If she looked closely, though, she could see strands of silver weaving their way into the gold. Her eyes still shone with intelligence and depth, but lines had begun to crease their corners. And the natural radiance of youth had been replaced by a painted perfection: her skin matted with powder, her lashes brushed with mascara, her cheeks contoured with rouge, her pout the false red of brandied cherries, her brows plucked and penciled into a long, thin arch.

What would Junius see when he looked at her for the first time in so long? Would he even recognize the woman she had become? She searched the mirror for any trace of the girl she had once been. She stared for so long her face morphed, distorted into unfamiliar shapes. Who was that person in the mirror? The woman behind the glass was a stranger.

For the first time in years, Ilse felt insecure. The locus of her self-worth had always been external; she had always needed it to be reflected in the approval of others—that was a failing she had come to terms with long ago. But she couldn't remember the last time she had felt unsure of her ability to gain the approval she sought. Tonight was different, though. Tonight she was shaken. She didn't know what to do. She wanted to cover her face in cold cream, wipe it clean. But even then, she knew the face staring back would not be the same one Junius once held in his hands.

Disgusted by her own vanity, she closed her lipstick, cast it into a drawer, and turned away from the mirror.

Ilse was strangely aware of her body as she stepped out of her room. She felt the whispered breath of the air blowing past each hair on her arms, the lapping of her hemline around her ankles with each step. For the first time in her life, she found herself actively considering her hands. What unseemly things they were! Should they be doing something more than just hanging at her sides? Should her fingers be clenched or released? Surely, they were not supposed to wriggle, but holding them still felt stiff, unnatural.

At the top of the stairs, Ilse stopped. She was panicking; she knew she was panicking. Her mind and heart were competing to see which could race fastest. Her head was beginning to swim. She had to reel herself back in.

Remember your exercises, she told herself. *See the paper, grab it, fold it, make it smaller, smaller, smaller. Until it disappears. Like it never even existed.*

She took a breath, shook off the nerves. Raising her chin high, forcing her shoulders back, she descended the stairs with the poise of a Hollywood starlet, even as crimped Fortuny silk clung to sweat at the small of her back.

Thank God I wore the navy, she thought. *Navy will hide anything.*

She was early, but Heinrich was already in the drawing

room, reading a well-used copy of *Candide* and wearing a dinner jacket that now hung a bit too loosely on his shrinking frame. Another reminder that life was slipping away from him. Ilse made a mental note to have the jacket taken in before he could notice. Though, in all likelihood, he already had.

Heinrich put down his book and smiled up at her. "You look lovely this evening, Coco," he said. They had not exchanged a word since their argument that morning, and he hoped the compliment would help subdue any lingering hostilities.

"I look the same as I do on any other evening, I should think," she replied flatly.

Heinrich sighed. "You are still upset with me, I see." He knew she would not make a scene. He had watched her bottle her feelings a thousand times, coasting through even the most irksome circumstances. Still, he hated being the object of her irritation.

Standing over the bar cart, Ilse let her fingertips graze the tops of the decanters but did not pour herself a drink. She had little tolerance for alcohol and would not risk loosening her tongue. "I am not anything," she replied. "We have company coming. We are the very picture of conjugal contentment. Just as we have always been."

Heinrich threw back his head and sighed again. He wasn't going to justify himself; he wasn't going to press her. With any luck, the evening would go well, and all would be forgiven.

After a few strained minutes, they heard a knock, and muffled voices began echoing through the grand foyer. Eager to escape the prickliness that had settled over the drawing room, Heinrich did not wait for his guests to be announced. He pushed up from his chair and made his way out to greet them.

With one last breath to center herself, Ilse followed, her sense of duty overpowering her instincts for flight.

She stood back, allowing Heinrich to conceal her, to block her line of sight, for just one moment more. She heard Heinrich greet Martin. Backslapping and performative, their usual public manner. Then came the formal welcome, the exchange of civilities. The instinctual tensing of every muscle as her body recognized Junius's voice, deeper than she remembered but still resonant, still musical. And then Heinrich was saying, "Allow me to present my wife," and stepping aside.

There he was. Right there in front of her. Just a few feet away. Tall and broad and solid flesh.

For the first time in twenty years, Ilse was face to face with the only man ever to have possessed her heart. His dark hair was slicked back, revealing the gray that now peppered his temples. His face was tanned, slightly weather-worn. But his eyes . . . His eyes were still the eyes of the boy she'd loved. That steely, icy blue. The intensity that burned away her layers, letting them char and curl until the only thing left was her, naked and exposed. She met his gaze, and for an instant, her breath caught. But then she felt herself gliding forward, extending a hand.

"Welcome to our home, Herr Oberst," she heard herself say, her voice liquid velvet.

Her hand did not tremble, even as Junius caught it in his own, bent to kiss it. She felt his rough lips, his warm breath on her skin, and she was suddenly transported. The sound of a rushing river, the smell of rain-dampened grass . . .

"It's lovely to see you again after all these years, Gnädige Frau,[33]" Junius said, still holding her hand. The aloofness in his voice snapped Ilse back into herself. She had never heard him produce so dignified a tone.

"I half expected to hear you call me *Fraulein Eder*," she said in her deliciously teasing manner, offering an inviting smile. It was not a choice, meeting his coolness with warmth. It was a reflex, her body's innate response, born of instinct and habit.

"And disrespect the venerable Baroness Jörger, of whom everyone speaks so highly? I wouldn't dream of it," he replied. His expression softened slightly, and Ilse felt herself in danger. She disengaged her hand from his and turned to greet her other guest.

"Marty dear, lovely to see you, as always," she said, placing a peck on each of his cheeks.

"Marty?" Junius quirked an eyebrow and looked dubiously at his friend.

"Only *she* gets to call me that," Martin chuckled, nodding in Ilse's direction. "It is a fair trade. The baroness tolerates my haunting her hallways and monopolizing her husband's time with my never-ending parade of business prattle, and in exchange, I allow her to call me *Marty*."

"Not quite a fair trade," Ilse rejoined, "but I suppose we can call it even. You are, after all, so kind as to dig up old friends to entertain me. Truly, I never was more surprised than when Heinrich told me this morning who you were bringing to dinner!" She laughed, smiled, tossed her head in Junius's direction. But she couldn't bring herself to look directly at him again. Not yet.

"Had I realized the connection before, I would have brought him to you long ago," Martin replied amiably, oblivious to any pain or embarrassment the meeting might be inflicting on either of his friends. "Actually, that is probably stretching the truth beyond recognition. Had I known, I'm sure I still would have kept you in ignorance. Your poor husband and I probably are now doomed to spend an entire evening listening to the two of you reciting your biographies in painstaking detail to catch up on years' worth of missed memories."

"I haven't the least intention of doing anything of the sort," Ilse assured him.

"No, nor I," Junius concurred.

"Though perhaps, Marty, you will indulge us for just the abridged versions?"

"I suppose I could be convinced to suffer through that," Martin conceded. "As long as they are *very* abridged."

"I think I can meet that challenge," Ilse smiled. Turning to Junius, she relayed the briefest of histories. "Went to America, came back to Vienna, married Heinrich, and have spent eleven lovely years plaguing a man by the name of Martin Rezek with my ridiculous schemes to fritter away the money he so ingeniously earns for my husband."

To this, Junius countered simply: "Fought a war, got married, and had four children who have proved far more difficult to manage than an entire company of soldiers."

Ilse accepted Junius's offering with a business-like nod and then turned back to Martin. "There now, are you satisfied?"

Martin grinned. "Yes, tolerably."

"Now, before someone requests an egg timer to regulate our dinner conversation, shall we go in?" Heinrich suggested.

With that, Ilse placed her hand on her husband's awaiting arm and allowed herself to be led back into the drawing room, conscious with every step that Junius followed just a few paces behind.

***

As the evening progressed, insecurity again wrapped its tentacles around Ilse, tightening its grip. She allowed her husband and Martin to steer the dinner conversation, not wanting to draw more attention to herself than necessary. Even so, she frequently felt Junius's eyes resting on her. Whenever she returned his gaze, she sank to discover that he appeared to find her lacking. His expression was sober, bordering on dour. Any smiles were civil, any laughter contained. It was clear he took little pleasure in his present company.

But from what Martin has told Heinrich, Junius takes little pleasure in most company these days, Ilse reminded herself. This was her one consolation.

The Junius sitting at her table was as different from the boy she had known as she was from the girl she had been. Though his conversation was intelligent and engaging, the fire that once animated his address had been extinguished. Had their parting doused the flame? Had it been the war? Or could such a change have been wrought wholly by the loss of his wife? Though Martin blamed Junius's dullness on the latter, Ilse found it a difficult notion to swallow. Accepting it would mean admitting that Junius had given himself to his wife entirely, had loved her with depth and sincerity. Feelings Ilse had never allowed herself to indulge.

Not since him.

After dinner, the conversation veered into current affairs, and Ilse was obliged to take on a more active role in the dialogue. It was expected. After years of marriage, it was one of those little habits that had emerged. Heinrich took no interest in politics, so Ilse became the Jörgers' mouthpiece when such subjects arose.

It was Martin who initiated the topic. "What is the mood in Linz these days, Junius?" he asked.

"By 'these days,' I suppose you mean since February."

"Naturally."

Junius cleared his throat apprehensively. His eyes flitted from Martin to the Jörgers and back again.

"Do not worry, old friend," Martin assured him. "You are free to speak your mind here. No one in this room is going to report you for a dissident."

Junius shifted in his chair. His posture relaxed a bit, but his muscles remained tight. "In answer to your question, it's difficult to say. Linz has always been dominated by Christian Socials, and most of the city still supports the regime. But having been the epicenter of the violence, people undoubtedly are shaken. Drop a glass in a restaurant, and half the diners will dive under their tables."

"Now there's a diversion. I'm tempted to try it next time I'm in town."

Junius was used to Martin's sarcasm and rolled past it without comment. "There is a fear that Dollfuss has gone too far, that he's unleashed a beast he won't be able to control."

"Do you speak on behalf of your neighbors or for yourself?" Ilse probed.

"For myself, I suppose," Junius admitted. "Outside Vienna, politics is discussed so little that one can never be certain of their neighbors' views. Still, it's clear what everyone is thinking. Among the workers, there's a bitterness brewing, a resentment. What happened in February won't be the final word, I fear. And whether they'll say so or not, everyone seems to know it." There was resignation in his voice. It seemed he was simply awaiting the inevitable, preparing to sit back and endure whatever might come.

"I quite agree, I'm afraid," Ilse replied. "Dollfuss, he's gone to such lengths to quell unrest, but I worry he has done little more than to breed more extremists. And with these contemptible Nazis parading around like heroes, sweeping in to defend the fighters in court, supplying aid to the imprisoned . . . I shudder to think what will happen in the next election if the Social Democrats end up aligning with them."

"I dare say that's their general strategy," Junius said grimly. "Already we've seen propaganda circulating in Linz, claiming the Jewish leaders in the Christian Corporatist government have betrayed the people, that the only way to bring down the regime is to combine forces with the National Socialists. It's all nonsense, of course."

"Sadly, there are plenty of weak minds that will be convinced by it."

"Well, look on the bright side," Martin offered. "Your fears assume there will *be* a next election. I'm quite confident old *Dollface* has no intention of allowing that."

"A bright side indeed. Your optimism never fails us, Marty dear," Ilse replied caustically. "Herr Oberst, you must excuse our Martin. In his twisted mind, *to shock* and *to amuse* are synonyms."

"You forget, I have known your Martin longer than anyone else in the room. I'm well acquainted with his rather warped sense of humor. I remember once, we came under heavy fire outside Dragoslavele, and he said to me, 'Shore up. At least if we all die, we won't have to shiver our way through another winter in the trenches.'"

From here, the conversation veered from politics to war stories, war stories to general reminiscences, and back to friendlier terrain by the time Heinrich rose on weak legs and excused himself to an early bed.

"I'm afraid we have overtired you these past two days," Junius said as he shook his host's hand.

"Please, do not trouble yourself," Heinrich replied, waving away his guest's concerns. "I am quite used to it by now."

"Do you need help getting upstairs, darling?" Ilse enquired.

"No, no, please, you stay here. See to our guest. Martin can deliver me safely up."

"Of course, my friend," Martin agreed.

And with that, the clandestine lovers retreated to the privacy of Heinrich's apartments, unremarked by the gentleman from Linz.

Ilse and Junius sat in silence, save the occasional clearing of Junius's throat, the creaking of his chair as he shifted in his seat. Both felt the awkwardness of having been left to themselves. Ilse perhaps felt it more, given her suspicion that Heinrich had contrived his exit by design, but displayed fewer signs of discomfort. She was readying herself to engage in small talk until Martin's return when Junius abruptly rose.

"I really should be going."

"Please don't feel you have to leave so soon. I'm sure Marty will join us again in a moment."

"Thank you," Junius said, his eyes darting around the room like he was prepared to leap from a window if no other exit was offered, "but I have a very early morning tomorrow. I should return to my hotel."

"Of course. I'll not keep you. Allow me to see you out." Ilse rose and escorted him into the grand foyer.

"Thank you for your hospitality this evening, Baroness," Junius said as they reached the front door. Ilse noted that his voice had again taken on the hardness he'd exhibited at the start of the night. "Please express my gratitude to your husband and offer him my best wishes if I don't see him again." Catching himself, Junius added, "During this visit to Vienna . . . is what I meant."

But they both knew that was not what Junius meant. They both knew he meant *in case he is no longer here when I return to Vienna.*

Ilse winced, almost imperceptibly. The change in her expression was so slight that it would have been lost on most. Junius was not most people, though. He saw it, and he reproached himself for having been so tactless. But Ilse quickly recovered and accepted his words with the cordiality with which they had clearly been intended. "Thank you, Junius," she said.

It was the first time she had slipped and addressed him by his given name. For a moment, her guard dropped, and Junius saw a flash of the old Ilse. Artless, innocent, unsure. He took her hand, pressed it. He did not release it immediately. Instead, he held it, clenched it, like he could not bear to let it go. He looked into her eyes, searching for what he wanted to say. But words failed him. The only thing he could manage was, "Good-night, Ilse." Then he dropped her hand, turned, and left her.

Ilse locked the door behind him and stood alone and confused in the cold, empty hall.

THE PERVERSE PLEASURE OF PAIN

It was over. She had survived it.

He is gone, Ilse thought as she leaned against the door, pressing her eyes shut, feeling the air rush back into her lungs. *Gone from this house and gone from my life. I can go on as before, as though nothing has changed.*

After all, nothing *had* changed. Not really. She and Junius had behaved civilly, but there had been nothing more than civility. There would be no renewal of past sentiment. And why should there be? She was not a lamp to be flicked on and off. Her feelings could not be dialed up and down like the volume on a Victrola. Neither could Junius's.

Were there things left unsaid? Of course there were. Junius had wanted to say something more before he left her; Ilse had no doubt about that. But if he had decided those things were better left in the past, she would not try to resurrect them.

And besides, she told herself, *he is leaving Vienna in a matter of days. Even if Heinrich persists in promoting the acquaintance, our paths are not likely to cross much in the future.*

But it seemed Junius was less convinced they should continue inhabiting separate spheres. His business in Vienna detained him for much longer than anyone had anticipated. No one knew what that business was, and no one thought it fit to inquire. He was simply there, prowling the margins of Ilse's life long after she expected him to have gone.

Having so quickly established a rapport with Heinrich, Junius's visits to the baron were frequent, and though Ilse's responsibilities at the office and engagements around town kept her from home much of the time, she could hardly avoid seeing him altogether.

One Sunday in early June, Heinrich took to his bed, lacking energy for much of anything beyond his books. Refusing to let Ilse and Martin waste their lives out of charity to him and his failing body, Heinrich sent them out to take in the fresh air of the nearby Volksgarten, silencing their protests with pleas for rest. Ilse and Martin had walked about a block when they happened upon Junius, who was on his way to pay a visit to Heinrich. On hearing that the baron was indisposed, Junius accepted Martin's invitation to join their walking party.

They wandered into Volksgarten in silence, each absorbed in their own melancholy. But few tonics can rival a clear June sky and the fragrance of spring floating on a gentle breeze; they subdue even those most firmly attached to their misery. As the trio meandered among the box hedges, drenched in sunlight, one by one, they found their spirits lifting.

Ilse loved these gardens. As a girl, she had often come with Therese and their mother. She and Therese would run through the labyrinth of paths, darting past bushes bursting with roses of every color. Ilse would pretend she was a princess in a faraway land and this was her garden, one she shared with all her people, bringing them together to admire its beauty. Lords walked side by side with peasants. Ladies rested clean white gloves in the roughened hands of farmers and smiths, undeterred by their blackened nailbeds.

Ilse supposed, in her heart, it made her something of a socialist, this childhood fantasy of hers. It still had a certain idyllic allure. But she knew she didn't live in her utopian garden. She lived in a world of incentives and interests, where actions, even well-intentioned ones, always provoked reactions. They could spin out consequences no one desired. In the real world, pragmatism was almost always more productive than standing on principle. Concessions might have left a sour taste in the mouth, left you questioning if you might not have done more. But by bending, you could at least achieve *something*. If the alternative was nothing at all, wasn't *something* a worthy goal?

As they ambled, Ilse found herself pondering, as she often did, how her own compromises might be judged in the end. The path she had chosen, the line she had walked, the bargains she had made, the lies she had told. The wounds she had inflicted. Even as she carried no malice in her heart.

She dropped back from the group and watched Junius walk away from her. Still so impassive, so distant. He held himself rigidly, as if constantly bracing for a blow. Ilse wondered whether that was simply his way now or if his body adopted a defensive posture in her presence.

Noticing her absence, Martin and Junius stopped and looked back, waiting. She smiled and said airily, "Don't mind me! I was just having a closer look at the yellow roses. I would swear they are the exact variety our neighbor, Mrs. Kenyon, grew in Washington. My father always admired them. I'll have to bring him to see these."

Another lie. They came as naturally as breathing.

As they were about to turn onto the path leading to the memorial to Empress Sisi, Martin spotted an associate he felt he should greet. He bade Ilse and Junius to continue walking, promising to catch up with them shortly. With a quick bow, Martin was off.

The tree-lined promenade and the monument to which it led were infrequently trafficked—in plain view, yet surprisingly hidden away. Few ever made their way back to pay respects to the beloved Sisi, and despite the throngs elsewhere in the park,

Ilse and Junius found themselves alone for the first time since the night of their reunion. Without the constant chatter of passing strangers, they felt obliged to make an effort at conversation. They talked of their delight in the garden and the irony that something so beautiful could result from an act of vengeance.[34] They traded tidbits of trivia about the empress. When small talk had been exhausted, and Martin still did not come, Ilse ventured to ask Junius to share more of his personal history. Out of consideration for Martin's impatience, she had restrained her curiosity during their prior encounters, yet with Martin seemingly so well entertained in another part of the park, she hoped Junius might now indulge her.

Junius did not go all the way back. He dared not venture too near their previous time together but was otherwise happy to fill in the more recent gaps in his history.

Junius had stayed with the army after the Great War, past the dissolution of the empire, even after the deaths of first his brother and then his father. "Had he lived for many more years, I'm sure I would have refused to make a career of it. But rebelling against the man's wishes seemed somehow indecent once he was no longer here to enforce obedience," Junius explained. "And so, I stayed on. Worked hard, distinguished myself, rose in the ranks. I was posted as an attaché in Budapest when my youngest was born and my wife . . ." His voice trailed off. He had never spoken of Arabella's death to Ilse, and he seemed unable to bring himself to do so now. He brushed past it and went on.

"Well, after that, I requested a transfer to Enns. The Theresianum, you may have heard, was relocated there shortly after the War, and given its proximity to Linz, my teaching position has allowed me to be home with the children for the last several years. The school is now in the process of moving back to its home at Wiener Neustadt, though, and that's been pulling me away from them more and more frequently. I suppose once the move is final, I will probably just retire altogether. Service to the state has lost its luster, I'm afraid. These days, rather than calling on me to step up, honor and duty seem to be telling me to stand aside. Things being what they are . . ."

Junius paused his narrative, thinking. Ilse could see the subject was difficult for him, and she was not surprised. He had dedicated his life to the Bundesheer.[35] As romantic as Junius had always been, he must have convinced himself that service was a moral calling. How disheartening it must have been to find himself serving a government he could no longer respect.

"It surprises me," Junius said after a moment, changing the subject, "that you should have been in this city for twelve years, and yet our paths have never crossed until now. Every time I visit Friedrich, part of me expects to walk in and find you there, beating back your nephews or sharing a tea party in the salon with that darling niece of yours."

"I confess," Ilse said, laughing, trying to keep their conversation light, "I have never had that expectation."

"I find that somewhat remarkable."

"Not at all," she shrugged. "I had the benefit of knowledge on my side. For one thing, I know that little Krista quite despises tea. And for another, I know how fastidious Therese is and how tirelessly she's worked to prevent our meeting."

"Therese?"

"She is my sister, after all; she loves me," Ilse replied simply. "She has always worried that seeing you would cause me pain . . . or at the very least, it would make for an awkward evening for everyone involved."

"Why would she think that?"

Ilse raised her brow and threw him a look that conveyed just how dense she thought he was being.

"But surely . . . surely, Therese knows nothing of our history. You were always so insistent that she not find out about us. You can't expect me to believe you would have told her."

"It certainly was never my *intention* to tell her." Ilse hesitated, considering her words, then said flatly, "She simply found out. That's all."

"Found out? I don't understand. How could she have *simply found out?*" Junius demanded. The indignation of long-buried resentments seeped into his voice. He waited for his answer, watching as Ilse realized what she had done, the path she had led them down. For the first time, he was seeing distress wash over her lovely face. For weeks, he had been the one in constant torment, bristling at Ilse's ability to sail through each of their encounters, as though she had edited the whole affair out of her memory. He had searched in vain for any sign that a feeling heart still beat somewhere beneath her porcelain exterior. But now, that shell was cracking, and he took a certain satisfaction, bordering on smugness, in being the one to have broken through it. He knew there was something she wasn't telling him, and he would hear it.

"Ilse," he said quietly, softening his tone. "Please. It's me. You can tell me. How did she find out?"

In Ilse's confusion, she thought she heard in his voice the Junius of old. The Junius who loved her. The Junius who had held her on the banks of the river, who had kissed away her tears and made all her fears disappear.

Emotion spread before Ilse in a great sheet, a gaudy display of green and orange paisley. She knew Junius would not protect her this time. It was up to her to stamp out her own fears. *Breathe in.* She reached out with both hands and crushed the paper. *Breathe out.* Summoning all her dignity, she made herself as tall as possible.

"Because I was pregnant, Junius."

She had said it. The words were out in the open. They hit Junius with force, knocked him back, throwing off his equilibrium. He sat hard on the steps of the monument, like the earth had suddenly shifted beneath his feet.

Ilse had been pregnant.

Seconds ticked by before he found words to reply. Even then, he could only stammer half-formed thoughts.

"You were . . . ? We had a . . . ? But where . . . ?"

Ilse spared him the trouble of assembling a complete sentence. "I lost it, of course. Our child. Before I even realized I was pregnant, it was lost. And Therese was there, and she saw, and she knew, and how could I then hide the truth from her?"

Junius sat on the unforgiving steps, struggling to process what he was hearing. Ilse lowered herself a few feet away, saying nothing, watching him, trying to read his thoughts. She had had many years to inure herself to the fact of it. Having shouldered the burden for so long, she scarcely felt its weight anymore. But Junius was absorbing a twenty-year-old truth in a single moment. She needed to give him time to reorient himself to this new version of history. Not just the pregnancy but the fact that Therese had known of it for years. Therese had dined with him, talked with him, looked him in the eye, sat before God and raised no objection as he married another. All while knowing and never saying a word.

As Ilse waited, she kept herself tethered by focusing on every physical sensation. She felt the silk of her blouse rippling against her back as a breeze swept over them. She felt the coolness of the marble steps seeping through the fabric of her skirt. Running her thumbs across the corner of the cut stone, she felt the bite of each rough nick and notch. But then her body sensed the closeness of Junius, the heat radiating from him, and she stopped herself from feeling anything more.

After a few minutes, Junius collected himself enough to speak. "This is why you never wrote then, never tried to find me?"

"How could I have?"

Silence again fell over them. Ilse longed to say more but hesitated, worried Martin might suddenly return and overhear. They sat for several minutes, and Martin still did not come. The longer they waited, the more unbearable the silence became, until Ilse felt compelled to keep talking, to clear the air between them that had been obscured for so long.

"You know," she began, "for a long time, I fancied you as Orpheus; and I, your Eurydice. Did you ever learn that myth?"

"Remind me of it," Junius replied, finally trusting himself to look at her again.

"Orpheus was the son of Apollo and a muse . . . I believe her name was Calliope. They passed down to him both the brilliance of the sun and the inspiration of the muse, and the two combined to endow him with the ability to make the most extraordinary music the world had ever known."

Junius let out a chuckle, both rueful and self-deprecating. "Sounds fairly accurate so far."

Ilse allowed herself to smirk and roll her eyes but then pressed on with her story. "Well, one day, Orpheus comes across the wood nymph, Eurydice. He is drawn to her beauty; she, to his music. Like magnets pulled by an unseen force, their hearts become bound." She paused and smiled wistfully, remembering the bittersweet first days of her affair with Junius. "So, naturally, Eurydice dies."

"She dies?"

"Of course. It is a myth. Did you really think a myth would end happily?"

"A man can hope."

"Well, it doesn't. She dies," Ilse continued. "I don't recall how exactly, but somehow or other, she does, and she descends into the Underworld. Unable to live without her, Orpheus works up a plan: he is going to use the power of his music to mesmerize the beasts that guard the Underworld and then enchant Hades and convince him to return Eurydice to the world of the living."

"Seems a bit of a fool's errand, but I suppose you must make allowances for youth and hubris."

"Foolhardy or not," Ilse said, "his plan works. On listening to Orpheus sing of his love, Hades weeps and relents. He agrees to release Eurydice to follow Orpheus back to the surface. *But* he warns that only the purest of loves can break the chains of death. Orpheus must prove the strength of his love. He is to lead Eurydice out of the Underworld, but he can't look at her until they've returned to the light. It must be an act of faith. He must trust that she is there. If he turns back to ensure she's following him, she'll be pulled forever into the dark.

"So, Orpheus begins his trek back to the world above. He stumbles through the dark caverns of the Underworld, fords the river Styx, again passes all the sleeping beasts he's enchanted. At first, he's filled with joy that he'll soon be reunited with his love, who he has no doubt is close behind him. But as he walks, the darkness infects him. Shadows slide further into his heart, seep into every corner of his mind. His faith falters. He begins to question if Eurydice really is there, to doubt whether she ever loved him as he loved her.

"As he approaches the surface, a ray of light shines into the cave, and Orpheus can no longer resist the pull of his paranoia. He looks back. But he has looked too soon. The moment he catches a glimpse of Eurydice's haunting face, just a step behind him, that face is shrouded in darkness, and she's ripped away, pulled forever into the land of the dead."

"And how, exactly, did you see us in this rather morbid tale?"

Ilse stared ahead, unable to look at him. She watched the water spilling from a fountain not far from where they sat, praying its burble concealed their conversation from anyone nearby.

"You flinched," she said frankly. "You didn't seek me out, didn't wait for me to return. I know it was silly and childish to have expected it. I was gone for so many years. But you were the only man I had ever loved. No matter how rational I tried to be, this small part of me always believed you would wait. But then I returned to Vienna and found that you had moved on. You'd built a life. Like Orpheus, you went on to live in the light, while I, like Eurydice, would be forever falling, destined to live my days in darkness."

Junius stared at her, at the sad remembrance that had clouded her exquisite face, and for a moment, he felt something like pity. But this was quickly replaced by rage, seeping from a twenty-year-old wound that had suddenly been exposed and ripped open. "I *flinched? I* flinched?" He shot up, unable to contain his emotions. He stormed to the fountain, back to her, away, and then back again. Not wanting to make a scene, he sat back down, taking deep, quivering breaths to calm himself. He sent his fury into his fingertips, digging them fiercely into his thighs. "I *never* flinched," he spat through clenched teeth, his eyes drilling a hole in the ground between his feet. "*You left!*"

Ilse could say nothing. She was too stunned by the strength of his reaction. All she could do was watch as a passion Junius had kept bottled for years finally burst forth.

"You left me without a word!" he went on, his voice hushed but the power of his resentment clear. "I woke up that morning, and you were just gone. After what had happened, you simply discarded me, as though what we shared had meant nothing."

"Meant nothing? I loved you, Junius! You were my entire world."

"And how was I supposed to have known that? What was I supposed to think? One moment you're in my arms, and the next thing I know, you've vanished. Poof! Without a word, without a trace, seemingly without a care."

"I was terrified! I was little more than a child. I didn't know what to do. We had done something I had been taught was the worst thing I could possibly have done, something that could have ruined me."

"And I had done it too."

"But it's not the same for you. You know very well that it's not. You're a man. You can never understand what I felt in that moment. The thing you were raised to believe it your mission to take, I was raised to believe it my duty to protect. And I had failed. How could I bear facing you after that?"

"And you thought so little of me? You thought I would have judged you?"

"No, I—"

"Rather than take that chance, you chose to send me into a war with a broken heart, believing you despised me, not caring whether I lived or died. The safety of my fellow soldiers was the only thing that sustained me. I cared nothing for my own life, but I refused to take them down with me, so I carried on. But you *devastated* me. You changed me. And then the war ended, and I found someone who brought something resembling joy and beauty back into my world. What was I supposed to do? I saw a path back to life, and I took it. And never, not for one single moment, have I regretted that choice."

Exhausted, they sat again without speaking, blistering at the words that still hung around them like poisoned gas. These were the injuries that had defined their lives, lent them distinction in their own minds, made them feel superior. As if there was unique wisdom to be gained through heartache. Now that they had picked the scabs, they watched with fascination the ruby-red beads that rose from under the skin. Sitting close enough to touch, they turned away from each other, choosing instead to swaddle themselves in the perverse pleasure of a pain relived.

Eventually, Ilse emerged from the embrace of her wounded

pride. "I don't blame you for being angry," she said. "For years, I was angry with myself. For not being braver. For putting you through that. I longed to offer you an apology, an explanation, anything. It was always fear that held me back. I know it cannot mend what was broken—what I broke—but for whatever it is worth to you after all these years, I want you to know, I was sorry. I *am* sorry."

Junius looked at her, at the helplessness that shone in her eyes. They were the eyes of a child, lost and confused, at odds with the sophisticated clothing, the perfectly placed hair. She looked like a girl, caught playing dress-up in her mother's wardrobe. He relented, sighed. "The blame is not all yours, I suppose. I should not have been so quick to injury, so quick to doubt you."

"It seems we *both* doubted when we should have had faith." Ilse looked at him earnestly, a look that could have thawed all but the iciest of hearts. "We cannot go back," she said, resigned. "We can never change what is past."

"No," Junius agreed, "we cannot."

"But perhaps we can finally put that past behind us? Might we hope to move forward as friends?"

"Perhaps." Junius smiled, tight-lipped, strained. His expression conveyed a determination to end their conversation, but not warmth, not forgiveness. He stood, dusted himself off, adjusted his hat, and began making his way back up the tree-lined avenue that had brought them to the monument, motioning for Ilse to follow.

As they reentered the central rose garden, they were joined again by Martin, who apologized for having been detained for so long. "I do hope, old chap, that you haven't bored our lovely baroness to death in my absence."

"I should hope not," Junius replied. He did not look at Ilse.

Ilse smiled at Martin and took the arm he offered her. As

they began to walk on, she glanced over at Junius. She caught his eye, but only for a moment; he would not hold her gaze. She tried to read what he was thinking, this man who was so different in so many ways from the boy she had known. But he had closed himself off from her again.

No, she thought as they left the garden. *We can never go back.*

FIDGETING WITH A LOOSE THREAD

All around them, the city buzzed with life. Car horns blared, the cries of children drifted down from apartments above, newsboys called out, passersby laughed without care. Ilse heard none of it. She was in a world of her own as they walked the short distance from the gardens back to the house. She heard only the echoes of her thoughts and the clicking of her heels against the bricks.

Mercifully, neither of her companions seemed in the mood for conversation. She was not called on to be sociable. She was not asked to say a word.

As they approached the house, Junius took his leave. "Urgent family business calls me back to Linz, so I will be leaving Vienna in the morning," he explained.

It was the first Junius had mentioned this urgent business, and Ilse couldn't help suspecting that his abrupt departure was an outgrowth of their conversation in the garden.

"I hope it is nothing serious," Martin said.

"No, no," Junius assured him. "Time-sensitive, yes, but not serious. Not yet, at any rate. My unruly brood has chased away another governess, and I must go see to her replacement before the rest of the regiment mutinies."

"Won't you at least come in and take your leave of Heinrich?" Ilse asked, driven more by politeness than any desire to extend their afternoon. "I'm sure he would want to say goodbye and bid you a safe journey."

"You are most gracious, Baroness Jörger, but I would not wish to disturb your husband today, knowing he is unwell. Please offer him my best wishes."

There it was again, that formality. Ilse nodded and forced her lips into an upward curve. "Of course. You are very thoughtful, Herr Oberst."

"Safe travels, my friend," said Martin, grabbing Junius's shoulder.

"Thank you, Martin." Junius patted Martin's arm and then shook his hand vigorously. He directed only a tip of the hat toward Ilse and a curt, "Good day to you." Then he left them, without another word, without a look back.

Martin and Ilse stood for a moment on the sidewalk, watching Junius walk away. Ilse thought she noticed his posture relaxing as he put distance between them, as though he had been bound by almost unbearable restraints in her presence.

"Bit of an odd fellow," Martin observed, "but a man never had a more loyal friend. I am glad Heinrich finally had a chance to know him."

Ilse said nothing, just nodded and started up the steps to the front door, expecting Martin to follow.

"Actually . . .," Martin said, looking down at his watch, "I think I will also take my leave of you now. There are some things that I must see to."

"Of course. What shall I tell Heinrich?"

"Tell him I'll check back in on him this evening."

"Take all the time you need. We will see you tonight."

Martin smiled and nodded, then turned on his heel and strode away. As Ilse watched his retreat, she was struck by his manner of walking. Not just hurried but urgent, almost agitated. Veiled agitation. He moved as swiftly as he could without drawing notice. It was like watching a shoplifter flee the scene of his crime. Strange . . .

Ilse glanced back in Junius's direction, but he had already disappeared around the corner. She inhaled deeply and blew the air out in a quick puff. She felt . . . unsettled. Not dismayed. Not disappointed. Not even offended, really, that everyone seemed in such a hurry to be away from her. Just unsettled. As if invisible insects were skittering up her arms, and she couldn't shake them off. Like someone had raised her center of gravity, and she could be knocked off balance by the weight of a single feather.

Staring at the empty street corner, she was hit by a sudden pang. It wasn't a longing but something unfamiliar, physical and deep. It emanated from somewhere beyond her heart, below the pit of her stomach.

She decided it was her feet. Her feet ached. She couldn't remember the last time her feet had had the audacity to hurt. They lived in the shoes she required them to wear, the shoes that befit a woman of her role and social standing, the shoes of the Baroness Jörger von Tollet. Ilse did not tolerate anything so pedestrian as cramping feet. But there they were. Throbbing. It was like her hour of honesty had given even her appendages permission to reveal their true feelings, to protest the years of being crammed into patent leather peep-toes, strapped into Spanish heels.

Right there on the steps, Ilse slipped off her shoes. It was a quiet rebellion, witnessed by no one, but it made her mind feel instantly freer, as though a valve had been released, relieving pressure, averting catastrophe. Picking up her shoes, she glanced up the street again and then continued into the house.

No sooner had Ilse closed the door than she was met by the housekeeper, Frau Radak. "Oh, Gnädige Frau, you've finally come back!" Frau Radak cried, her face contorted with worry. "It is Herr Baron. He has taken a turn. The doctor has been called; he is with him now."

Ilse wasted no time. "Herr Rezek, he is headed north. Have someone fetch him back here this instant!" Having given that instruction, she dropped her shoes and flew to the stairs. As she rounded the end of the forged banister, her long strand of pearls caught the curling ironwork and snapped with the force of her speed, sending pearls clattering down the steps in her wake. They spilled across the foyer floor, but Ilse did not stop to watch them fall. She did not look to see Frau Radak wince or wonder how many pearls the maids would pocket as they swept them up.

The pearls didn't matter.

Her aching feet did not matter.

Junius von Hess didn't matter.

Only one thing in her world mattered at that moment. She was running to him.

***

Hours later, as Heinrich slept under the watchful eye of a nurse, Ilse and Martin sat below in the drawing room, each immersed in their own thoughts.

The day had left Ilse emptied, confused, dissatisfied. The more she thought on it, the more she saw that, rather than helping to put the past behind them, her confrontation with Junius had merely opened old wounds.

She had always known there was a possibility—no, not just a possibility, a *likelihood*—that the manner of her parting had damaged her in Junius's eyes. But she had not foreseen the depth of his antipathy. Far from giving her feelings due consideration, he seemed determined to invalidate them. He was so consumed by his pain he allowed Ilse no room for hers. Even the revelation of her pregnancy, appropriately shocking when she first disclosed it, seemed to have been eclipsed by the unyielding sway of pride.

This was not the same Junius she had loved, just as she was

no longer the girl who had loved him. How could she have been so open? What had she been thinking? Perhaps the first disclosure had been unavoidable, but she should have ended it there. What had she expected to gain by admitting to harboring feelings for him for all those years? Did she simply want his pity? Had she hoped that arousing some residue of past sentiment in Junius might slake her vanity? Whichever objective animated her in the heat of the moment, it had obviously failed.

And now, instead of focusing on Heinrich, who lay upstairs, unable even to rise from his bed, she sat there obsessing over a conversation with a man she likely would never see again. She was utterly ashamed of her weakness. Heinrich deserved better than this. She owed him all her care and attention. Even if it had been Heinrich himself who had contrived and encouraged her and Junius's reacquaintance.

Heinrich. Her lovely, vexing, infuriating Heinrich. Perhaps allowing Junius to dominate her thoughts was simply avoidance, a way to ignore for one miserable evening other ideas that had been harassing her for months. That her dear husband's time was growing shorter. That each Monday, each ordinary Tuesday, might be their last together. Heinrich may have come to terms with that, but Ilse could not. He looked at death as a consummator that would somehow make him complete. But for her, it was the opposite. Death was a pillager set to steal away the one person who made her feel whole. Looking over at Martin, who was staring morosely into the dwindling fire, she couldn't help wondering, *Will he, too, drift out of my life when Heinrich is gone?*

Ilse sighed and shifted in her chair. Her sudden movement roused Martin from his meditation. He watched for a moment as she fidgeted mindlessly with a loose thread in the upholstery. "Have a care, Ilse," he said. She started at the sudden break in the silence. "Heinrich won't thank you when he sees you've pulled his favorite chair to pieces."

"Always the optimist, Marty dear," Ilse replied with a thin smile, flicking the thread back and forth with her forefinger. "Believing that Heinrich will ever see the results of my handiwork."

"You think he won't, then?" Martin asked gravely.

"I don't know," she sighed. "I hope so. But I'm finding faith a difficult concept today. And I can tell from your face that you are as well."

"You could say that." He rose and stepped over to the fireplace, picking up the poker and jabbing mindlessly at the empty grate. "But I'm ashamed to admit, it's not only Heinrich on my mind."

"Oh?"

"I can't bear to keep this to myself any longer. Normally I would tell Heinrich, but how can I burden him right now?" Martin stared at Ilse with an intensity that surprised and alarmed her. "Can I trust you?"

"Trust me to do what?" she asked tentatively.

Martin heaved a sigh. "I hardly know." He sat back down, leaned forward, wringing his hands and digging his elbows into his knees. "To tell me what is to be done, I suppose. To not blame me."

"Blame you? Martin, you're scaring me. What is it?"

He sighed again, heavily, and steadied himself. "Perhaps you noticed that I was a bit quiet this afternoon, a bit more distracted than normal."

"I think there are few who would not have." This was not a lie, not exactly. A quiet Martin Rezek was always notable. But in this case, Ilse had not, in fact, noticed anything unusual in his behavior. She, too, had been lost in thought. Not that she would admit that to Martin.

"You'll recall that I left you and Junius for a time in the gardens to go and greet an associate of mine."

"Of course. And I remember being surprised at how long you were away."

"My clients, as you know, are of all stripes. The only thing they have in common is their money. They trust me to advise them on their finances, and I am paid handsomely when my advice succeeds. Beyond this, we are strangers. They rarely share anything of their political views, and I never have cause to ask. Their beliefs are of no interest to me."

"Yes, I know. You are as amoral a creature as I ever met," Ilse said wryly. "But we love you anyway."

"That's not quite fair. It's not so much that I'm amoral. I have beliefs, strong ones. It simply doesn't pay to have them out in the world for all to see. If my beliefs were known, I would alienate half the country and, with them, half of my potential clients. Not to mention, why should a man in my shoes give people any reason to find him suspect? Having adversaries is too great a risk."

"Fair enough," Ilse allowed. "But what has this to do with today?"

"I'm getting to that," Martin assured her, rising to refill his snifter with brandy. His hands shook as he poured, and the lip of the bottle clinked revealingly against the crystal. He took a deep drink to shore up his confidence, then continued.

"The gentleman I was speaking with today is a long-time client. We go back many years, almost as far back as the war. But I've only ever seen him at his office or mine, and our conversations have always been limited to business. But today . . . I don't know . . . perhaps it was the fresh air and atmosphere . . . he was *chatty*. Much more so than I've ever known him to be. He talked to me as though I were a close friend. Griping about the impacts of recent labor policies and anti-inflationary measures. Saying how it's no surprise things are such a mess since we've all been shoved into a state that has no business being a state, how we will never survive on our own, that sort of thing. I neither concurred nor disagreed with him; I simply let him talk. But he must have assumed I was of the same mind when I didn't contradict him because he just kept *going*. And he said something that made me nervous. He said to me, 'Don't you worry, though. Our boys will take care of all that. Just you wait. Won't be long now.' I asked what he meant, but he just raised a finger to his lips, winked, and walked away."

"How odd. What do you think he meant by it?" Ilse asked.

"I hardly know," Martin replied, "but it can't be *good*, can it?"

"You think he knows of some new agitation being planned?"

"Doesn't it sound like it to you?"

Martin was clearly disturbed. But Ilse wondered. "If something truly noteworthy is afoot, would this man have been so open about it? Even if he assumed you were an ally in his cause, it still seems unlikely."

"I see your point. But you didn't see his manner, his expression. I don't know how to describe it . . . It was practically fanatical."

"And you know nothing of this man's leanings?"

"Nothing at all," he said. "Simply knowing his bank balance, I can hardly think him a socialist. I would be shocked if he was referring to a strike or some repeat of February."

"I wonder . . .," Ilse mused. "His derision of Austria, his thinking the country unviable . . . Is it possible he backs the reunification?[36] You don't suppose he could be a supporter of this Herr Hitler?"

"It's entirely possible. And I must admit, that is what has me worried. Could the Nazis be planning more bombings or hoping to stoke unrest? Or worse?"

"These days, anything is possible," Ilse conceded. She

considered for a moment everything he had told her. "Do you plan to report it?"

"What would I even report? That someone may or might not be planning something, somewhere, at some time? It is hardly firm intelligence. I could always report him for questioning, I suppose. But then, what if he is simply a braggart and was referring to some completely legitimate form of protest? I can hardly expect the Heimwehr[37] would treat him with leniency, not after February. How could I chance it?"

"That's true . . ." Ilse sunk into rumination. To condemn a man based on mere suspicion was unconscionable. But to do nothing, if Martin's fears proved well founded, would be unconscionable, too. She did not envy her friend the position in which he found himself. Of course, she now found herself right there along with him.

"What do you advise?" Martin asked, his eyes imploring her to provide a solution where he could see none.

Ilse thought on it a moment more, then said, "I would advise you to do nothing."

"Nothing?"

"At least for now," she went on. "Let me talk to my father. It's been several years since he retired, but he still has contacts inside the government who respect him. He can put people on guard without putting your client at risk. The warning from a trusted source might cause the security forces to give weight to rumblings they might otherwise ignore. Your client may still get swept up in it, especially if he is already known to the government. But at least this way, you can be assured he will not be targeted without cause. Not because of you, at any rate."

"But what if they ask your father how he came by the information. You might get him, or yourself, into an awful jam."

"I'll simply tell him I overheard a conversation in the park. Even if someone does come knocking, I am not afraid to stick with that story. They'll ask me who said it, and I'll say I don't know. And that, at least, is the truth."

"I suppose that makes about as much sense as anything else," Martin concurred warily. "But it seems you're taking an awful risk on my account."

Ilse reached over and patted Martin's hand. "We've fibbed on each other's account these past eleven years. I don't see any reason we should stop doing so now."

A SCULPTURE FORGED IN BRONZE

Everything went as Ilse had planned.

A few days after her conversation with Martin, her father called to check in on Heinrich, and Ilse pulled him aside to share the information Martin had given her. Dr. Eder shared the tip with former colleagues, who shared it with the appropriate points of contact, who developed scenarios as to what the intelligence could portend and strategies to confront them all.

Yes, everything went just as Ilse had planned, and her father commended her shrewdness in anticipating the proper course.

It was not enough, however. In the end.

June passed into July, and summer engulfed the city. Heat tormented the light, refracting it and setting it writhing in a seductive dance above the pavement. The gendarmes spent their afternoons lackadaisically chasing children out of fountains and away from hydrants. And still, no reports of anything untoward reached Ilse and Martin.

They allowed themselves to be reassured. If anything *had* been planned, it must have been either abandoned or foiled by this time. More likely, they had simply blown the whole thing out of proportion. They could rest easy, they told themselves. Everything was fine.

But everything was not fine.

Their sense of security was a false one.

Late in July, as the mercury peaked, the news arrived on

their doorsteps. The chancellor's office had been stormed by Nazi zealots. Dollfuss had been gunned down. The conspirators were overwhelmed quickly enough, their clumsy coup thwarted. Still, the revolt had not been contained. It spread like a poison taken up by the bloodstream. In Linz, Tyrol, Styria, Carinthia, and beyond, the country erupted. And though the army quelled the violence, Ilse resisted the temptation of comfort. Austria was coming apart at the seams. History would look back on this week, she was sure, and see another step taken on the path to annihilation.

She did not voice her concerns to Heinrich. About the turmoil, Heinrich knew nothing. He had not left his quarters in over a month, and Ilse and Martin agreed that, at this point, no good could come from sharing with him the muck of the world beyond his walls. He never requested a newspaper, preferring to lose himself in his books. And as his usual well-wishers were far away on summer holidays, there was little risk that anyone else would let the news slip.

In any other year, the Jörgers would have been among those fleeing Vienna for the cool of the mountains or the refreshing coastal breezes. But as the summer of 1934 approached, Heinrich's doctors had warned against moving him. "He is not strong enough," they whispered to Ilse. "The journey would be the end of him."

Heinrich dismissed these concerns. "The doctors don't advise it. *Pah!* Doctors, who can take them at their word? I am their research subject, not their patient. They just want to poke and prod at me for another month."

But Ilse would hear none of it. "Oh, hush," she said. "Don't pretend to cling to those nihilistic prejudices. You know perfectly well such attitudes are long since obsolete. We will follow the doctors' orders."

And so, they stayed put. Together, Ilse and Martin built for

Heinrich a literary sanctuary where he could spend his few waking hours in the unspoiled company of poetry and books. For the conspirators, too, Heinrich's room became a refuge. A place without coups, without barricades and barbed wire. A place where they did not find themselves looking over their shoulders, jumping at every backfiring car or distant rumble of thunder. Once they stepped over Heinrich's threshold, the outside world lifted away, and their only cares were for his comfort.

***

"Don't you think it a bit odd to ask your lover to secure the future happiness of your widow?" Martin asked one night in late August as he reached behind Heinrich to fluff his pillows. As the weeks passed, this was one of the few ways Martin had found he could contribute to Heinrich's comfort. He attended to these pillow-fluffing duties relentlessly, almost to the point of annoyance.

"Not at all," Heinrich replied, groaning with the effort of leaning forward while Martin went about his work. "You are the two people I love best in the world. Why should I not want some sort of assurance that you will both be taken care of?"

"Is Ilse setting her sights on someone for me, then?"

"No. Of your happiness, I have not a fear. 'Man has one love; it is the World. Woman has one world; it is love.'"[38]

"Altenberg?"

"Very good." Heinrich smiled his approval. "So, you see, you will do just fine on your own. You will have a thousand sources of contentment."

"Not that I'm questioning the infinite wisdom of Peter Altenberg, but what makes you so certain?"

"Because, of all your brilliant qualities that I adore—and rest assured, there are many—your scruples are not exactly among them. You seek not good in life but advantage, which is the one thing you cannot help but find."

"I think I might resent that."

"You might resent it, but you don't deny it, do you?"

Martin made no reply beyond flumping down in a chair next to the bed.

"There, you see? I'm right; you know I'm right. And it's that unflinching self-awareness that I love. You have no delusions. You know exactly who you are. Oh, you will mourn me, of course. Of that, I haven't the slightest doubt. But then you will move on. Soon enough, you'll find some lovely young Adonis to be your playmate. Perhaps you won't adore him as you do me, but he'll make you happy enough."

"You know, if you were able to chase after me, I would march right out that door. But seeing as you cannot, I will stay. I have far too much pride to come back of my own accord after making such an exit, and I'm not ready to be rid of you quite yet."

"It's wonderful to have such security in my feebleness," Heinrich laughed.

Martin could not hold onto his disgruntlement in the face of such self-deprecating charm. He chuckled silently and rolled his eyes to signal that all was forgiven. Heinrich reached out his hand to Martin, who took it and pressed it against his lips. No flesh remained to cushion the bones, and beneath the petal-soft skin, Heinrich's knuckles felt sharp as flint. Martin wrapped his grimace in a smile.

"But where was I?" Heinrich continued. "Ah, yes. Now I remember. You will move on. We both agree that you will move on. But it won't be that way for Ilse. Ilse has such an overinflated sense of duty. She will always choose what she thinks is right and proper over what makes her happy. Left to her own devices, she will be an unhappy creature for the rest of her days."

"So, for the sake of argument," Martin mused, his resistance already waning, "let's say I do agree to do this. Shouldn't Ilse have some say in the matter? How are you so certain Junius is the man she will want to be with?"

"Ah, about that, you will simply have to trust me. I can't tell you why, but believe me, I am not mistaken in this."

"Well, if you're so confident, why not leave it to work itself out?"

"Because I know Ilse, and I know she will resist it. She is always overthinking. She wants so badly to do best by everyone but herself that she makes a muddle out of things that should be perfectly simple. Mark my word, unless she has someone nudging her along, she'll avoid seeing Junius altogether out of some misplaced loyalty to my memory. She will spend the rest of her life alone, and *that* I refuse to allow. Not if it's in my power to prevent it."

"There's just one problem. Ilse, as you well know, is not your typical woman," Martin pointed out. "You can't just dangle the prospect of romance in front of her and expect her to leap at it."

"There is more of the typical about her than she lets on."

"I still say that unless Ilse has resolved to be with Junius, there's little I can do. If I force her hand, she'll resist it all the more. You know she—"

Heinrich raised a hand to silence Martin. "All I ask is that you bring them together. Don't try to convince her of anything. Just bring them together. As often as you can contrive without arousing their suspicions."

Martin sighed. He knew he'd been beaten. "You know I will do anything you ask. But I still don't much see the point. Ilse is a big girl with a mind of her own. She won't be manipulated into a connection that she does not otherwise desire."

"But you'll do it?"

***

Down on the street, Ilse was wishing the chauffeur a

pleasant evening and stepping out of the car onto the first yellowing leaves that had started to litter the sidewalk. Autumn was approaching. *Soon the city will fill back up*, she thought. *Soon there will be dinners and balls, and Therese and Friedrich and their line of little Kassners will come tramping through the house once more. Soon we will have some sorely needed distraction.*

She entered the house, climbed the stairs, and, hearing the murmur of voices, made her way down the hall to Heinrich's room.

Having heard the door close below, Heinrich and Martin had let their conversation about Ilse drop. Martin was now casually reading aloud to Heinrich, who sat with his eyes closed in appreciation.

Ilse recognized the book as Rilke's *Duino Elegies*, one of Heinrich's favorites. She had never heard Martin read poetry before, not once in all the years she and Heinrich had been married. To her surprise, he read with sincere, almost melodious feeling. She stood in the doorway listening, lulled by the rise and fall of his voice.

> *. . . Here is the time for what you can say;*
> *this is its country. Speak and acknowledge.*
> *More than ever, things are falling away—*
> *the things that we live with—and what is replacing them*
> *is an urge without image. An urge whose crusts*
> *will crumble as soon as it grows too large*
> *and tries to get out. Between the hammerblows,*
> *our heart survives—just as the tongue, even*
> *between the teeth, still manages to praise—*[39]

"Oh, Ilse!" Martin stopped his recitation, pretending to be startled by her sudden appearance. "I did not hear you come in."

"I have not been standing here long," she replied, walking into the room. "Hello, Heinrich darling." Heinrich opened his eyes and greeted her with a smile as she gently kissed his forehead, as one would a sick child. "I see you are well entertained this evening."

"I could not ask for better," he said, looking fondly in Martin's direction.

"Marty dear, I've never known you to be much for poetry," Ilse said. "You read remarkably well."

Her praise was more earnest than Martin's pleasure in receiving it. In truth, he rather despised poetry. Poetry dripped with mawkishness and sentiment, and his logically bent mind preferred to convey ideas in more direct language. "Even I have hidden depths," he said, closing the book. "But I am glad you are here, as I must be off."

"Can I not tempt you to stay for dinner?" Ilse asked, genuinely disappointed. More and more, she had come to depend on Martin's society during these newly solitary evenings.

"I'm afraid not." He rose, stretched, yawned. "No, tonight I keep company with Countess Almeida and her cousin. I confess, I rather miss the days when these great houses couldn't mingle with the likes of us lesser beings. There was a time I could keep my work safely confined to the daylight hours. Nowadays, the invitations to social engagements flow freely, and I dare not refuse and risk giving offense . . . even if I would prefer other company." He stepped over to the bed and pressed Heinrich's hand. "Rest well, Heinrich. I will see you tomorrow."

Ilse watched Martin walk out, smiling sadly to herself.

"And what is that look for?" Heinrich asked after Martin was safely out of earshot.

"Oh, nothing." Ilse waved away her wistfulness, forcing a cheerier expression. "Just that I have always thought it a pity the two of you never call each other anything but *Heinrich* and *Martin*. Even when it's just the three of us. Even when it's just the two of you, I suspect."

Heinrich shrugged. "It is safer that way. Get used to calling each other anything else in private, and we risk letting it slip out in public. It's not so different from what you and I do, how we always call each other *Coco* and *Heinrich darling* at home, so it seems more natural when we do it among others."

"Oh, I don't question the logic of it. I just find it a shame that after all these years, you still must have these little barriers between you."

Heinrich gave a lopsided smile that said, *It is what it is, and I cannot change it.* More than anything, perhaps, this resignation broke Ilse's heart. Because she knew he was right. It was what it was. Heinrich would not live to see the day he and Martin would be accepted.

Ilse patted his leg, then took up the chair that Martin had vacated. "So," she said, "what is it you and Marty were speaking of that I could not hear?" Her husband gave her an innocently quizzical look. "Oh, come now. I've never known Martin to read poetry. Not even to indulge you."

"You know us too well for your own good," he said, straining to shift his position. "If you must know, we were discussing funerals," Heinrich invented. Even resting in bed, he was quick on his feet.

"Funerals? That sounds rather maudlin."

"Not at all. I was telling him about Hugo Wolf's funeral. You remember Wolf, that composer who died so young?"[40] Ilse nodded that she did. "I was acquainted with him a bit during my university days. We met one evening at Café Griensteidl and had the most fascinating conversation. He was already slightly off by the time we met but still positively brilliant. When I learned of his death a few years later, I don't know . . . I felt duty-bound to pay my respects. His funeral was on Mardi Gras, and we had to fight through crowds of drunks and costumed jesters just to get out of the church. I was telling Martin that I think I should like that. No one should have to mourn me for more than an hour. As soon as they leave the service, it should be a sea of frivolity."

"Oh, Heinrich, be serious," Ilse reproved.

"I am perfectly in earnest! We have been so dull around here for so long. I can hardly expect a party while I'm still lying in this bed, but I certainly expect a celebration when I am finally free of it. Grief is a completely selfish emotion, after all. You grieve because of how much *you* will miss me and because *your* life will be so different. I challenge you to be totally selfless in my death and think only of *me*. And if you think of me, you will throw up your hands and rejoice that I am no longer trapped in this prison of a body."

Ilse still looked unconvinced.

"There now, you see?" Heinrich said, with a little laugh that turned to a cough, which wracked his body for several seconds before he could go on. Ilse reached for the water glass on his bedside table and held it out to him, but he waved her away. "That is precisely why we didn't want to say anything about it to you. I told Martin to wait and tell you after I'm gone. That way, you can't argue with me about it.

"Now, tell me, Coco," he continued, skillfully changing the topic, "how was everything at the office today?"

"Oh, you know how it is. There is a problem with the supply chain for tin. The Hungarians have raised their export taxes, so the canneries are trying to identify domestic or Italian sources that will be less expensive. And one of the breweries would like to expand production to increase exports. Naturally, the board has divided itself into two camps: those who are certain the demand is there and those who are convinced the markets will never materialize. And, of course, there are the usual arguments around the quarterly wage analysis."

"In other words, absolutely nothing has changed," Heinrich said dryly, wincing as an acute pain radiated through his body.

"I shouldn't be troubling you with this," Ilse said, watching helplessly as he shifted, trying to find a more tolerable position.

"No, no, I want to hear it. I hate being handled with kid gloves all the time, like I'm going to crumble with the least little bit of bad news."

There was certainly truth in his accusation; Ilse could not deny that. She and Martin had curated their conversations for weeks. Even in discussing the troubles at the office, she had left out much. That the Hungarians' new tariffs owed to the weakened state of the alliance. That they questioned Schuschnigg, Austria's new chancellor, and doubted his ability to hold the line against an increasingly assertive Germany. That the board feared what Austria's increased diplomatic isolation meant for trade prospects. Ilse shared none of this with Heinrich. Instead, she said, "Oh pish, we do nothing of the sort. Kid gloves? Not at all. We handle you with the mangiest, most grizzled pair of old driving gloves we can find."

To this, Heinrich blew out a breath and rolled his eyes.

"Shall I pick up reading where Martin left off?" Ilse asked, nodding toward the book.

"No, no, thank you. I am tired. I think I'll rest a bit."

"Of course, darling," she said, her smile easy. "I'll leave you for now and look in again after dinner."

Ilse rose to leave, but Heinrich called her back when she reached the door. She paused where she stood and turned to her husband. "What is it, Heinrich darling?"

"Can you do me one favor?"

"Anything at all."

"Please stop treating me like you do the rest of the world."

"I don't know what you mean," Ilse lied.

"Yes, you do," he replied. He didn't look at her. He was staring across the room at a small statue sitting on the corner of his bureau. It was carved bronze, about two hands high. A miniature replica of Rodin's "The Kiss." The man's hand rested lovingly on his lady's hip, her arm wrapped his neck in a passionate embrace. It had been a wedding gift, and Heinrich and Ilse had laughed when they opened it. Their ruse had undoubtedly succeeded if someone felt such an intimate rendering was an appropriate gift. Through the years, Heinrich had kept it close. A symbol of his devotion to his wife to stop the tongue of any impertinent or suspicious servant.

"For all the time I have known you," he went on, his eyes still glued to the sculpture, "you have always been honest with me, and I with you. There has been no pretense between us. I've watched you drift through life like a work of art, a sculpture forged in bronze or marble, exquisitely beautiful but hard, impenetrable. You convince everyone around you that you have not a care, not a pain, no opinions that are not perfect reflections of their own. By hiding yourself away, you make others feel seen. But it never was that way with us. I saw you. Always, from the very beginning, I saw *you*. While the rest of the world worshiped an idol—unbreakable, formidable perfection—I have seen the woman, with all her beautifully human flaws. I'm asking you not to hide that woman away. Don't vanish on me. Please, in what little time we have left together, don't make us strangers."

What could Ilse say to him? That every day that woman died a little watching him slip further and further away from her? That just looking at his once hale form, now thin and frail, was a torment? That she had to steel herself and choke back tears just to step into his room? That the whole world seemed to be spinning out of control, and she was paralyzed, unable to move forward?

No, she could never say any of this to him. She would not force him to carry the burden of her sorrows. Not now.

And so, she merely laid a hand upon her heart, offered him a warm smile, and left him to his rest.

WITH HUMILITY AND FONDEST AFFECTION

Fasching season came again. Christmas markets sprouted up in every square. Shop windows draped in greenery and red ribbon displayed shining baubles to hopeful and hopeless eyes alike. At every parade and festival, children screamed in delight at the sight of St. Nicolas and delighted to scream at the Krampuses following close behind him, their wooden faces snarling out from beneath curled and menacing horns.

Ilse did not join the revelry. There was no place for her in such a joyous season. Looking down from Heinrich's bedroom, she watched the children skipping along the sidewalk. Her pale face stared back from the glass, floating like an orb above her somber mourning dress, starkly contrasted with the merriment below.

She knew this was not what Heinrich had wanted. He had wanted her to embrace his death. He had hoped it would usher her into a future of infinite possibilities. But Ilse could not seem to rise to his expectations. In the two months since Heinrich's passing, the best she could muster was gratitude.

For his release from suffering.

That the release had been quick.

In the end, Heinrich had not spent months wasting away as she and Martin once feared he might. One morning in mid-September, Ilse was roused before dawn by the nighttime nurse.

Suspecting a stroke, she bade Ilse to come at once. The nurse had left Heinrich's room for less than a minute, but that was all it took. By the time she and Ilse arrived at his side, Heinrich was gone. No signs of life animated his body. There was no rise and fall of his chest, no curling of fingers around her own when Ilse clutched his hand.

Even now, when she closed her eyes, Ilse still saw Heinrich's as they had been in that moment. The image haunted and comforted her. His face slightly contorted, his mouth screwed to one side. But in his wide-open eyes, she had seen no trace of pain. Their expression was closer to awe, rapture. Like he had seen something so overwhelmingly beautiful he had given in to it. Surrendered. Just that quick.

For all the months she'd spent preparing for his death, when the time came, Ilse was deprived even of the chance to say goodbye to her most cherished friend. He was simply there one moment and gone the next. Yet, somehow, Ilse suspected Heinrich had sensed the end was coming. He seemed to have known that their conversation on his last night would be his final chance to say all he needed to say. Out of nowhere, he had asked if she had heard anything of Oberst Hess since his return to Linz. Ilse had sighed vexedly, begged him to let go of his ridiculous fantasy that she and the oberst would somehow live happily ever after. Heinrich had allowed the subject to drop for a time; they'd moved on to discussing something more mundane, less provoking. But he returned to it, determined to have his say.

"I'll never understand why you think closing yourself off to love makes you stronger, that it makes you brave somehow," he'd admonished her. "Can't you see, when it comes to love, being strong is only evidence of cowardice? It is in vulnerability that you prove your strength."

He hadn't been cruel. His words were not angry. No, there had been something entirely different in his voice, something closer to pity. But it hadn't been pity, exactly. It was more like *concern*. He had been afraid for her, and that fear opened a well of sorrow. Listening to his words, seeing the despondency on his face, it had been like she was seventeen again, sitting in her father's study, stubbornly resenting him as he implored her to understand his reasons for spiriting her away to a safer place.

Heinrich had been right, of course. He had known her better than she knew herself. It took losing him for Ilse to open her eyes to what he had seen all along. That she was a coward. She had let fear shape her entire life. In fear, she had hidden her affair with Junius all those years ago, and in fear, she had run from him. Fear of moving on led her to accept her father's conditions for joining him in Washington. Even her marriage to Heinrich had been an act of spinelessness, fueled by her refusal to ever again lay herself open.

The trouble was, she had failed. Hardened though her heart was, she *had* let love into it. The weight of her grief proved it. Her relationship with Heinrich may have been strictly platonic, but she had loved him. And she was lost now that he was gone.

In the first throws of anguish, Ilse had had to remind herself that she was not alone in her despair. Though he could not risk a public display of emotion, Martin, surely, had felt the loss as much as she did. Very likely more. She regretted how little she saw of him in the first days after Heinrich's death. Outside the formal events, she scarcely saw him at all. And as she was constantly surrounded by family, she had no opportunity to speak with him privately. She had not even been able to break the news or comfort him through his initial shock. The information had been conveyed to him by one of the nurses as she left the house. Well-meaning in her efforts to prevent Ilse from being disturbed, the nurse told Martin of Heinrich's passing right there on the street. As though he were some common business associate to be chased away, someone to whom she did not owe the respect of mourning.

Yet, though Ilse saw little of it, she did not doubt that Martin's suffering was great, and as the weeks wore on, she did not question or resent his method of coping. Where Ilse threw herself into work, Martin threw himself back into Vienna's social scene. She poured every ounce of energy into salvaging the crumbling foundations of Heinrich's company. Martin poured drinks. He laughed his way through cocktail parties and dinners, was seen at every smoke-filled jazz club in the city. Ilse did not read heartlessness into these actions. She saw only desperation. A longing to fill the empty spaces with anything resembling pleasure. How long it could last, Ilse did not know, but she would not begrudge Martin anything he needed simply to endure.

***

It was now the evening before the Feast of St. Nicolas, and Ilse was bracing for a night of celebration with her father and the Kassners. For years, she and Heinrich had hosted all three generations of the Kassner family on this day. Though Therese had offered to take on the burden of hosting, Ilse stubbornly insisted their traditions should remain unchanged, even without Heinrich at the head of the table. Earlier that day, the maids had hidden treats throughout the house, and now Ilse was awaiting the moment when she could release her niece and nephews to scavenge whatever riches they could find. Some years, the children managed to locate every last treasure; other times, a maid was too clever by half, and months later, someone would uncover a moldering marzipan Krampus hiding behind books in the library or a foil-wrapped chocolate Nicolo peeking out from a Fabergé egg.

As she sat alone in the drawing room waiting for the first of her family to arrive, Ilse was delighted to hear in the foyer the voice not of her father, not of her sister or brother-in-law, not even of the venerable elder Kassners, but of Martin, chatting pleasantly with the butler. She rose as he entered the drawing room, dapper as ever in his evening black and white.

"Marty dear, what a lovely surprise!" she exclaimed, taking his hands and kissing his cheek. "I wasn't expecting to see you tonight. After all these years, have you finally decided to join our little party?"

"Grubby-handed children running about the house with sugar coursing through their veins? I think I will pass," he laughed. "No, tonight I'm on my way to a concert. I just thought I would stop by on my way to the opera house to see how you are faring. You always seem to be at the office when I drop in, no matter the time of day. But tonight, at least, I knew I'd find you at home."

"Find me you have, and I am so glad." She smiled and motioned to the chairs by the fireplace, and the two sat down next to the roaring blaze.

"How have you been?" he asked.

"Oh, about as well as you, I imagine," she replied, offering him a sympathetic smile.

"That I find hard to believe. My distractions have been of a much more amusing variety. I hear you hardly leave the house except to go to work."

"It's a busy time. My duties keep me engaged."

"But there must be someone else who could—"

"Oh, you know me," she interrupted, waving off his concern.

"Yes, I'm afraid I *do* know you, which is precisely why I worry you may be trying to take too much on yourself. Rome wasn't built in a day, and it wasn't built by a single set of hands, either."

"Oh, pish!" She scrunched her face into a charming pout. "If I was a man, you'd be congratulating me on my drive and determination."

"If you were a man," he corrected, "I'd be taking you out

and getting you good and soused."

Ilse laughed. She couldn't remember the last time she had done so.

"But since I can hardly do that," Martin continued, "I'll simply encourage you to come up for air every now and then."

"Oh, the air is highly overrated. Every time I come up, I find it is not much worth breathing, and I ask myself, *Why not just stay under?*"

Martin shook his head, tutted, drew a silver cigarette case out of his pocket. He did not take out a cigarette, simply moved the case between his hands. Ilse recognized it instantly; it had been a Christmas gift from Heinrich three years before.

"In all seriousness," Martin said, "what are you doing, Ilse? You can't be happy, spending all your time alone, hiding your head under a mound of work like an ostrich in the sand."

She sighed. "It's complicated. I wouldn't want to bore you."

"Try me."

Her eyes were drawn again to the cigarette case, the light reflecting off it as it flipped back and forth in Martin's hands. Flashing like Morse. A message coded in light.

"If you must know," she said, "I feel I owe it to Heinrich to secure his legacy. He never could stomach the idea of able men sitting idle and watching their families starve just because no one had the gumption to employ them. Nor can I, for that matter. And I know you and I have never seen eye to eye on this," she said, putting up her hand before Martin could protest, "but it was important to Heinrich, and it's just as important to me. Perhaps even more so . . ." Her voice broke off, and for a moment, she grew pensive, turning her gaze to the fire.

"It's not lost on me, you know . . . what an easy run I've had. I was spared the horrors of the Great War and its aftermath because my father had the foresight to ship me overseas and keep me there for years. Then I came back here and was spared the hardships of the Depression because a wealthy man happened to think me reasonably good company. I'll never understand why, but it seems fortune has decided to forgive my many failings. I'm almost ashamed when I think how little I've suffered compared to everyone else."

"And so, in exchange for your privilege, you must spend your entire life doing penance?" Martin put the cigarette case away and leaned forward, supporting himself on his forearms. His expression was equal parts empathy and accusation.

"Not exactly. But I do owe it to those who have been less fortunate to not forget their plight, to never forget that I am luckier than I have ever deserved to be. And besides," Ilse continued, blinking back a tear that was threatening, "I enjoy the work. I enjoy being *useful*. I can't imagine sitting around here doing nothing all day in this big empty house."

"Well, I'll not argue with you on that head," Martin conceded. "My friends have encouraged me to trade up, buy a larger place, maybe take advantage of some poor fool's misery and pick up one of the great houses in foreclosure. But I can't stomach having so much space to fill." He looked around the room with its high ceilings and intricately carved moldings. It was one of the cozier spots in the house but still far too large to be comfortable. "Do you think you will end up selling?" he asked.

"How could I?" Ilse answered. "Heinrich is here. I can still see him lounging in that chair at the end of a long night, reigning over the dining room table, greeting guests in the foyer . . ."

"Oh, I almost forgot!" Martin suddenly exclaimed, fishing through his pockets. "I have something for you . . . somewhere . . . *ah-ha!* Here it is." He pulled an envelope from the inside of his dinner jacket and handed it to her. "Just call me Nicolo," he said, grinning.

"What's this?" she asked, examining the letter. On the back was simply written *The Baroness Jörger von Tollet.*

"It's a letter," he stated matter-of-factly.

"Yes, thank you, I had worked that much out for myself. But who is it from?"

Martin cleared his throat. "It's . . . uh . . . from Oberst Hess. It was enclosed in a note I had from him the other day. He said he had mislaid your address and asked that I deliver it to you."

"Oh," Ilse said, trying to sound unbothered. "I am sure he is just writing to send his condolences. Very kind of him, after so short an acquaintance. I will read it later." She laid it calmly on the table between them.

I see I shall have my work cut out for me, Martin mused.

Just then, the laughter and squeals of the Kassner children were heard outside. "And that is my cue to depart," he declared good-humoredly.

In the foyer, Therese shouted, "*Your sister's hair is not a high-wire!*"

Martin and Ilse laughed, baffled as to what could have prompted such a scolding.

He rose to leave, and as soon as his back was turned, Ilse grabbed the letter and tucked it safely behind the strap of her brassiere. She did not know whether Junius had mentioned their reunion to Friedrich or if he or Therese would recognize the handwriting on the envelope, but she didn't want to take the chance. She was in no state to withstand interrogation.

"Thank you so much for stopping in, Marty dear," Ilse said warmly as she escorted him out. "I know I haven't been around as I should. I don't want us to drift apart. I promise I will try to do better, to be around more."

"And I promise to never stop trying to hold you to that." He pressed her hand and braced himself before opening the door, hoping to slip undetected through the pandemonium on the other side.

***

Later that night, after the adults had been wined and dined and the children had been taken away to set out their shoes and dream of the delights Nicolo would leave in them, Ilse wandered into Heinrich's bedroom.

Even in its emptiness, she found comfort here. It was as if Heinrich's spirit had latched onto the thick fibers of the crimson carpets, lodged itself in the many curios he'd always kept about him. A bone box from Tibet. A rusted Bariba dagger. The opera glasses through which he watched the premiere of *Salome*. A rock from the top of the Matterhorn. A marble elephant with jewel inlays, purportedly carved by the same hands that built the Taj Mahal. Little snapshots of Heinrich Jörger.

And then there were the books. Covering every surface, spilling out of shelves, stacked in corners, lining the baseboards. Giving off musty smells of leather and dust and dried-out leaves. The maids secretly longed to clear them out but knew better than to suggest it.

Sitting on the edge of the bed where Heinrich had suffered his last days, surrounded by his most precious possessions, Ilse breathed his spirit in and felt bolstered. She reached into her dress and pulled out the letter from Junius Hess.

For several minutes she sat there, holding the note in her hand, staring at the neat lettering on the outside of the envelope. It occurred to her that this was the first time Junius had ever written to her, the first time she had even seen his handwriting. Its sensible precision surprised her. Rather than the slanted scrawl of a troubled artist, as she might once have expected, his writing was upright and legible. Like a stenographer. Or a shop attendant. Would the letter's contents be equally reserved, or would Junius's words contain the eloquence she'd once known him capable of producing? She hardly knew which she preferred. Finally convincing herself that it didn't matter one way or the other, she pulled open the seal.

November 23, Linz

Gnädige Frau,

News very recently reached me of your husband's passing. Our acquaintance consisted of only a few weeks, but I esteemed the Baron highly, and I am sure you and all those who loved him must feel his loss keenly. Though I can hardly hope any sentiments I offer could bring you comfort and peace, it is my dearest wish that you will find them.

Indelicate as it is, I must also beg your indulgence in allowing me to offer my apologies for the coldness of our parting. In the months since I last saw you, I have come to regret having left things the way I did, and I ask your forbearance as I clear my conscience and attempt to provide something resembling an explanation.

For a very long time, I had been used to believing myself the victim in our sordid history. Hearing that you, too, had suffered was incongruous with an assumption I long ago settled as fact. At first, I had great difficulty accepting it. Since we parted, though, I have had time to think about what you said. I now realize your words had more truth than I was willing to allow.

I see now that you were right to be hurt. You had every cause to feel frightened. I took liberties with you, and, looking back with a renewed perspective, I am now rightly ashamed of having taken them. And I do not refer only to the last night we shared. From almost the moment of our meeting, I took liberties with you that I would never have taken with a woman of my own station. It is not that I thought you low—I knew you were from a very respectable family—but I knew that you were not someone I could ever consider marrying, so I felt few qualms about carrying out our affair. Quite ironically, had I hoped to marry you, I would never have gotten to know you half so well and would never have loved you half so well. But now I see that, even loving you as I did—especially loving you as I did—I was wrong. Knowing I was raising expectations I could never fulfill, I still never had the decency to tell you the affair would go nowhere. I led you down a dangerous path, willfully blind to everything but my own selfish pleasure in being with you.

Even now, I continue to take liberties simply by recording these confessions on paper. I am risking that this letter might fall into the wrong hands because I cannot continue in this world without your forgiveness. I cannot bear to think you might somehow elude me for another twenty years and I might carry this regret for the rest of my life.

I know I should not be saying these things. Please do not think me disrespectful of your husband's memory. Grief must have its time; the heart must have space to recover. But one day, after enough time has passed, I hope you will not refuse to see me. I pray that we can start again.

With humility and fondest affection,
Junius Hess

END VOLUME III

I once read a theory of time. It purported that time divides among infinite realities. Every action, each possible choice splits onto a separate path, creating a million parallel worlds where different versions of us thrive or falter.

I don't know if there is any truth in this. But it's a lovely idea, isn't it? To think that somewhere out there is a world where I said no instead of yes, paused instead of pressing forward, turned left instead of right. I followed an entirely different path and found myself an entirely different person in an entirely different place.

In one world, I grow old, surrounded by family, drowning in children and grandchildren. Their husbands and wives, their wayward in-laws. When I depart that world, they mourn the loss of their matriarch but laugh over stories of the joy I brought them, the love and confidence we shared. They cherish each blessed memory.

In another world, I am warm and eccentric. My beauty lies in the mistakes I make every day and the humor with which I accept them. My grace is shared through the music of my laughter. It rings out as I poke fun at myself.

In another world, I am kind. Well, clearly kind. My kindnesses require no explanation. They are not shrouded by layers of logic and economy and intent.

In another world, my heart is open, and I follow it. Choices present as black and white, not some constant smudge of gray. Nothing is complicated. Interests do not conflict. One choice is good, the other is bad. And I choose only good. Always.

But we don't live in any of those worlds.

CONCEIVED TO BE HUMBLED

"Misery is fertile soil for the seeds of hate to take root in," her father warned. "Hate springs up from the bare land, spreads invasively as a weed. Once it emerges, even hope cannot be trusted. Hope convinces us these strange new plants will blossom into flowers. By the time we see them for the blight they are, they have proliferated beyond control."

Rather a poetic turn from the mind of a jaded public servant, but still very like Dr. Eder. When all was well, his thinking was linear and logical; when saddled with worry, he expressed himself in metaphor. As though the beauty of his words could somehow make reality less frightening, make men less depraved.

Dr. Eder could speak in elegy, but even his most florid prose would not erase the blight creeping over the land. Ilse saw it everywhere. It darkened the hollow eyes waiting on the bread line and ravaged once idyllic villages, leaving swaths of destitution in its wake. It even burrowed into the hearts of her workers who, though thankful for their employment, begrudged the guilt they felt in simply providing for their families when so many others could not.

Victimhood. Anger. Resentfulness. Distrust. Blame.

Combine with all this the continued weight of oppression, of democratic hopes doused by an increasingly repressive regime, and the soil was indeed tilled and ready for planting.

But what could be done? Ilse knew well that little could be

done. She threw herself into her work, employing hundreds in a failing enterprise. What more could she do? Sell Heinrich's house? Even if she were willing to part with her memories, there was no one to buy it. And suppose she were to bleed her accounts dry, endow her inherited millions on the suffering thousands, any relief she might provide would be fleeting. She could change a year for a lucky few or a day for the many. But the sun would still rise on the same battered world.

The cruelest part of a broken system is its resistance to being mended by well-meaning hands. And increasingly, Ilse was becoming convinced the system was, indeed, broken. Her country was failing because it had been *designed* to fail. Their failure was the punishment meted out to an empire that no longer existed. How could they thrive when they were conceived to be humbled, to be humiliated? A country of eight million desperate souls—a quarter of them packed into the once flourishing capital, an imperial city that had swelled when it had half of Europe to feed it.

She had not always been so pessimistic. For years, Ilse resisted despair. She had believed in her and her father's work after the Great War, chiseling a foothold for Austria in a reimagined world. She had been so proud when he decided to continue working for the new republic after their return to Vienna. They had both trusted that if good men only kept plodding for long enough, it would all come together eventually. It would because it *had to*. There was no alternative.

But few had shared their optimism. Where the Eders placed their faith in the state, others pledged loyalty to faction. Factions with such diametrically opposed dreams for the country—one a pastoral idealism seeking return to some imagined harmonious past; the other a fantasy of a modern, classless society—that they were blind to common enemies. While their weapons were trained on each other, radical notions spread like a virus, a pestilence devastating the land.

No, Ilse was convinced, their best days were not ahead of them. Nothing she nor anyone else did could steer a country craving self-destruction onto a different course.

And so, she chose to endure. For herself, for her tenants, for the men and women whose livelihoods depended on her. No matter what it cost her, she would continue Heinrich's legacy. No family would be made homeless if she could keep a decent roof over their heads. No man would go hungry if she could afford to employ him.

Ilse vowed to persevere in a world gone mad.

ON THE INSIDE OF HER WRIST

Snow blanketed Vienna's frozen streets, but the air in Ilse's room was close and warm. She sat at her writing desk, staring at the letter in her hands. She read its contents, then reread them. Just as she had done so many times before. She had lost count of how many times. So often that the corners of the pages had softened and curled. So often the edges of the paper had grown as feathery as the frost painted across her window.

She didn't know what she hoped to accomplish. No answers would leap from the careful lettering that had not emerged on a hundred other reviews. But she read it again anyway. It was the only thing she could do to still her mind as she waited for the clock to tick away enough minutes for her to depart for Restaurant St. Annahof.

She had been there many times over the years. Each time, it brought back memories of the first time she dined there, the night Heinrich introduced her to Martin. She recalled how petrified she had been that night. Sensing how important this man was to Heinrich—and thus how important it was that they learn to coexist—Ilse had been desperate to secure Martin's approval. She spent the evening releasing nervous energy however she could without drawing attention. Threading her napkin through her fingers under the table. Scrunching and releasing her toes within her shoes. No one had seen, no one had known. Outwardly, she was the definition of calm. *Positively charming,* as

Heinrich had assured her afterward.

Years later, Ilse told Martin how flustered she had been that first night. He had laughed heartily at her expense, comparing her to a swan, regally serene above the surface, frenzied effort beneath. For days, he insisted on calling her *Swannie*, but as the name never seemed to ruffle her feathers, Martin soon lost interest in his joke.

Swannie. Ilse smiled, remembering. The glimmer in Martin's eye each time he tested it. Heinrich's satisfaction as he realized the two of them had grown close enough to needle each other.

Tonight, Ilse's nerves had another source. Far from being determined to please, she was unsure what her objective for the evening was. It was this uncertainty that rattled her.

She read the letter again.

More than a year had passed since Martin had placed it into her hands. At first, she was astonished by its contents and completely torn as to how to feel about them. A part of her, naturally, had been gratified by the tenderer sentiments the letter contained, the feeling poured so palpably into its pages. To think she could inspire such emotion, especially in a man as reserved as she then believed Junius to be, was astounding. And she felt validated by its professions of past affection. At the same time, she could not overlook Junius's more offensive confessions. That he never had serious designs, had thought only of passing pleasure, had been as careless with her heart as he had been with her reputation. At the green age of nineteen, he had approached her as little more than a *süsses Mädel.* Someone just high enough to make her manners pleasing, but low enough that she might love him for love's sake alone, without any thought to a future together. As if she'd been a shopgirl. A dancer in the opera.

Of course, he had not come right out and said so. But his meaning was perfectly clear.

It was not just that he had affronted Ilse's pride. His honest words stung her. Deeply. And yet, she knew that in offering them, Junius was trying to make amends, to wipe clean the mistakes of the past so they might have some hope of a new beginning.

Ilse had been so disarrayed that it was two weeks before she could bring herself to answer him. Even then, she had to force her hand to take up the pen. She knew that every day she delayed must be Junius's torment, and undecided as her feelings were, she did not want that. Even reading the worst of his words, she hated to think of him suffering. Not knowing what to say, her response had been concise and respectful. *I thank you for your sympathy and kind condolences. The sentiments you expressed were most welcome during what has been a difficult time. I wish you and your family peace and joy during this holiday season.* Her words were vague, neither cold nor encouraging, and would, she'd hoped, buy her time to learn her own mind.

To his credit, Junius kept his distance, just as he had promised. He gave her space to grieve. He made no special trip to Vienna. He did not rush her door with roses the moment a year had expired. Weeks, then months passed, and in wondering where Junius was, why he did not come, Ilse's wounded pride healed over. Her hardened heart softened toward him. There were even times when she felt a strange stirring, a tingling, like ants crawling beneath her skin, and she almost thought she yearned to see him. But then she reminded herself that she was thirty-nine years old, well beyond the age of being susceptible to such itches. *I probably just drank too much coffee today*, she convinced herself.

In the end, Junius waited nearly a year and a half. Six months longer than the minimum respectable for mourning. After being so reckless in the past, it was like he was taking extra care now to ensure his pursuit carried no whiff of scandal.

Or perhaps it wasn't respect that had kept him away. Maybe

his mind was simply as unresolved as Ilse's.

Whichever was the case, he was here now, waiting with Martin at Restaurant St. Annahof. Ilse was to meet them there at eight o'clock, and she was determined to wait until that time to leave her house. By arriving late, she could ensure Martin and Junius would both reach the restaurant before her. Ilse abhorred tardiness but could stomach a bit of hypocrisy if it meant sidestepping the awkwardness of sitting alone with either of them.

At last, the chiming of the grandfather clock in the study echoed up through the house. Ilse folded the letter and stowed it with care in the back of the desk. With unanswered questions still swirling through her mind, she walked down the stairs and out of the house. Stepping outside, she raised her ermine collar against the snow and the wind, and with a cordial greeting to the driver who held open the door, she stepped into the car.

Like many of Vienna's finer restaurants, St. Annahof had sprung up in one of the city's many ballrooms that long ago had fallen out of regular use. In the center of the room, two crystal chandeliers, reminders of a more elegant time, were suspended from high, ornate ceilings. Drifting through their soft light at the heels of the maître d', Ilse spotted Martin on the far side of the room.

Martin rose when he noticed her approaching, as did Junius, whose back was to her. He turned to watch Ilse's progress across the crowded room. As Ilse drew closer, her reservations began to dissolve. Gone was the hardness and restraint she had seen in Junius when they met two years before. In their place, she saw echoes of the warmth and earnestness of former days.

Echoes of her Junius.

She arrived at the table and greeted Martin with her usual breezy "Hello, Marty dear," along with a peck in the direction of each cheek. She then extended a trembling hand toward Junius. He took it and held it gently, as if handling something fragile and precious. Bowing down, he turned her hand and kissed the inside of her wrist, softly, his lips barely brushing her skin. It was a subtle gesture that would pass unnoted before the gawking restaurant crowd, the gossips eyeing them from behind their menus. Anyone watching would have assumed nothing more than a polite and sociable kiss of the hand. It escaped even Martin's notice.

But Junius's message was received by the person for whom it was intended. Ilse knew it for what it was. An intimacy. An invitation. To feel something more. To want something more. To ask it of him. Ilse had extended such an invitation once. All those years ago. Standing next to the river in the rain, huddled beneath the overhang of the boathouse. Soaked through and shivering. She'd invited Junius to be the one who removed her chill. And now, all these years later, he was asking the same of her.

When Junius straightened up, he looked into Ilse's eyes, and a weight lifted. Each released a breath that had been held for more than twenty years. They exhaled it in quick, nervous laughter, like two jittery teenagers who had misstepped during a dance.

Martin could only look on in amazement and mentally curse Heinrich for being right once again.

***

For over a year, a question had been frequently posed at dinner tables and in drawing rooms of Vienna's best houses: *Whatever has become of Baroness Jörger?* For over a decade, Ilse had established herself as a fixture of Viennese society, charming the men, delighting the ladies, and providing a model of aspiration to awkward young daughters of every house she entered. Of course, Heinrich's illness had been no secret, and Ilse's right to mourn was respected. Still, a widow need not shut herself away once the freshness of first mourning has passed.

Ilse knew her absence had not gone unnoticed. She knew she had withdrawn from society for too long. Far too long. But being the Baroness Jörger von Tollet took effort. Pretense demanded energy, exertion, and since Heinrich's death—since his diagnosis, really—she had simply lacked the stamina to maintain the façade. Rather than risk a slip, or worse, a fall from grace, she shut herself away. She went to the office, prevented disasters, did everything she could to keep the whole endeavor from collapsing. She welcomed her family and closest friends into her home and appeared at the occasional dinner with the Kassners. But attending to society more broadly had been out of the question.

After their dinner at St. Annahof, Ilse and Junius each knew instinctively that the other wished to further the acquaintance, see if anything worth salvaging remained between them. Also implicit were the challenges they faced. Junius could not call on Ilse privately. He would not risk scandal and rumor. And as much as Ilse esteemed Martin, she loathed the idea that she and Junius would only ever meet under his close and curious eye.

And so, Ilse found her way back into the wider world, and she discovered that, with proper motivation, she could summon the fortitude to endure it.

Only Martin discerned how Ilse's reentry coincided precisely with Oberst Hess's stays in Vienna and how the oberst's business in the capital was calling him there more and more frequently. Martin noticed because he had orchestrated it, pulling the strings so skillfully his puppets didn't even feel the tugs. He would simply mention to Ilse that he had heard she received an invitation from Countess Paar or Ritter Beranek and encourage her to rally her spirits enough to join them. If he should drop into their conversations the names of common acquaintances he expected to be in attendance, what could be more natural than that? And why should these lists not include Oberst Hess when he happened to be in the city?

On such occasions, Junius studied Ilse as an anthropologist might observe an unknown civilization: at a distance but with keen interest. She was so very different from the girl he had once known. No longer did she endeavor to fade into the background. When Ilse Jörger entered a room, the tides parted to admit her. If she but shifted her weight from one foot to the other, the world paused to find the source of the tremor.

Even in middle-age, Ilse held every man in Vienna under her spell, from the youngest upstarts to the staunchest old imperialists. Their eyes followed her with rapt attention. Like a Siren of the western sea, her laughter, practiced though it was, called them into her orbit. More incredible still was the reverence in which the women in her company held Ilse. Rather than forcing smiles when they met her, rather than jealously pursing their lips, these women seemed to compete for even the slimmest share of Ilse's notice. To be permitted to kiss her cheek or press her hand was a luxury, a rare opportunity to absorb a bit of the baroness's grace. To be singled out for her attention was to be honored among women.

To Junius, though, there was something contrived in the way Ilse engaged with the world. Something artificial, plastic. Her expression was too serene, her smiles too consistent, her manners too fawning. Her banter read like a *feuilleton*, sparkling but safe, lacking in depth. There was nothing to pique genuine interest.

And yet, at every gathering they attended, the devoted flocked to worship at the altar of Ilse Jörger. Watching from the periphery, Junius, who had known and loved Ilse *Eder*, struggled to match the world's adoration.

But every now and then, when they chanced a private conversation, if he unraveled the dignity and poise, looked past the wit and easy charm, Junius could see flickers of Ilse's former self.

In the crack of a smile, in a suppressed roll of an eye. He convinced himself the old Ilse still resided behind the immaculate mask. In time, she might trust him enough to let him resurrect the woman she once had been.

Ilse, too, was busy forming opinions.

The tenderness Junius displayed in that fleeting moment at St. Annahof had by no means established itself as a fixture of his character. Junius had always had a tendency toward dejection; Ilse knew that. Even before the Great War, his earnestness and fervor had been intermixed with moodiness. Indeed, Ilse's ability to pull him out of these sulks was one of the things that had endeared her to him, and vice versa. But now, even as the frost had thawed, even as she could feel him warming to her, gravity remained the dominant trait of his personality. It was like he was so accustomed to gloom he struggled to break the habit. Ilse grew determined to make him laugh or smile despite himself, and she felt immense pride at how quickly she became adept at doing so.

Martin watched their progress with satisfaction. Each time he saw Junius whisper some private remark in Ilse's ear, whenever she playfully reprimanded Junius and a bit of the oberst's stiffness chipped away, Martin congratulated himself on a job well done.

He had delivered on his promise to Heinrich. He had thrown them into each other's paths.

Now all they needed was time.

ALL COMING BACK

"What would you say about the three of us getting out of the city for a bit?" Junius looked expectantly at Ilse and Martin, who glanced at each other, trying to decide who would be the first to respond.

It was a flawless June day. Sapphire skies. Warm but not yet oppressive with the sun beating down on the small sidewalk café where they awaited their lunch. Ilse, in what had become her trademark style, wore an ivory silk blouse paired with a linen pencil skirt. The ensemble was sophisticated yet simple, made with expensive fabrics and quality construction to maintain the respect of her social sphere but cut into basic enough designs that her employees would not dismiss her as frivolous. Martin sported a seersucker suit he'd picked up the year before during a business trip to New York, which he insisted was the height of style and summer practicality, despite Ilse's endless teasing. Only Junius still sweated away in his winter wool suit.

"Get out of the city?" Junius's proposal had caught Ilse in a rare flat-footed moment. "What did you have in mind?"

"Well," he continued, "as I sit here roasting inside this portable sauna, it occurs to me that I cannot possibly manage for much longer in the city this summer. I will either have to return home to change out my wardrobe or hire a servant to follow me around with a poultry baster. And as much as I would love to be in a position to put a good man to work, I'm not sure the sight would be appreciated in many dining rooms around the city. To make a long story short, I must head back to Linz soon. I thought the two of you might relish the chance to escape for a couple of weeks."

"It's unexpected," Ilse replied. "I'll have to check my calendar and see if things can be adequately sorted out. When were you thinking of going?"

"I suppose I can tough it out here through Derby Day and then head out after."

"Oh, hang your calendar, Ils!" exclaimed Martin. "I'm sure they can manage without you for two measly weeks."

"Hang nothing," she said coolly. "If I miss a board meeting, I'm sure I'll come back and find they have shuttered a cannery or locked up one of the mills, and fifty more men will be standing on the breadline."

"And with fifty fewer salaries drawing on your savings, your bankers will sing praises to the skies!"

"Savings," Ilse replied with a flippant scoff. "What good are savings? What use is comfort if everyone around us is miserable?"

"So, why not spend down to the last, and then you can all be miserable together!"

This was a familiar debate for Ilse and Martin, one they had engaged in countless times. Though their manner of discussing it oscillated between playful and sardonic, the issue of what to do about the Jörger Corporation remained as intractable a dispute as it had been when Heinrich was alive. Martin could never bring himself over to the Jörgers' perspective. It was one of the few areas of their lives together where he forever felt like an interloper.

"Oh, come now, Marty, you exaggerate. You know you do."

"I do no such thing! Don't forget, unlike you, I know what it is to teeter on the edge of insolvency. I watched my father toe the line every year of his life, even in the best of times. I know how fickle the world can be. One day you're up; the next day, you're down. You may have money to throw away now, but who can tell what tomorrow will bring. I say this as your friend. It makes no sense to keep taking such risks. It would be one thing if you were a man, but you are a woman."

"Keenly noted, but irrelevant," she remarked glibly, lowering her chin and glaring over the rims of her sunglasses.

"You know very well it's not. Don't try to pretend otherwise. How many times have I heard you rail that men are more than happy to take your money but will never take your ideas? Even a woman as capable as you will have few means to build back up if everything should one day come crashing down. Junius, surely, you agree with me. Tell her I am right!"

Sprightly as the tone of this conversation was, Junius knew Ilse well enough to know there was genuine sentiment behind it. Ilse was not obstinate for obstinacy's sake. When she cared little, she would drop a point without a second thought. But if something *really* mattered to her, and she truly believed she was in the right, she could fight as fiercely as any man. And Heinrich's company was something that really mattered. Keeping her men in jobs was Ilse's way of affecting a tiny bit of good in a disappointing world. She felt a duty to them, and nothing anyone could say would convince her to let them down. Her manner may have been silk, but her will would be iron. As much as Junius wished them to join him at Hess Manor, he would not force Ilse's hand.

"I will own that you are correct about one thing, Martin," Junius replied with a sly glance at Ilse. "Ilse is, as you say, a woman. The rest I leave to the two of you."

"Exceedingly wise, Junius dear," Ilse said, reaching across the table and squeezing his hand. "But, Marty, I know you have my best interests at heart, and so I will concede that, should there be nothing on my calendar requiring my presence in the city, I will be exceedingly happy to leave town for two weeks."

It was a trifling concession, given that it left Ilse exactly where she had started, but it was enough to satisfy Martin. "That is all I ask," he declared, unfolding his napkin and dropping it across his lap with a victorious pat. "Because you deserve a break, and so do I. Junius, old chap, I will speak for the both of us: we would be delighted."

For his part, Martin did not much relish the idea of spending half a month on Junius's estate. If he was going to be dragged out of the city, he would much rather go to one of the mountain resorts, where there might be a chance of finding a decent bit of action. But he could see through his friend's ruse. Junius needed to get Ilse to Linz. He needed to introduce her to his children, to see if their worlds could be knitted together. Ilse could not go alone, of course, and after the humiliation of losing their adjoining estate, her sister and brother-in-law would never agree to go there with her. And Ilse's curious knack for collecting admirers without forging actual friendships meant she could not conceivably call on anyone else for such an errand.

Whether she would admit it or not, Ilse needed him.

***

Junius took in a contented breath as they finally reached full speed away from the clutter of city traffic. "Can you think of any greater felicity than driving through the open air in the front seat of a Mercedes-Benz 500K cabriolet?"

His question was directed at Ilse, but it was Martin who answered, shouting from the back seat. "I shall tell you once I have experienced it!" He made rather a pitiful figure in his green-tinted driving goggles, his neck scarf flapping unforgivably, swatting him in the face as he spoke. He gripped his hat with both hands to prevent it from taking flight.

"Terribly sorry about the wind!" Junius shouted back. "If it gets to be too much, just let me know. We can always pull off, and you can hop over to the luggage car!"

Ilse looked back at Martin just in time to see him wrap his scarf around his head and knot it below his chin to keep his fedora from blowing away. He then swung his legs up onto the seat, crossed his arms like a petulant child, and wedged himself in for a nap. Ilse laughed, as much at Martin's display of displeasure as at the foolishly ingenious bonnet he had fashioned. "Poor Marty is such a good sport," she said. "He will suffer any indignity before he stoops to joining his servant."

Unlike Martin the Martyr, Ilse had little cause for complaint. She was ensconced next to Junius, gazing across the verdant expanse of the Wachau Valley, protected by the windshield and an airy silk chiffon headscarf.

They whipped past lush vineyards and quaint farmsteads, slowing only to drive through villages along the way. Ilse bade her eyes not to linger on the more disheartening sights as they drove. Men sitting on crates outside dormant factories, staring out like sleepwalkers, their expressions blank, their hands idle. Children picking through piles of rubbish for any scrap their mothers might use, hock, or barter. *In two weeks*, Ilse reminded herself, *you will be home again. Then you can continue doing your part to keep the dam from breaking.*

But for today, she was resolved to be happy. Whether she *felt* happy or not was beside the point. She was with Junius. He was taking her to see his home. He was taking her to meet his children. If she couldn't marshal a bit of happiness now, what would it possibly take to get her there?

She forced herself to focus on Junius's conversation. Admittedly with some difficulty at times. She had always been baffled by the ability of men to talk about their automobiles, and Junius was proving no exception. The car was clearly his pride and joy. He spoke at length about its independent suspension, the double-joint rear swing axle, the double wishbone axle at the front. The subject could not arouse Ilse's interest, but she could still take pleasure in indulging him.

They had set out from Vienna early that morning while smoke from the Derby Day fireworks still clung to the humid air, catching the dawn and filling the city with a haunting orange haze. Junius drove Martin and Ilse in his sparkling roadster while Martin's valet followed behind in a more sensible sedan.

For years, Ilse—who had managed to walk the earth all her life without a lady's maid—had ridiculed Martin about his insistence on still employing a valet. But today, even she had to admit the arrangement had its benefits. After all, without someone to drive the second car, she would have faced strict limits on her suitcases, hardly desirable when one hopes to make an impression.

About an hour into their journey, they stopped in Melk to fuel the cars. While there, they decided to take breakfast at an inn in the shadow of the abbey church, which loomed high on the cliffs above the town, a constant reminder to residents that no sin was committed in secret.

As much from interest as from charity, Ilse invited Martin's valet to join them for their meal. She even managed to coax enough words from him to learn he had once trained as a violinist, but his father had lost all his savings in the inflation of 1922.[41] With gratitude and pride, the young man said he owed everything he had to Herr Rezek, and Ilse silently vowed never to tease Martin about his valet again.

After breakfast, they continued toward Linz. Coming in from the south, they drove through the heart of the city before crossing the Danube and catching the road out to Hess Manor. Ilse found herself awash in memories as they worked their way through streets she had not traveled since she was a girl. Up the bustling Landstrasse they drove, past the magnificent Ursuline

Church and the busy central square. And then, before she knew it, they had emerged from the city center and were winding their way back into the countryside.

They passed the gates of what had once been Bergesschatten. An ostentatious sign indicated it was now the Glasenbach Country Retreat for Rest and Restoration. Ilse heaved a sigh for her in-law's fall from grace, but a moment later, they were turning off the main road and motoring up the crushed-gravel drive that led to Hess Manor.

Ilse's breath caught when the house came into view.

It was just as she remembered it.

The exterior of the house was less impressive than its neighbor's. In his attempt to signal his family's consequence, the former Herr Kassner had lavished on Bergesschatten every embellishment that Baroque style could excuse. Hess Manor, on the other hand, displayed a dignified simplicity. Its builder had nothing to prove. He had been a man of unquestioned import with no need to flaunt it. The medieval manor house was merely a large and efficient residence. Its flat stucco walls rose four stories to a red clay-tile roof, with space for eleven windows to spread across each level in the front and six stretching to the back.

Outside and waiting to greet them, the household staff was lined up to the right, each standing erect as a soldier in formation. To the left, a young lady, a young man, two smaller children, and a respectable-looking older woman were similarly posed.

The guests were helped from the car, and Junius introduced Ilse and Martin to his children one by one.

First was Juna, a striking young woman of fifteen with jade eyes and her mother's flaxen hair. Lips pursed, eyes scanning for flaws, she greeted Ilse with the kind of unvarnished contempt only a girl of fifteen can muster.

Next was Kurt, a strapping boy of thirteen who was his sister's twin in coloring, but far more congenial in his greeting.

Then came Sebastian, dark-haired and solemn, who would doubtless grow into a faithful copy of his father. At nine years, Sebastian insisted he was a man. He shook Ilse's hand with a firmness that made her smile despite her best efforts to mirror his serious expression.

And finally, there was little Arabella, who bore her mother's name and for whom that beautiful lady had given her life. With sharp, clever eyes and a head full of wild curls, six-year-old Ari stole Ilse's heart even before she presented her visitor with a cluster of primula, roots and all, and then shyly hid her face in her nurse's skirt.

After they'd met the children, Junius introduced the lady standing at the end of the row holding little Ari's hand. "Ilse, Martin, allow me to present Frau Varga, the children's governess. Frau Varga, this is the Baroness Jörger von Tollet and my old friend, Herr Rezek. They will be staying with us for the next two weeks."

"It is a pleasure to meet you both," she said, bowing her head in polite obeisance.

Martin merely nodded his acknowledgment. A governess was hardly worth his notice. But Ilse was more gracious. She knew winning over the governess would go a long way toward gaining the children's favor.

"The pleasure is mine, Frau Varga," Ilse fawned. "The oberst has told me you are quite the miracle worker, able to teach French, mend scrapes, and chase monsters from under beds without ever batting an eye. *J'espère que nous serons de grandes amies pendant mon séjour ici.*"[42]

The governess nodded and smiled, gratified by such unexpected condescension. But any efforts toward building that friendship would have to wait. Junius abruptly dismissed her, and she shepherded the children into the house ahead of her employer and his party.

For all the time she and Junius had spent together, Ilse had never crossed the threshold of Hess Manor. Junius had been alone at home during Ilse's two months at Bergesschatten. He had never had a reason to host the Kassners, and it would not have been proper for her to visit him there on her own. Even in the carelessness of youth, they never dared to go that far. Ilse had often been curious about his home, and now that her curiosity was being satisfied, it was an effort to swallow her dismay. The rooms through which Junius led them were austere. Their stone walls were unadorned—not a painting or tapestry to be found—and the ancient wood floors were unsoftened by carpets.

Junius anticipated the disappointment hiding beneath Ilse's smiles as she surveyed the empty spaces and quickly explained, "Only for the summer."

"Hmm?"

"My father always ran the house with a naval efficiency. I have tried to carry on his traditions, at least in that regard. We roll up the carpets and put the paintings in storage during the hottest months to help keep the house cool."

"Rather ingenious, I'd say," Martin remarked encouragingly.

Ilse allowed the practicality of this ritual but silently reflected that it could not make the manor a very pleasant place to live. The grand residence took on a lonely, rather institutional aspect. But Ilse refused to let something so trivial as furnishings dampen her mood. Rather than ruminating on the bare rooms, she followed Junius and Martin onto the terrace.

Now this, she thought as her eyes took in the vista, *this I remember.*

Beyond the terrace, the land had been painstakingly carved out, gradually stepping in broad green flats down to the river, which glittered in the distance. A cascade of wide limestone stairs, buttressed by urns overflowing with fuchsia and violet blossoms, descended toward the water. To her left, Ilse could see through the trees to the gazebo and beyond it to the boathouse, where, long ago, she and Junius had shared their first kiss.

It was all coming back to her. Every flutter of her heart, every tingle on her skin, every heady, weak-kneed moment. Ilse breathed in the long-forgotten sensations like they were the air itself, like she would suffocate without them.

A few feet away, Junius was in unusually high spirits, chatting with Martin and pointing out features of the landscaping. As she watched him, Ilse couldn't help wondering whether Junius's mind was flooded with the same thoughts as hers or if memories of another lent such animation to his expression.

NEVER MIND THE RUBBISH

Away from the meddling eyes of Vienna, Ilse and Junius began to find their way back to each other. They inched closer to intimacy without worrying about what speculation they might raise. Strolling along the river in the cool of the dew-kissed mornings, she dared to brush a windblown hair from his eyes. He presumed so far as to take her hand and lift her fingers to his lips.

But even here, breaking through the reserve that had restrained them in the city felt uncomfortable. Unnatural. Wrong, somehow. They had lost themselves once before. Neither was prepared to do so again. Not yet, at least. They stepped tentatively, taking stock of each footfall, searching the ground for any root or rut that might trip them up.

Martin knew his role in all of this and played it admirably. He would lounge about with books, pretending to savor the peace and quiet after unmitigated months in Vienna's din. He did not begrudge Junius and Ilse their time alone and was always happy to swap in when either needed a break from the other's company.

They were far from a solitary trio, however. After Junius's series of increasingly extended absences, news spread quickly of the oberst's return home, and visitors converged on Hess Manor. To most, Junius proudly introduced Ilse, the Baroness Jörger von Tollet, noting her connection to the Kassner family, formerly of Bergesschatten. Over afternoon tea or evening cocktails, Ilse was happy to oblige such guests with updates on the Kassners. How they had been lucky with their investors. How Martin's expertise had helped Friedrich navigate the choppy waters of the last decade. How the family had thrived, particularly the three rowdy members of the youngest generation.

There were other visitors, however, to whom Ilse was not introduced. Several times during their first week, a footman brought in a card on a silver tray, and instead of welcoming the callers in, Junius chose to excuse himself, receiving them in the privacy of his study. Sometimes he would return quickly, seeming slightly rattled but unwilling to waste his breath to say who the visitor had been. Other times he stayed away longer, shutting himself up in the study for an hour or more after escorting the intruder from the house. He would emerge reticent and withdrawn. When directly called on, he would force a smile and offer vague replies. Then his mind would drift off, consumed by cares he was not yet ready to own.

***

One morning about a week after their arrival, Ilse found herself in a rare moment alone. Junius was in his study, attending to some estate business, and Martin was off exploring the surrounding country, a pastime in which Ilse no longer permitted herself to partake. Instead, she curled up in a small morning salon with a translation of Tolstoy's *Anna Karenina*.

Ilse's mind was a thousand miles away in an overheated Russian ballroom. *She saw that Anna was intoxicated with the wine of admiration she had aroused. She saw the trembling light flashing in her eyes and the smile of happiness and excitement that involuntarily curled her lips* . . .

"Oh!"

Ilse was yanked from the fantasy by a surprised Juna Hess.

"I am so very sorry to interrupt you, Gnädige Frau," Juna exclaimed, scanning the room. "I was looking for my father. I would never dream of intruding on your personal time."

"Think nothing of it, my dear," Ilse said warmly, setting aside her book. "Your father has gone off to attend to something, but I am sure he will return soon. Won't you join me?"

Fraulein Hess looked as though she would rather do anything other than engage in a tête-à-tête with her father's friend, but she was too well bred to own it. She politely sat, perching on the very edge of her chair, straight as the barrel of a shotgun, ready to bolt at the earliest excusable moment.

Juna avoided Ilse's eye, choosing instead to look at the works of art that hung around the room. For Ilse's comfort, Junius had refitted this one common room of the house. The rough floors were once again covered in a Persian rug, resplendent with the loveliest hues of turquoise and pink woven into a medallion motif. On the formerly naked walls now hung paintings from the Italian Renaissance, the Dutch masters, the French impressionists. Junius had judiciously selected only the finest pieces to bring out of storage.

"They are lovely, are they not?" Ilse offered. Watching Juna gawk at the artwork, Ilse's heart began to warm to the girl. It had been so long since she'd encountered such a shamelessly unworldly thing. Ilse could almost pity the girl. *So young, so entirely unaware of the relentless trauma that is life.*

"Oh, yes, they are lovely. But I was not thinking about that."

"Oh?"

"No." Juna looked at the paintings for another moment and then locked her gaze squarely on Ilse. "Actually, I was thinking how you must be congratulating yourself."

"Congratulating myself? I'm not sure I follow—"

"Seeing all the trouble Father has gone to for your sake. But then, I'm sure people always go out of their way for your sake, so perhaps you had not noticed."

The warmth Ilse felt evaporated almost as quickly as it had

kindled. Juna's tone was respectful, her mouth curved into an innocent smile, but her eyes flashed a challenge. Ilse refused to rise to it. Juna was little more than a child, after all.

"I'm not sure I would put it that way," Ilse replied evenly. "I try to make all my friends feel welcome, and they do the same in their turn. It is mutual goodwill. And your father is a wonderful man. He simply wants me to feel welcome in his home."

"And you seem more than happy to be welcomed here."

"Yes. I am."

Ilse refused to be rolled, but she could not afford to make an enemy, either. Juna's disapproval had been so instantaneous, was so decided. Ilse knew it had little to do with her personally. A strong-willed girl of fifteen, shut away on a country estate, must want nothing more than to be heard. Juna obviously felt threatened by someone else claiming a share of her father's attention. Ilse needed to show her that, though she might pull away some of Junius's notice, she could also expand Juna's society and open her world to other sources of validation.

"You know, visiting here has been something of a home-coming for me," Ilse shared, her voice still relaxed, still completely unperturbed. "I've lived most of my life in Vienna, but I met your father not far from where we're sitting. That was many years ago, of course, and I've seen many places since then. America, France, Italy, Greece . . . But I always wanted to come back here one day. I have such very fond memories of this place."

Juna, unmoved, was as impassive and taciturn as the portraits on the walls. Ilse tried a different tack.

"Of course, when I was here before, I never had the opportunity to see any of these wonderful paintings. I've been sitting here all morning trying to work out whether that one there is a Botticelli or a Masaccio . . ." Ilse gestured to a painting of a woman in profile wearing a green Renaissance dress. Her blond hair was barely visible beneath a fawn French hood, from which flowed a sheer veil. She was exquisitely beautiful, with a virginal purity. And yet, everything about the woman spoke to discomfort. Her expression was pained, the skin of her face drawn by her tightly secured hair. Bejeweled fingers fidgeted with the neckline of her bodice and the fabric of her sleeve. On the whole, she gave the impression of being imprisoned in the heavy folds of her velvet gown.

"It is Lippi," Juna corrected.

"Lippi?" Ilse asked, sensing that she had hit her mark with the girl this time. "Are you sure?"

"Quite sure," Juna replied, her determined dislike giving way to an irresistible interest. "It has the look of a Masaccio, but that's because it is one of Lippi's earlier works. You see, he started out as a Carmelite priest and watched Masaccio working in a church. That's what inspired him to become a painter. So, before he became confident in his own style, he was heavily influenced by Masaccio. And as for Botticelli . . . well, he eventually was Senor Lippi's student. So, I am not surprised that you saw elements of both. Lippi learned from Masaccio, and Botticelli, in turn, learned from Lippi."

"How very extraordinary!" Ilse exclaimed, pleased with how successfully she had drawn the girl out. "You seem to know a great deal about art history."

"I am certainly no expert," Juna said, more shyly than before, "but I confess, it is a particular interest of mine. It's not just the beauty of the paintings, but the element of . . . detective work, I suppose you might call it. How you can trace influences through time and place. For instance, if you look, you can see in Lippi's suggestion of movement in the fabric of her veil the beginnings of techniques Botticelli would later master."

"I think you may be more of an expert than you give yourself credit for," Ilse said. She smiled as she watched a blush flood the girl's cheeks. "You are fortunate to have such remarkable works at your fingertips. Although I imagine it is a very hard day for you when they are packed away for the summer."

"It is, indeed. I have tried to convince Father not to do it, but he can be a bit rigid when it comes to such things. He says it is for my own good, and if I had ever spent a summer in a house that did not go to such lengths, I would thank him for it."

"I can certainly relate to that. I, too, have a father who can be quite the mule. When I was your age, he was forever doing things *for my own good*. It was devastating to grow up and learn just how often he was right," Ilse said archly.

Juna grinned and blushed in humble concession.

"Do you paint?" Ilse asked after a pause, hoping to continue chipping away at Juna's reserve.

"Whenever I can. Though Father is always telling me I should focus on more rational pursuits. But why should I waste my time on rational things when the world only wants me to curtsy and smile and nod? I'm sure I am much more obliging when I have spent the day with a brush in my hand than with my nose in a book."

Ilse couldn't help laughing at Juna's satirical turn of mind and the offhanded way she delivered this little diatribe. Sitting here with her, watching the girl's face illuminate now that she had been pulled out of her preconceived scorn, Ilse was struck. Juna's eyes sparkled in a rare shade of blue-green, almost teal. Like oxidized copper. Her unruly golden locks were modestly tied back with a ribbon at the base of her neck, but frizzled strands had either pulled loose or refused to be subdued in the first place. The eyes, the hair, the ready exuberance and un-guarded ramblings, the chin that jutted forward as she spoke, like she was daring the world to contradict anything she said. Juna Hess was a younger version of Ilse, the version Ilse had cast aside so long ago.

Therese had once said that Junius's wife reminded her of Ilse, and those same features had clearly been passed down from mother to daughter. The resemblance between Juna and Ilse was uncanny. It was as if Ilse was looking at her own child. Like she had stepped into another life, another world where she had carried and delivered her baby, watched her blossom and grow. Another world where Ilse was not the Baroness Jörger von Tollet but the Baroness von Hess and always had been.

"I should very much like to see your work," Ilse said, stopping her mind from veering into unconstructive territory. "If you would allow me the privilege, that is."

"I don't pretend to be an artist, but I would be pleased to show you sometime," the girl said, glowing. "Only please, don't say anything about it to Father," she added hastily. "I'm not sure he would like me showing them to you."

"It will be our little secret," Ilse agreed.

"Juna." Junius's voice boomed into the calm that had settled over the room, startling Juna and Ilse both. He stood in the doorway with a severe expression on his face.

"Oh, Father, there you are!" his daughter exclaimed, looking mortified at having been caught speaking so freely. For Juna's sake, Ilse hoped he had not overheard much. "Please excuse me, Gnädige Frau." She rose and, with a quick bob of a curtsy, scampered out of the room.

After chatting in the hall with his eldest child, Junius returned and lowered himself with a groan into the chair next to Ilse's.

"Sorry about that," he said, trying but failing to force good humor convincingly into his voice. "She can be a bit of a chatterbox when the mood strikes her. She's still learning how to take stock of her surroundings. Not having a mother's example has been difficult for her." He smiled then, softening as he looked at Ilse.

"There is no need to apologize," Ilse assured him. "I was enjoying our conversation. And I feel for her, you know. I was about her age when I lost my own mother. I know what it's like to figure out how to be in the world without a mother to guide you."

"Yes, and as I recall, you, too, were rather an uncut gem when I met you." Junius grinned and took Ilse's hand, lightly stroking her fingers with his thumb. Each movement sent jolts of electricity up Ilse's arm. "But just look at the bewitching creature you've managed to mold yourself into. I do hope Juna will learn from your example. One day, she might even know you well enough to look to you in her mother's absence."

Junius did not need to say more. His look conveyed the depth of his meaning.

Blood rushed to Ilse's ears. She could hear the beating of her own heart, felt heat prickling her face as she worked to suppress the flush creeping up her neck. She knew what Junius was alluding to, but somehow, she could not bear to hear it. For so long, she had trained every fiber of her being to revolt against intimacy. Detachment was more than merely a habit; it was who she *was*. Letting Junius in meant letting go of herself.

His sweet and suggestive words terrified her.

"Well," Ilse said, forcing a casual tone, "she's a charming girl, and I should be proud to be of any use to her that I can. And she reminds me of someone, you know . . ."

"She is the very image of her mother."

"Well, actually, I was going to say she reminds me of a younger version of myself. But you certainly do have a type, don't you?"

Junius started. An expression crossed his face that Ilse couldn't interpret. Was it confusion? Surprise? Distress? It passed before Ilse could decide. He gave her a strained, closed-lipped smile, squeezed her hand, and slipped into quiet contemplation.

Accustomed as Ilse was to his reticence, at that moment, the silence was agonizing. She grasped for another subject. "Junius, why don't you play anymore?"

"Play?"

"Your guitar," she clarified. "Music was once such an important part of who you were. You loved it better than anything. It didn't surprise me not to hear you play while in Vienna. After all, you were traveling, and why should you have brought a guitar with you? But we've been here for a week, and I've still not had the pleasure of hearing you."

He released her hand and leaned back, seeming almost annoyed at the question. "I don't play anymore," he said flatly.

"But whyever not?"

"Do I need a reason?"

"Yes, I should think so. It just seems so uncharacteristic of you to give it up."

"And can characters not change?" He rose and moved to a window overlooking the terrace.

Ilse could tell she had struck a nerve, but she didn't regret having done so. If Junius was going to allude to a future together, she had to understand the man he was now. All of him.

Junius relented. "I have not played since Bella . . . my wife, Arabella . . . passed. Before I met her, my life for years was nothing but darkness. You had abandoned me, or so I had convinced myself. I had been to war and seen all its horrors. I thought I would live in that darkness for the rest of my days. But then one night, I met Bella . . . well, I didn't *meet* her that night. We had known each other as children but hadn't seen each other for many years. But on that night, she was loveliness itself. She was everything I'd lost when I lost you. Bella brought me back to life. And when she left us, it was like all the light had been removed from my world again. Music and anything else beautiful and good belonged in the light . . . with her."

"You loved her very much, didn't you?" Ilse asked, her voice laden with the crushing certainty that he had given his heart to another, even as he still possessed her own.

"Yes." He turned to her and smiled weakly. "Yes, I did. And for a long time after she left us, I felt the way I had before I met her. That the rest of my days were doomed to be cold and empty."

"I saw her once, you know," Ilse said, going to him, taking his hands in hers. "She was everything you say she was."

"You saw her? When was this?" He did not bother hiding his surprise.

"Oh, years and years ago. Shortly after I returned home to Vienna. I saw the three of you—you, Arabella, Juna—playing in Stadtpark. Juna couldn't have been even two years old at the time."

"You saw us? And you didn't even say hello?"

"Well, I was with Therese, who was very pregnant at the time, and she looked as if she was about to have a heart attack. She was so petrified I was going to confront you and make some big, awful scene. And, really, what good could have come from us meeting then? At best, it would have confused you. At worst, it would have caused you pain."

"I suppose you're right," he said, drawing her hands up around his neck, sliding his own behind her waist, setting Ilse's heart racing again. "I found my way back to you just when I was supposed to."

"Good morning, my friends! Is it safe?" Martin was feeling his way into the room, his right hand covering his eyes. He had teased Ilse and Junius this way for days, even though the most intimate gesture yet to pass between them was a lingering kiss on the cheek.

"Oh, for heaven's sake, Marty!" Ilse stepped away from Junius and sank back into her chair. "You look a perfect fool."

Martin withdrew his hand from his eyes and dramatically clutched at his chest. "Ouch! The lady's daggers are sharp!"

"You are certainly in high spirits today," Junius observed. "Don't tell me, you found some poor milkmaid to defile?"

"Please! Unless she sells her milk to the Duke of York, I haven't the time."

"Well, something certainly has you chipper."

"*Chipper* may be a bit of a stretch. *Self-satisfied* is probably a more apt description."

"Fine, then. What, might I ask, has you feeling so *self-satisfied?*"

"Nothing more than the suspicion that I will very soon be proven right. The fact of the matter will be quite appalling, of course. But, you know, I do so love being the smartest person in the room, so I've decided not to focus on anything beyond that."

"Have you any idea what he's talking about?" Junius asked Ilse.

"None at all," she replied. "And I think we would be safer not asking."

"Oh, come now, that is unfair," Martin protested. "When I have gone all the way to Linz and back just to bring you this intelligence!"

"Linz? Is that where you were? Here I thought you were out clambering over the foothills."

"Clamber? Me? In these? These, my dear lady, are Italian leather!" he exclaimed, displaying his freshly shined shoes. "No, no, I took the car into town this morning, hoping to hear some news of the outside world besides the sanitized drivel they print in the papers. I went to one coffeehouse and then another, but I did not get on at all. The moment I sat down at a table, the fellows sitting there would stop talking and just *stare* at me like I was some sort of circus oddity."

"I keep telling you, this is not Vienna," Junius said. "You're not going to find some total stranger here who will share all their most profound thoughts with you. This is a small community, and the people tend to follow the old ethic. We don't have the benefit of anonymity that you get in the capital, so they will only ever say to you what they know you will agree with."

"Ha, sounds like Ilse at a cocktail party!" Martin quipped while Ilse shot him a look to signal he was on thin ice. He cleared his throat. "Well, it turns out you were right."

"About my own city? Shocking, indeed."

"And so, I left the coffeehouses behind and went to the train station. I thought, surely, if I sat there for long enough, someone useful would pass through. And sure enough, I was right."

"And that is what you are so self-satisfied about?"

"No, no. That, old chap, has to do with what the man told me," Martin explained, finally coming to the crux of his story. "The man was from Frankfurt, passing through on his way to Bratislava. And he told me the news in Germany is that Schuschnigg is on the verge of signing some big agreement with Herr Hitler. Was I not just saying last week that Schuschnigg is about to yield? I swear, the man is totally spineless. He's even worse than the Peasant's Bastard!"

"He means Chancellor Dollfuss," Ilse interpreted for Junius.

"I'm glad to see you have moved so far on from the late chancellor's assassination that you no longer feel any need to respect the dead," Junius reproached.

"Forgive me, my friend, if I fail to properly mourn our dearly beloved dead dictator. He did not respect me in life, and so I see no need to respect him in death."

"So," Ilse jumped in, not wanting her companions to quibble over niceties, "you say this Frankfurter is certain Chancellor

Schuschnigg is getting ready to sign some sort of agreement? Did he say what sort of agreement it was?"

"He did not. But I'm sure it must be something setting us on a path to reunification. What else could it be? Old Schusch has lost Mussolini's backing, and he certainly can't check the Nazis for much longer based on internal support alone. One man in five still holds to the old fantasy of *Anschluss* that was stamped out at St. Germain,[43] never mind the rubbish rotting at the top of the Reich. Of the other four, half are so miserable they would cheer any change so long as it's disruptive enough. As for the rest . . . well, Franz Joseph cowed them into complacency so well they confuse resignation for patriotism."

Whether it was the news itself or Martin's flippant handling of it, something in the conversation was more than Junius could stomach. With a grave expression, he rose, muttered a quick, "You'll have to excuse me," and strode out of the room.

UNWELCOME COMPARISONS

You are not drunk, Ilse willed herself. *You are not drunk. It is not possible. You do not become drunk.*

Well, that was not, strictly speaking, true. It was entirely possible. Ilse knew this because she had been drunk once before. Very much so.

After dinner one night, late in the Great War, Aunt Selde had poured them glass after glass of wine from her dwindling stores. It seemed they had not smiled in years, and maybe they hadn't. But that night, they laughed. Oh, how they laughed! Ilse and Therese fell into a heap on the floor, gasping for air, tears streaming down their faces. Of course, neither knew what was so funny. Once it occurred to them, that fact only made everything all the more hilarious.

Ilse never forgot the feeling. The weightlessness. Her arms light, practically floating; her feet not touching the floor. She'd thought a breeze might come along and lift her up, carry her away. On that breeze, she would float across the sea. On that breeze, she would drift back to a better time. After years of being present and solemn, to feel so disconnected had been delicious.

But then Selde, crafty sprite that she was, had asked Ilse to fetch her copy of *Metamorphosis* from a shelf on the far side of the room. Ilse had righted herself with difficulty, her gangly limbs not fully under her control. Suddenly, she found that her feet were not weightless at all but heavy, clumsy things. She crossed the room in a stagger, tripping on the hem of her dress, knocking painfully against a side table. Even with only Selde's and her sister's eyes upon her, Ilse had felt foolish.

When she reached the far wall, her brain seemed incapable of grasping the organizational scheme of the small library, and no matter how many times she blinked, her eyes refused to settle on the letters scrawled across the spines of the books. Defeated but not humbled, Ilse had brought Aunt Selde a copy of Mark Twain's *Huckleberry Finn*. Selde, lips suppressing a bemused smile, noted it was not the volume she had requested. Collapsing onto the sofa, Ilse claimed she had, in fact, found just the book Aunt Selde wanted. In slurred and over-articulated words, she declared, "Huck met-o-mor-pho-sized on th' river, and aren't I th' clev'rest woman in the world for having thoughtuvit!"

That was the last thing Ilse remembered.

Morning came, and Ilse awoke with burning eyes, a dry mouth, a pounding head, and a surging stomach. But the lesson was worth a day of misery. Selde's point had been well taken. A lady can be a drunken fool, or a lady can be admired, but a lady cannot be both.

It was a truth Ilse had lived by for nearly twenty years. She was very nearly religious in her moderation, often spending an entire evening with the same half-full glass of warm champagne swilling in her hand.

But a week into her stay at Hess Manor, Ilse's unflinching self-control cracked.

Because a week into her stay at Hess Manor, everything started to unravel.

***

It was a peculiar thing, the feeling that she controlled her destiny.

After a lifetime of forcing herself to conform to the needs of others, it was strange to think that, for once, she could make a decision that depended only on her own desires. Ilse was no longer beholden to her father's career. No longer concerned with upholding Therese's reputation. No longer worried about safeguarding Heinrich's secrets. There was no expectation to be met, no one to disappoint or let down.

Well, except for Junius, of course.

For there was no longer a question in Ilse's mind of *whether* Junius would propose; it was simply a matter of *when*. That much had become excruciatingly clear. He had brought her to his home. He had paid her every attention. He had been on the precipice of saying the very words that morning. Looking into Ilse's eyes, Junius had seen his future, and in that vision, they were together. Ilse was sure of it.

Was she ready for Junius to utter those sacred words? Well, perhaps not.

Did she *want* him to? She hardly knew.

That was the trouble of it.

To make a decision without reference or deference to anyone outside herself should have been liberating. So why did she feel like she was in a freefall any time she imagined Junius asking her to marry him? Why did her insides rearrange themselves when she remembered him pulling her close, his hands sliding low around her waist, his lips coming dangerously close to her own?

It was not desire that shoved her heart into her throat and tied her stomach around her lungs. It was fear. Fear that she was about to lose herself. Fear that she had somehow defrauded him, tricked him into wanting her. Fear that he might suddenly awake from his trance. Fear that, when the time came, she would make the wrong decision. Fear that, when it all fell apart, she would have no one to blame but herself.

These are the thoughts that haunted her all morning. After Martin had shared his bit of political speculation and Junius had strode out of the salon, Ilse had plenty of time to ruminate. She and Martin saw nothing of Junius until hours later when he took his place at the head of the table for luncheon.

The meal had done little to quiet her misgivings.

Junius usually insisted the younger Hesses take their meals in the schoolroom when there was company in the house. After a week in residence, Ilse had scarcely laid eyes on them. The night before, though, she had suggested that the children be allowed to join them for just one afternoon, and Junius put up no resistance. But his instruction to the governess, Frau Varga, seemed to have slipped his mind. He started when he entered the dining room and saw his children around the table, waiting expectantly, sitting stiff and straight, like they had bolts glued to their spines. After muttering a greeting, Junius sat and made such a to-do of cutting his salad that the children were afraid even to lift their forks.

Ilse was her usual, breezy self. *Someone* had to prevent the luncheon from spiraling into an unmitigated disaster. She did her best to engage Frau Varga in conversation and made small talk with Martin while stealing nervous glances at Junius. She tried to ignore how frequently his eyes drifted from herself to Juna—studying the girl, assessing Ilse, making unwelcome comparisons.

Could it be the resemblance between them, and by extension, between the late Arabella and Ilse's younger self, had never occurred to him until Ilse had pointed it out that morning? She strained to believe it possible but could think of no other way to account for Junius's behavior.

Through the first two courses, the children were largely silent, their youthful energy suppressed by the unfamiliar charge in the atmosphere. But then Ilse made the mistake of directing a question to Juna, assuming that, after one civil conversation, she had converted the girl into an ally.

"Oh, how I wish we had some music! Herr Rezek will attest I'm always saying that a bit of music can make any meal feel like an *occasion*. Fraulein Hess, do you play? I've noticed a beautiful instrument in the drawing room. Might we have the privilege of hearing you later?"

"You'll excuse me, Gnädige Frau," Juna replied, "but I'm sure my attempts would only bore a great lady from Vienna. Especially one who has traveled to America, France, Italy, and Greece. My abilities are surely not worthy of your attention."

Juna smiled cloyingly, but the undercurrent of insolence was enough to open the floodgate. Little Ari began to fidget, then fuss, then cry and scream that it was unfair she had to sit by Frau Varga; she wanted to sit by Uncle Martin. Kurt began inexplicably drilling Ilse with random, trivial questions: "How many men did Napoleon lose on his march to Russia? Do you know why oil floats on water? How can you tell the difference between an African elephant and an Asian elephant? I bet you don't know why a peacock cannot fly!" He quickly tired of his target, though. Ilse's broad knowledge made her bad sport for his little game, so he turned his attention to pestering Juna, who bore the harassment with far less composure. Only Sebastian continued his silence, brooding like his father and looking rather embarrassed by his siblings' behavior.

The ruckus built to a fever pitch. At the end of the table, Junius's neck tensed. He stared at his plate, furiously chewing his meat. A vein in his forehead swelled and pulsed. At last, he could hold back no longer. Junius erupted. *"For God's sake, will you not leave us in peace!"* He punctuated the outburst by slamming his fist onto the table, rattling the glasses and the fine Biedermeier porcelain.

The room froze. The only sound was the clatter of Ari's spoon as she dropped it on her plate. Junius glared at his fist, still tightly clenched, its knuckles whitening, as he drew in ragged breaths. With effort, he contained his voice to a seemlier volume. Through gritted teeth he pushed out the words, "Frau Varga, take these children away and do not bring them back until you have taught them some manners."

The stunned governess blinked twice, then rose and hastened the four children out before the inevitable tears flowed. They left behind a jarring void, a black hole that stole the air right out of Ilse's lungs.

Junius leaned forward, elbows pressing into the table, eyes scrunched tight. Every muscle in his body contracted. He rubbed his temples so forcefully Ilse thought he might blot out his entire consciousness, rub out all knowledge of the world. Perhaps that was the intent. She had never seen him like this. Serious, yes. Withdrawn, cold, distant. But she had never seen him lose his temper in such a violent way, and based on the flabbergasted faces of his children, neither had they.

Ilse left her chair and knelt beside him. She let her hand hover just over his arm, barely grazing his sleeve, worried he might crumble under the force of her touch. Junius reached over and covered her hand but continued in silent anguish.

"Junius, please," Ilse intreated softly, her voice just above a whisper, like she was shushing a child who had awakened from a nightmare. "Something has upset you. I can see you are terribly upset. Whatever it is, we are here. But we cannot help you if we don't know what is wrong."

After a moment, Junius collected himself. When he spoke, he did not look at Ilse. He would not remove his eyes from the glistening vein of fat on his plate. "The two of you talk as if life is one never-ending fête, and if you can just smile and be clever and droll, everything will somehow right itself. You have no idea what I have been going through."

"You're right; we don't. How can we know what you will not tell us?" Ilse asked. Her eyes continued to search his expression for even the slightest clue as to what might have unsettled his mind.

Junius sighed and knitted his fingers in front of his face. He drove his thumbs into his brows, wincing from the pounding in his head. Even if he could not bring himself to look at them, he could explain, and he did so, slowly and deliberately.

"You have noticed, no doubt, how often I have been visited over the past week. Doubtless, you also gathered that some of my visitors have been unworthy of an introduction."

Neither Ilse nor Martin spoke. They held their breath and waited for Junius to continue.

"I am being pursued. I have been for some time, but they are becoming increasingly determined."

"Who is becoming increasingly determined?"

Junius hesitated. He could taste the shame of the words that sat on his tongue. Saying them out loud would make them real, would taint him by association. "The Austrian Nazis," he finally managed to ground out. "Their representatives. They are trying to recruit me to their cause. The Bundesheer has always stood firmly behind the Christian Corporative,[44] so they think a defecting military voice will lend them credibility, gain them a stronger footing in the district."

"But you are retired," Ilse said dumbly, knowing even as the words slid across her lips that Junius's status was irrelevant.

"And I have tried to tell them that. I've tried to tell them that I only want a quiet life, to raise my children in peace. And I've told them in none too delicate terms that I do not support their philosophy. But they refuse to accept it."

"But they have no authority over you, old chap," Martin reassured him. "They cannot force you to do anything you do not wish to."

"No, for the moment, they cannot force me to do a thing. And up until this morning, they were little more than an annoyance, flies to be swatted away. But what of this new agreement you told us of? What happens if it is the *Anschluss* that so many are calling for? What right would I then have to refuse? I could be conscripted, forced to serve against my will, against my conscience."

Ilse wanted more than anything to be the one to suggest an escape that Junius had overlooked, but she could see none. She wanted to tell him that together, somehow, they could find a solution, but she doubted one existed. As much as she longed to assure him everything would be fine, she could not bring herself to do it. It was against her nature to coddle. She abhorred empty consolation. And she knew Junius was right. When it came down to it, if his fears were realized, her love and support would bring little relief. All she could think to say was, "Then we shall pray it never comes to that." She poured into those words all the empathy she was capable of feeling, willing it would be enough.

It had to be enough.

She had nothing but prayers to offer him.

At last, Junius looked at her. His expression was strange. Like he had raised his eyes in search of safe harbor and found only her—not Ilse Eder, not even Ilse Jörger, but the Baroness Jörger von Tollet. It was as though he had seen straight through her, had suddenly peeled back all the layers of pretense and found that precious little was left beneath them.

Ilse could have sworn at that moment she heard his thoughts. A low growl whispering that the prayers of a woman like her were not worth much.

Junius released her hand. "You'll both please excuse me," he said. "I think I need some time alone." And then he was gone.

***

That night they were to host the Baron and Dowager Baroness von Auersperg. Ilse had been astounded earlier in the week when Junius mentioned who was coming. "The dowager baroness is still alive?" Ilse had met the Auerspergs long ago at Bergesschatten—the evening had been one of her early encounters with Junius—and the dowager had been ancient even then. Junius laughed and assured her the current dowager had been the baroness when Ilse met her; the present baron, the woman's nephew, was a young man about thirty years of age.

Junius's guests arrived, and the dowager greeted Ilse graciously. "My, my! When I heard you had returned, I did not know quite what to expect. You were such an odd little bird when I met you! But the years have molded you into something far superior to anything I could ever have imagined."

Ilse thanked her for the compliment. As clumsily as it had been delivered, it was clearly well meant.

As the evening progressed, Ilse kept a watchful eye on Junius. He seemed to have summoned his countenance tolerably well. His mind was still occupied, that much was clear. Yet he was a polite host, considerate even, and there seemed little risk of a repeat of the afternoon's outburst.

But the conversation veered into perilous territory as the dinner plates were cleared. The Baron von Auersperg, having learned Martin's occupation, asked his opinion on some financial matters.

"What currency are you recommending these days, Herr Rezek?"

"Well," replied Martin, eyeing a chance to impress a potentially significant prospect, "times being what they are, I think a disbursed portfolio is best. I've advised my clients to diversify. Pounds, Swiss francs, even American dollars."

"And what of German marks?" the young baron inquired.

"If you are looking for something short-term, the mark is certainly stable at present. You might even be able to turn some fast gains. But for longer-term holdings, I cannot recommend it.

The former Allied powers were not at all pleased in March when the Wehrmacht decided to tramp back into the Rhineland.[45] They may still be dithering about it, but I assure you, it will not be long before they rally themselves enough to make an effort at reining in the führer. Whether those efforts take a military or diplomatic form, the currency is bound to suffer."

Ilse saw this conversation for what it was. She knew how Martin compartmentalized. "Leave politics to the politicians and morality to the priests," he would say. When talking with clients, especially prospective clients, Martin could switch off his personal opinions and approach questions from a purely economic perspective. And sitting before Martin that night was a young man who had recently risen to wealth and influence. Better yet, Baron von Auersperg hadn't the slightest idea what to do with either. He was simply too enticing a catch to let off the hook. Ilse knew all this through years of constant close association, but she doubted whether Junius would dismiss Martin's apoliticism so easily.

At the head of the table, Junius maintained his composure. He sipped his wine, replaced the glass gently on the table, dabbed the corner of his mouth with his napkin. But in his eyes, Ilse could see storm clouds gathering.

Ilse shot subtle warning looks at Martin, but he was determined to ignore them. She tried to engage Junius and the dowager in another subject while Martin and the baron talked business, but the dowager was far too interested in her nephew's aggrandizement to be distracted.

Ilse wanted to upbraid Martin, scream at the top of her lungs that there are more important things in life than exchange rates and appreciation. But she could not make a scene at Junius's table, in front of Junius's guests. The shackles of decorum were too strong, too unyielding; she could not break free of them. She would not insult Baron von Auersperg, a veritable stranger, by pointing out he sought direction from an untrue compass.

As she fought to maintain a placid expression, the image of the Lippi hanging in the morning room flashed in Ilse's mind. She could see the woman in the portrait perfectly. The skin pulled tight across her forehead because the world dictated her hair be tamed. The eyes flaring with the agitation of a caged animal. The fingers that gripped her sleeve to stop her hands from shredding her velvet prison.

Suddenly, Ilse knew everything about that woman.

The woman was watching a disaster.

The woman felt helpless to stop it.

For the first time in a very long time, Ilse sensed something like panic stirring. It started in her stomach and metastasized into her shoulders, condensing at last into a knot that wedged into the base of her neck. And there it sat, throbbing. So forcefully, Ilse could hear it.

She could not show her distress, so she chose to suppress it. A nearly full glass of wine was on the table in front of her. Ilse raised it to her lips and took a deep drink. She felt the knot loosen. She downed several more heavy gulps, savoring the warmth that spread through her as the wine slid down her throat, as the knot melted back into her bloodstream.

The ever-observant butler saw Ilse's glass was low and refilled it without a word.

A few minutes later, when Junius suggested they all move into the drawing room, the glass was again empty. Ilse's head swam as she rose from her chair, but her anxiety had receded.

With the change of scenery came a welcome change of subject. At Junius's asking, the dowager told stories of a recent visit to Rome. She spoke of the fascinating ruins, her love of the cypress trees, the exquisite sculptures at Galleria Borghese, and the remarkable soprano she had heard at the Teatro Reale dell'Opera. This last triggered a memory and sparked an idea.

"Baroness Jörger, you have a charming voice, as I recall. Won't you sing something for us?"

The knot of panic returned. Ilse feared she was in no condition to play. She feigned modesty, tried to refuse, but when Junius added his voice to the dowager's urging, Ilse surrendered and walked cautiously to the shining black medium-grand piano in the corner of the room.

She sat on the bench, feeling four pairs of eyes rip into her. *You are not drunk*, she willed herself. *You are . . . not . . . drunk.*

She lifted her arms and let her hands hover over the keys, inhaling deeply, exhaling slowly. And then her fingers took over. Relying entirely on muscle memory, Ilse struck out the first mournful notes of Brahms's "Die Mainacht."

The song swelled, and Ilse sang of doves cooing, their ecstasy an insult to her sorrow. She did not think about the lyrics. She did not connect the words to the agony of love lost. She would not admit the arpeggios of the *lied*[46] painted the story of her life. Inverted. Diminished. Broken. Ilse propelled forward as a perpetual machine, her constant motion not requiring human intervention.

At last, she approached the end of the song, not a note missed, not a break in her voice. As she sang the final stanza, telling of a lonely tear burning upon her cheek, she allowed one practiced drop to escape her eye.

Ilse closed her eyes and released the keys, letting the final vibrations resonate from the instrument, absorbing its trembling breath into her bones. Then she opened her eyes and bowed her head to the room, smiling her most gracious smile as Martin and the Auerspergs applauded and praised her performance.

Junius merely said, "You have improved."

His words were a compliment, but Ilse knew their true meaning.

He meant she had gained the skills for superior execution

but had lost all artistry in the process.

He meant she had traded goodness and purity for grandness and artifice.

What he meant was he didn't even recognize her anymore.

What he meant was he despised her.

"I have studied," Ilse replied unemotionally.

Martin and the dowager pressed her to sing again, but Ilse had no intention of obliging. She rose from the bench, accepted their accolades, and returned to her chair. With each step, she felt Junius's eyes following her, tarring her with his aversion.

A short while later, Martin noted that Ilse looked unwell. She thanked him for his concern and acknowledged having a bit of a headache. With profuse apologies to the dowager and the baron, Ilse retired to the solace of a fitful sleep.

IN THE GOLDEN RAYS

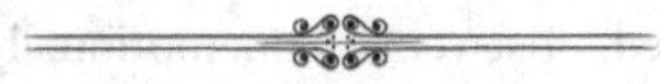

The disastrous day was behind them. There were no more outbursts. Junius's visitors continued to come, but he dealt with and dismissed them with the dispatch they merited. With Ilse, he continued to make determined references to the future and to her place in it.

But Ilse could not relax. In a single day, everything had changed. Junius may still have been saying all that was right and honorable, but the tenderness that lately had emerged in his address all but evaporated. Duty, not desire, nudged him along. It was as though he had pressed so far forward he felt obliged to continue plunging down the path on which they had started.

For nearly a week, they tiptoed around each other. They told stories, joked. Junius made amends with his children and brought them more frequently to see Ilse, to get to know her. But for Ilse, winning their trust now seemed secondary to simply getting through the week.

Something had come undone.

It all seemed an enormous, laughable mistake.

And then the news came.

***

It was the day before Ilse and Martin were to return to Vienna. Ilse and Junius sat on the terrace, watching ducks glide past on the river below. The past being the safest refuge for those avoiding the present, Junius was telling Ilse of pranks he and Kurt Kassner used to play on Friedrich. They were laughing heartily at Friedrich's expense when Martin appeared with a newspaper tucked under his arm.

"Have you seen the afternoon post yet?" Martin asked, skipping over the usual pleasantries.

"No . . . ," Ilse replied. "Why? What has happened?"

"Read for yourself." Martin tossed the newspaper on the table between them, and Ilse's heart stopped. The words "Chancellor Signs Historic Settlement" were slashed across the top of the page in large, triumphant letters.

"Don't worry, my friend," Martin assured Junius, "it's not what you think. It is not the *Anschluss*. Not yet, at any rate. Germany has lifted some sanctions and recognized our independence. In exchange, Schuschnigg has agreed to act in Germany's interest on the international stage, to conduct our foreign policy as a German state."

"Conduct our policy as a German state? What does that even mean?" Junius asked, snatching up the paper and running his eyes over the story's contents.

Ilse did not need to read it to know the answer. She closed her eyes, took in a breath through flaring nostrils, and blew it out through pursed lips, working to suppress the froth of acid stiffening in her stomach. "It means our country now exists at the pleasure of the Third Reich. Schuschnigg will never have sufficient domestic backing to stay in power without being propped up by some outside party. Until recently, that was Italy. But with Mussolini now firmly in the führer's pocket, the chancellor will need someone else. And Germany can now dictate who that someone can be. Or if, indeed, there will be any outside party at all."

"I'm afraid I'm of Ilse's mind," Martin concurred. "Oh sure, the propagandists will paint this as some sort of grand diplomatic victory. But the way I see it, this is little more than a pathetic attempt at appeasement. All it does is delay the inevitable collapse."

"I hardly know what to say," Junius replied, stunned. "To leave us at the mercy of the Reich . . . How could the chancellor agree to it?"

For a moment, no one replied. Neither Ilse nor Martin had an answer to Junius's question.

"Well, I know what Heinrich would be saying if he were here with us," Martin finally offered, trying to come up with something to push them through their collective stupor. "Whenever he was stumped into speechlessness, he would steal words from someone else. He'd be quoting Adler or Kraus. Saying something like, 'The devil is an optimist if he thinks he can make men worse than they are.'"[47]

"Kraus?" Junius replied dubiously. "You really think Heinrich would censure a regime of anti-Semites by quoting an acknowledged anti-Semite?"

"Most especially," Ilse nodded. "The Heinrich I knew would have delighted in the irony of it."

"But, surely, your late husband, of all people, wasn't a fan of Kraus."

"Why, because Heinrich was Jewish? You forget that Kraus was Jewish himself. The man practically perfected the art of self-loathing. Besides, for better or for worse, Heinrich always had an uncanny ability to seek out the worth of a man. He could disagree with fifty percent of a man's character and still find value in the other half. I suppose it's not all that surprising, considering . . ." She nearly said, "what he faced his entire life," but cut herself short when Martin cleared his throat to warn her off.

"Considering what?" Junius asked, looking from Ilse to Martin, trying to decode the understanding that existed between them.

"Oh, you know . . . just the kind of person he was." Ilse

waved Junius off casually. "Always so good-natured, always wanting everyone to be amicable. It was both his greatest gift and his greatest failing."

"But even someone as charitable as your late husband had his standards."

"*Pfft*, standards? They can be troublesome things, my friend," Martin retorted. "I make it a point never to have any unless they somehow benefit me. You'd do well to adopt the same practice. We will all be German soon, after all. If I were you, I'd practice rolling out the red carpets now to make sure you're on their good side. Next time one of your visitors comes calling, you'll have to invite him in for tea."

Martin wasn't serious, of course, but Junius was in no humor for sarcasm. Glowering at his friend, Junius threw the newspaper down on the table and stormed into the house.

"Marty, must you always be so vulgar?" Ilse rebuked, shooting him a piercing look as she rose to rush after Junius.

"And this is what I get for trying to lighten the mood," Martin said to no one. Deserted by his companions, he sat, poured himself a cup of tea, and settled back to finish reading his paper.

***

Inside the house, Ilse was quick to track down Junius. She found him pacing back and forth in his study, muttering under his breath. "*Unpardonable!*"

Not wanting to crowd him, she positioned herself in the doorway, leaning against the frame. "Pay him no mind. You know that's just Marty being Marty," she said offhandedly, hoping to mollify Junius's nerves and maintain some semblance of peace in the household. She and Martin were departing the next day; there was no point in a rift emerging between the two men now.

"Just Marty being Marty?" Junius lobbed the words back to her, his expression incredulous.

"Now, don't give me that look," Ilse chided, walking over and gently brushing the dust of the outdoors off Junius's shoulders and lapels. An excuse to pet him, to make him feel fussed over. "Remember, Marty is your friend by choice. He came to me as part of a package. Like the coconut cream hiding in the otherwise lovely box of chocolates that was my Heinrich."

"Coconut cream?" Junius quirked his eyebrow inquiringly.

"Of course. If I have my own way, you know, I always avoid them. Oh, they might taste fine at first, but after you've chewed on them for a bit, you notice that something about the texture is not quite what you would have it be."

Junius's expression softened, and he snorted out a bemused chuckle. "If Martin is a coconut cream, then you, my dear, are a toffee," he said, gripping her shoulders and placing a conciliatory kiss on her forehead. "Sweet on the outside but with a center so hard it could crack a tooth."

Ilse gave him a playful shove and meandered to one of the study's large arched windows. She felt something shift and tug as she regarded the mountains in the distance, as though she was already missing what was right there in front of her. She may not have been of it, but this land was part of her, had formed her. It affixed itself to her soul long ago and never left. So often during those years away, she would wake in the night and know this was where her unconscious mind had journeyed. For a moment, Ilse lost herself, so much that she did not notice Junius coming to stand beside her. When he spoke, she started.

"Remarkable how a face so lovely can suddenly become so serious," he said.

Ilse lifted her eyebrows and offered a half-hearted smile before her face again fell.

"Dare I ask the source of that little crinkle between your eyes?" he inquired.

"I was just thinking about Marty," she answered.

"Ah, yes, the ignominious Herr Rezek. The source of many a furrowed brow."

"You know, he might lack finesse, and his incentives can be slightly perverse at times, but he's not entirely wrongheaded . . ."

"What?" Junius searched her face for some trace of sarcasm or a flash of twisted humor. "You can't be serious. Or if you are, then you don't know what you're saying."

"As a matter of fact, I know exactly what I'm saying. And I am perfectly serious."

Ilse crossed the room and eased herself into the wingback chair in the corner. It was the kind of chair she usually avoided, deep and plush and sunken in from years of being favored by its owner. Absolutely impossible for a woman in high heels to gracefully rise from. But it was perfect for this moment. If she couldn't move, she couldn't flee; if she couldn't flee, she had no choice but to make it through this conversation without breaking.

She smoothed her skirt, tucked one foot behind the other, and sucked down a bolstering breath. "I've been thinking about this a great deal, and not just since I've been here with you. I know you like to convince yourself that you are the only serious thinker here. You imagine that because Marty and I are able to carry on a sociable conversation, our entire depth lies in drawing room prattle. But believe it or not, the space between our ears is not entirely empty. We do have some idea what is happening in the world."

Junius watched her narrowly from across the room but said nothing to contradict or affirm her, so Ilse continued.

"Today's news . . . it's just further confirmation of something we've all sensed was coming for a while now. There is a storm rolling in, Junius. You know it; I know it. A man standing on the shore cannot stop a hurricane. He can only get swept up by the surge.

"These visits you've been receiving aren't going to stop. They will not simply fade away like some nightmare you struggle to recall after waking."

"And what would you have me do, Ilse?" Junius asked. "Roll out the red carpet as Martin suggests? Stand and salute? Serve . . . serve *them*? It's unconscionable!"

Junius's anger resurfaced as quickly as it had receded, but this time, it was directed at Ilse. She had not been the object of his ire since their fight in the Volksgarten two years before, but she recognized the signs. The clenched jaw, the slight twitch of his right eye as every muscle in his face tightened. She knew an eruption was coming, but she would not be diverted.

"Of course, I would not have you serve *them*. I would have you serve Austria. This *Anschluss*, it is coming, Junius. It *will* come. That's inevitable now. None of us can change a history that is already written. We can only decide what part we will play in it. Will you sit in the wings and watch the horror unfold, or will you try to shape the performance?"

Black clouds crowded the corners of Ilse's vision as her pulse quickened and blood flooded into her head, but she kept her eyes focused, her voice measured. She folded her hands in her lap and straightened her posture as well as she could while being swallowed up by the chair.

"Someone out there will serve, Junius. *Someone* will lead. We both know there are plenty who would eagerly sign up only to add kindling to the fire. Call me crazy, call me unconscionable if you will, but I, for one, would far rather the role be played by someone filled with misgivings, someone whose soul will cry out in agony with each move and countermove—a man who might stand a chance at blunting their worst instincts."

"Are you out of your mind? You're talking absolute madness!" Junius declared, his voice quaking with emotion. "You would have me toss aside everything I've ever believed, stand side by side with men whose ideas I abhor with every fiber of my being?"

"I would have you *survive*, Junius," Ilse urged, "and maybe, just maybe, help others survive in the process."

"Oh, I see! How marvelous!" he cried, mocking her sincerity. "So, I should destroy five lives to stop someone else from destroying ten? Is that the general idea? Is that what you want?"

"It's not about what you or I *want* anymore. Can't you see that? It's about containing the damage. And yes, since you ask, I do happen to think those you might shield would consider a bit of your honor a worthwhile sacrifice."

Ilse felt emotion creeping into her voice, tears beginning to prick the corners of her eyes. But she would not let them overrun her. She *would* get through this. For two decades, she had choked back every emotion. She had flirted casually with men whose misogyny enraged her. She had smiled and bit her tongue as bigots unknowingly demeaned her dearest friends, screaming on the inside but knowing that to rise to her friends' defense was to seal their undoing. After all that, her self-control would not fail her now. She would not permit it.

Ilse strangled her feelings. "Can I ask you something, Junius?" she said, forcing calm. "What do you think to gain by antagonizing them?"

Ilse's composure chilled Junius to his core. "What kind of question is that?" he demanded. "What will I *gain*? Is moral integrity not trading at a fair market price these days?"

"Don't cheapen my position by suggesting I'm looking at this as some kind of economic proposition," she said evenly, with terrifying coolness. "It demeans me, and it's beneath you. What I'm asking is not a question of commerce, and you know it.

"What do you think will happen if you continue to refuse them, Junius? Worse, what happens if you *offend* them? When the *Anschluss* comes, do you think they will just say, 'Very well, then,' and you'll go your separate ways? No, I know you're not so simple as to think that. You're setting yourself up to be at the top of their list of dissidents. Say you are imprisoned or worse. What good can you be to anyone then? What higher purpose would you then be serving? What's more, what do you think will happen to those around you? Think about your children. What will become of them if you are locked away?"

"Do you honestly think I haven't thought about my children? But would you really have them raised by a man who can't even look them in the eye?"

"I would have them raised by their *father*. They have already lost their mother. I would not have them grow up with everyone they've ever loved and everything they've ever known ripped out from under them."

Junius did not respond to this. He stared at Ilse with an expression unmoved and unreadable. She continued cautiously, hoping rather than sensing that she was starting to gain ground.

"And what of me? When we are wed—if, indeed, you still wish that—all that I am and all that I have will be yours. Everything Heinrich and I worked so hard for so long to sustain—"

"Ah, now we come to it!" Junius interrupted. "You're worried about Heinrich's little business, is that it?" His voice dripped with derision. It was the first time he had ever disparaged Ilse's husband, and it stung her more than a direct insult ever could.

"Not Heinrich's business. Heinrich's *legacy*. My Heinrich!" she cried, desperately trying to quash the lump driving up her throat. "You know very well it's not just a business, that it's *never* been just a business. What happens if it all falls into Nazi hands? What of the men who depend on our wages to keep food in their children's mouths? And what of the hundreds of families, almost all of them Jewish, who live under our roofs? Do you think they will be allowed to keep their homes? And when they are turned out on the streets, who will take them in? How much collateral damage would you be willing to stomach so you can sit in a cell with your morals intact? While you're busy protecting your principles, who will protect *everything else?*"

Junius had heard enough. "I won't listen to this any longer! Not in my own home!" he exploded, no longer caring to contain himself for her sake.

But still, Ilse pressed on. She spoke with urgency and conviction but would not rise to his fury. If she quaked, she would crumble. If a fault opened, she would fall into it. "You think the only way to have integrity is by being unyielding. But we are where we are today *because of* principled men who were unyielding, who for decades refused to compromise and ended up grinding this country into—"

"*Enough!*" Junius barked, throwing Ilse a look so cold it would silence her on the subject forever. "We are done here." He dropped the words at her feet and stormed out, leaving Ilse in silence so brittle she dared not move, not even to breathe. She held her breath until her vision flickered with a thousand black sparks.

She knew she had gone too far. Junius's eyes had radiated disdain, a venom Ilse had not known him capable of producing. But she did not regret her words. *This* was what it was to control her destiny. She had chosen to crack open the door and give Junius a glimpse of the room in which the real Ilse lived. What he had seen there was not some ghost from his past, not some phony society creation, but the living, breathing, thinking, feeling woman Ilse had become.

Yes, Junius had finally seen her.

He had seen her, and he had recoiled.

He could no longer mistake her for that idealistic child from his youth. The real Ilse had been tried and bruised, exalted and used. She was a woman who saw the world for what it was, with all its ambiguities, all the messy inconveniences. She was a cynic, and she was an optimist. She was clear-eyed about what was coming, but she had to believe that from all the grime and grit, there was still a chance to wring out something resembling good. She just couldn't be afraid to fight for it. If achieving *something* rather than *nothing* required her to sift through the muck, she was prepared to blacken her hands. Even if it meant losing a bit more of herself in the process. Even if it meant hating herself a bit more every day. She was not yet powerless. She refused to surrender the one means she had of doing something worthwhile.

Not even for Junius.

When Ilse pushed up from the great chair, she realized she was trembling. She shook her head quickly, as if doing so would flick away the memory of the last five minutes. She smoothed her skirt and straightened her blouse. Then, she slowly walked out of the study, across the austere stone hall, and up the cold stone stairs. Her posture was regal. She took care that each step was a picture of dignity. She reached her room, entered, and closed the door without a sound.

And there, away from any eyes that might see her with a hair out of place, she collapsed onto the floor and wept, bathed in the golden rays of the late afternoon sun.

IF THE WHALE RISES UP

Hours later, as evening glazed the grass with a misting of dew, Ilse emerged from her room. Her eyes were still rimmed with red, but any other trace of distress had been cleverly concealed. The tear-streaked makeup had been washed away and replaced. Her hair was pinned back in its proper place. She had changed out of her rumpled clothing and slipped into a flowing evening dress, though she had no intention of joining Junius and Martin for dinner.

She found Junius on the terrace, watching his daughter stroll in self-contained harmony along the river. Ilse stood back, observing him—this man who once had been her entire world—not knowing if she should interrupt his solitude. She didn't have to decide. Sensing her presence, Junius looked back and offered a strained smile.

Ilse walked out and joined him at the edge of the terrace. Neither spoke a word. For a time, they just stood there, leaning against the balustrade, side by side in the moonlight. Two people who time had ripped so far asunder in so many ways.

Below them, Juna moved along the water's edge, untroubled, with a nymph-like grace, one with the river and the hills beyond.

"I wish I could be like that again," Ilse said, her voice distant and dreamy. Junius turned to her inquiringly, and Ilse nodded toward the girl. "Like your Juna. As I once was. Back when things were simple. Before the Great War. Before living for years under Therese's thumb. Before navigating the cities of America from behind a glass curtain . . ." She sighed. "Before I cut myself off from the world and everyone in it. The way I was when I first met you. So unsure, yet so open. Innocent and untamed. The girl you fell in love with."

Junius said nothing. His eyes drank her in, searching desperately for the woman he loved. Not finding that woman, he turned back to the river.

"It wasn't far from here," he said after a moment, as much to himself as to Ilse. "The place where we met. Do you remember it? That day I caught you spying." There it was again, the lopsided grin that stole across his lips whenever he thought about something that amused him. That smile that tore at Ilse's heart.

"How could I forget?" she answered. "It was just down the river, about halfway to Bergesschatten. You were playing 'Evening Song,' and the music called me to you. It drew me in, and I was lost. The rest of my life seemed to have been ordained."

They slipped into silence, listening to the hollow twitter of the nightjars. Ilse lapped up the sound, drew strength from it. Each birdsong, each chirping cricket, every flicker of the fireflies assured her there were plenty of lone creatures out there. It was not such an unnatural state to reach for love and come up emptyhanded.

She looked at Junius, the moon shining behind him, his face shrouded in shadow, and she knew what she had come to say. "Do you remember, back in Vienna, before that wretched fight in the gardens, when I told you the story of Orpheus?"

"You mean how you had spent so long thinking of me as Orpheus and yourself as Eurydice?"

"Yes." She paused to collect her thoughts, wanting to be sure they were arranged before saying anything more. "I see now that I was wrong."

"You were?"

"Yes," she replied. She did not try to cover the pain in her voice. She needed him to know this did not come easily. "I was. As it turns out, you were never Orpheus."

"I wasn't?"

"No, you weren't. Ironically enough . . . as it turns out . . . I am."

Ilse paused, steeling herself for the words she knew she must say.

"You don't love me, Junius. You love the simple creature I used to be. We both know I'm not that girl anymore, just as you are not that young man singing by the river. I could try to ignore it. I could stay and fight for us. I could insist on wearing blinders as I walk through Hell, clinging to an illusory faith that you are following . . . all the while knowing that if I ever turn to look, I'll see you are already lost to me. If I stay, it will be to spend every day watching you pine for the girl I used to be, with a constant reminder of just how very different a woman I have become." She looked again to where Juna was still ambling alone by the river.

Junius didn't protest. He didn't try to convince Ilse she was wrong. Deep down, he knew she was only saying things he had been trying for months to deny.

Ilse's eyes followed the water downstream, toward Bergesschatten, toward the place they had met, where they had kissed, where they had held each other on a night that felt like the end of the world. "I will always love that boy by the river," she murmured.

Junius reached out, touched her cheek, and turned her face to him. "And I will always love the spy."

She pressed her face into his palm, lingered there, allowed herself for just one moment to feel the warmth she had run from so long ago.

"What will you do?" he asked.

Ilse sighed and forced herself to step away. "I will go home," she said resolutely. "I will carry on. Just like I always have."

He nodded, swallowed, and raised his eyes to the sky. Combing the stars for answers, he asked wistfully, "And what will I do?"

He looked so lost, so helpless, that for a moment, Ilse thought she might not be able to tear herself away. She almost allowed herself to believe that simply being by his side would be enough. She could pretend to be the woman he needed her to be. She could be lithe and comforting. She could hold him until he forgot to be afraid. She could bite her tongue and hold her breath; she had done it all her life. Why could she not put on a new charade, for Junius's sake? Why couldn't that be enough?

But she knew it never would be. Not where the two of them were concerned.

Stepping back to him, she gently pulled down his chin so she could look into his eyes, so full of longing and reservations. "You will do the same as me," she said firmly. "You will do what you *must*. Somewhere between your heart and your head, between impulse and obligation, you will find whatever that is. You will question it a thousand times. You will torment yourself to the point of madness. Yet, in the end, you will do it. Because in your core, you will know you could never have done anything else."

She started to move away but paused and turned back. "But if the whale does rise up and swallow you whole, please, just promise me one thing."

"What's that?" He gulped.

Ilse smiled dangerously. "That you won't sit easy in its stomach." She chucked him under the chin, and he smiled back then. It was a look of both reconciliation and farewell. With one final brush of her hand against his face, one last look into his eyes,

Ilse Eder finally said goodbye to Junius von Hess.

Walking back to the house, Ilse could have sworn she heard the sound of a lone guitar. A lilting melody floating along the river. Like a breeze off the mountains. Ethereal as rain falling on the water. She paused by the door and looked back. Junius had turned away from her, but she could tell from the tilt of his head that he, too, could hear it.

She imagined that somewhere nearby, some hopelessly vain child was stealing into the night, running toward the music, toward a young man who was passionate and sulky and entirely, brilliantly *hers*.

Ilse tried to envision what was in store for these furtive lovers. How often would they stumble and stray? How many times would they break each other's hearts? Would they be the lucky ones whose lives were marked by tears of joy? Or, like so many others, would they fill jar after jar with ashes and dust?

As quickly as it had started, the music stopped. But the impression of the young lovers stayed with Ilse. Much later, after the house had draped itself in quiet and dark, she would stand in the window of her room, thinking of them as she gazed out at black hills silhouetted against an indigo sky.

Perhaps there had been no bright-eyed girl slipping off into the countryside that night. Maybe that girl belonged to Ilse's memories. But love was still real; she hadn't the slightest doubt about that. Even if it wasn't hers, even as the world spiraled toward disaster, love was as real as ever, always out there, somewhere, just waiting to be unearthed. It still cast its spell on those who least expected it, soldering souls, tethering once chainless hearts with binds that tug and ache.

Ilse wanted to rush out, find all the young lovers, throw her arms around them, make them swear they would cling to each other, no matter what was coming, no matter what hideousness might get thrown in their paths. But she knew she could not.

They each must find their own way. All Ilse could do was hope, against all evidence and every intuition, that life might handle them with care.

END VOLUME IV

EPILOGUE

Time and again, we tell our stories. Over the years, the stories become myth. Our actions remain the same, but the motives we assign to them change to suit us in the moment. Have you ever noticed that? We want so badly to be the heroes of our own lives that we convince ourselves we were always blameless, our aims were always pure.

Decades later, I look back at that time, and I ask: Was I fooling myself? Did I even believe those things I said? Did I really think we could somehow make a difference?

Maybe I was well-intentioned, grasping at some sort of utilitarian outcome when anything better seemed beyond reach. Father used to call me his child of June. He would say I liked to suppose myself wizened and hard, but my perspective reeked of naïveté. I was too quick to empathy, too prone to underestimate man's capacity for malice. I always took great umbrage at this, but perhaps he was right. Maybe I was naïve, plain and simple.

But maybe I was egoïstic, refusing to let go of the one thing I could control, so desperate for my life to have meaning that I would not cede my means of imprinting my mark on the world. I would not leave the house, even as it burned. Even as the beams splintered and popped and the roof collapsed in on me.

Or maybe it was all just a pretext to push Junius away. The craven excuses of a gutless woman.

Some will say it does not matter, that what counts is not our intentions but the results of our actions. I used to be one of them. Now, I'm not so sure. If we are callous and calculating and, by some fluke, all ends well, are we suddenly absolved of culpability? If we operate within the purest of moral codes and still manage to leave a trail of ruin, are we condemned? And how do you factor in fear, conflicts, indecision, doubt? What if we choose to help someone, knowing full well their salvation is reaped from the suffering of others? And what of mistakes and regret? What of ignorance? It is not always willful. Sometimes it is simply ignorance. Sometimes it is learned, taught, preached from revered tongues. Sometimes it accumulates through a slow drip-drip, *like the precipitation of a stalagmite. Sometimes it is cleverly disguised as insight, fed to us the way we trick children into taking their medicine.*

When an entire country is led astray, how much of the guilt rests with the sheep, and how much do we heap on the backs of the wolves?

The Anschluss came. Just as we knew it would. Not immediately, of course. Fate likes to leave us dangling. We wriggled on the line for nearly two years, waiting as the drip-drip-drip *of lies laid a proper foundation. In the terrible suspense, I wrote letters. I sent alarm bells across the sea to everyone I'd ever known there. They must not wait, I urged. They must act now. They must lift their visa restrictions. A few thousand places a year would not be enough; it would not be nearly enough.*

My appeals were snowflakes landing in a pool. They made only the faintest ripple before melting away to nothing. Who was I, after all, to command anyone's attention? No one. Just some woman they'd met at a party once. Perhaps from somewhere in the recesses of their memories, they recovered a vague impression of a foreign lady; just as quickly, they crumpled that impression and tossed it in the trash alongside that lady's pleas.

When the inevitable day arrived, I recoiled at the joy of my neighbors. I looked down from the window of Heinrich's room as throngs made their way to the steps of the opera. They joined their voices in a sickening chorus. "One people, one Reich, one leader, one victory." Knowing many simply cheered that war had been averted offered scant comfort.

Night fell, and I sat there still, clutching Heinrich's robe to my heart as the city's most putrid demons oozed out from their hiding places. They tore through Leopoldstadt with their torches and their bricks, victory cries intermingling with wails of terror.

Later, my neighbors threw roses as the triumphant motorcade drove into the city. And still, I sat there, helpless, trying desperately to drown out the hideous song of the peeling church bells.

Eventually, the celebrations settled into a vile smugness. I left my refuge and stepped into a city dripping with red flags, their hateful sigils cutting like knives across everything that once had been beautiful.

Night after night, I pleaded my prayers to an indifferent God; day after day, I silently questioned whether each man and woman I passed had taken to the streets. Did you cheer? Did you sing? Did you wield a sign or a rose or a stone?

I dared not ask such things out loud. I kept my head down. I held my breath. I bit my tongue. I gave no offense. I vomited, rinsed my mouth, went on. I swept glass, righted shop shelves, ladled soup. I held a widow in my arms and promised that her children would have a roof over their heads for however long I had it in my power to give.

I knew it would not be for long.

For nearly a year, I managed to draw no notice. I kept my employees fed, kept my tenants housed, tried to keep them safe as the gates of hell opened all around us.

It was not enough.

It was never going to be enough.

I often wonder, how grim was the toll of my good intentions? If I hadn't insisted for so many years on making life a little more tolerable, just to ease my own conscience, how many might have left before the horrors? How many might have been spared?

They did leave, of course. Eventually. Tens of thousands poured out of Leopoldstadt and Vienna's other once-thriving Jewish communities. They left everything behind, and still they paid a heavy bounty to the beasts of the Reich for the luxury of escaping with their lives. Those who could not afford such luxury also left but by a very different train.

We can never know what could have been, just as we cannot change the past. But that doesn't mean we move on. When I lie awake longing for the solace of dreams, I'm met only with questions. Might I have done more? Should I have done less? Should I have known better? Was I a fool? Was I cruel? What if I'd done differently? What if I'd only been different?

The answers never come.

But if I close my eyes long enough, I can go back to the beginning, to a time when the world was full of promise.

Beauty is possible, I remind myself; I saw it once.

Love is possible, I remind myself; I had it once.

Can we ever get them back? I catch glimpses here and there, but they are fleeting. I see them, and already they have begun to fade. They slip away because, even after all that has happened, we still have not learned how to keep them. Learning is too inconvenient, too uncomfortable. Easier to forget what we've lost. Better to ignore what we will miss.

We leap into the void, and we let ourselves fall.

Forever swaddled in darkness.

Pretending there never was a light.

THE END

ENDNOTES

---

[1] Count Karl von Stürgkh was prime minister of Austria from 1911 until his assassination in 1916. He dismissed the Reichsrat (the imperial legislative body of Austria-Hungary) in March 1914 and, after that, governed by decree.

[2] Under the excessive bureaucratic state of Emperor Franz Joseph, the press was heavily censored. Preliminary copies of newspapers were submitted to censors for review. Articles pulled at the last minute would be replaced by a blank space and the word "*konfisziert*," or "confiscated."

[3] Central train station

[4] A long skirt that was so named because its narrowness restricted the movement of women's legs. The silhouette was popularized in the early 1910s but quickly fell out of style. Therese wearing one here signifies her trying but failing to stay current with the changing fashions.

[5] A traditional German lullaby.

[6] From Greek mythology. A legendary musician, poet, and prophet.

[7] The Theresian Military Academy, or the "Theresianum," as it is commonly known, was the principal training institution for officers of the Austro-Hungarian army.

[8] The Roman Catholic Shrovetide carnival as celebrated in German-speaking countries. Fasching season festivities officially begin in November and stretch through the beginning of Lent.

[9] Paul Poiret (1879-1944) was a popular French fashion designer. The preeminent dress designer of pre-World War I Paris, his work heavily influenced women's fashion of the era, including the incorporation of Eastern and Neoclassical styles and the introduction of hobble skirts.

[10] French for *fish*.

[11] A traditional Austrian entrée of beef or veal boiled in broth with root vegetables. It is rumored to have been a favorite dish of Emperor Franz Josef I.

[12] Henri Bergson gave a lecture entitled "Philosophical Intuition" at the Philosophical Congress in Bologna, April 10, 1911. The actual quote is, "Faced with currently-accepted ideas, theses which seemed evident, affirmations which had up to that time passed as scientific, it whispers into the philosopher's ear the word: Impossible!" It is imperfectly paraphrased here, as it is unlikely that Ilse would have memorized it perfectly.

[13] "Erlkönig," by celebrated German poet Johann Wolfgang von Goethe (1782), was set to music by Austrian composer Franz Shubert in 1815.

[14] A controversial novel by Galician author Leopold von Sacher-Masoch, which eventually gave rise to the term "Masochism."

[15] Archduke Franz Ferdinand, the nephew of Emperor Franz Joseph and heir-presumptive to the throne of Austria-Hungary, was assassinated on June 28, 1914.

[16] Montmartre, or "the martyr's hill." It is said to be the site where St. Denis, the first Bishop of Paris, was beheaded by the Romans in 250 AD.

[17] A rank of the Austro-Hungarian Army indicating an officer aspirant.

[18] U.S. President Woodrow Wilson addressed a joint session of Congress on April 2, 1917 to request a declaration of war against Germany. Congressional approval of the declaration came on April 6. The U.S. declaration of war against Austria-Hungary did not occur until December 7, 1917.

[19] The first chancellor of the Austrian Republic after the fall of the Habsburg Empire. He served in this role from November 1918 until June 1920.

[20] The Treaty of St. Germain set forth the peace terms between the Allied Powers and Austria after World War I (similar to the better-known Treaty of Versailles between the Allies and Germany). The

Austrian delegation to St. Germain was excluded from the negotiations, but facing an ultimatum from the Allies, Renner signed the treaty in September 1919.

[21] Emperor of Austria-Hungary from 1848 until his death in 1916. The five-kilometer Ringstrasse was built in response to an 1857 dictate from the emperor that Vienna's suburbs would be connected to the center of imperial power. The boulevard is lined by numerous important and historical buildings.

[22] Vienna's City Hall

[23] The former imperial palace

[24] After the Austrian nobility was officially abolished, Count Adalber Sternberg (1868-1930) famously changed his calling card to read "Adalbert Sternberg. Ennobled by Charlemagne 798; Unnobled by Karl Renner 1918."

[25] Similar language appeared in Schnitzler's Buch der Sprüche und Bedenken/*Book of Sayings and Scruples*, published in 1927: "There are all kinds of flight from responsibility. There is a flight into death, a flight into sickness, and finally, a flight into stupidity. The last is the least dangerous and most comfortable, since even for clever people the journey is not as long as they might fondly imagine." It is implied here that Schnitzler came up with the concept for these words before he ever wrote them down.

[26] Shapeshifter of German folklore.

[27] Heinrich is paraphrasing Grillparzer's 1847 poem "Abschied von Wien/Farewell from Vienna."

[28] He is quoting Karl Kraus here. "Die Welt ist ein Gefängnis in dem Einzelhaft vorzuziehen ist." See *Die Fackel*, no. 264/5 (Vienna, 18 Nov. 1908).

[29] The fall of 1897 saw a filibuster in the Reichsrat (imperial advisory council, similar to parliament) and the beginning of a period of unprecedented legislative obstruction that would last for the next decade. The various factions frequently brought noisemakers—cowbells, whistles,

brass instruments, drums, etc.—into the assembly to drown out speakers from the other side.

[30] A reference to Gottlieb Biedermeier, a satiric figure of a pious and law-abiding schoolmaster created by humorist Ludwig Eichrodt. The term "Biedermeier" would eventually be used to describe the apolitical bourgeois culture that emerged during the reign of Emperor Franz Joseph.

[31] Austrian military rank equivalent to a colonel.

[32] Heinrich paraphrases a quote from Hermann Bahr's essay "Selbstinventur/Self-Inventory," which appeared in a 1912 collection of essays, *Inventur/Inventory*. The full quote is: "I am fond of death. Not as a savior, for I do not suffer from life, but as a consummator. It will bring me everything which I still lack . . . Death takes nothing from me yet gives me so much."

[33] Gracious lady; the accepted form of address for ladies of baronial families.

[34] When Napoleon Bonaparte's troops withdrew from Vienna following the 1809 Peace Treaty of Schönbrunn, they blew up some of the city's fortifications on their way out. A part of the cleared space was eventually turned into a public park, which opened in 1823.

[35] The Austrian army.

[36] Ilse is referring to proposals to reunite Austria with German, which had been barred by the peace treaties after World War I but still had widespread support in many parts of Austria.

[37] A network of paramilitary groups that operated across Austria between World War I and World War II. Dollfuss's government was heavily dependent on the Heimwehr's political arm to retain power in the final years of the Republic; after the establishment of the Christian Corporatist government, the Heimwehr took on formal police and security duties, including reconnaissance.

[38] Heinrich is quoting from Viennese writer and poet Peter Altenberg's 1896 collection *Wie ich es sehe (How I See It)*. *"Der Mann hat eine Liebe—die Welt. Die Frau hat eine Welt—die Liebe."*

[39] From "Ninth Elegy," from *Duineser Elegien*, Rainer Maria Rilke, 1923, translated by Gary Miranda (Tavern Books, 2013)

[40] Composer Hugo Wolf died in Vienna of syphilis in 1903.

[41] Austria experienced hyperinflation in the early 1920s—reaching nearly 1,500 percent in 1922—throwing much of the middle class into poverty.

[42] "I hope we will be great friends during my stay here."

[43] *Anschluss*, or the reunification of German Austria with greater Germany, was explicitly barred by the treaties of St. Germain and Versailles after World War I, as the Allies feared reunification would give Germany too much power. Most German-speaking citizens of the former Austro-Hungarian empire considered themselves German even during the imperial era and had hoped for reunification when the empire fell, so this provision of the truce was a significant psychological blow. As the Austrian economy faltered throughout the 1920s and into the early 1930s, calls for *Anschluss* remained a part of Austrian political life.

[44] The authoritarian regime established by Chancellor Engelbert Doll-fuss in 1933, which combined principles of fascist Italy with conservative Catholicism. Though immensely unpopular, the government retained power through the support of the Bundesheer, the bureaucracy, the Catholic Church, and Mussolini's Italy.

[45] On March 7, 1936, 20,000 German troops entered the Rhineland region of western Germany. Following World War I, the region—which borders the Netherlands, Belgium, Luxembourg, and France—was occupied by Allied forces until 1930. The remilitarization of German territory west of the Rhine River was a direct breach of the Treaty of Versailles.

[46] *Lied* (plural: *lieder*) literally is German for "song;" however, in classical music, *lieder* refer to 19th century songs for a single vocalist and piano that set poetry to music.

[47] "Der Teufel ist ein Optimist, wenn er glaubt, daß er die Menschen schlechter machen kann." See Kraus, Karl. 1912. *Ausgewählte Schriften (Selected Works)*. Albert Langen, Munich.

ACKNOWLEDGEMENTS

It always seems strange to me, seeing just one name on the cover of a book . . . my own included. The world has yet to witness a solo achievement; everything we do is supported by a thousand others in a thousand ways. I could not possibly acknowledge everyone who assisted and inspired me throughout this journey, but I would be remiss if I did not mention a critical few.

No book stands alone. Writing comes from reading. William M. Johnson's *The Austrian Mind: An Intellectual and Social History 1848-1938* and Evan Burr Bukey's *Hitler's Austria: Popular Sentiment in the Nazi Era, 1938-1945* provided an indispensable foundation for understanding the cultural consciousness of early 20th century Vienna and the political and economic environment of interwar Austria. Numerous other scholarly articles and websites covering everything from 1910s immigration policy, to the evolution of Austrian marriage laws, to make-up trends of the 1930s helped fill in the blanks and bring Ilse's world to life. To all these experts, I am forever grateful to you for sharing your knowledge.

To my first readers: Sarah McKeown, Lynn Pedersen, Louise Rothschild, and Margaret Richardson. You are saints for suffering through my early drafts! Your comments and advice pushed me from version three to version fourteen.

A huge thank you to Janet Fix, editor-in-chief at The-WordVerve. Your frank critiques made me a better writer, and your kind encouragement gave me the confidence to send this book out into the world.

And finally, I'm so grateful for Laurice Grae, who was so enthusiastic in her support for the original concept of this novel, and for Heather David and Jerry Pedersen, who didn't have the heart to rip into my drafts but who kept me tethered to this world, even as I immersed myself in Ilse's; Rachel, Ali, Laura, Beth, April, John, Michelle, Tori, Frank, Jackie, Tony, Sean, Gita, Karen, Iona, Gary, Brian, and countless other friends, colleagues, and neighbors who cheered me on and kept me sane for the last two years; and the awesome staffs at St. Elmo's and Busboys and Poets, who kept me caffeinated and fed through long months of writing and editing.

About the Author

Child of June is Quillen deBruney's first novel. Born and raised in the Midwest, Quillen has spent two decades living and working in the national capital region. After receiving a Bachelor of Arts in political science from Truman State University and a Master of Arts in public policy from The Johns Hopkins University, Quillen dedicated her career to public service. She currently resides in Alexandria, Virginia, with her beloved mutt, Anne Elliot.